Vintage

Vintage

SUSAN GLOSS

WM

WILLIAM MORROW

An Imprint of HarperCollins*Publishers*

VINTAGE. Copyright © 2014 by Susan Gloss. All rights reserved. Printed in the United States of America. No part of this book may be used or reproduced in any manner whatsoever without written permission except in the case of brief quotations embodied in critical articles and reviews. For information address Harper-Collins Publishers, 10 East 53rd Street, New York, NY 10022.

HarperCollins books may be purchased for educational, business, or sales promotional use. For information please e-mail the Special Markets Department at SPsales@harpercollins.com.

FIRST EDITION

Designed by Jamie Lynn Kerner

Library of Congress Cataloging-in-Publication Data has been applied for.

ISBN 978-0-06-227032-0

14 15 16 17 18 ov/rrd 10 9 8 7 6 5 4 3 2 1

For my grandmother Sally Baker who taught me that every seam has a story

Vintage

Chapter 1

INVENTORY ITEM: *wedding gown*

APPROXIMATE DATE: *1952*

CONDITION: *good, minor discoloration on lining*

ITEM DESCRIPTION: *Ivory, tea-length gown with scooped neckline and cap sleeves. Silk taffeta with crinoline understructure.*

SOURCE: *Dress acquired from the couple's daughter.*

Violet

BENEATH THE ASH TREES on Johnson Street, just east of campus, Hourglass Vintage stood in a weathered brick building, wedged between a fair-trade coffee shop and a bike-repair business. Behind the boutique's windows, Violet Turner was buttoning a mannequin into a smocked sundress.

She sighed as undergraduates with bright scarves and red faces rushed by the shop without glancing at her or the garments on display. Gray spring days like this one were all about hurrying and practicality, and Violet didn't like either concept. People in practical moods didn't wander into the shop to buy Bakelite jewelry or turn-of-the-century kid gloves. Even the hearty street musicians—bearded bluegrass players who usually staked out a spot near the crosswalk—had packed up their banjos and left.

Violet tucked a strand of short black hair behind her ear and bent down to tie an espadrille sandal onto the mannequin's ankle. When she got back up, a pair of blue eyes stared back at her. A girl stood outside, just inches from the window, clutching a 1950s wedding dress against her fleece jacket.

Violet remembered the girl. She had come in a few weeks earlier and tried on half a dozen bridal gowns before selecting the full-skirted one she held now, which flapped in the wind like a surrender flag.

The girl entered the shop and spread the dress on the counter. "I need to return this."

"I'm sorry, but we don't allow returns." Violet took her place behind the register and smoothed her checkered skirt against her hips.

"Can't you at least give me back part of what I paid?" The girl ran her hands over the silk fabric of the wedding gown, letting them linger on the tulle rosettes along the hem.

"I wish I could, but it's store policy," Violet said. She felt a blast of dry heat from the old radiator affixed to the wall and peeled off her pearl-buttoned cardigan—a find from her grandma Lou's closet after she passed away.

The girl stared at the tattoo of a flame-licked phoenix on Violet's freckled bicep, then looked away when Violet caught her staring. "I guess I hoped you could make an exception," the girl said. "I could really use the money." Her eyes clouded with tears—a layer of water over blue ice.

Violet started to bite her lip, then remembered she was wearing red lipstick. She felt sorry for the girl, but she needed to be firm on her rule. Since she sold secondhand items, there was no way to tell if an item had been worn when a customer brought it back. If she allowed returns, she worried that her shop would become like a lending library for vintage clothes. She handed the girl a Kleenex from a crocheted tissue-box holder.

The girl took the tissue and wiped her wet cheeks. "Sorry, I'm a mess."

"It's okay." Seeing the heartbreak in the girl's face reminded Violet of a time in her own life she didn't like to think about—the pain that had permeated the breakup of her marriage and culminated in her moving to Madison five years earlier.

"I don't usually cry in front of strangers," the girl said.

"I helped you pick out your wedding dress. I'd like to think I'm not a *total* stranger. I'm Violet, by the way."

"I'm April Morgan." The girl shoved the crumpled tissue into her purse—a battered leather schoolboy satchel.

"I like your bag," Violet said. "It looks like it's from the seventies."

"Yeah, it belonged to my mom."

Violet sensed the girl had a story to tell, and listening to other people's stories was her specialty. Every item in the boutique had a story behind it, from a Missoni caftan to a Fendi baguette bag with the tags still on it. If Violet didn't know the real story behind something, she liked to fill in the blanks with her imagination. She knew the caftan, for instance, was from an Italian professor who bought it when she studied abroad in Italy as a college student in the seventies. The professor said she'd had a short but passionate love affair with a distant cousin of Vittorio Emanuele, the last crown prince of Italy. Violet believed her, too, because of the way the woman's cheeks had burned as she recounted the story.

Violet didn't know the details behind the baguette bag. A young journalist from the local alternative newspaper had sold it to the shop

for rent money and simply said it had been a gift. Violet liked to imagine that the journalist received it from a cruel but brilliant New York
fashion editor who gave it to her to try to entice her into a life of re-
porting on runway shows and seasonal trends. Perhaps the journalist
had turned down the job in favor of writing about what she saw as
more important matters, like politics and environmental issues, but
kept the bag for a while as a reminder of the road not taken.

"Do you want something to drink?" Violet asked. "A cup of tea?
Shot of whiskey?"

The girl looked startled. "I, uh, no. I'm only eighteen."

Violet laughed as she plugged in an electric kettle on a small table
behind the counter. The midcentury table, all angles and Scandina-
vian oak, held a silver Victorian tea tray and an assortment of mugs.
The effect was a hodgepodge of styles, like the boutique and like
Violet herself.

"I'm kidding about the whiskey," Violet said. "I don't have any
booze in the store."

"You sure have a lot of pretty old bottles, though." April pointed
toward a shelf full of vintage glassware in every shape and shade—
green, cobalt, ruby red. "What's that big jug for?"

"I'm not sure." Violet went over and took down a stoneware crock
with a tiny finger-sized handle. She plunked it on the counter. "It
doesn't have a mark or a label or anything. Maybe someone used it to
make moonshine."

April picked up the jug and examined the blue floral design on
the front. "Where did you get it?"

"Bent Creek, where I grew up. The owner of the local tavern gave
it to me."

"Is that here in Wisconsin?" April asked. "I've never heard of it."

Violet nodded. "There's no reason you would have, unless you're a
hunting and fishing enthusiast. It's a tiny town up near Lake Superior.
Population of less than a thousand."

"Huh," April said, eyeing Violet's tattoo again. "I wouldn't have guessed that."

"Yeah, I didn't fit in very well there," Violet said. "When I was a kid, my mom used to scold me because I'd wear my flapper Halloween costume to school on a regular Tuesday or put on my First Communion gloves for a trip to the grocery store."

Violet remembered with a smile that on such occasions, her maternal grandmother would stick up for her if she was within earshot. Grandma Lou would wink at Violet and say, "Some people were just meant to sparkle more than others, honey."

Violet waved a hand to avoid any more questions about her past. She opened a mahogany caddy and thumbed through rows of tea bags nestled inside the satin interior. "Are you sure you don't want some tea? I'm making some for myself anyway, so it's no big deal to make another cup."

"Okay, sure." April put down the jug and unzipped her jacket. "Thanks."

"And here, lemme hang up that dress. It'll get wrinkled." Violet whisked the wedding gown from the counter. She smoothed it out and put it on a tall rack next to the register.

"I don't care if it gets wrinkled," April said.

"I do. That thing took me over an hour to steam before I put it out on the sales floor. Silk taffeta is a bitch to press."

Shit, thought Violet, scolding herself for swearing in front of a customer. *There goes my mouth again.* She cast a glance at April, who didn't seem to have noticed or, at least, seemed not to have minded.

"What kind of tea do you want?" Violet asked as she poured hot water into two hand-painted china cups. "I've got green, Earl Grey . . ."

"Do you have anything without caffeine?" April asked, placing her hand on her stomach.

Violet noticed a bit of roundness at the girl's waist and wondered if April was pregnant. Her speculation came with a wave of jealousy and pity. Violet had always loved babies, but lately the desire for one of her own had kicked in with unexpected ferocity. This new longing bothered her, not because she was thirty-eight and single, but because she liked to think she was content with her life the way it was. She had Miles, her pit bull, and an eclectic group of customers who had become her friends. Babies and biological clocks were, in her opinion, conventional. Violet prided herself on being independent and nonconformist—never mind the fact that she sold vintage aprons and corseted dresses in her shop.

"I like chamomile, if you've got it," April said. "My mom used to make it for me."

Violet put tea bags into the cups and handed one to April. "So what made you decide to buy a vintage gown?"

"I live down the street, so I walk by here a lot," April said. "And I like old things. I don't know why. I guess I like the idea that everything has a life behind it, that the past has meaning."

"I know what you mean," Violet said. "I also like to think things were simpler years ago, though I'm sure I'm kidding myself."

"I still remember what you told me about the dress, that the lady who wore it ended up being married for fifty-five years."

"Wow. I'm glad someone actually listens to my stories," Violet said. "I mean, I tell customers details about the merchandise all the time, but I figure most people kind of nod politely and tune me out. I realize not everybody is quite as obsessed with old stuff as I am."

"What you told me about the dress is one of the reasons I chose it. Well, besides the fact that it's beautiful, and so unique."

"Isn't it?" Violet cast a wistful look at the gown, which kept its shape even while hanging on the rack. "It was handmade by the bride. You just don't see that sort of detail on something mass-produced."

"Did the lady who made it bring it in?" April asked.

Violet shook her head. "The couple's daughter did. Her parents died within a week of each other."

"That's so sad."

Violet sipped her tea. "I suppose, but they had a long, happy marriage. That's more than a lot of people get."

"I meant sad for the daughter." April's voice wavered. "Were you in the middle of something? I don't want to hold you up if you have stuff to do."

"Business isn't exactly booming today." Violet gestured around the empty store. "Do you want to talk about what happened? Why you wanted to return the dress, I mean."

The girl shook her head, whipping strands of blond hair against her cheeks. "I don't want to take up any more of your time."

"I'm just changing out the window displays for summer. It's nothing that can't wait." Violet glanced over at her two mannequins in the window, now mismatched with one in a sundress and the other in a peach mohair sweater.

April placed her teacup on the counter next to the register, knocking over a pile of papers. "I'm so sorry," she said, bending down to pick them up.

"Don't worry about it. It's my fault for having my filing lying around. One of these days I should probably get all my records computerized, but I just don't know where to start. Plus, pages full of numbers aren't exactly my strong suit," Violet said. "I'd rather spot-clean a silk blouse or iron vintage linens any day."

"I love numbers," April said. "I got a scholarship to study math at UW starting next fall."

The bells over the door jingled, and a dark-haired woman in a pink sari walked into the store. The shiny folds of the fabric rustled as the woman approached the counter.

"Excuse me for a minute," Violet said.

"I'll get out of your way." April zipped her jacket. "Thanks for the tea."

"No, you don't have to go. It'll probably just be a couple of minutes."

April took a few steps toward the door, then turned around. "Oh, I forgot the dress." She gave Violet a pleading look. "Is it okay if I just leave it here? I don't have any use for it, and I don't want to have to look at it every time I open my closet."

"Sure, that's no problem," Violet said, thinking perhaps she could make an exception to her return policy, just this once. She reached toward the cash register—a hulking metal thing with round buttons similar to a vintage typewriter. When she pulled the lever to open the cash drawer, it stuck. She jiggled it, but it wouldn't budge.

"If you can just hang on a minute, I'll get this thing open," Violet said. But when she looked up from the register, April was gone. Instead, the woman in the sari stood in front of the counter, rummaging in her handbag. Violet noticed stripes of gray hair near her part.

"Hello," Violet said, hiding her surprise with a smile. "What can I do for you?"

The woman's hands emerged from her purse with a red fabric pouch. She turned it upside down and a rainbow of bangle bracelets clattered onto the counter. "I would like to sell these," she said.

Violet picked up one of the bracelets—a thin gold band embedded with blue stones. "They're lovely. Are they costume jewelry?"

"I don't understand what you mean." The woman wrinkled her forehead, creasing the red bindi in the middle of her brow.

"What I meant is, are they real gold?" Violet asked.

The woman shook her head. "I have some eighteen-karat gold bangles at home, but these are just inexpensive ones. The blue ones were a gift from my husband, back when we were young and didn't have any money."

Violet set the bracelet down. "Oh, perhaps you want to keep the blue ones, then? It sounds like they mean something to you."

"No. Not anymore." The edge in the woman's voice signaled that she didn't want to talk about her husband, and Violet respected that. She knew from personal experience that some stories were too painful to tell.

Violet picked up a bracelet with a pink and orange design etched into the metal.

"That one belonged to my daughter," the woman said. "I have been cleaning out her room because she got married recently and bought a condo across town with her husband. That is why I am wearing a sari and bindi and all of this." She touched her forehead. "I only wear them for special occasions. This morning we held a small prayer ceremony, a *puja*, for the newlyweds. My daughter refused an Indian wedding, so her father and I had to settle for a *puja* and brunch after they returned from their honeymoon."

"Are you sure your daughter won't want this?" Violet asked, placing the bangle on the counter.

The woman nodded. "She is the one who told me I should get rid of the things she left behind. I told her I did not mind keeping some of her belongings around, but she said it is time to—how did she put it?—'move on.' She says I hold on to too many old things."

"You and me both."

"Do you have children?" the woman asked.

Violet shook her head and said with forced brightness, "My dog is kind of like my baby, though." She opened the leather-bound inventory journal where she kept records of everything that came into and went out of her store, from a Chanel suit to a crocheted halter top. After checking a couple of entries for similar pieces of jewelry, she said, "I can give you twenty dollars in cash for the lot, or thirty dollars in store credit. Which would you prefer?"

"Cash, if it is not too much trouble," the woman said. "I have so many more things at home. Not just bracelets, but other items, too. I could bring them in sometime this week if you are interested."

"Sure," Violet replied. "We're open every day from ten to seven."

"And what is your name so that I may ask for you?"

"I'm Violet. But you don't need to worry about finding me. I'm the only person who works here, and I'm *always* here. I live upstairs."

"My name is Amithi."

"Nice to meet you." Violet smiled. "I'll just need to see some ID. I have to check it for anyone who sells something to the store. It's a state law, to prevent people from trying to sell stolen stuff, I think."

Amithi produced her license, and Violet opened the register drawer and handed Amithi the money for the bracelets.

"Thank you." Amithi tucked the bills into her purse and glanced toward the windows with a worried look. "And now, I hope you will not think I am being strange . . . it is probably nothing, but I wonder if you know that man who is parked outside your store. I did not think anything of it when I came in, but I noticed that he is still parked in the same place and that he keeps looking over here."

"What? Which car?" Violet went over to the large display window and looked out at the street, where vehicles crammed the curbs, parked bumper to bumper as usual in this college town.

"The silver one there, see?" Amithi joined Violet near the window.

Violet pushed her blunt-cut bangs out of her eyes and saw a gray Nissan across the street, idling in front of the acupuncture clinic. A man sat in the driver's seat, but she couldn't make out his face. "Did you see what the guy looked like?" she asked. "I can't tell from here."

"I did not see him up close, but I think he has brown hair, balding a bit," Amithi said. "He looked to be a large man. Bulky."

Jed, her ex, might have been losing his hair by now. And at the rate he consumed cans of Busch, at least back in their married days, Violet wouldn't have been surprised if he'd put on some bulk, too. In the early days after their divorce, Jed used to drive three hundred miles just to get drunk and show up at her doorstep with threats to drag her back to Bent Creek, but he did so less often now.

The man in the Nissan couldn't be Jed, Violet thought. He wouldn't have been caught dead in anything but an American-made pickup. She forced herself to take a calming breath, like she'd learned in the yoga classes she'd taken a few months before, in an unsuccessful effort to get more balance in her life.

Across the street, the door of the gray car opened, and out stepped a man with muscular arms bulging from his white T-shirt. He wore the tough, poker-faced look of a person who did someone else's dirty work.

"Do you know him?" Amithi asked.

"Never seen him before."

The man came in and pushed the door closed, clattering the bells. "Oops, sorry 'bout that." He shrugged and looked down at a clipboard. "Violet Turner?"

"Yes?" Violet touched her hand to her chest.

Amithi stepped away and went to examine the racks of shoes in the back of the store.

The man handed Violet a thick stack of paper. "I've been asked to give you this." He didn't move from his place on the welcome mat—perhaps because he sensed he wasn't welcome.

Violet pushed her horn-rimmed reading glasses up on the bridge of her nose and scanned the heading on the first page silently: "Notice to Vacate Premises."

"Am I being evicted?" she asked.

Without making eye contact, the man thrust his clipboard at her. "I'll just need you to sign on the line here to acknowledge that you've been served."

"I think you have the wrong person," Violet said. "I have a rent-to-own agreement with my landlord, and a right of first refusal on the building. So I don't see why they'd be evicting me. A portion of my rent each month is credited toward a future down payment."

"I'm just a process server, ma'am. I don't know anything about what the papers are about. You'll have to take that up with your lawyer."

"I don't have a lawyer," she said in a low voice, glancing over her shoulder at Amithi. Violet scribbled her signature.

"Thank you, ma'am. Best of luck to you." The process server bent his head in a slight bow. "Seems like a real nice store you've got here." He tucked his clipboard under his arm and left.

Amithi came back toward Violet. "I am sorry I did not leave. Since you said you did not know the man, I was afraid for you and did not want you to be here alone."

Violet's hands shook as she clutched the documents. She appreciated Amithi's concern, but the only thing worse than getting served with an eviction notice was having a customer there to witness it.

"Is there anything I can do for you?" Amithi asked. "I sensed that man did not have good news for you."

"No," Violet said. "Not good news at all."

Chapter 2

INVENTORY ITEM: *plates, set of six*
APPROXIMATE DATE: *1988*
CONDITION: *fair; small chip on the rim of one of the plates*
ITEM DESCRIPTION: *Assortment of Fiesta ware dinner plates: two apricot, two rose, and two turquoise.*
SOURCE: *estate sale*

April

APRIL SAT AT THE round kitchen table, eating buttered toast and two hard-boiled eggs. She didn't want to eat them, didn't want to eat anything, but the obstetrician told her she needed to add more protein to her diet, and eggs were cheap and easy to cook. She sliced one of them and examined the two halves split open on her plate. The oblong pieces rocked back and forth on the pink Fiesta ware she'd inherited from her mom—if you considered the mess she'd left behind, the half-baked business venture and the cluttered house, an inheritance.

April grabbed the plate and dumped its contents into the trash, but not before catching a whiff of something spoiled. She ran over to the sink, where she vomited up her breakfast. So much for trying to do something good for the baby.

The nausea subsided, but April didn't feel better. It wasn't fair, she thought, that Charlie would be graduating from college in just a few weeks and would go off to med school in Boston in the fall. He'd forge ahead as if nothing had changed, and meanwhile, she'd be stuck here in Madison in this sagging bungalow.

She'd grown up in this house, nestled on an isthmus between Lake Mendota and Lake Monona, just blocks from the white-domed capitol building and the State Street pedestrian mall. The house was one of half a dozen bungalows on the block, mixed in with Victorians and American Foursquares shaded by wide front porches. One of the houses on the street, a Prairie-style beauty with clean lines and a low-pitched roof, had been designed by a student of Frank Lloyd Wright.

Some of the homes, like this one, were still occupied by families, but many of them had been converted over the last several years from student rentals and single-family residences to yoga studios, art galleries, and swanky condo developments. As a kid, April would sit on the front steps on fall Saturdays and wave to college students walking to football games. She'd imagined that someday she'd be one of them, sporting a red sweatshirt and a carefree smile. Now she wasn't so sure.

She was more than twenty weeks into the pregnancy and there was no turning back now. Even if she could find a clinic that would perform an abortion this late, she couldn't go through with one. This baby was her only hope for having anything that resembled a family.

April paged through a pregnancy book she'd checked out from the library. She didn't relate to any of the smiling, shiny-haired women in the pictures. She wished her mom were there so she could ask her about all the weird things happening to her body and emotions, and whether they'd go away. She thumbed through a chapter on prenatal complications, running her finger over all the strange-sounding words for things that could go wrong. "Ectopic pregnancy." "Polyhydramnios." "Preeclampsia." The numbers, especially, stood out for her on the pages, and she fixated on probabilities and percentages. *After twelve weeks, the chance of miscarriage is three in one hundred.*

April also wished her mother were around so that, for once, the focus could shift to something other than her mom's problems. A baby, even an unplanned one, might have injected some normalcy into the frantic highs and bottomless lows that had characterized her mom's last years. Medication kept her bipolar disorder at bay, but just barely, and only if she took it. On more than one occasion, April had found full prescription bottles in the bathroom wastebasket.

April swished some water in her mouth and spit it out in the sink, then sat back down at the table to sort through the mail. Most of the envelopes were addressed to Clutter Consulting LLC, the business her mother had thought up in the middle of a manic streak. Her mom had quit her longtime secretarial job to start the business but never got it off the ground. When April questioned her mom about the feasibility of helping other people organize their lives when she could scarcely manage her own, Kat Morgan had said, "Oh, honey. Not everything comes down to mathematical certainty. Sometimes you've gotta take a chance."

Saliva pooled in the back of April's mouth and she got up and ran back to the sink, thinking she was going to be sick again. Despite what her mom had said, April knew quite a bit about taking chances. She'd taken a big one five months earlier, on the December morning after her eighteenth birthday.

She should have known better than to have sex for the first time just a few days before she had to retake the SAT, but she and Charlie had already waited for what felt like forever. When the condom broke, he'd held her and told her not to panic. They'd gone together to Walgreens to get the morning-after pill, where the pimply young pharmacist told them about the likelihood of side effects like nausea, vomiting, and severe cramping. *About one in four women experiences unpleasant side effects.*

April couldn't live with those sorts of odds of getting sick during the SAT. She had bombed it when she took it in November, just weeks after her mom's accident. She needed to do well the second time around to have a shot at getting any of the scholarships she'd applied for. With that in mind, she had thrown away the white paper pharmacy bag without opening it. She went on to ace the SAT, earning a perfect score on the math section. Unfortunately, she also aced the at-home pregnancy test she took two weeks later.

And that was how she'd ended up here, dry-heaving over the kitchen sink.

The doorbell rang and April straightened her back, startled. She went out to the foyer, where, through the leaded glass window, she saw a gray-haired woman in a suit and sunglasses standing on the front porch.

Shit, thought April. It was Mrs. Elizabeth Barrett, a member of the local women's organization that had awarded her a full college scholarship. April had forgotten about the meeting they'd scheduled.

April opened the door and tried to shield her body with it. She hadn't yet told anyone from the scholarship committee about her pregnancy. "Hi, Mrs. Barrett."

The older woman stepped inside. "Good morning." She removed her sunglasses and tucked them into her handbag, which was enormous and bright yellow. And probably expensive.

"I like your purse," April said.

"You don't need to suck up to me, dear. You've already got the scholarship. Unless you're trying to get me to leave you something in my will, which seems to be the reason most people kiss my rear. And if that's it, I've got news for you, honey. I'm not planning on dying any time soon."

"Okay," April said, taken aback. "But I wasn't sucking up. I really do like the bag. And I'm *definitely* not after an inheritance. I've got enough problems trying to deal with my mom's estate."

The word "estate" was misleading, April thought. Before her mom died, she'd always thought the word implied some sort of wealth. She learned she was wrong after seeing all the letters from banks trying to collect debts from the nonexistent assets of her mom's "estate." Now she just piled all the letters up and dropped them off periodically at the lawyer's office.

"Can I get you anything to drink?" April asked.

"No, thank you, I'm fine," said Mrs. Barrett. "Let's just have a seat."

April led her into the living room. They sat down opposite one another in worn wing chairs.

"So." Mrs. Barrett leaned forward. "One of the other committee members stopped by your school to drop off some forms for you the other day."

April sucked in her breath. She was busted.

"The front office said you've been absent lately. Have you been ill?"

By reflex, April folded her arms in front of her midsection. "Not exactly."

"April," said the older woman after a pause. "Why do you think I'm here today?"

April sat up straighter. "I thought I was required to meet with you as a condition of my scholarship. That's what you said on the phone, anyway."

"That's not entirely true. Well, for you it is." Mrs. Barrett repositioned a gold watch on her bony wrist. "What I mean is, in the past we haven't required other scholarship recipients to meet with a committee member. But because of your special circumstances, having lost your mother so recently, we thought it would be a good idea to make sure someone checks in on you."

April couldn't decide whether to be touched or annoyed. She was so tired of everyone feeling sorry for her. Most of her interactions lately were stripped down, sanitized through a filter of pity. What people didn't know, though, was that April had been taking care of herself for years, even before her mom died. There were plenty of times when her mom was so out of it that April had to do everything around the house: grocery shop, renew the license plates, make sure the bills got paid.

"You can tell me what's going on," Mrs. Barrett said. "I won't tell the rest of the committee, not if you don't want me to."

"Okay, but you can't tell anyone else. Not yet, anyway," April said. She figured there was probably no point in lying. It would be impossible to hide her condition soon enough, if it wasn't already. Recently she'd caught a lot of people staring at her belly. That shop lady with the tattoo, Violet, had done it the other day at the vintage store.

"I won't tell anybody," Mrs. Barrett said. "That is, unless you've committed a crime."

"Well, it's not a crime as far as I know," April said. "I'm pregnant."

April had only uttered those words aloud once before, to Charlie, after she'd taken the home pregnancy test. He'd responded with a marriage proposal.

Mrs. Barrett's response was less enthusiastic. She looked shocked, and April was certain she was going to lose her scholarship on the spot. Surprisingly, the realization didn't sting very much. April *wanted* it to sting, wanted to feel any sort of sensation other than the hollow ache she'd been feeling since Charlie left. Losing him so soon after losing her mom, though in a different way, burned like ripping the bandage from a still-seeping wound.

"You can't just drop out of high school," Mrs. Barrett said. "If you're embarrassed or worried about what your classmates will think, I'm sure we can talk to your teachers and figure something out."

"I'm not embarrassed," April said. "I didn't stop going to class just because I'm pregnant. I was also bored."

Mrs. Barrett put a hand to her temple. "I have to say this is terribly disappointing. How will you be able to go to college if you don't graduate high school?"

"I'd still like to go to college. I took the GED already."

There, thought April. *I'm not a* complete *fuckup.*

Mrs. Barrett opened her mouth, then shut it again. She shook her head.

"I passed," April said. "And I already sent my scores to the University of Wisconsin. The admissions committee said they were fine, in terms of holding my place in the freshman class. I should have taken the GED months ago, really. I could have saved all that time I spent sitting in class."

April knew she was acting defensive with Mrs. Barrett, maybe even cocky. But one of the main reasons she'd stopped showing up at the high school was that everybody, from her guidance counselor to the lunch lady, seemed to think they knew what was best for her. They didn't hesitate in sharing their opinions but never asked April about her own.

"I'm assuming the fact that you're telling me all of this means you're planning to keep the baby," Mrs. Barrett said.

April nodded. She knew Mrs. Barrett probably expected her to say what a difficult decision it had been, how she'd considered all of her choices, including adoption, but that would have been a lie. April knew what it was like to lose a mother, and she couldn't put another person through it.

"I don't have children," Mrs. Barrett said. "But I've managed to stay busy all these years with my charity work. I'm not sure I would've had time to do it all if I *did* have a family."

April realized she must have looked scared, because Mrs. Barrett continued. "Not that I'm saying you can't have children and still do other things you want to do in life, necessarily. And *that's* what we should talk about. If you haven't been going to your classes, what have you been doing with your time?"

April looked out the window. The peony bush her mom had planted several summers ago on the side of the house was now blooming a brilliant pink. Peonies had been her mother's favorite flower. April thought they were a rather unstable plant. The flowers were too showy for their own good; the stems often flopped toward the ground under the weight of the huge blossoms.

She turned her face back toward Mrs. Barrett. "Well, I'm still going to my advanced calculus course at the university, so I can get the credits, but that ends in a couple of weeks," she said.

April didn't mention that the main reason she kept going to her college-level class was that she hoped to run into Charlie on campus. She knew he had some science classes in the same building she went to for calc. They'd met when the building was evacuated for a fire alarm in the fall. April had stood shivering on the sidewalk waiting for the firemen to let the students go back inside, and Charlie had offered her his sweatshirt. She still remembered the way it smelled, of pine needles and Ivory soap.

After that, they'd started studying together. April also began spending the night sometimes at Charlie's apartment on campus, telling her mother she was staying at a girlfriend's house. She hated lying to her mom, but she was willing to do almost anything to spend a series of uninterrupted hours with Charlie, lying skin to skin and sharing secrets underneath the billows of his down comforter—a shield from the petty, perpetually boring world of high school, which April couldn't wait to leave behind.

Her mom didn't approve of the relationship. The few times April had brought him over for dinner, Kat had thought Charlie was sweet enough, but she worried that, because he was older, he would soon move on and break her daughter's heart.

Charlie's parents didn't approve of the situation, either, but for different reasons. Judy and Trip Cabot thought it was inappropriate for their son to be dating a girl who was still in high school, and they worried about what people would think. Even before they had a chance to meet April, they pressured Charlie to break up with her. After April's mom died, though, the Cabots softened their stance. They didn't accompany Charlie to the funeral, since they'd never met Kat or even April, but they did invite April to spend Thanksgiving with them just a few weeks later.

April remembered how intimidated she'd been, not just by the Cabots' towering Tudor-style home, but also by Judy Cabot's forced smile and sharp gaze, which seemed to absorb and assess everything upon which it fell. Though Judy was coolly polite that day and Trip bordered on friendly, April sensed that if it weren't for her dead mother, she wouldn't have been invited.

Once during the evening, when April was returning from a visit to the marble-tiled powder room, she overheard Judy say, "Charlie, you only need to set three wineglasses at the table. April is barely old enough to drive, let alone to drink."

"I don't get why April's age is such a big deal to you, Mom," Charlie had said. "Dad is seven years older than you."

"That's different. I didn't have four or more years of medical school ahead of me when we started dating. And anyway, I was twenty-one when we met. April is seventeen."

I'll be eighteen next week, April had wanted to say, but she didn't want them to know she'd heard.

As the weeks went by and the accident inched further into the past, the Cabots became less subtle about their objections to Charlie and April's relationship—or Judy did, anyway, taking every opportunity she could to express her displeasure. Trip didn't say much, not even when Charlie broke the news of the pregnancy and engagement to his parents that March. Judy had started crying at the dining room table, tears dripping down her tastefully made-up face and onto the grilled salmon on her plate.

Mrs. Barrett, too, looked disappointed now as she shifted in her chair and asked April, "So other than the few hours a week when you're in class and the time you spend studying, what else have you been doing? Do you have a job?"

April looked at the hardwood floor. "No," she muttered. She'd been living off the small stores of cash her mom had hidden around the house during her bouts of paranoid mania—behind the micro-wave, in the cookie jar, under the loose tile in the bathroom. April saved money by spending most of her time at home, watching reality TV and feeling sorry for herself. In fact, she'd been so lethargic and listless that she wondered if she was starting to show symptoms of her mom's mental illness. Her mother had been diagnosed with bipolar disorder when she was in college, and the disease had a strong genetic component—a heritability rate of 71 percent, according to an article April had read. As she approached her twenties, she lived with the fear that she could develop it any day now.

"Well, you'll need to get a job, or an internship or *something*," said Mrs. Barrett. "It's only May. We can't have you just moping around until you start college in the fall. Speaking of which, when is this baby due?"

"Labor Day. Ironic, isn't it?" April let out a halfhearted laugh. "Can I delay starting college until the spring semester?"

"I'm afraid not," said Mrs. Barrett. "If you decide not to enroll in the fall, the committee will have to offer the scholarship to someone else."

"I guess I'll need to find someone to watch the baby when I'm in class." April figured Mrs. Barrett was probably right about getting a job or an internship. She needed something to get her out of this house and, if possible, keep her from going crazy.

"Have you thought about what sort of summer job might interest you?" Mrs. Barrett asked.

April played with a strand of hair. "Who's going to hire a pregnant teenager?"

"I'll make some calls." Mrs. Barrett got up and slung her purse over her shoulder. "I've got a lot of connections in this city."

Chapter 3

INVENTORY ITEM: *sari*
APPROXIMATE DATE: *1968*
CONDITION: *good; small water stain near the hem*
ITEM DESCRIPTION: *Orange sari made from silk dupioni with gold paisley design.*
SOURCE: *Amithi Singh*

Amithi

IN A METERED PARKING space in front of Hourglass Vintage, Amithi turned off the car ignition with one hand and clutched her cell phone with the other.

"Dad keeps leaving me messages," said her daughter, Jayana, on the other end. "I'm not calling him back until you tell me what's going on with the two of you."

"That's between your father and me," Amithi said.

It had been almost a month since she had accompanied her husband, Naveen, to Chicago for an engineering conference at which he was scheduled to present a paper. They'd driven there together in the same silver Honda Amithi sat in now, looking forward to spending a weekend in the city. The trip hadn't gone the way either of them had planned, though, and culminated with Amithi driving back to Madison a day early, alone, in the middle of the night.

Naveen had returned to Madison by bus after the conference on Sunday evening, and though he called her from the bus station to apologize for everything that had happened, Amithi refused to pick him up from the station. Since then, they'd hardly spoken to one another, even though they were living in the same house. They passed each other in the hallways of their two-story Colonial like strangers on a crowded city sidewalk—except that the house was empty, but for the two of them. And silent.

Amithi didn't want to talk about what had led to their rift, though, not even with Jayana. So she shifted the focus of the phone conversation to her daughter instead.

"Have you thought any more about when you and Jack will go to India to see your grandparents?" Amithi asked. "They are disappointed that they have not yet had a chance to meet him."

"They could have come to our wedding if they'd really wanted to," Jayana said.

Amithi was not surprised when her parents declined her offer to pay for their plane tickets to come to Jayana's wedding. She tried to picture her mother and father, both in their eighties, at O'Hare airport—first shuffling their way through customs, then boarding a tram to take them to their connecting gate, all with a crippling case of jet lag. She then tried to imagine their expressions if they'd seen the location of Jayana and Jack's wedding ceremony—a peeling red barn in the middle of an overgrown meadow. Jayana had called the setting "simple" and "intimate." Amithi had thought "insulting" was a better word. Her husband had worked hard all his life, and for what? To see his daughter get married under the beams of a hayloft, in a dress that looked like a nightgown.

"You do not understand," Amithi said. "Even if Nana and Nani had made it to the wedding here, it would still be important for you to go to visit them, and the rest of the family, too. It is the least you can do, since you decided not to have the wedding in India."

"I'm not sure I want to drag Jack from temple to temple all over Rajasthan," Jayana said. "I know Nana and Nani don't approve of me being married to a non-Indian man, anyway. Just like you and Dad don't."

It was true that Amithi and Naveen would have preferred for their daughter to marry an Indian boy with roots near Jaipur, where they'd grown up and still had family. They'd spent years bringing their daughter to their Indian friends' parties and *pujas,* hoping she would hit it off with a potential match. But that was the most they could do. They had learned long ago that their daughter made her own decisions—a fact that was both a source of pride for Amithi and an endless well of frustration.

She did not know when the sea between her and Jayana had begun to swell. They'd had so many differences in recent years. First, there had been the fact that Jayana had chosen to move to the West Coast for college, rather than attending the local university where Naveen taught. When Jayana had moved back home for graduate school, again taking up residence in the room where she'd grown up, Amithi had rejoiced to have her daughter under her roof again—that is, until Jayana announced that she was getting a PhD in art history.

Amithi had tried to point out why she was worried about Jayana's choice of academic focus—that she wanted the girl to have a good job so that she could be financially independent. Amithi herself had never had the freedom that came along with making one's own money. As a young woman in India, she'd begun coursework for a BA but left school when she moved to the U.S. and never reenrolled. And though Amithi never complained—she was grateful for her health and the prosperous life she and Naveen had built—she had the sense that Jayana was all too aware of the fact that her mother's choices in life had been limited. All through her twenties and into her early thirties, Jayana had repeatedly told her parents she had no intention of getting married. Then she met Jack, and within a matter of months, she had not only gotten married but also had bought a condo with him and moved across town.

"What does Jack think?" asked Amithi. "Does he want to make a trip to India?"

"Oh, he's all for it," said Jayana. "He sees it as a great opportunity to do some research. I told him there won't be any time for research because he'll be too busy getting introduced to relatives *I* don't even know. He thinks I'm exaggerating."

Amithi thought it was strange that Jack, a graduate student in political science, was doing his master's thesis on the rule of Warren Hastings, the first British governor-general of colonial India. When Naveen and Amithi were still on speaking terms, Naveen used to joke sometimes that Jack was trying to colonize their daughter.

Amithi didn't think it was funny. She'd been protective of her only child since she was born, more than three decades earlier, through a premature and difficulty delivery that the doctors said would have to be Amithi's last. Though Jayana later grew strong and healthy, catching up to her peers at a miraculous pace, Amithi never ceased to picture her as she came into the world—as a tiny, blue-faced baby, wheezing for life.

"All I'm asking is that you respect your grandparents' wishes," she said. "You do not know how much longer they will be around."

"I know," Jayana said. "But that doesn't mean I have to let them dictate my life from halfway around the world."

Furious, Amithi banged a hand on the steering wheel and accidentally set off the horn.

"Mom, what are you doing?"

Amithi took a deep breath. "I did not bring you up to speak that way about your grandparents. Call me when you are ready to have some respect for your family."

She hung up, thinking about how cell phones were not nearly as satisfying as older phones had been for ending angry conversations. She used to be able to slam down a receiver. Now all she could do was press a tiny, glowing button.

According to the clock on her dashboard, Amithi had been sitting in front of the boutique for fifteen minutes. She realized that her car, a silver Honda, looked similar to the car of the process server from the other day. Amithi hoped her being parked here for the last quarter of an hour hadn't caused Violet any unnecessary alarm.

In the bicycle lane next to Amithi's parked car, a girl whizzed by with her bike basket full of vegetables and flowers, probably on her way back from the Saturday morning farmer's market on the Capitol Square. The Prius parked in front of Amithi had a bumper sticker that said IF YOU'RE LOOKING FOR A SIGN FROM THE UNIVERSE, THIS IS IT.

Amithi picked up a shopping bag from the passenger seat and went inside the boutique.

Violet was helping a customer, a woman in a belted trench coat, but smiled when she saw Amithi.

The lady in the trench coat held up a red dress. "Are all of your items *used*?" she asked.

Amithi cringed when she heard this.

"I prefer to say pre-loved," Violet said. "We take beautiful, high-quality items and give them new life. We save them from neglect in someone's basement or, worse, a landfill."

The woman dropped the dress she'd been holding as if it were crawling with lice. She hurried past Amithi without making eye contact.

"That was quite rude," Amithi said after the woman had left.

"She didn't even bother looking at the label." Violet picked the dress up and cradled it for a moment before hanging it back on the rack. "I mean, this is a 1970s Diane von Furstenberg wrap, for God's sake. It's probably one of the first ones she ever designed. It's not exactly something you throw on the floor. Go into any department store, even now, and you'll see half a dozen knockoffs of this very same style."

"Some people only pay attention to something if it is new and flashy," Amithi said. "I think they overlook a lot of beauty in the world that way."

Violet smiled. "I'm glad you came back in. I was hoping I could talk to you about what happened the other day."

"I have not mentioned it to anyone, if that is what you are wondering."

"I appreciate that." Violet tipped her head to one side. "What did you hear, exactly?"

The polite thing to do, thought Amithi, would be to say she heard nothing. But Violet did not seem like the type of person who would be satisfied with that answer, so she said, "I heard you say it had something to do with your lease. Something about eviction."

"Oh, Jesus." Violet paced the wood floors in her red heels. She put a hand over her mouth. "Sorry, that was probably really unprofessional. It's just that, well, the shop is my life."

Amithi nodded, even though she'd never had a business. She had never even had a paying job, for that matter. But she knew what it was like to put her whole heart into something and not have it turn out the way she'd expected.

Violet stopped pacing. "I hope you won't mention this to anyone else. My reputation in the community is everything to me. When I first moved here a few years ago, no one knew who I was. I've had to work hard to build up a name for myself and my business."

"Of course. I will not say anything." Amithi tugged at the folds of her tunic top. She'd made it from some floral fabric her sister sent from India, and though she'd designed it to fit loosely, today it seemed to stretch around her middle. She made a mental note to stop snacking as a way to pass the time at home.

"Thank you," Violet said.

"It is nothing. Is there anything I can do to help?"

"I don't think so. Unfortunately, it's one of those things I need to handle on my own," Violet said. "So what brings you in today?"

Amithi lifted up her shopping bag. "I brought in some more things I thought you might be interested in for the store."

"You really must be doing quite a bit of cleaning and organizing, to come in twice in one week," Violet said.

"Ah. Yes," Amithi said. Though it was true that she *had* been culling items from her closets, one of the main reasons she'd come back into the shop was that she needed someone to talk to, something to do to give her day some structure. Amithi remembered feeling exhausted every night when Jayana was young, wishing for just a few more hours in the day. Now she felt there were far too many, and she often longed for evening simply because it came with a set of concrete duties: prepare dinner, eat, clean up, and go to bed. Today, Naveen had gone into the office before the sun came up. Amithi felt relieved to have him—and the hushed tension between them—out of the house. Yet she wasn't sure how to fill the long, lonely hours of the day.

"Let's see what you brought," Violet said.

"If you cannot use these things, then please do tell me. I will not be offended." Amithi emptied the bag onto the counter with care.

Violet unfolded a swath of orange fabric about six feet long.

"It's a sari," Amithi said. "I have so many, and I hardly ever wear them anymore, so I brought in several. That one has a small stain on it, though."

Violet examined a spot near the hem. "You can barely see it." She refolded the fabric and picked up another item—this one a short, sleeveless blouse.

"That's the shirt that goes under it. It's called a *choli*."

"These are gorgeous," Violet said. "I'll buy this orange one from you, but I'll have to pass on the others for now. I'll have to see how this one sells first. I've never carried anything like this in the shop before."

"What if I made them into something else?" asked Amithi. "A shorter skirt or dress?"

"You know how to do that?"

"Sure," Amithi said. "I like to sew."

"That might work," Violet said. "But I can't guarantee I'd be able to buy whatever you make. What sort of inventory I take depends on what's selling well in the store at any given moment."

Amithi didn't care as much about the money as she did about having a project to keep her occupied. "Maybe I'll make one or two and bring them in for you to see. If you are not able to buy them, I will not be offended."

"That sounds fine, as long as it's not too much trouble for you."

"Not at all. It will be good for me to have something creative to do. Oh, and I almost forgot. I brought something else, too." Amithi put her hand inside her purse and felt around for the small velvet box she'd been carrying with her for the last few days. She took it out and flipped it open to reveal a pair of gold, dangly earrings. A sizable red stone in the center of each piece glittered under the overhead lights.

"They are real this time," Amithi said. "Not costume jewelry like the bangle bracelets."

"I see that." Violet's eyes widened. "Are those rubies?"

"Yes. I brought in the appraisal, if you'd like to see it." She searched for it in her purse.

Violet held up her hand. "That's okay. I don't need to see what they're worth to know I can't pay you anything close to a fair price. You'd probably be better off taking them to a jeweler."

"Do you know of any that take vintage jewelry?"

"Sure." Violet scribbled the name of a jeweler on the back of a business card. "This place on the west side deals in a lot of vintage pieces. If you'd like, I can call ahead to let them know you're coming. But before I call, I have to ask—are you sure you want to sell these?"

Amithi nodded. She'd been debating selling the earrings ever since her daughter said she didn't want to wear them for her wedding. Amithi had offered to give them to her anyway, but Jayana had refused, claiming they were gaudy. She'd told her mother that, rather than jewelry she'd never wear, she'd prefer to have money to buy furniture for her and Jack's new condo. Amithi thought of her conversation with her daughter earlier that day. She decided she would sell the earrings to the jeweler and give her daughter the money, like she wanted.

June 20, 1968

Last week at this time, Amithi had sat on the patio of her mother and father's house, chattering in the humid shade with her aunties and drinking mint tea to calm the anxiety fluttering around inside her. Now she sat on an air-conditioned plane next to a man she barely knew, but for the few, short conversations they'd exchanged before the wedding, the touch of one another's hands as they'd circled the sacred fire during their Hindu ceremony, and the shy but urgent lovemaking the night before.

Despite the giggles and anticipation, the whole intimate episode had been over in a matter of painful, but not unpleasant, minutes. Before the wedding, Amithi's older female friends and relatives—

her "aunties"—had whispered all sorts of seduction secrets to her as they wrapped her in her beaded bridal sari and pulled the crimson folds around her slender waist. They'd made such a fuss over sex that Amithi expected it to be either miserable or spectacular. She wasn't disappointed when it was neither. Afterward, she'd curled up like a child and slept in a fatigued haze on the flower-strewn bed until, in the blue dawn, she'd risen to check the contents of her luggage for the last time.

Now they were flying to a place called Chicago, where Naveen, her husband—the word tumbled around inside her head like a monkey in a treetop—was pursuing his doctorate in chemical engineering. Although he was the only Indian student in his program, Naveen had assured Amithi she would feel at home in their suburban community west of the city. There was an Indian grocery store not far from their apartment, he'd told her, where he claimed they could buy ready-to-eat samosas that tasted almost as good as his mother's. This news came as a relief to Amithi. She hated frying the triangular, potato-stuffed pastries. She always ended up spattering grease on her clothes, resulting in dark spots she couldn't wash out.

As Amithi peered out the rounded window at the clouds, she marveled at how everything had happened so quickly. In March, she and her younger sister, Priya, had been watching the Beatles on their family's little television set. All anyone could talk about—from the music teacher to the man who sold savory *chaat* from the snack cart on the corner—was the arrival of the British rock band at an ashram in Rishikesh. No matter that it was almost five hundred kilometers away from Jaipur. That didn't stop the entire city from gossiping about the star musicians. Amithi did not understand why these men would fly so far from home and pay money to a gray-haired man to learn to meditate—something that anyone could do for free with just a little bit of time and discipline.

One moment, Amithi had been staring at the band members and their fair-haired wives on the black and white screen, and the next, her parents had marched into the room, turned off the set, and announced that they'd "spoken with the Singhs at the club." The Singhs' son was home from school in America, they'd said, and the three of them were coming over for tea that afternoon.

Even before that day, Amithi had already heard a lot about the Singhs and their only child, Naveen. Her parents found a way to work his name and his accomplishments into even the most mundane conversations.

"Do you like the *paneer* I made for this dish, love?" her mother had asked one day at the dinner table. "Mrs. Singh shared with me her method for making it. She uses lemon juice instead of whey from the last batch. It makes it a little firmer."

Her father had raised a piece of the white cheese to his lips. "Oh, yes, dear. Very good."

"Mrs. Singh says it's her son's favorite."

"Excellent taste that boy has."

Based on her parents' endorsements, when Amithi finally had the opportunity to meet Naveen on that March afternoon, she'd expected to see a modern god, a gilded prince. Instead, into the sitting room walked a gangly boy with shy brown eyes and sweaty skin. Amithi had felt sorry for him for having to venture out in the heat and dust with his parents, while she'd sat in the comfort of her room, combing her black hair and selecting a perfect, sky-colored sari with her mother. The Singhs lived just a few miles away, but even a couple of minutes in the early-summer humidity were enough to soak a person's clothes with perspiration.

Amithi and Naveen had not done much talking at that first meeting. Their parents did most of it, exchanging questions and answers about one another's relatives—where they lived and what they did.

They'd spoken of nieces with beautiful, healthy children and nephews at the top of their classes.

In her seventeen years, Amithi had never interviewed for a job, but she imagined it would be a lot like that first meeting with Naveen's parents.

"And you, Amithi? What do you enjoy doing?" Mrs. Singh had asked her.

"I like to sew and design clothing," Amithi said.

"She made the *salwar kameez* I'm wearing," her mother bragged, running her hand over her loose blouse and pants set. "I've never been good with working with silk, so slippery, but Amithi makes it look easy."

Mrs. Singh nodded in appreciation. "It's a good skill to have, sewing. A woman who knows how to mend can save her husband a lot of money."

Amithi had never mended men's clothes before and didn't have much interest in doing so. She preferred to sketch elaborate embroidery patterns and Hollywood-style gowns, but she kept that fact to herself. It was just a hobby, and would probably be thought silly by the Singhs.

During that initial encounter, she hadn't made much eye contact with Naveen. She did not want to be thought too forward. She'd snuck glances at him, though, when he reached down for his cup or to stir his tea. He was not overly handsome, she'd thought, nor was he ugly. She'd decided she was glad of that. She had always thought it would be a burden to have a husband who was prettier than she was.

Amithi hadn't seen Naveen again until their engagement ceremony, where they had exchanged rings while a pious pandit chanted in Sanskrit and selected a wedding date from the astrological calendar.

Now, on the airplane, Amithi leaned back in her seat and wrapped her shawl around her shoulders. In the weeks before her departure, she had spent a lot of time worrying about the flight. Now she could see that the flying part was not so bad—it was the cool, sterile space that made her feel uneasy.

Amithi felt a warm hand on her arm, and a stewardess offered her a cup of tea. Amithi accepted but spilled a few drops onto her orange sari as she tried to take a sip.

Naveen pulled the handkerchief from his pocket and handed it to Amithi.

"Thank you," she said, touched by this small gesture. It meant he had noticed. "Your mother told me it was not a good idea to wear a sari on the plane, that I should have packed something more practical. But I always wear a sari for important occasions, and today is one of them."

"Never mind my mother," Naveen said. "You look beautiful."

Amithi blushed as she dabbed at the spot, hoping it wouldn't stain. She had purchased the sari from a stall at the bazaar near her parents' house. On subsequent trips to the market, she had never been able to find that particular vendor's stall again, nor had she ever seen another shade of silk in such a brilliant, sunny hue. It reminded her of the marigolds that dotted the flower beds along the pink avenues of Jaipur, the only home she'd ever known and was now leaving behind.

Amithi looked over at Naveen, who was nodding off to sleep. She studied his hands, resting still in his lap. Despite the week of festivities in their honor, the couple had had little time to talk with one another during the continuous stream of music, praying, and arriving relatives. She noticed now that Naveen had slender fingers and very clean fingernails, fitting for someone whose chosen profession required precision.

She looked down at her own hands, covered in swirls of fading henna. She touched the place between her thumb and forefinger where the *mehendi* artist had scrolled Naveen's name, hidden between drawings of lotus petals and meandering vines. She wondered how long it would take for the henna to fade completely. She didn't want it to. She feared that her connection to India, her childhood, her family would fade along with it.

She could not let Naveen know that homesickness was already tightening her throat and chest. In the days leading up to the wedding, between the *puja* prayer ceremonies and elaborate meals, her aunties warned her never to complain to Naveen that she missed her family. One of the reasons the Singhs had approved of Amithi as a match for their son was her reputation for being strong, sensible, and resilient. Naveen's doctoral program required him to work long hours in the lab, sometimes straight through the night. A needy young bride, pining away for her parents and her homeland, would not be a good partner for him.

Amithi had nodded at her aunties' advice but largely ignored it. Intoxicated by the scent of jasmine flowers in a garland around her neck, and blinded by the gleam of gold jewelry, she could not see the future as anything but a beautiful and unceasing adventure. And marrying Naveen was the fastest way there.

She had not comprehended then, as she did now, on the humming plane, that she would not see her family again for a very long time. She wondered when she would next taste her mother's roti flatbread, laugh at her sister's jokes.

Amithi felt a pulling sensation on her scalp. A few strands of her hair were tangled in one of the ruby earrings she'd received as a wedding gift from her mother, who had received them as a gift at her own wedding many years ago. Amithi reached up and touched the earring to free her hair from it. The precious metal, which previously had danced with light, felt cold and sharp to the touch.

Chapter 4

INVENTORY ITEM: *suit*

APPROXIMATE DATE: *1980s*

CONDITION: *excellent*

ITEM DESCRIPTION: *Black skirt suit in summer-weight wool. Shoulder pads and tapered waist on jacket. Fitted skirt with back slit.*

SOURCE: *former president of Madison Chamber of Commerce*

Violet

WHEN VIOLET HAD MOVED to Madison five years earlier, she thought she'd put the worst behind her. With Bent Creek three hundred miles away and her divorce all but finalized, she thought the only thing that stood between her and her dream of running a successful vintage boutique was a little bit of start-up money and some hard work.

She chose Madison because of its reputation as a place where being different was not only accepted but celebrated—like Austin or Portland, but with more snow in the winter. In Bent Creek, Violet had always felt like an oddball. While everyone else wore jeans and

Carhartt jackets, Violet ran errands and waited tables wearing 1940s shirtdresses or tie-bottom rockabilly tops with pedal-pusher slacks. In Madison, with its experimental theater groups, unicyclists, and near-constant political protests, it was easy to express oneself without standing out *too* much. Violet liked that about it.

She remembered sitting in her landlord's wood-paneled office on the day she signed her rent-to-own lease, initialing each page, then passing it over to Ted Mortensen, the "and son" of Mortensen & Son Properties Inc. As she'd waited for Ted's assistant to make her a copy, Violet had thought about the perfect shade of blue she'd paint the walls of the shop and the vintage gold and white chevron fabric she'd use for the dressing room curtains. She tried to picture how she'd arrange her sparse furniture in the apartment above the shop.

Violet hadn't expected then that she'd now be sitting in the same wood-paneled office, begging Ted to let her sign a new lease, or give her some more time to come up with a down payment to buy the building, or something, *anything,* to keep her from getting kicked out. Her current location was ideal for foot traffic, and for attracting the types of customers she'd come to depend on for her livelihood.

The building she rented was just blocks from the government and office buildings on the Capitol Square, which meant that professional women and elected officials with money to spend often came into Hourglass Vintage to shop during lunch or after work. The building also sat on the fringe of the sprawling University of Wisconsin campus. This meant not only that stylish professors were regular customers, but also that the boutique enjoyed a steady influx of gently used designer garb from sorority girls who shopped in New York and L.A. with their parents' credit cards when they went home for breaks.

There was no other street in town that was both zoned for retail and would allow Violet to reach her broad range of customers the way she did now. Leases seldom turned over in the area, and when they did, they went for premium rent rates. In the years since she'd signed her rent-to-own agreement, real estate prices in the neighborhood had skyrocketed. Academics and young professionals had begun to snap up the sprawling old houses on surrounding blocks for inflated prices, which sent rent rates soaring. Violet had been lucky to lock in a good rate just before the market turned. If she couldn't get Ted to honor their deal, she didn't have a prayer for finding another space in the neighborhood within her budget.

Violet leaned forward in her chair. "So tell me what's going on, Ted," she said. "I haven't missed any rent payments, so why is a process server showing up at my door?"

The fluorescent overhead lights reflected off Ted's crew-cut hair, which appeared to have been styled with gobs of polyurethane. His tie listed to one side of his bulging belly.

"It's true you haven't missed any payments," he said. "But there's a clause in your lease that says we can terminate the contract at any time if we opt to put the property on the market."

Violet made a mental note to look at her lease again or, better yet, to go over it with her friend Karen, a lawyer. "I didn't know you were thinking of selling the building."

Ted turned his head toward his office window, which offered a view of the white dome of the state capitol, topped by a gold statue reminiscent of a Greek goddess.

"I'm sure you're aware property values have gone up in that area," Ted said. "Which is remarkable, given that they've gone down almost everywhere else. So we're better off selling our holdings in that neighborhood and reinvesting in other areas."

Violet cringed at hearing her shop and her home referred to as a "holding."

"I thought I had a right of first refusal," she said.

"You do," Ted replied. "And if you can come up with the rest of the money to purchase the building at market rate, you can do so. But in the meantime, the terms of the lease allow us to actively market the building until you either exercise your right of first refusal or relinquish it."

"What's market rate? I mean, what are you listing it for?" Violet asked. "Because I *am* interested in buying it."

"Just under a million."

Violet blinked. "I had no idea it was worth that much."

"The building is on the only double lot on the block, so it's attractive to developers."

"There's no way I'll be able to get a million-dollar mortgage."

"Nine hundred and ninety thousand, actually," Ted said.

"Oh. Well in *that* case . . ." Violet gave him a wry half smile, even though she wanted to scream. "Why didn't you just tell me you were putting the building up for sale instead of sending a process server to my door with eviction papers?"

"It's not technically an eviction yet," Ted said. "It's merely a notice to you that we're exercising our right to sell the property under the lease. It will only become an eviction if you don't move out by the end of August."

"Or buy the property by then," Violet said.

"Right." Ted smirked, as if he knew just as well as Violet did that coming up with a down payment and close to a million-dollar mortgage was very, very far out of her reach.

"Can't I just rent the property from the new owner?" Violet asked.

"I think that's unlikely. It's being advertised as redevelopment property," Ted said. "Having a retail and a residential tenant in here really limits the way we can market the property, so we'll need you out by the end of summer anyway. Unless, of course, you want to make a deal." He leaned back in his chair and folded his arms.

"I'm not sure what you're getting at," Violet said.

"We're hoping you'll be motivated to move out voluntarily before the end of the summer, and sign papers releasing your right of first refusal. If you do so, we can offer you a little incentive."

His smirk made Violet uneasy. Nonetheless, she asked, "What sort of incentive?"

"A little start-up cash for your next location. We'd give you back your last two months of rent."

Violet had to bite her lip to keep from laughing. Two months' rent wasn't nothing, but it certainly wasn't enough to make up for the higher rent rates she'd have to pay if she moved to another building.

"I don't want my last two months of rent," Violet replied. "What I want is to not have to move out of my shop *and* my apartment, with only a couple months' notice. What I want is to buy the building. I thought I was on course for doing that, with the rent-to-own arrangement."

"Think about the offer," Ted said. "There's no need to decide right now. You can always come back if you change your mind."

"Well, in that case, I won't be back," Violet said.

She muttered good-bye and left Ted's office, realizing that the black eighties power suit she'd worn for the occasion hadn't given her much power after all. As she walked through the reception area, her spectator pumps clicked on the marble floor. She thought she caught the receptionist giving her a sympathetic nod.

When Violet returned to Hourglass Vintage, Betsy Barrett, her friend and longtime customer, stood waiting outside the locked shop.

"Betsy, good to see you." Violet hugged her. "I hope you haven't been waiting a long time. Come on in." She put her key in the door.

Betsy followed Violet inside. "I've only been waiting a few minutes," she said. "But what are you doing closing your shop in the middle of the day?"

Betsy never hesitated to say what was on her mind. It was one of the things Violet loved about her.

"I had a meeting," Violet said. She saw no reason to mention what the meeting had been about. The fewer people who knew about the trouble she was having with her landlord, the better. Plus, Betsy would probably want to help, and Violet felt like she owed her too much already. When she'd first opened her shop, Betsy had sat on the board of a women's business organization that gave Violet a start-up grant. If it weren't for that grant, Violet would have had just enough money for rent and fixtures, and nothing left over to pay herself even the very small salary that she needed to survive in those first few months.

"Don't you think it's about time you got some help around here?" Betsy asked. She sat down in one of two orange Eames lounge chairs outside the dressing room—gems Violet had found at a yard sale and had gotten reupholstered.

"I'm doing okay," Violet said.

"Well, in the five minutes I was waiting, three different customers came to the door and turned away when they saw you were closed," Betsy said. "You can have all the lovely merchandise you want, but if you're not open when people want to buy it, it's not gonna do you much good."

Violet sat down in the other chair. She slid off her shoes and buried her toes in the white shag rug. If only Betsy knew how much help she needed. She tried to change the subject. "I see you've brought out your silks, even though it's been chilly lately."

Betsy looked down at her cream shantung jacket and skirt. "I say screw it. At my age, I figure I've only got a few seasons left to wear my favorite warm-weather stuff."

Violet didn't like to think about it, but there was probably some truth to Betsy's statement. Betsy never told anyone her exact age, saying instead that she was "somewhere on that highway north of seventy and south of eighty." That didn't stop her from aiding not only small businesses like Violet's, but also a large chunk of the Madison creative community. From her hilltop mansion on Lake Mendota, Betsy steered and funded the ballet, the youth symphony, and countless other arts organizations. Her energy level rivaled that of someone decades younger. She reminded Betsy of her grandma Lou in that way—or at least the way she had been up until her stroke.

"Did you bring stuff to sell?" Violet asked. "You know I love it when you clean out one of your closets."

"No," Betsy said. "I need a favor."

When Betsy asked for a favor, it usually meant donating an item from the store to a charity raffle or auction, and Violet was happy to do it. It was good publicity, and she felt like she owed Betsy a hell of lot more than a couple of retro dresses or poster prints. If it hadn't been for Betsy, and Betsy's wealthy friends who liked to buy rare antiques and vintage accessories, the shop might not have made it through its first couple of years.

"Anything," Violet said. "What do you need?"

"I need you to consider hiring someone."

Well, almost anything, thought Violet. "Oh, I don't know . . ."

Betsy continued. "Before you put me off, let me just tell you that it wouldn't have to be for a whole lot of hours a week, and probably just for the summer. I've got a girl—she's our scholarship recipient this year—and, well, she's struggling. She has a lot going on, personally. She's smart as can be, pretty much a savant in math, but I think she just needs a little structure. I thought of you because, well, I know you haven't always had it easy, either."

Violet doubted that a troubled eighteen-year-old would be of much help around the shop, math whiz or not. She had hired college students before but had stopped doing so because she couldn't count on them to do things the way she wanted. Their attention spans ebbed and flowed with the academic calendar, and Violet found it nearly impossible to get anyone to staff the store on a football Saturday or during exam week. In the end, having employees always seemed to create *more* work, not less.

"Betsy, I'm flattered you thought of me," she said. "But I don't think I can afford to hire somebody right now. I'm saving every penny for a down payment on my building."

"Oh, don't worry about it," Betsy said. "You were the first person on my list, but I've got some others to ask. I'll figure something out." She got up from her chair with visible effort. "Oh, and I'll come back soon with some things for the store. I'm trying to do some spring cleaning. You can't imagine how much stuff I've got after living in the same house for forty years."

After Betsy had left, Violet pulled the legal papers out of her purse. It had already been a week since she was served, and she'd been counting on her meeting with Ted to clear things up. Apparently it wasn't going to be that simple. She needed a lawyer, but she couldn't afford to pay what she imagined would be steep fees.

She picked up the receiver of her blue rotary phone and dialed the number of the only lawyer she knew who would work for clothes in lieu of legal fees—her friend Karen Young.

"Violet, hi," Karen said when she picked up. "I'm so sorry I've been out of touch."

"That's okay. You've got a good reason. How *is* that sweet baby girl of yours?" Violet asked, trying to keep envy out of her voice.

"Edith is great," Karen said. "I don't want to talk about babies, though. I need some adult conversation. Maybe we can go out some night soon like we used to?"

"Sure," Violet said, though she doubted either of them had the energy to run around to bars and burlesque shows like they did before Karen got married.

"Have you been on any dates lately?" Karen asked. "If you have, don't leave any details out. I need to live vicariously."

"I had coffee with an IT guy I met through a local online dating site," Violet said.

"Wait, what's his profile? I'll look him up."

"He doesn't have a profile," Violet said. "He's one of the tech support guys for the site. I couldn't figure out where to go to upload my picture, and there was this box that said 'Click here for twenty-four-hour tech support.' So I clicked on it. While he was helping me, we got to chatting about other stuff, and he asked me out for coffee. He was funny, so I said yes."

"That is *so* you, Violet." Karen laughed. "I'm pretty sure that breaks about a dozen of the site's terms of use, though. Not to mention probably his employment contract."

"Oh, why do you have to be so lawyerly about it? Anyway, he turned out to be a lot less conversational in person than he was online. He would barely make eye contact. Needless to say, we haven't gone out again."

"That's it?" Karen asked. "You don't have anything else for this poor, cooped-up mama?"

"Sadly, no," Violet said.

The truth was that, although she'd been on the occasional date, Violet spent most of her nights lately either going over shop inventory and bills or snuggling with Miles on the couch, watching old Rodgers and Hammerstein films. She knew she'd never meet anyone that way, but she would also never get hurt, never again have to make the difficult decision to leave anyone or be left. Or to give up the independence to which she'd grown accustomed. Besides, Violet was pretty sure no straight man would tolerate watching *State Fair* and *Carousel* as frequently as she did. And God, did she ever love the tight-waisted dresses and Technicolor makeup all those musical starlets wore.

"Anyway," Violet said, "I've been pretty distracted with some stuff that's been going on with my store. That's actually why I was calling. I wanted to see if I could come over to talk to you about some legal issues. I hate to bother you when you're on maternity leave and everything, but I really need your advice. I can't pay you, but you can do a raid on my inventory if you want."

"Hell yes," Karen said. "I am in desperate need of new clothes. None of my PE clothes fit me."

"PE? You mean like gym?"

"Pre-Edith."

Violet laughed. "Okay, so when can I come over?"

"Any time you want. I'm kind of a shut-in these days. How about Friday night? I'll get us some wine."

"Friday works. Once you see what I'm dealing with, though, you might want to make it whiskey."

On Friday evening, Violet drove to Karen's house under a still-bright sky, even though it was past eight o'clock. Soon it would be the summer solstice, marked in Madison every year by a bonfire celebration near Olbrich Botanical Gardens. Old hippies and families with cloth-diapered kids would gather, pounding drums and waving silk scarves to celebrate the longest day of the year.

The sun floated in a bath of pink above the sturdy rows of corn and soybeans bordering the two-lane highway outside the Madison city limits. Despite the apparent order of things, Violet thought, life was far from predictable. She had grown up in a small town, had married young and anticipated having a lot of babies. Now Violet lived alone on a busy downtown street, while Karen, who swore she'd never settle down, lived out in the suburbs.

When Violet rang the doorbell of Karen and Tom's sprawling home, there was no dog's bark or sound of pattering paws to greet her. If she ever lived in the country again, Violet thought, she would adopt another dog—a buddy for Miles to play with. He was getting old, and a younger dog might be good company for him.

Karen opened the door cradling a pink-cheeked baby. The child's tiny fist clutched a handful of her mother's red hair.

"Ow," said Karen, freeing her curls from the baby's hand. "Come on in."

"Thank you so much for meeting with me. It's good to see you." Violet stepped inside the house and hugged her friend, being careful not to squish the baby. "Oh, my God, Edith has gotten so big."

Karen's face lit up with a proud smile. "Do you want to hold her? You don't have to if you don't want to. I know I used to get annoyed when people always assumed I wanted to hold babies, just because I was a woman of a certain age."

Violet held out her arms. "I would love to hold her." She took the warm bundle from Karen. Edith's creased white arms and legs stuck to Violet's own heat-damp skin in a way that should have been unpleasant but actually felt quite heavenly. She smelled the little girl's fuzzy hair and kissed the top of her head. "Hi, little one," she said with a spark of longing.

Though Violet knew that splitting up with Jed was an essential chapter in her story, the possibility of never having an Edith was the price she'd paid for her independence and new start. It sucked, really, the way that possibilities narrowed as she got older. Sure, Karen had had a baby at almost forty, but Karen had also already been married at that point, after two years of dating Tom. Barring a calculated one-night stand or a visit to a sperm bank, Violet figured she was a long way from ever being pregnant, even if she met the man of her dreams tomorrow.

"Do you want anything? A glass of white wine? Water? Frozen breast milk?" Karen asked.

Violet recoiled. "Wine sounds good, thanks. Where's Tom?"

"Work trip, as usual. I'm like a single parent these days. Come on, let's go sit in the kitchen."

Still carrying the baby, Violet followed her friend into the massive kitchen with its Restoration Hardware fixtures and faux-weathered, farmhouse-style cabinets. It perplexed Violet, the way people tried to make the insides of new homes look old. She sat down at the table. Karen grabbed a half-full wine bottle out of the fridge. She poured a glass and set it down in front of Violet.

"I opened it a couple of days ago," she said. "Sorry if it tastes a little off. Wine doesn't disappear as quickly as it used to around here."

"It's fine," Violet said after taking a sip. She noticed a picture of a seahorse etched on the base of the glass. "Hey, we have some Water-ford goblets just like this in the store. My friend Betsy brought them in. Since when are you so fancy?"

"We got them for a wedding gift. I figure we might as well use them."

"Aren't you gonna have any?" Violet asked.

"Maybe in a little while. I need to nurse Edith soon." Karen sat down in a chair opposite Violet and put her elbows on the table. "So, what are we dealing with here?"

Violet dug in her purse to retrieve the papers she'd brought. She pushed them toward Karen. "This is what the process server gave me. And there's a copy of my lease in there, too."

Karen bent her head and paged through the document while Violet rocked Edith in her arms.

When she was finished reading, Karen asked, "So it looks like you either need to move out or act on your right of first refusal. Are you in a position to buy the building?"

"They're listing it for almost a million."

"So I'm gonna guess the answer is no, unless you've been hoarding a big pile of money somewhere that I don't know about," Karen said. "Have you had a chance to talk to your landlord?"

"Yeah, but . . ."

"Spit it out," Karen said. "It's never a good idea to keep secrets from your lawyer."

"Okay, yes. They made some sort of offer."

Karen leaned forward. "What do you mean 'offer'? What were the terms, exactly?"

Violet repeated what Ted had told her, and was surprised to see Karen nodding.

"Wait, do you think I should take the deal?" Violet asked when she'd finished explaining.

Karen shrugged. "Look, I know it seems counterintuitive, but the deal they're offering might actually be a decent option."

"I don't see how. The money they're offering me as an 'incentive' is a joke."

"We could negotiate and try to get them to offer more."

Violet shook her head. "Even if they double the amount they're offering me, it won't be enough to cover my costs of moving, plus the increase in rent I'll surely have to pay if I can even find another location in the neighborhood. I've done some searching already in the classifieds, and the couple of places that are available are much more than I can afford to pay and still keep the lights on. I don't see how what they're offering could possibly be a good option."

"Taking the deal is less of a risk," Karen said. "See, if you aren't able to buy the building and you don't move out on their terms, you can pretty much bet Mortensen & Son will take you to court over it. And if they win, they can go after you for their attorneys' fees and court costs. I can see from the name of their lawyer on the last page of the lease that it was drafted by a very expensive firm in town. It could end up costing you thousands if you fight them and lose. And, unfortunately, from what I see here, the terms are in your landlord's favor."

"That doesn't seem fair," Violet said. "It seems sneaky."

"Sneaky, yes, but that doesn't mean it's not legal."

Violet shook her head. "You've got to be kidding me."

"You asked me for legal advice, Violet, not for me to be your cheerleader."

As if to break the tension, Edith reached a tiny hand toward Violet's face and touched her lips. Then the baby started to fuss and writhe around, so Karen took the warm little body out of Violet's arms in order to feed her. Although it was a hot evening, Violet felt a chill, a sense of loss.

"I'm not taking the offer," she said. "I refuse to just hand over the keys to my place, and meanwhile get priced out of the neighborhood and having access to my customer base."

Karen pushed her shirt up and put the baby to her breast. Edith cooed and began to make smacking noises. Karen looked at Violet. "You don't mind, do you?"

"Of course not," Violet said. "Come on, we've been to strip clubs together. You think I'm gonna be offended by a little bit of breast-feeding?"

"Well, if you're not interested in their offer, then I think our best bet is stalling," Karen said.

"Seriously? That's the best option I've got?"

"It's the only option you've got, if you're not willing to take the deal and if you're not willing to move. We need to buy you as much time as possible so that you can try to figure out a way to raise some funds and get yourself in a better position for a mortgage, or to be able to afford a higher rent elsewhere in the neighborhood."

"So how do I do that?" Violet asked.

"What, raise funds? Hell if I know. If I knew how to come up with money out of nowhere, you can bet I wouldn't be working for a bunch of white-haired men at the law firm."

"No, how do we stall?"

"Oh," said Karen. "That. Now *that* I know how to do. No one graduates law school without knowing how to drag out a legal conflict."

That night, Violet sat on the couch with a notebook while Miles snoozed with his wrinkly face in her lap. She listened to his raspy breathing while she brainstormed as to how she might make more money, and quickly. She could raise prices, but she feared that might have the undesired effect of driving her already-loyal customers away. She could auction some of her more expensive items online, but she hated the idea of taking people's treasured items and shipping them off to strangers.

When the phone rang at ten thirty, Miles leaped off the couch and growled.

Violet patted the bulldog's head. "It's okay, buddy," she said, even though she almost never got calls this late. She picked up the phone. "Hello?"

"Violet, I'm sorry to bother you," said a familiar voice.

"Betsy? Is everything okay?" Violet sat up straight. She had once told Betsy that she could call anytime if she needed help. She worried about her friend alone in her big house. Betsy was healthy and boisterous, but still . . . at her age, a slip on the travertine floor or the varnished staircase could be disastrous.

"Yes, yes, I'm fine," Betsy said. "You can put the ambulance on hold."

Violet tried to laugh, but it came out as a dry cough. It was too close to the truth to be funny. "What's going on?" she asked.

"After I left your shop the other day, I thought about what you said about not being able to afford to hire our scholarship recipient."

Violet's pulse quickened, and she wondered if Betsy had somehow found out that she was in danger of losing her apartment and store space. If Betsy knew, God love her, the whole city would know, from the governor to the man with the orange-dyed beard who played the piccolo on State Street.

"Uh-huh," Violet said, not sure what else to say.

"I suppose I could have just called somebody else to find her a job, but I had my heart set on her working with *you,* specifically. She lost her mother recently, and if that weren't enough to handle, she's also pregnant."

Jesus, thought Violet. She felt sorry for the girl but had the feeling that whatever Betsy had in mind could be a real disaster. Violet had too many problems of her own at the moment to be confident in her ability to mentor anyone.

"I was thinking an internship would be the answer," Betsy said.

"You mean she would work for free? I don't know how I feel about that," Violet said. "I think I'd feel like I was taking advantage of a teenage mother."

"Not for free. She'd get college credit, which would help her out a lot since she might have to miss some classes in the fall when the baby is born. I already made some calls to my contacts over at the university—Walt was on the board of trustees, you know, before he died—and it will take some paperwork before we can finalize it, but I think it would be a wonderful opportunity for both you and April."

"I'm sorry, did you say April?" asked Violet.

"Yes, April Morgan. She was a senior at East High this year. She stopped attending, though, and got her equivalency diploma instead. Do you know her?"

Violet pictured the blond girl who'd stood outside the store with the wedding dress swirling around her in the wind.

"I'm not sure. How old did you say she was?" Violet asked.

"Eighteen."

Violet thought about herself at that age. Her life had been defined by two loves: fashion and Jed Cline. In her one-stoplight hometown, she'd had little access to one and all too much access to the other. Jed had singled Violet out when she was a sophomore and he was a junior at Bent Creek High. He'd plucked her from the ranks of farm kids and metalheads who sat at the peripheral lunch tables and elevated her to the status of "Jed's girlfriend." Being Jed's girlfriend meant a lot of things. It meant Violet sat next to him every day in the center of the cafeteria, surrounded by his contact-sport-playing friends with their orthodontically corrected smiles and car keys. It meant losing her virginity in the middle of a cornfield, in the bed of Jed's Ford truck under an endless June sky. And it meant accepting a proposal from him at her high school graduation party and enrolling in community college rather than the out-of-state schools many of her classmates had chosen.

None of it had mattered, though, at the time. Violet hadn't seen sacrifice in any of her choices. Jed had been the goal, a goal she had achieved without really trying, and when something everyone else deemed as desirable came so easily, it hadn't occurred to her to question it. Not at the wedding reception in the grade-school gym, where she'd danced in a blissful fog of tulle and tap beer, wearing Grandma Lou's satin gown from the 1940s. And not in the rented duplex behind the gas station where she and Jed had lived out the decade and a half of their married life—or at least, not until the very end.

Grandma Lou hadn't wanted Violet to get married so young. She'd said so when Violet and Jed first got engaged, and again in the tiny room in the back of the church, just minutes before Violet walked down the aisle.

"You're sure about this, honey?" Grandma Lou had asked while Violet's mother pinned a long veil to her daughter's dark hair.

Violet had looked in the mirror and traced her lips with another coat of gloss. "Uh-huh."

"'Cause if you're not, you just say the word," Grandma Lou had said. "You and I will pile into my Buick and keep driving 'til you say when."

"Mom, don't make trouble," Violet's mother had said. "We've got half of Bent Creek out there in the pews. Violet's father is already standing at the foot of the aisle, waiting to walk her down."

"All I'm saying is that you're not stuck." Grandma Lou had leaned over and whispered into Violet's ear, "You never are, and don't you forget it."

Grandma Lou had never promised that getting unstuck would be easy or quick, though. It had taken Violet a long time to untether herself from the choices she'd made in those critical years of early adulthood. Betsy knew it, too. She'd listened to Violet's whole story when she'd interviewed her for the start-up grant for Hourglass Vintage. Betsy had told Violet she was a "sucker for second chances" and had rallied the other board members to award her the grant funds.

And now Betsy was asking her to help give someone else a similar chance.

Violet couldn't say no.

Chapter 5

INVENTORY ITEM: *suitcase*
APPROXIMATE DATE: *1950s*
CONDITION: *good, no scratches or scuffs*
ITEM DESCRIPTION: *Yellow Samsonite suitcase with ivory, quilted lining.*
SOURCE: *Lucille Rollins. Not for sale.*

Violet

THE BELLS ABOVE THE door jingled and Violet caught a glimpse of her new intern through the glass. Violet hadn't been expecting her for another half an hour, and she'd been counting on that time to finish reading through the packet of legal information Karen had printed for her to better help her understand what was going on with her lease. She opened a drawer underneath the counter and put the papers away.

April made her way to the register. She had on a navy dress with gathered sleeves and a Peter Pan collar (1950s, Violet guessed), paired with tan cowboy boots and a chunky turquoise bracelet. Although April's dress fell loose from an empire waist, Violet noticed with a twinge of envy that her belly looked rounder than the last time she'd seen her, just a couple of weeks earlier.

"Hi," April said. "I'm a little bit early. I hope that's all right. I didn't want to be late on my first day."

"It's all right," Violet said. "If you ever drive here, you can park in back of the store. The street parking on Johnson has a two-hour limit, and the police are pretty vigilant about handing out tickets."

"I won't need a parking spot. I live just down the street. And anyway, I don't drive." April clutched the strap of her brown satchel.

"You mean, like, you don't have a license?"

"No, I just don't like to."

Violet noticed a defensive edge in April's voice and decided to drop the topic. So what if the girl didn't like to drive? Violet certainly had some neuroses of her own.

"Do you remember me?" April asked.

"Of course," Violet said. *It's not every day that someone comes in to buy a wedding dress, let alone return it a few weeks later,* she thought. She wasn't sure what she should do. On one hand, she wanted to give April her money back because she regretted not doing it in the first place. On the other hand, she feared bringing up the dress would remind April of whatever had made her want to return the dress in the first place, and Violet didn't want to upset her.

To break the silence between them, Violet said, "It's hot out there today. It's nice to finally have some warm weather."

"Yeah," April said, pulling her hair from the back of her neck. "Listen, I want to say thanks for letting me do this. I know it wasn't your idea, even though Betsy tried to act like it was. She told you I'm pregnant, right?"

Violet nodded, thinking. *This is gonna be awkward.* It was too late to change her mind, though. She had already signed the paperwork the university had sent over to formalize the internship.

April took off her satchel and set it on the register counter.

"Oh, I can show you where to put your purse in the back room," Violet said. She hoped she didn't sound too uptight. She'd spent years getting the aesthetics of her store just right, from the orange and blue palette to the gilded mirrors and Lucite stools in the dressing rooms. She didn't mind clutter, necessarily—clutter was part of her store's charm—as long as it was *her* clutter, and carefully curated.

Violet led April into the storage room in the rear of the shop and showed her the hooks where she could hang her coat and personal items.

"So why did you decide you wanted to intern here?" Violet asked. "I mean, I know Betsy made the connection, but she knows plenty of other business owners in town, too. You probably could have worked at one of the designer boutiques on Monroe, or at one of the trendy shops on State Street that cater to students. Why did you pick a vintage place?"

April shrugged. "I guess I just think vintage stuff is more interesting. Anyone can walk into a chain store and buy the same sweater all their friends have. But there's no story there."

"Exactly," Violet said. For her, vintage items also represented other lives, other choices, and drew the focus away from her own.

April inclined her head toward a wall of shelves stacked high with canvas containers. "Wow, you have a lot of stuff back here."

"This is where I've got all my stock that's out of season or doesn't fit on the sales floor. Everything is organized by decade."

April pointed to a box labeled *1990s*. "Is stuff from the nineties really considered vintage?"

"Sure," Violet said. "Especially the early nineties." She lifted the container from its shelf and took off the lid. She pushed aside a layer of tissue paper to reveal a black dress with hot-pink triangles all over it.

"Okay, I guess that *does* look vintage," April said. "I was just a little kid when the nineties ended, so I don't remember the fashion except for a few things my mom wore. Looks like I didn't miss much."

"Careful," Violet said with a smile. "This type of stuff is selling really well right now."

Violet remembered driving thirty miles from Bent Creek to the nearest JCPenney to buy a similar, neon-patterned dress to wear to her first homecoming with Jed. When he offered her a swig from a flask he'd snuck into the dance, she was so nervous about getting caught by one of the chaperones that she spilled it all over herself. Knowing she couldn't go home with her dress reeking of peach schnapps, she'd had to wash it with liquid hand soap in the girls' locker room and then hold it under the hand dryers, wearing just her underwear and bra.

"Why do you have to wrap everything in tissue?" April asked.

"It's acid-free paper." Violet replaced the lid. "Some fabrics can get damaged or discolored over time just by being in contact with other surfaces."

"My mom tried to start up a professional organization business," April said. "She would've loved to see how you've got everything set up back here."

Violet remembered what Betsy had said about April having lost her mother. She wondered what had happened but knew better than to ask. Instead, she said, "I guess you could say I'm kind of obsessive about my merchandise. But my store is my baby. Besides my dog, Miles."

Violet put the box back on the shelf.

"Do you ever bring Miles in with you?" April asked. "I love shop dogs. The manager of the hardware store down the street from me brings in his Lab. The dog is always there when I go in looking for some obscure fixture for the house."

"I'd like to bring Miles in here, but he's a pit bull and some people are afraid of them." Violet paused. "Did you say you're fixing up a house?"

"Just little stuff here and there. It's the green bungalow a block east of here, next to the natural foods co-op."

"Oh, yeah, I know that house. It's beautiful."

"Yeah, but it needs work—work that I don't know how to do and don't have money to pay for. My mom left it to me when she died."

"I'm so sorry to hear about your mom." Violet didn't know what else to say.

"Yeah. Me too." April's shoulders slumped. "The house is actually on the market and I'm hoping it sells soon. The Realtor has brought a bunch of people through, but so far no one has made an offer. I guess I can't blame them. Why would they want to buy a hundred-year-old house when they could buy a brand-new condo right down the street?"

"If you inherited the house, that means your dad's not in the picture, huh?" Violet asked.

"He and my mom got divorced when I was two. He lives in Ohio with his wife and their kids. He used to visit a couple of times a year when I was younger, but I haven't seen him in a long time. And to be honest, I'm fine with it. It was always awkward when he visited." April turned to the shelves. "So *you* know where everything goes, but how am I supposed to figure it out? I mean, I can't tell just by looking at something what decade it should be shelved under."

Violet knew her perfect system was perfect only for *her,* and she'd organized it that way on purpose. She'd never trusted any of her employees enough to do more than fold clothes and ring up sales.

"If you need something from back here, just ask and I can show you where it is," Violet said.

"But what if you're not here?"

"I'm almost *always* here," Violet said.

"What's all that?" April nodded her head toward a folding table covered with heaping stacks of paper.

Violet let out a nervous laugh. Of course April had to notice the one area of the store she didn't have under control. "Just more records I don't need, but need to save for tax purposes and stuff. I put stuff there to file away later, but I never seem to have time."

"Have you thought about getting them all scanned, so you can save them electronically?" April asked.

"Sure, but I don't know when I'd possibly have the time."

"Isn't that what interns are for?"

"Getting everything loaded onto the computer is only the first baby step, though," Violet said. "Then I'd actually have to learn how to find everything again."

"I could show you. Do you have an inventory system, too?"

"Oh, yeah, hang on." Violet went over to the table and retrieved her leather-bound journal. With pride, she ran her hands over the worn cover, then handed the book to April. "This is where I have my records of every piece that comes into the store, where it came from, and what condition it's in."

April squinted as she peered down at Violet's looped handwriting. "Okay, well, we can get all this information computerized, too. You *do* have a computer, right?"

"Upstairs in my apartment," Violet said. "For e-mail and stuff. And sometimes I go online to look for vintage stuff for the store."

"If you brought it down here, I could set everything up for you so you wouldn't have to deal with all these receipts and notebooks and everything."

Violet took the inventory book back from her. "I'm not sure we really need to. I mean, things may look disorganized, but believe it or not, I actually know where everything is." She took a step toward the door, anxious to end all the talk of records and technology. "Come on, let's go up front. I'll show you how to work the register."

On the sales floor, Violet admired the neat, round racks of dresses and the rainbow of shoes and handbags lining the shelves. She liked it so much better out here than in the back of the shop. It always made her feel calm to be surrounded by beautiful things, like the stacks of hemstitched Irish linen tablecloths she'd folded that morning and placed on the main display table. Beautiful things distracted her from the uglier parts of life, the parts filled with divorce and disappointment.

"Do you just have the one register?" April bent over the hulking machine with its roll of receipt paper and a corkscrewed change slide.

"Yep," Violet said. "She's a bit fussy, but you'll get the hang of her. These buttons open it." She tapped a combination of keys and the cash drawer sprang open. A few thin stacks of bills lay nestled in the compartments. Like everything else in the store, the register was secondhand.

"Sometimes the receipt roll gets jammed, and if that happens, you can use this high-tech device to fish out the paper." Violet held up a bobby pin that had been sitting next to the register. "I also recommend swearing a lot. Seems to help."

"What if someone needs to return something?" April asked.

"We don't take returns."

"Oh, yeah." April's expression turned sad for a second. "The wedding dress."

"About that . . ." While she had the register open, Violet counted out a stack of bills and handed them to April. "This is for you, for the dress."

April stared at the money in her palm. "But what about your policy?"

Violet smiled. "I can make an exception for my intern."

April looked Violet in the eye, seeming touched by the gesture. "Thanks," she said. "I won't tell anyone."

The bells over the door jangled and a barefoot woman walked in, clutching a plastic broom with one hand and holding a lit cigarette with the other. Her long, white hair obstructed her face, but Violet needed only to look at the woman's bare feet to know that it was Erma, the neighborhood drifter.

"Erma, I've told you before, you can't smoke in here," Violet said. "State law."

The old woman went back outside, grumbling something about fascism.

"You know that lady?" April asked.

"Everyone knows her around here. It's hard to miss somebody who doesn't wear shoes, even in winter."

"What's her story?"

"No one really knows. Some people say she's a witch." Violet looked out the window, where Erma stood on the sidewalk finishing her cigarette. "She's been coming in here since I first opened. Sometimes she brings me mushrooms or herbs that she says are edible—she calls herself an urban forager. She never buys food, only eats what she can find."

"So she's homeless."

Violet shook her head. "She says she has an apartment."

"Do you ever try the stuff she brings you?" asked April.

"Are you kidding me? I'm afraid to. I've seen Erma pretty tweaked out at times. Hard to know if it's from the stuff she eats or if it's just her."

"Don't people get annoyed with her loitering around?"

"I think people are afraid of her."

As if she'd heard them, the old woman stuck her face to the window glass and looked inside the store. Because of Erma's lazy eye, Violet couldn't tell whom—or what—she was looking at. Erma stubbed out her cigarette on the sidewalk and came back into the store.

"How can we help you?" asked Violet.

Erma held up a knobby hand. "You've got it wrong, honey. Old Erma is here to help *you*." She pointed the bristles of her broom toward the ceiling and walked the perimeter of the store, humming to herself. As she passed the cash register, her humming grew louder. She paused and rocked with intense, jerking movements.

"What's she doing?" April whispered.

Violet shrugged.

Erma fished a flask from the pocket of her men's shirt and took a long pull from it. "I'm clearing the energy. It's bad, very bad." Erma screwed the cap onto her flask. "You know the store that used to be here didn't make it."

Violet nodded. She'd known that fact before she leased the building, and she tried not to think about it. She'd gone, once, into the shop that had been in this space before hers. It had been a clothing store that sold garments made from environmentally sustainable textiles, like hemp and organic cotton. The concept had sounded good to Violet, until she actually went inside and saw that, at least in the case of that particular store, "sustainable" had been synonymous with "shapeless, sacklike, and outrageously expensive." She'd hoped that Hourglass Vintage, which was environmentally friendly in a different way, would do better. But now she wondered if Erma was right, that the location had bad energy.

Erma walked over and stuck her face just inches from Violet's. "You've had an unfortunate turn of events, too, haven't you?"

Violet didn't answer. She smelled liquor wafting from the woman's words.

"I'll need to come back," Erma said. "Too much residue. I'm tired." She shook her head and left the store, dragging her broom on the wood floor.

"What was that all about?" April asked.

Violet hesitated. Part of her wanted to open up to April about the eviction, or notice to vacate, or whatever the technical term was. It was a lot to dump on the poor girl on her first day, though, and even if it weren't, Violet had too much pride to admit there was anything she couldn't handle on her own. So she just shrugged and said, "You can never really be sure with Erma."

April seemed to accept this, and pointed at something on the wall. "Hey, are those real?"

Violet turned around to look at a pair of deer antlers that she'd painted white and repurposed as a jewelry rack. "Yeah," she said. "My ex was into hunting. Those are from a prized buck he shot one year. I took them in the divorce just to piss him off. I certainly wasn't going to get any money, since we didn't have any. He spent whatever he made working at the packaging factory every payday at Vern's Tavern."

"Is that the same tavern you got that cool moonshine jug from? The one you showed me last time?" asked April.

"Yeah. I guess the owner felt like he owed me something, since my ex was always spending our money at his bar. He said he knew I liked old stuff." Violet looked up at the necklaces hanging from the antler rack and noticed that some of them had gotten tangled. She took them down. "Hey, do you think you could sort these out for me?" she asked.

April took the necklaces. "Sure. Do you mind if I sit down? My feet are kinda sore."

"Oh, sure. I guess I didn't think of . . . that you might . . ." Violet felt her cheeks burning. "I've never been pregnant, so it didn't occur to me that you might be uncomfortable."

"Normally, I'm fine on my feet, but it's kind of hot today and they're really swollen." April settled into one of the orange chairs outside the dressing room.

Violet sat down in the other chair. "So I guess I should ask you what you're expecting to get out of the internship, so I can make sure we're on the same page."

April furrowed her brow as she unknotted the wad of tangled jewelry. "Well, Betsy said I'm supposed to be getting some exposure to math stuff—you know, like accounting and that sort of thing. To justify getting college credit. I have to write a report about it at the end of the summer and submit it to some professor who's supposed to be my adviser. So I was hoping to be able to help you out with getting your files organized so I can learn about your bookkeeping."

When Violet agreed to take on an intern, she'd been picturing someone who would be willing to hang up clothes and dust shelves with a smile. She hadn't been expecting to be told how to run her business by a teenager.

"Look," Violet said. "You want to get some good experience. I get that. And hopefully I can provide that. But can't we just slow down for a minute here? It's been a while since I've had anyone work for me, and I can be a bit . . . *particular* about the way I do things. So it's gonna take me a little while to get used to this whole thing, okay?"

"Okay." April's eyes widened. "Sorry, I just . . . I don't know, I guess I can be kind of pushy for my age. My mom was sick, so I had to take over for her sometimes."

"I didn't know your mom was sick. I mean, I know you lost her, but—" Violet paused, not sure if she and April knew each other well enough yet to have this conversation. "I'm sorry."

April waved a hand. "It's okay. She wasn't, like, physically sick, like with cancer or anything. She had some mental health problems, I guess. But anyway, she died in a car accident."

Violet must have looked shocked because April said quickly, "I know what you're thinking, and no. She didn't kill herself. It was during an ice storm, in early November. Her car went off an overpass. She was dead before the paramedics arrived."

So that explains the driving phobia, Violet thought. "Jesus."

"Yeah." April looked down at her cowboy boots. "So anyway, I've been on my own for the past few months, and even before that, sometimes, when my mom was going through one of her bad times. I've gotten used to doing things my own way, because I knew I couldn't count on anyone else."

Violet leaned back in her chair and said, "Well, then, we have something in common."

As April untangled the necklaces, Violet resolved to sort out the girl's story, even as she struggled, still, to sort out her own.

Five years earlier

Violet trudged through the snow to the mailbox. She went back inside the house, stomped her boots against the doormat, and opened an envelope from the registrar at Bent Creek Community College. The letter informed her that her tuition check for Course #405: Fundamentals of Fashion Retail hadn't cleared.

When she came into the house and stomped her boots against the doormat, Miles jumped up and put his paws on her thighs. She and Jed had adopted the pit bull pup just a few months earlier from a rescue shelter, and he was still learning good house behavior.

"Down, Miles," Violet said. She put the dog's paws back on the floor and stormed over to Jed, who was on the couch, watching a college football game. Empty beer cans created a miniature scrap heap on the coffee table. She stood in between Jed and the TV, gripping the letter.

"It says here that my tuition check bounced, so the registrar gave my spot in the class to someone off the wait list."

"Oh." Jed craned his neck so he could see past her to the TV.

Violet took a step to the side, so that she was still blocking his line of sight. Her boots dripped dirty puddles on the worn carpet.

"I know there was enough money in the account when I wrote the check on Monday." Violet put her hands on her hips. "And I haven't done anything but put gas in the car since then. The gas sure as hell didn't cost eight hundred dollars, which is what the balance in our account was when I sent this check out."

Jed swiveled his body to the other side, and Violet moved again to block his view.

"The class is five hundred dollars, so the check should have cleared," she said. "What happened to the money?"

"I don't know," Jed mumbled.

"Really? I guess I'll just have to call the bank to find out."

"Hang on a minute, lemme think." Jed scrunched up his booze-slackened face as if trying to concentrate on a physics equation instead of a simple question. "Monday was Smithy's birthday, so we went to the bar after work."

"And you spent eight hundred dollars? How is that even possible? Beers are two dollars there. What else did you spend it on?"

Jed scratched his stubbly cheek. "I can't remember. I had a lot to drink and I kinda blacked out. We mighta gone somewhere after the bar, but it's fuzzy."

"If you 'kinda' blacked out, then I'm sure the bank can help me fill in the gaps. They should be able to tell me where you withdrew money." Violet took a few steps in the direction of the phone.

"Wait, it's coming back."

Violet turned toward Jed. "How convenient."

"We went to Chubby's Bunnies." He looked at the floor.

"You spent my tuition money at the strip club?" Violet dug her fingers into her palms to keep from throwing something.

"Don't be mad, Vi. Smithy's my best friend."

"Oh, I see," Violet said in a dry tone. "A special occasion."

Jed nodded, not catching her sarcasm.

"I'll *tell* you what a special occasion is." Violet threw the envelope with such force it skidded across the coffee table and knocked over an empty can. "A special occasion is when the only institute of higher learning in this goddamn town offers a class I'm interested in for once. That actually applies to what I want to do, which, in case you forgot, is open a vintage store."

"Yeah, I know you've said that's your dream and everything, but I kinda thought that's all it was—a dream."

"You know, some people actually take steps to achieve their goals,"

Violet said. "And that's what I was trying to do, by taking the class. You think I've been accumulating all those old clothes and things in the garage just for some dream I never plan to act on?"

"Can't you take the class next semester?"

"Sure, maybe if we lived in, say, Madison, where they need a phone-book-sized course catalog just to list all the classes in one department of the university. But the class is only being offered this one time at the community college, by a visiting professor."

Jed let out a snorting sound. "You think you're better than everybody else, don't you? That Bent Creek is okay for some people, but not for you because you're *special* or something. You want to open a store? You want to go live somewhere else? Then do it. I'm not stopping you."

Violet knew she should be irate, but the prickly sensation running through her body wasn't anger. It was numbness. She and Jed hadn't even exchanged Christmas presents that winter. When Violet learned that there would be an executive from a well-known retail chain teaching the fashion course at the community college, she'd started stashing away a portion of her tips to save up for it. Fearing that something like this would happen, she had kept the cash hidden in her underwear drawer. She hadn't deposited the money into their joint account until Monday morning, the same day she wrote the check. It had taken Jed less than twenty-four hours to piss away her dreams.

Violet went into the bedroom. She ignored Jed's distracted apologies, which were muddled by the football announcers debating a penalty. She opened a suitcase—a yellow, 1950s Samsonite that her grandmother had given her the last time Violet was at her house, "just in case"—and started packing.

Chapter 6

INVENTORY ITEM: *necklace*
APPROXIMATE DATE: *1970*
CONDITION: *fair; a few rhinestones missing*
ITEM DESCRIPTION: *Gold-plated necklace with oval pendant set with rhinestones.*
SOURCE: *Amithi Singh*

Amithi

ON A SUNNY FRIDAY in May, a month before she first set foot inside Hourglass Vintage, Amithi had accompanied her husband to Chicago for an engineering conference. Naveen had booked them a hotel in Oak Park, a western suburb. In addition to being a work-related trip, the weekend was supposed to be a getaway for the two of them. Amithi and Naveen had lived in Oak Park in the early days of their marriage, and they both had fond memories of the place—the historic neighborhoods where they'd walk when they needed to get out of their tiny apartment without spending any money, the corner diners that weren't great but were cheap and gave Amithi a break from cooking every now and then.

Yet as they exited the interstate that Friday, all Amithi could see out her car window were strip malls and gas stations. The streets looked different now from when they had lived there all those years ago. Gone were many of the family-owned restaurants and shops, re-placed by fast-food franchises and retail chains.

Naveen steered their car through the downtown district, and Amithi cheered up at the sight of the Lake Theatre, with its art deco columns and neon blue sign. This, at least, remained unchanged. On weekend nights when Naveen wasn't in the lab, they used to go to films here: *Jaws, The Godfather,* the latest James Bond. Though she always pretended to be outraged by the violence and nudity in Amer-ican movies, Amithi relished those hours in the dark when she could immerse herself in risk and adventure without suffering any of the consequences.

After checking into their hotel, Naveen took a shower while Amithi changed into a purple sari decorated with tiny silver mirrors. Over the years, as she'd grown more accustomed to American life, she'd found fewer and fewer opportunities to wear saris. A pair of chinos with a blouse or the loose lines of a two-piece *salwar kameez* were so much more accommodating for housework, cooking, run-ning errands. But for special events, nothing felt quite as right as a sari's feminine folds and six feet of silk.

Amithi finished securing the sweep of purple fabric around her frame, then took a necklace out of her suitcase. It wasn't expensive, just a gold-plated chain with a large pendant made of rhinestones, but Naveen had purchased it for her at a trinket shop on Devon Avenue back when they were newlyweds. She wore it tonight to remind her-self of how far they'd come. When they'd left Chicago years earlier, they'd had very little. While Naveen was in graduate school, earning the salary of a teaching assistant, they'd lived from one measly pay-check to the next. Since then, they'd managed to obtain something that both of them valued: security, both in their finances and in the familiar cadences of their relationship.

Naveen came out of the bathroom, toweling himself off. Amithi noticed how his chest no longer looked smooth and tight like it once did. Instead, his skin sagged around the ribs, and the chest hair that was once dark and thick was now gray and sparse. Still, she felt tenderness at the sight of him.

"There's a reception tonight for the conference attendees. Did you remember to bring the schedule they sent us?" he asked as he buttoned his shirt.

"It's somewhere downtown, I think." Amithi pulled a card out of her purse. If it weren't for her, she was certain, Naveen would never find his way anywhere. "It says here it's at the Signature Room on Michigan Avenue. Starts at seven o'clock."

They caught a taxi downtown to the towering, trapezoidal Hancock Building and rode the elevator to the ninety-fifth floor. The host led them into a private banquet room where men in suits and women in black cocktail dresses milled around a bar and a long table stacked with hors d'oeuvres. Floor-to-ceiling windows revealed a sweeping view of the city and the periwinkle evening sky. Amithi went over to the window to get a better look. Fog billowed around the twinkling lights of neighboring skyscrapers, and the cars on the streets below looked like children's toys.

Amithi turned away from the window and followed Naveen as he made his way around the room and shook hands with people. Each time they approached someone, Naveen would say, "You remember my wife, Amithi." The acquaintance's eyes would light up with recognition. She realized people probably remembered her because she stood out from the crowd, with her dark complexion and the bright clothing she usually wore. She looked down at her purple and gold sari and wondered if she should have made a different choice, gone with something more western to blend in with the dark jackets and dresses of the other guests.

Although Naveen's colleagues seemed to remember Amithi, she did not remember them. Several of the conference attendees had been classmates of Naveen's, but their names all blurred together in her mind: Kevin, Carl, Kent. Even harder to tell apart were their spouses. Many of them had the same shade of grayish-blond hair. Every conversation seemed the same to Amithi—an endless discussion of who was living where, working on what, divorcing whom.

For the seated dinner, Amithi settled in with Naveen at a table near the window. Two other men joined them, and Amithi vaguely recalled that they'd been some of Naveen's closer friends when he was in school. One of them—a loud, round-faced man the others called "Mel"—was now a famous researcher for a pharmaceutical company. They'd only been seated five minutes when he launched into describing how many patents he held (nine) and how many vacation homes he had (three).

After the salad course, Amithi excused herself to use the ladies' room, grateful to have a break from all the boasting. When she returned, Mel was still talking. He had his back to Amithi and was leaning toward Naveen, saying, "You know, I ran into Paula Sorensen at the Miami conference this spring. Boy, is she looking good. But you probably already know that even better than I do, don't you, Naveen?"

Naveen, who was facing Amithi, caught sight of her. "There you are, love," he said.

His response made her suspicious. Although she and Naveen sometimes used terms of endearment privately, they never did so in public.

"Please do not stop your conversation because of me," she said as she sat back down. "I think you were talking about a Paula someone?"

"She was a classmate of ours," Naveen explained.

"She was more than that to Naveen," Mel said with a boorish laugh.

"I don't know what you're talking about." Naveen looked down into his scotch and swirled the melting ice cubes.

Amithi had known Naveen dated an American girl from his class before they were engaged. He'd told her as much before the wedding. Perhaps this Paula person they were talking about was she. But what Amithi did not understand was why Mel would be bringing her up now. There were so many questions she wanted—needed—to ask Naveen, but she would have to wait. Personal matters were not to be discussed in public.

During the main course, Amithi ate little of the beautiful food in front of her: pan-fried halibut with lemon butter, whipped potatoes, and slender asparagus. What concerned her was that Naveen, too, seemed distracted. She told herself not to worry, that whoever Paula was, she was in the past. Amithi and Naveen had been married for over forty years. She tried to relax and enjoy the chocolate tart that the waiter placed in front of her.

During the taxi ride back to their hotel, Naveen kept up a cease-less commentary on the people they'd seen. He expressed surprise at those who had been successful despite their poor grades, and disappointment at those like Mel who, in his opinion, had wasted brilliant minds on making quick money with big corporations instead of contributing to scholarship.

At the first pause in his diatribe, Amithi asked, "And what about Paula?"

Naveen turned toward her. A passing car illuminated just one side of his face, but Amithi could see surprise in his expression. "What about her?"

"Well, why was Mel talking about her tonight? Is she the girl you dated before we were engaged?"

He paused before answering, "Yes. I told you about her, remember? It was never serious. I knew I couldn't marry her."

"Because she was American?"

"Not only that. She was a radical, always getting involved in some sort of political struggle or another. I suppose you'd call her a hippie. My family never would have approved of her, and I never would have put them through it. I suppose I was rebelling a bit, being so far from home. But it was just a fling."

A fling. Amithi frowned. She had trouble imagining her serious, professorial husband participating in a fling. A thousand thoughts spun around in her head. She'd been so shy and inexperienced when she and Naveen got married. She wondered if Paula, the radical hippie, had been a better lover. She wondered if Naveen still thought about her. Or worse, if he still saw her.

"Are you still in touch with her?" Amithi asked.

"I see her from time to time at conferences and such." Naveen put his arm around Amithi. "I know what you're thinking and you needn't worry. She is my professional peer, nothing more."

Amithi's shoulders tensed at his touch. "Mel made it sound as if you still know her quite well."

Naveen put his hands back in his own lap. "Mel likes to exaggerate, if you hadn't noticed."

"You're right about that. But why have you never mentioned Paula to me? At least, not since we were young."

"Because she hardly seemed worth mentioning," Naveen said, meeting her gaze.

Amithi searched the brown eyes she'd trusted since she was seventeen years old and found nothing there to doubt. "You're sure, then, that you've told me everything?" she asked.

"There is nothing else to know."

Back at the hotel, Amithi realized she was exhausted from worrying and making small talk all evening. She imagined that being tired had a lot to do with the way she'd reacted to Mel's crass comments. She got into bed and closed her eyes while Naveen leaned back on a pillow, reading a scientific journal.

Just before Amithi dozed off, she remembered that she still had her rhinestone necklace on. She unclasped it and set it on the nightstand. As she did, she felt a hot hand on her arm.

"What is it?" she asked, turning to Naveen. He was clutching his chest and wincing as if in pain. "Are you sick?"

"I feel terrible," he said. "But I am not sick."

Amithi realized, then, that Naveen had not told her everything.

"Paula," she said.

Naveen nodded. His face contorted to show every wrinkle—most of them earned during the years of their marriage.

"I knew it." Amithi jumped up from the bed, as if touching the same surface on which Naveen sat would burn her. "How long has it been going on?"

"It is not going on anymore," Naveen said. "That is why I did not go to the Miami conference this year. I did not want to see her."

Amithi's throat swelled with anger and tears that she refused to cry. She remembered thinking it had been strange that Naveen had skipped his trip to Florida that spring for the annual biochemistry symposium he always attended. She remembered, too, all the times she'd offered to go with him, wishing for a sunny respite from spring in Wisconsin, which was cold more often than not. Year after year, Naveen had discouraged her from coming, promising that it would be busy and boring.

Now Amithi knew why he'd have had so little time for her. It was not that he'd been spending all of his time at lectures and events. He'd been spending time with another woman.

"You did not answer my question," she said, surprised at how cold her voice sounded despite the anger boiling inside of her. "How long has this all been going on?"

Naveen exhaled. "Remember that time you took Jayana to India when she was a baby and I stayed home to—"

"To go to the Miami symposium," Amithi said, finishing for him. "You said you were presenting a paper that year."

"I did present a paper that year," he said. "Paula came up to me afterward to congratulate me on my research findings. I hadn't seen her in years, and we had a drink to catch up and—"

"Enough. I can guess what happened next." Amithi put a hand to her stomach, which seemed to drop to her feet.

She remembered the trip to India that Naveen was talking about, back when Jayana was a year old. She'd carried the restless child from one relative's house to another, not just on her side of the family, but on Naveen's side as well. She'd lain awake in the spare bedrooms of his distant uncles and cousins. She'd endured their parenting advice and answered their tiresome, repetitive questions. And at the very same time, Naveen had begun to cheat on her. Not just with any woman, but someone who was his educational equal. Amithi wondered if Naveen thought her stupid. She had never even finished her BA, let alone a PhD.

"So you have been seeing one another for more than thirty years?" Amithi asked, almost unable to get the words out.

"No!" Naveen cried. "No. After that one time, Paula stopped attending the Miami symposium for several years, even though she lives in Florida. We both felt terrible about what had happened and agreed it should never happen again. But then she started coming again when she got the tenured position in Gainesville. There was a fair amount of pressure on her, I think, from other faculty to go and to present . . ."

Amithi couldn't believe it. Naveen was making excuses, not only for himself, but for Paula, too. "Just because she was *there,* Naveen, does not mean you needed to sleep with her."

"I know," he said in an almost inaudible voice. "So that was about ten years ago, and it's been every year since then, up until just a few months ago, when I told her that it was over and I wasn't coming."

Amithi was afraid to ask her next question but had to know the whole story, now that she was this far in. "Was it just in Miami, then, or did you see her other times, other places?"

"There were other times, I'm ashamed to say. Sometimes she would meet me in Chicago, when I was there for work. She even came to Madison once. She came to speak on a panel and stayed in a hotel—"

Amithi gasped. "How could you?" she shouted. "It is bad enough that you cheated—*and for so long*! But to carry on with her in our home—"

Naveen shook his head. "I never brought her to our house."

"It does not matter," Amithi said. "Madison is our home. We have built our life there. As far as I am concerned, you brought her to our home."

It occurred to Amithi that other hotel guests might hear her. Ordinarily, she would have cared about a thing like that. Not tonight.

"It is terrible, I know. Unforgivable." Naveen shook his head so forcefully it reminded Amithi of a dog shaking water off its back. If only it were that easy to rid oneself of the past.

"Why have you never told me?" Amithi asked. She clutched the folds of her nightgown as if holding on to one small, tangible thing could keep the rest of her life from disintegrating. "Did you think I was too dense to figure out the truth?"

Tears now flowed down Naveen's cheeks. Amithi felt no sympathy for him. In fact, this broken, whimpering man bore no resemblance to the husband she thought she'd grown to love.

"I knew it was a mistake, all along," he said.

"You had the chance to stop it, though, after that first time." She pressed her lips together, a line against the rage inside of her.

The sound that came out of Naveen's mouth was a cross between a cry and a whisper. "Yes."

Yes had always been one of Amithi's favorite English words. It had such a crisp, uplifting sound. In this context, though, its indisputable finality rang in her ears.

"How could you have kept such a secret all these years?"

"Because I was a coward." He would not look her in the eye.

Amithi walked over to the door of the hotel room and opened it. "Get out," she said.

"But where will I go?"

"I do not care. Get your own room. Or sleep in the car. Just get out."

Naveen got up and shuffled toward the door with his head down. Before he stepped into the hallway, he lifted his eyes and looked at Amithi. "Do you think you can ever forgive me?"

Amithi shut the door and locked it without answering. She did not get back into bed. Instead, she turned off the light and sat in an upholstered chair near the window without opening the drapes. She wanted to cry but couldn't. Finally, when she could sit there no longer, Amithi left the hotel room. She walked down the empty hallway and took the elevator down to the parking garage.

As she drove westward on I-90 toward Madison in the dark hours of early morning, memories of her married life flickered at fast-forward speed in the back of her mind. The holidays, the birthdays. The endless shirts ironed, the countless meals cooked.

It had all been a lie.

Chapter 7

INVENTORY ITEM: *shoes, formal*
APPROXIMATE DATE: *1960s*
CONDITION: *fair; some wear on bottoms and insoles*
ITEM DESCRIPTION: *Red satin d'Orsay pumps with closed heel and toe.*
SOURCE: *Brought in by a law professor from the university*

April

ON A JUNE MORNING two weeks into her internship, Violet handed April the keys to her Jeep.

"Do you think you could go pick something up for me on the north side of town?" she asked. "A lady is moving her mom into a nursing home and she posted pictures on Craigslist of a whole box full of amazing jewelry she's getting rid of—enameled brooches and big, mod beads. I called ahead and the lady said we can have it for free as long as we come get it today."

"I'd be happy to, but is it okay if I take the bus?" April asked, embarrassed to have to remind Violet of her driving phobia.

"Right." Now it was Violet's turn to look embarrassed. "Sorry, I

forgot you don't drive." She took back the keys. "Forget about it. I'll go
get the stuff. Do you think you could keep an eye on things here for
half an hour or so while I'm gone?"

"Of course," April said, glad to finally be entrusted with something other than polishing old silverware or ironing pleated skirts.

While Violet was gone, a middle-aged woman in yoga pants and
a zip-up pink sweatshirt came into the shop and struggled her way to
the register with a heap of velvet and sequins in her arms. She deposited them on the counter with an exaggerated exhale.

"Good afternoon. What can I do for you?" April asked.

"I need more room in my closet." The woman repositioned a piece
of highlighted blond hair that had escaped from her ponytail. "So I
decided it's time to finally get rid of all my old theater stuff."

April held up a garment from the top of the pile—a burgundy,
empire-waisted gown with gold trim on the bodice.

"That was from when I played Juliet," the woman said in a wistful voice.

"You're an actress?" April tried to picture her on a stage, commanding the attention of an entire audience. It was a stretch.

"Was," the woman replied. "In New York, in my twenties. Then I
moved to Madison after I got married. My husband landed a tenure-
track position to teach history. It was the only offer he had, so we
couldn't pass it up."

"I can't believe you got to keep the costumes."

"I usually didn't." The woman ran her hand over the gauzy skirt
of what looked like a dance costume. "I got to be friends with the
costume designer, though. She convinced the head of the theater company to let me have a few pieces as a good-bye gift when I left New
York."

The sadness in the woman's eyes bothered April. She wished she
could offer some bright and hopeful words but didn't know what to

say. "We have a couple decent theater groups in town," she said after a pause. "Have you ever acted in any of their plays?"

"I auditioned for a few things when I first got here, and even landed the part of Eliza Doolittle in a production of *Pygmalion*— God, that would have been fun." The woman shook her head. "I had to back out, though, because my youngest had a lot of ear infections when he was a baby. I missed too many rehearsals for doctor appointments and visits to the ER. It wasn't fair to the rest of the cast, so I had to quit."

April wondered why the university-professor husband couldn't take the kid to the doctor once in a while but didn't say anything. Insulting customers by judging their spouses was probably not good for business. "So are you looking to sell these?"

"Uh-huh. I'd been saving them for my kids to play dress-up with someday. My three sons don't seem to be interested, though. At this point, the stuff is just taking up precious space in my closet."

"It will probably take me a while to look through everything. It's my first time in the shop without my boss here. Do you want me to give you a call and you can come back when I'm done?"

"Oh, I'll just stay and browse. My husband's got the kids for once, and I want to stretch this time out as long as I can. If I go home, someone will need a ride somewhere, or need me to make a sandwich or wash a baseball jersey. I'd rather just stay here while I'm free."

"I'll need to check your ID," April said. "We need to see ID for anyone who sells items to the store—I know that much."

The woman dug around in her canvas tote bag and produced an overstuffed vinyl wallet. She removed her license and set it down with an exaggerated sigh. "I hate that picture. I wish I could have a hair and makeup crew now, like I did for all those shows."

April looked from the picture to the woman and back again, and read the name: Lane Lawton. She copied down Lane's name, driver's license number, and birth date. The photograph, despite the too-bright lighting, showed a woman with a confident, commanding smile. In the smile, April could see a hint of the dramatic diva that didn't come across in the role of frazzled mom that Lane seemed to be playing right now.

April handed back the driver's license. "Thank you. If you just want to take a look around, I'll call you over when I'm done going through everything."

Lane walked to the back of the shop to study the purses and shoes. April put her hands on her growing stomach and tried to calm the anxiety fluttering around inside her. Or maybe it was the baby she felt. Either way, April wondered what motherhood would do to her, if it could make a New York actress leave the stage to make sandwiches and drive carpools.

Except that April didn't drive. She was embarrassed that her fear had gotten in the way of her doing her job duties that morning. She knew she'd have to get back behind the wheel eventually, probably before the baby was born. But every time she sat inside her mother's Toyota parked in the garage—the car her mom *didn't* crash—her hands shook and she couldn't breathe.

She looked down at Lane's heap of costumes. It spanned many places and times. There was a denim dress with a cowgirl vibe and a blue ball gown with petticoats, reminiscent of the Civil War. April wondered again how Lane could have given up acting. What a gift, to be able to morph into someone else, even if only for a couple of hours under hot lights.

April realized that Violet hadn't really told her much about pricing. She looked for Violet's leather-bound inventory book to try to get an idea of how much she should pay Lane for her items. She spotted it on the counter, serving as a coaster for a red Moroccan tea glass half-filled with water. April set the glass aside and leafed through the inventory entries until she felt she had an idea of how to pay for the costumes.

"Lane?" she said.

The woman looked up. "Yes?"

"I'm done going through your things, so I'm ready if you are. Sorry it took me so long. I've only been working here a couple of weeks."

"It's okay. Trust me. This is most peaceful half hour I've had in a long time. I've gotta come in here more often." Lane smiled. "Oh, and I found these." She dangled a pair of red d'Orsay pumps from her hand.

"Those are great," said April. "Violet—my boss—said they came from a professor at the law school who has a closet full of black suits and hundreds of pairs of wild shoes. You're lucky you're her shoe size. If you come back in a few weeks, we'll probably have more. I guess the lady goes through her collection at the end of every school year and brings in the ones she doesn't want anymore."

"I'm not sure where I'll wear them," Lane said. "Preschool field trips to the farm aren't exactly conducive to heels—but I'll *make* an occasion for them if I have to."

Lane agreed to take store credit instead of cash for her costumes. She used some of the credit to purchase the shoes and said she'd be back soon to spend the rest. "I have plenty more costumes at home," she said. "So feel free to call me if there's anything specific you need."

Lane wrote down her contact information, then headed out the door swinging an orange paper shopping bag with HOURGLASS VINTAGE printed on the side.

April was proud of herself for successfully handling her first solo transaction and couldn't wait for Violet to return so she could tell her all about it.

When Violet got back from her errand, though, she looked critically at the bundle of costumes on the counter. "What's with all these?"

"Some lady who used to be an actress brought in a bunch of her old costumes. Look at this one." April held up a shiny red leotard that looked like it could have been a circus outfit. She touched the sparkly band around the neckline.

Violet sorted through the pile of garments, furrowing her forehead. "Wait, are they *all* costumes? We don't carry costumes."

"Oh," said April, feeling like an idiot. "Well . . . maybe you should, or at least have a supply you can haul out around Halloween. As a way to bring in people who wouldn't otherwise shop at a secondhand store."

Violet looked skeptical. "It's an interesting idea, but I'm just not sure how my customers would feel about seeing something that they actually wore to an important event, like a wedding or a prom, on the costume rack."

"I'm sorry. I guess I should have waited for you to come back before buying the stuff," April said.

"In the future, you can always call me if you have a question and I'm not here." She surveyed the costumes and sighed. "I guess I'll hang on to these until Halloween, like you said, and see if we can sell them then."

April felt like she'd had a shot at proving herself to Violet and blown it. She needed to redeem herself.

"You know," she said, "when I was looking through the inventory book, it was really hard for me to find the information I needed. If you're okay with it, maybe I could try to figure out a better way to organize everything. If we get all your records computerized like we talked about, they would be searchable. Seriously, I don't mind doing that sort of thing."

Violet threw up her hands. "Okay, okay, you little data wizard. Have at it."

That night, April sat at her mom's old secretary desk, paging through the ledger and file folders she'd hauled home with her from the boutique. The deeper she waded into Violet's documentation, the more convinced she felt that she could come up with a better system of storing and sorting all the numbers and records.

She heard a dinging sound and, by reflex, opened up her e-mail on her laptop screen. A new message from Charlie sat in her inbox, with the subject *In Boston for orientation*. April felt a little kick somewhere deep inside her and looked down at her belly. "E-mail from your dad," she said. Sadness clutched her chest, and she deleted the e-mail without reading it.

During the weeks following April and Charlie's engagement, Judy Cabot had refused to speak with or see April. By default, this meant that Trip hadn't uttered a word to April, either. Charlie had served as intermediary, pleading for his parents to accept his fiancée and the baby they would soon have.

Then, one Saturday, April had gotten a call from Judy, asking her to come over without Charlie. As soon as April arrived at the Cabots' home, Judy had pressed an Emily Post wedding handbook into her hands and led April into the living room, where an overeager brunette in a sweater set stood with a white binder under her arm.

"April, meet Lila," Judy had said. "She's the best wedding planner in Madison."

"Um, hi." April had given Judy a questioning look.

Judy's eyes had met April's. "Not a thing about this . . . *situation*"— she glanced at April's still-small but expanding waistline—"is how I would have chosen it. The wedding, at least, will be done my way."

April still couldn't decide what had been worse—the silent treatment she'd received at first, or being forced to sit for hours while Judy and Lila debated different variations of monogram fonts and boutonnieres. None of it mattered now that the wedding was off.

Even though she and Charlie were no longer together, April still hated the idea of his moving out east in August. She had at least hoped he'd be able to see their baby on a regular basis. But Charlie had only gotten into one medical school out of the fifteen to which he'd applied. He'd been wait-listed at his first choice, the University of Wisconsin, and from what the admissions office told him, his name was pretty far down the list.

She tried to focus on entering data into her computer from the receipts and sales records from the shop. Unlike April's past, numbers usually made sense. Today, though, connecting all the pieces proved to be frustrating because her mind kept wandering to Charlie and everything that had happened.

She'd be lying if she wrote him back to say she didn't want to see him. She did. She didn't know if it was because she still loved him or if it was pregnancy hormones, but she craved his smile, his warm body curled around hers, the implicit understanding of each other they used to have.

Three months earlier

"Hey, wake up. It's okay. You're okay."

April heard Charlie's voice, as if from far away. She felt his arms encircling her, his lips kissing her forehead, her temples.

She opened her eyes, and he wiped her wet cheeks with the corner of his bedsheet. Outside his apartment window, the February wind stirred the bare trees, casting spindly shadows on the wall.

"You were crying in your sleep again," he said.

Charlie held her tighter as the realization set in, as it always did, that her mom was still gone. April longed for the day when she would no longer wake in the middle of the night, wondering whether her mom's accident had been a bad dream. For the day when she could smile without feeling like something under the surface of her skin might break.

April leaned into him, facing him, so that her arms, her stomach, her legs aligned and intertwined with his. At moments like this, the only thing more visceral, more palpable than her grief was her overwhelming desire for Charlie, and his for her. All around was darkness, all around was death. But here, under the folds of his comforter, under the weight of his body—and between them in her growing belly—was life.

Chapter 8

INVENTORY ITEM: *hat*

APPROXIMATE DATE: *1949*

CONDITION: *excellent*

ITEM DESCRIPTION: *Bell-shaped hat made from lime-green felt and decorated with a black grosgrain ribbon and peacock feather.*

SOURCE: *Lucille Rollins. Not for sale.*

Violet

"EXCUSE ME, DO YOU have a men's section?" asked a male voice.

Violet looked up from folding a red Pendleton sweater. A man in a flannel shirt stood just inside the front door of the shop. He looked a little bit familiar, but she couldn't figure out why. She decided it must have been the brown eyes, broad shoulders, and solid build—he had that lifelong Midwesterner look about him.

"No, I'm sorry," she said. "I used to carry a few men's clothes, but they didn't sell well enough for me to justify keeping up with it, so I stopped. Is there anything specific you're looking for? Maybe I can point you in the direction of a shop that might have it."

"I need a hat," he said. "It's the last week of school. I promised my students that if no one out of my seven sections failed the final exam, I'd wear a ridiculous hat on the last day of classes. They kept up their end of the bargain, so I've got to keep mine."

"What do you teach?" Violet asked.

"Biology and earth science," he said. "Freshmen and sophomores."

"Well, some of our hats could probably pass as unisex. Or, if you wanted to look really ridiculous, you could get one of our ladies' hats. Come on, I'll show you what we've got."

Violet led him to a display in a corner of the shop, where vintage hats in felt, silk, straw, and velvet were arranged on a circular stand.

"Nice rack," Sam said, then clapped a hand over his mouth. "I can't believe I said that out loud. Sometimes I don't have any filter."

Violet laughed. "I'm guilty of that, too. And anyway, I'm willing to admit it's a nice rack."

It wasn't often that Violet got men into the shop, let alone good-looking ones. He was handsome, but not in a showy way. He had a short beard that looked like it wasn't so much a conscious choice but just the result of a few skipped days of shaving.

He tried on a gray wool fedora with a feather on the brim. "What do you think?"

"I think it looks great. I can get a mirror if you'd like to see for yourself," she said.

"Thanks. Hey, I'm Sam Lewis." The man extended his hand and smiled. Little lines crinkled around his eyes.

"Nice to meet you. I'm Violet Turner." She shook his right hand and noticed the lack of a wedding ring on his left.

"I knew it," Sam said.

"What?"

"You're from Bent Creek, right? We went to high school together. You were a year behind me."

"I thought I knew you from somewhere," Violet said. She picked up a silver-plated hand mirror from a table and gave it to Sam.

He looked at his reflection and cocked the fedora to one side. "Hmmm. I think the kids will be disappointed if I wear something this normal looking."

"It's very nineteen fifties Wall Street," Violet said.

Sam put the hat back on its stand and placed a red beret on top of his head. "It's okay if you don't remember me from school."

"Maybe I would remember you if you'd worn that beret," Violet joked.

"I just remember you because—well, you dated Jed Cline, right?" Sam asked. "He was in my class."

Violet hated that, even now, that single fact still defined her in some people's minds.

"I married him, too," she said.

"When did you guys move here?"

"Oh, we're not still married. I moved here on my own a few years ago to open this shop and finish a degree I'd started in fashion merchandising at the community college up there."

"You did both of those things at the same time? I'm impressed."

"I'd been planning for years to open a store, so I already had a lot of the details worked out. I'd also accumulated way more vintage stuff than I could justify owning if I *didn't* open up a shop. I thought about doing it in Bent Creek, but there just aren't enough people there to support a high-end boutique. Plus, I was too busy taking care of Jed. He needed me, and for a long time being needed seemed like the most important thing in the world."

"Yeah, I'd heard that he had a drinking problem. But you just never know what's true and what isn't with small-town gossip." Sam took off the beret.

"That's for sure." Violet didn't even want to think about what gossip must have circulated in the wake of her divorce. Small towns had selective memories, and despite the fact that Jed could be cruel and controlling, especially when he drank, he had also stayed put. There were those people who stayed in Bent Creek and those who didn't. Violet knew that the simple act of leaving had, in many people's minds, made her suspect. Even her parents were wary of her decision. They knew Jed and Violet had their problems, but they didn't see why she had to move away. They didn't understand, as Grandma Lou had, that Violet couldn't change her life if all of the people in it saw her a certain way.

"Roots are important, honey," Grandma Lou had said when Violet told her she was contemplating leaving. "But sometimes a flower outgrows its pot."

Sam grabbed a light blue pillbox hat and placed it on top of his head. He arranged the birdcage veil in front of his face and batted his eyelashes. "What do you think?" he asked.

Violet laughed. "If you're looking for ridiculous, you've found it."

Sam picked up the silver-plated hand mirror from the counter and inspected his reflection. "This will be perfect. My students will get a kick out of it."

"They're lucky they've got a teacher willing to make a fool out of himself for the sake of their education."

"Hey, whatever works." Sam took off the hat and ran a hand through his thick brown hair, speckled with gray. Violet wondered why she had never paid attention to him in high school, and then remembered that she had had tunnel vision at the time, focused only on Jed.

Sam looked around the store. "I'm not very into fashion or design or whatever, but it's a pretty cool store you've got. Is it just you who works here?"

"I have an intern, but she's at an appointment," Violet said. "So I've told you how *I* ended up here. What brought you to Madison?"

"I went to college here. And, like a lot of people, I fell in love with the place and never left. When I bike to work, I see a guy with a two-foot-tall Mohawk pushing his dachshund in a stroller along the bike path. There's a stilt-walkers' group that meets up at a bar in my neighborhood every Monday night. Where else can I get that kind of entertainment?"

"The circus?"

Sam smiled. "Anyway, even though I love it here, it's good running into someone from back home."

Violet returned his smile, wondering why she hadn't noticed in high school how cute he was.

"Listen, I've got to get back to work," Sam said. "I'm on my lunch break."

"Of course," Violet said, disappointed. "Here, let me ring that up for you." She took the hat from Sam and brought it over to the register.

He handed her a credit card. "I'd love to finish catching up sometime."

"That sounds great." Violet swiped the card and printed a receipt. She placed the blue hat in a shopping bag and gave it to him. Their hands brushed and she noticed goose bumps spring up on her arms, which were bare in her sleeveless dress.

"Thanks," Sam said. "Nice tattoo."

Violet blushed, hoping that he didn't notice the goose bumps. Or maybe she hoped he did.

"If you give me your number I can plug it into my phone," he said.

Violet opened a drawer and rummaged through a shoe box full of old black and white photographs. They were pictures she'd collected from thrift stores and garage sales, all of people she didn't know. There were babies in lace bonnets and soldiers in uniform, women on horseback and kids at the fair. Violet didn't know why she bought them, other than to save just a moment of these people's stories.

She searched through the box until she found what she was looking for—a picture of a woman in a birdcage veil similar to the one on
the hat Sam had bought. She flipped the yellowed photograph over
and scribbled her phone number on the back side.

Sam laughed when he saw the picture. "I have to say I've never
had anyone give me a phone number this way before."

Violet grinned. "I like to do things my own way."

"Hey, how come you didn't let me try on *that* hat?" Sam pointed
to the tangerine-colored wall behind the register counter. Beneath the
hammered metal letters that spelled out "Hourglass Vintage" hung a
green felt hat decorated with a peacock feather.

"Because that one is special," Violet said.

A year earlier

After the funeral, while her relatives mingled over coffee and cookies in
the kitchen, Violet snuck down the pile-carpeted hallway to Grandma
Lou's bedroom. She went into the walk-in closet and sat down on the
floor, between the racks of clothes, and breathed in the scent of ciga-
rettes and White Shoulders perfume. Her grandmother's scent.

She didn't know how long she'd been sitting there when she heard
her mother's voice. "Violet, where are you?"

"I'm in here," Violet called out.

Celeste Turner appeared at the doorway to the closet and put a
hand on her hip. Violet thought that her mom, with her pleated black
pants and shapeless sweater, seemed out of place in Grandma Lou's
closet full of sequins and silk. Celeste dressed for function. She didn't
share her mother's affinity for fashion. It seemed to have skipped a
generation and showed up in Violet instead.

"What are you doing in here?" Celeste asked.

Violet ran a hand over the surface of a lacquered black jewelry box. "Saying good-bye."

Celeste's eyes teared up. "I know. I miss her, too."

It had been six weeks since Grandma Lou had been admitted to the hospital after a stroke that put her into a coma. Violet's mother had had to make the difficult decision, based on her mother's advance-directive papers, to take her off life support.

Violet stepped into a pair of her grandmother's patent heels. "What are you going to do with all of her things?"

"I'm not sure." Her mother sighed. "I suppose we'll just give them to Goodwill, like we're doing with everything else. If your aunts and uncles were planning to stick around for a few days to help, I'd say they could pick out whatever furniture or keepsakes they want. But they're all headed back out of town tomorrow. And anyway, they all said they have enough junk already and don't have room for more."

"It's not junk," Violet said. She touched the hem of a black velvet cape lined with satin—an "opera cloak," Grandma Lou had called it. Never mind the fact that Bent Creek didn't even have a movie theater, let alone an opera house. It was a beautiful garment.

Her mother's expression softened. "You're right. I'm just overwhelmed about getting the house on the market."

Violet wished there were something she could do to make her mom less stressed, less weary. She pressed her cheek to the fox-fur collar of one of her grandmother's wool coats. "Can I have some of this stuff, if no one else is gonna take it?"

"Sure," her mother said. "I suppose you could sell it in your store. I don't know why I didn't think of that."

"I'm not going to *sell it,* Mom. Geez. I just want some things of hers, to remember her."

Her mother shrugged. "Well, I'm just saying. It would all just get donated anyway, so no one would mind if you did decide to sell it."

Violet shook her head, annoyed at the suggestion.

"Anyway, I came back here because everyone's asking questions about you," Celeste said. "And I don't know the answers."

Violet realized that was her own fault. Since she left Jed, she'd spent as little time in Bent Creek as possible, and her parents had yet to make the two-hundred-and-fifty-mile trip to Madison to visit her. Her mother didn't like to drive on the interstate, and living in a county crisscrossed by deserted two-lane roads, she'd never really had to conquer her fear. Violet's father, who operated a farm supply store, couldn't visit Madison for the same reason Violet couldn't often visit Bent Creek—he didn't want to leave his shop in anyone else's hands.

"Okay," Violet told her mother. "Just give me a couple more minutes."

After her mother left the room, Violet reached for a striped hatbox on the shelf. If she was going to go out there and answer a dozen questions about what had happened to her marriage and whether she was seeing "anyone special" in Madison, she would need help from her grandmother—a little piece of Grandma Lou's strength and style.

She opened the hatbox and, inside, found a lime-green cloche decorated with grosgrain ribbon and an iridescent peacock feather. She took the hat out of the yellowing tissue paper and put it on.

She stepped over to her grandmother's vanity, pushing aside trays of makeup and a crystal ashtray so she could lean closer to the mirror. The vibrant color of the hat lent a cheerful contrast to her black peplum jacket and pencil skirt. Violet could have sworn that, with the hat on, she looked a little bit like her grandmother did in pictures from when she was younger.

Violet turned off the closet light and left the room. With the hat on, she knew she was sure to get some raised eyebrows from her aunts and uncles, and probably even from her parents, but she didn't care. Grandma Lou would have approved.

Chapter 9

INVENTORY ITEM: *fur coat*
APPROXIMATE DATE: *1950*
CONDITION: *fair*
ITEM DESCRIPTION: *Blond, hip-length mink coat. Pink silk lining, some bare spots at the elbows.*
SOURCE: *moving sale*

Violet

THE NEXT EVENING, VIOLET leaned toward the bathroom mirror, humming to a bluegrass album while she applied red lipstick. Tonight was the night she'd promised Karen they'd go out for a night on the town like they used to do.

Back when Karen lived in an apartment down the street, she would often stop in at the boutique on her way home from work. She usually had a line on whatever was going on that night, whether it was the opening of a new restaurant or an indie film festival. Some evenings they'd just share a half carafe of Cabernet at their favorite bistro in Machinery Row. Other nights they'd dance to live funk music until dawn, sweating alongside strangers in a crowded bar.

Men were often a part of those nights, either men they met or men they invited along. Karen, with her long, pale limbs and fiery hair, fetched admiration everywhere she went. Violet never resented her for it, though. In fact, she usually was grateful for the deflection of attention. In the early days after her divorce, Violet wanted nothing more than to enjoy her newfound freedom. If she met some interesting men along the way, great, but they were beside the point. After Karen got married and built a house with Tom out in the suburbs, she and Violet's adventures became much less frequent, and they dropped off almost altogether when Karen soon got pregnant. Violet couldn't blame her. They weren't all that young anymore, and if she were in Karen's shoes, she wouldn't have wasted any time in starting a family, either.

Violet had some time before Karen arrived, even after she'd finished the always-difficult task of selecting something to wear from her full-to-bursting closet. For tonight, she'd selected an all-black pantsuit with a halter neckline from the 1970s. She'd added some beaded silver earrings made by a customer who sold jewelry, and she was set.

While she waited for Karen to show up, she pulled a box out from underneath her bed and lifted off the lid. Inside it, untouched for years, were all of her mementos from Bent Creek. She took out the dried, shriveled carnation corsage Jed had given her at the homecoming dance where she'd spilled schnapps on her dress, a teddy bear she'd taken everywhere with her as a child, and the gold band that had served as both her engagement and wedding ring. She set these all aside on the carpet. At the bottom of the box, she found her yearbooks. She took them out and curled up on the couch with Miles to page through them.

Inside the book for her sophomore year, Violet flipped to the index. She ran her finger down the list of names until she found Sam Lewis. Pages 39 and 94. Out of curiosity, Violet looked up her own name. It took three lines to list all the pages where pictures of her appeared.

She flipped first to page 39, where she found Sam's junior class photo. He smiled through braces and a face full of acne. She remembered who he was now. He'd been one of the kids whom Jed and his buddies picked on.

She turned next to page 94, where she expected to see a photo of Sam with the band, or chess club, or some other extracurricular activity. Instead, Sam's other photo in the yearbook was a candid photo taken in the lunchroom. The subject of the photo was a group of kids posed, arm in arm, around a crowded lunch table. Sam wasn't one of those kids. He appeared in the background of the photo, at a noticeably emptier table, with a slice of pizza stuffed halfway in his mouth. She peered at the awkward, teenage Sam and thought, *Hang in there. You're going to look a lot better in twenty years.*

She heard a knock, followed by barking and the sound of Miles's claws on the wood floor.

"Hello?" Karen called.

"I'm in here." Violet stepped out into the living room, where her friend stood holding two large tote bags. Karen's red hair curled around her face, competing for attention with the room's leopard-print pillows and ethnic textiles. She put down her bags and slipped off her trench coat to reveal a thin-strapped green camisole and tight black pants.

"Whoa, mama," Violet said, hugging her friend. "You look good."

"You really should lock your doors," Karen said.

"I usually remember to lock them when I leave, but I don't lock them when I'm at home. Well, except when I go to bed. Anyway, the neighborhood is safer than it used to be. Haven't you seen the trendy new restaurants up and down the street? The pet salon?"

"Well, when I lived in this neighborhood in law school, there was a crack house on the corner, and guys used to sit on their porches drinking forties every day. Sorry if I'm a little paranoid."

"Those days are long gone, honey. It's all professor types and hipsters now. I doubt the liquor store even carries forties anymore. They're too busy selling six-packs of microbrews made with organically grown hops." Violet gave her friend a teasing smile. "The neighborhood has changed a lot since you moved out to your country estate."

"Speaking of country estates, cabs won't go out there, so I'm sleeping over tonight."

"What about Edith?"

"Tom's got her. It will be good for me to have a night away."

"If you're worried about getting home after a few drinks, I can take you. I don't mind being the designated driver."

Karen shook her head. "I need a sidekick. And I need to have some fun. Do you have any idea what it's like to have a little person attached to you for most of the day?"

"Can't say I do," Violet said. Then she added in a wistful voice, "And I probably never will, either."

"Well, it's not easy." Karen walked over to the galley kitchen connected to the living room. She grabbed the bottle of whiskey from the top of Violet's refrigerator. With the familiarity of someone who'd been to the apartment many times, she opened up a cabinet and grabbed two crystal tumblers. Without asking Violet if she wanted any, she poured two fingers' worth into each glass. "Ice?" She opened the freezer.

"Oh, crap, I forgot to make some," Violet said.

"That's okay, I like mine neat anyway." Karen took a long sip from her glass, then scrunched up her forehead, which already looked more lined than the last time Violet had seen her. "How do you forget to make ice? You just refill the trays."

Violet shrugged. "No one's around to complain."

Karen handed her one of the glasses and Violet took a sip, feeling the pungent liquid warm the inside of her throat. She sat down on the sofa and patted the cushion beside her to invite Karen to sit down. Miles, misunderstanding, jumped up and settled in next to Violet. She rubbed his velvety ears.

"How's Edith doing?" Violet asked. "She's so adorable."

Karen sat on the other end of the sofa. "You don't really want to hear all of the sappy baby stuff, do you?"

Violet prickled a bit at Karen's assumption that she didn't want to hear about Edith just because she didn't have kids of her own. But Violet knew her friend was just trying to be considerate. In the pre-Edith days, Karen and Violet had often hung back in the corner at baby showers, drinking mimosas and rolling their eyes. It had been mostly Karen, though. Violet loved babies. She just didn't like all the pressure and worry surrounding them.

Karen crossed her long legs. "So have you heard anything from your landlord?"

"Nothing new," Violet said. "As far as I know, I still need to be out by the end of August or they'll get a court order to kick me out. Have you come up with any brilliant ideas in that legal mind of yours since we last talked?"

Karen walked over to the kitchen. She poured herself more whiskey and then held up the bottle. "This is the strategy the senior partners at my law firm always take in particularly hard cases."

"Don't you have to breast-feed?"

"Give a girl a break, will you? I can count the number of drinks I've had in the last year on one hand. And anyway, I'll be pumping and dumping tonight."

Violet held her palms in the air. "I'm not judging, just curious. Anyway, sorry for bugging you about legal stuff. That's enough for tonight. You said you needed to get out and have some fun, and I bet you weren't thinking you wanted to spend it talking about my landlord problem. So what should we do?"

"There's a drag show at the King Club I was thinking we could check out tonight," said Karen. "It's called 'Queens at the King.'"

"I was thinking we'd watch an old Marilyn Monroe movie and bake cookies—mostly so we could eat the dough. Any chance I can convince you?"

"No. But we still might see Marilyn."

And sure enough, on a blue-lit stage later that night, Violet and Karen watched a six-foot, buxom blonde belt out "Happy Birthday, Mr. President" while a drummer dressed as Rita Hayworth banged out a cymbal roll, ending in a "ba-dump-bump" rim shot. The performance concluded with a high-end fashion show, with pouting queens stalking up and down the stage in nineties Versace and sixties Pucci.

One of the drag queens even wore a mink coat that Violet could have sworn he (she) had purchased at Hourglass Vintage. She remembered the peach silk lining, which the model flashed when she opened the coat to show off a purple velvet wiggle dress underneath.

Seeing a garment from her store onstage sparked an idea in Violet's mind about how she might make some money to put toward a down payment and, just maybe, convince a bank to lend her money to buy her building.

When the house lights came back on after the show, Violet turned to Karen. "Hey, can I bounce an idea off you?"

"Pretty much everything bounces these days, as far as I'm concerned." Karen pinched her stomach, which boasted a barely perceptible fold of skin where there once had been nothing but flatness, even concavity.

"You're still less bouncy than me and I haven't had a baby," Violet said.

Karen tipped her head and peered at Violet with half-lidded eyes. "Do you think you ever will?"

"Considering that the thought of getting married again terrifies me, and that I'm not even in a relationship, the odds aren't looking good."

"You don't need a man, you know," Karen said.

A broad-shouldered queen passing by said, "That's right, honey."

Violet felt a lump in her throat, afraid to answer for fear of giving away the envy she felt toward her friend. But Karen was tipsy and the two of them always spoke freely with one another. They sorted through each other's clumsy and uncalculated words to look for the truth underneath, like panning for gold.

"I don't know." Violet stared down into her drink, which had started off as a whiskey and soda but was now just melting ice cubes. "I've always thought a baby would be part of my life, but I'm two years shy of forty. I've got to be realistic."

"No interesting prospects, even?" Karen asked. "Not for daddy-hood, necessarily, but just for dating?"

Violet though of Sam. "Someone interesting *did* come into the shop this week. I gave him my number, but he hasn't called yet. So we'll see."

"Oh?" Karen raised her eyebrows. "Tell me more."

Violet shook her head. "I just met him, and I don't want to make it all weird by obsessing. And anyway, I might not hear from him."

"Okay, fine." Karen pouted, then took a sip of her cocktail. "So what was the idea you wanted to talk to me about?"

Violet waved her hand toward the stage. "I was thinking I could do something like this to raise money for the store."

"A drag show?"

"Well, more like a fashion show, but sure. We could have drag queens, too. It would be a good way to show off some of my high-end merchandise and boost sales. What do you think?"

"I think it sounds great," Karen said, covering a yawn with her hand.

"Yeah, you look really intrigued."

"Seriously, I think it could work. But I'm exhausted. I haven't slept for more than a four-hour stretch in months. Forget what I said about you having a baby. You can have mine."

Chapter 10

INVENTORY ITEM: *formal dress*
APPROXIMATE DATE: *1970s*
CONDITION: *excellent*
ITEM DESCRIPTION: *Off-the-shoulder bridesmaid dress. Light green polyester and white lace, with matching cape.*
SOURCE: *Brought in by Karen's mother*

April

AS APRIL WALKED TO work on the last Saturday morning in June, she envied the customers leaving the coffee shop next door to Hourglass Vintage. She looked longingly at their paper cups of fair-trade Peruvian or shade-grown Guatemalan, or whatever the blend of the day was, wishing she hadn't already downed her one cup of coffee for the day before she even left the house. April felt exhausted from a sleepless night of trying to get comfortable lying on her side—the position her doctor had recommended during pregnancy. She preferred sleeping on her stomach, but that simply wasn't possible anymore. The fact that today would have been her wedding day didn't help April's insomnia, either.

It had been a month since she and Charlie had spoken—a month since he'd called off the wedding without so much as talking to her about it. April figured that in the weeks they'd been apart, Charlie's parents had probably already started introducing him to other girls to take her place—beautiful, well-bred girls without a history of mental illness in their families.

When April arrived at Hourglass Vintage, Violet stood hunched over the register counter, writing in a notebook with an intense expression on her face.

"Hi," April said. The weather had finally started to warm up, and she wiped a drop of sweat from her forehead. With it, she tried to wipe from her face any indicator of the pain she felt. She counted on work to distract her from it.

"I'm glad you're here." Violet set down her mug. "I have an idea. It popped into my head last night when I was at the King Club with my friend Karen. I thought, what if we put on a fashion show to raise some money?" She gave April a hopeful look. "We could call it the Hourglass Revue. We'd get women to audition as models and have them wear merchandise from the store."

"Hmmm," April said. The number-crunching part of her brain was already trying to estimate how much it would cost to put on an operation like that.

"You don't seem very excited," Violet said.

"No. I mean, yes. It sounds like it could be fun. It's just . . . well, how would you raise money, exactly? Wouldn't there be a lot of expenses involved?"

"Sure, but we'd make up for it in ticket sales and, hopefully, make a profit auctioning off the clothes and accessories we show on the runway," Violet said. "I have some really high-end things in the back that I don't put on the sales floor all at once because people don't tend to buy them. Madison is a pretty casual town, and most people are happier wearing a pair of Chaco sandals than a pair of Louboutin heels. It's really rare that someone comes into the store looking to drop eight hundred dollars on a fur coat or two grand on a vintage Hermès handbag."

Did you just say two grand for a purse?" April asked, blinking.

Violet nodded. "It's a gorgeous bag. Shiny red leather, with light blue suede on the inside. Remind me to pull it out and show you sometime. Anyway, two grand is nothing. Some vintage Hermès bags can go for ten thousand or more."

While Violet talked at a rapid pace about model auditions and renting theater space, April straightened a stack of vintage concert T-shirts on a table. She interjected as soon as Violet paused to take a sip of coffee. "I'm sorry," April said. "But did I hear you say something about drag queens? Where are we gonna find those?"

"Oh, honey, if we need drag queens, I'll get us drag queens. And good ones, too. Not just your cheap-wig-and-stuffed-bra variety."

April felt a thump inside her and put a hand on her stomach. "Oh, my God, I just felt a kick. I mean, I've felt little flutters before and stuff, but nothing like this." She looked at Violet. "Do you want to feel?"

Violet hesitated for a moment before taking a step forward with her hand outstretched. April placed Violet's palm on the side of her belly and said, "Feel that?"

Violet nodded, and April thought she saw her eyes misting over.

But then Violet took her hand away and said, "So even *she* thinks the Hourglass Revue is a good idea."

"I don't know if it's a she. I had an ultrasound a few weeks ago where I could have found out, but I didn't want to."

"An ultrasound? Was there a problem or something?"

"No," April said. "I guess it's just standard to check on things. I won't be having any more, though. I have free insurance through the state, but it only covers one ultrasound, unless there are complications."

Violet glanced at April's belly. "Well, *I* think she's a girl."

"Based on what?"

"I just have a feeling."

"We'll see," April said, turning her thoughts back to Violet's fund-raising idea. "Okay, so if we're gonna do this fashion show thing, we'll need to draw up a budget, get estimates on how much it will cost to advertise, print programs . . ."

"Maybe we should ask that actress who came in a while back with the costumes if she wants to get involved. I mean, I figure someone who has piles of theater garb in her closet probably knows a thing or two about putting on a show. Or at least more than we do. What was her name?" Violet asked.

"Lane," April said. "I don't remember her last name, but I know we have her contact information. I wrote it down in case we wanted to buy more costumes from her. And, for the record, I still think it would be a good idea for us to sell costumes in the shop."

Violet seemed to ignore the costume comment. "Sure, I'll give her a call," she said. "For the models, we should make sure we have people of different ages. Not just young girls. Young girls aren't going to be the ones with money to bid. I want the older women to be able to picture themselves wearing the stuff onstage, and that's not going to happen unless we actually have people their age up there."

April frowned. "They're not going to be able to picture themselves in something a drag queen is wearing, either."

"Oh, the queens are just for fun. Not many of them will fit into our sizes, anyway. We'll have to improvise a bit with their outfits. We'll go through all the stuff in the back room. It will be a good excuse for me to update my inventory records anyway."

"About that . . ." April pulled her laptop out of her leather satchel, sensing her opportunity to talk about the progress she'd made with Violet's records. "I downloaded some accounting and inventory software on my laptop that I think would really help you out around the store."

Violet opened and closed her mouth. "You don't have to buy

things for the store," she said. "I'm not even paying you, plus the baby is gonna cost—"

"Seriously, it's okay." April waved her hand. "The software was free. And anyway, it will make my life a lot easier. Your paper inventory system is stressing me out. It takes me forever to find any information in it. And, you know, my doctor tells me stress isn't good for the baby."

"How can I argue with that?" Violet's eyes let go of a little bit of their edge, but her lips looked tight when she said, "Thank you. You're gonna have to teach me to use it, though. And I guess I'll need to set up my computer down here, if I can remember how to put everything back together once it's all unhooked."

"I can help you with that later," April said. "In the meantime we can use my laptop."

"Want to help me start going through stuff?" Violet asked.

April nodded and followed her to the back room, where they sat on the floor. The pile of empty canvas containers grew as the two of them sorted through their contents—chinoiserie robes in rich red and pink, Halston one-shouldered gowns, and pastel cotton circle skirts from the fifties. A floral, woodsy scent clung to the garments from the cedar planks and lavender sachets Violet stored with them to keep moths away.

"What's this?" April pulled a swath of midnight-blue taffeta from one of the boxes. She stood up and lifted the item higher, but the fabric kept on coming.

"That's a Dior evening gown," Violet said.

With careful hands, April spread out the cool, crinkly fabric on Violet's worktable and straightened out its folds. The taffeta had a textured floral pattern on it, with black velvet and silver thread outlining the edges of each petal. A giant, sculptural bow adorned the strapless bodice.

"Where did you get this?" April asked. "And why isn't it on the sales floor?"

"It was, for a while. I had it on one of the mannequins," Violet said. "But no one was buying it, so I put it away. I got it from the wife of a former congressman. She wore it to a ball for Eisenhower's first inauguration in 1953."

"Why would she ever get rid of something like this?"

"It's a pretty funny story, actually. Her husband was a heavy hitter in the Republican Party, and she was a staunch Democrat. When I bought the dress from her and asked her why she was getting rid of it, she said, 'Because I voted for Stevenson.'"

"Well, it's gorgeous." April held the dress up to her chest. "Not that there's any way I could fit into this tiny waistline, especially not now. I'm just shocked it never sold. Maybe people just need to see it on someone—not just on the mannequin. We should definitely use it in the show."

"There should be black gloves in there that go with it, too."

"Ooh." April pulled a pair of long silk gloves from the box. She bent down toward her laptop and typed a description of the dress and gloves into her inventory program. She then moved on to the next box, where she unearthed a frothy, mint-green dress trimmed with white lace, as well as a nearly identical one in pink. "What's the story with these? Nightgowns?"

"Bridesmaid's dresses from the late seventies. Karen's mom brought them in, believe it or not. The green one has a matching cape with a hood."

"Are you kidding me?" April dug out the polyester cape and tied it around her neck. She walked over to the full-length mirror, with its spray-painted gold frame, and frowned. "I'm gonna say that capes are not a good choice for maternity clothes. I look like a hippo stuck under a giant tarp."

"You do not," Violet said. "You'll never believe this, but Karen's mom wore those dresses in two different weddings of the same friend."

"I hope that friend had better taste in grooms than in bridesmaid dresses."

"I don't think so," Violet said. "She told me both marriages ended in divorce. She found these in her attic."

April felt her cell phone buzzing in her pocket. She pulled it out and glanced down at the screen. It was Charlie. She looked at the bridesmaid dresses in her lap, thinking about her own canceled wedding. Pain throbbed through her chest and she felt dizzy all of a sudden. Still clutching the phone, she ran to the staff bathroom and shut the door. She sat down on the toilet and put her head between her legs—or tried to. She couldn't quite get it all the way there, with her stomach in the way, so she just leaned over, slumping her shoulders and hanging her head.

Her phone vibrated again, indicating that she had a new voice mail. She knew that listening to it would only make her more upset, but her hand moved of its own volition, punching the message button and lifting the phone to her ear.

"Hey, it's me," said the familiar voice. "I'm back in town and just wondering if maybe you want to get together. I sent you an e-mail a while back. Maybe you didn't get it? Or maybe you're still mad at me. Either way, I really need to talk to you. I keep thinking about how today would have been . . . well, anyway, call me. Bye."

She hadn't responded to Charlie's e-mail. She knew he was back in town—she'd been thinking about it all week, part of her hoping to run into him and the other part still raw and angry.

April exhaled, trying to slow her racing pulse. At her last prenatal checkup, her doctor had warned her about the effects of the stress hormone cortisol on a developing baby—how the hormone passes through the placenta and elevates the baby's stress levels, too.

"Try to avoid stressful situations if you can," Dr. Hong had said. "And if you do find yourself in a stressful scenario, leave the room if you have to, or imagine yourself somewhere else."

The problem with Dr. Hong's advice was that whenever she tried to imagine herself somewhere else, she imagined herself with Charlie, tucked safely under the nook of his arm. This image only exacerbated her distress.

She heard a knock.

"Is everything okay?" Violet asked.

April opened the door and nodded, embarrassed by her emotional reaction. She was at work, after all, and wanted so badly for Violet to take her seriously.

Violet tilted her head. "Want to talk about anything? Part of this job is listening to people's stories. I've gotten pretty good at it."

"That was Charlie." April was relieved to see Violet didn't seem to be annoyed by her display of emotion.

"As in returning-your-wedding-dress Charlie?"

"That's the one. The wedding was supposed to have been today." April grabbed a piece of tissue paper from the table and tore at the edges. "I didn't even want a fancy wedding. I just wanted to get married at a park. Have a barbecue afterward, invite a few friends. I couldn't exactly send formal wedding invitations to my high school friends. I mean, that would be weird, right? And I haven't seen my dad in years, so I wasn't about to extend *him* an invitation. But Charlie's parents hired this wedding planner. Booked the ballroom at their country club and invited a hundred of their friends."

"I know how weddings can get out of hand," Violet said. "If my parents had had the money, they probably would have invited the entire county back when I got married. It's important to do what's right for you, though. Were Charlie's parents disappointed when things didn't work out?"

April shook her head. "That's the thing. They don't even like me. They didn't want us to get married. But somehow the wedding became not at all about Charlie or about me, but just a way to flaunt their money." She looked down at her phone, still in her hand, and punched a button, deleting Charlie's message. "Anyway, I didn't answer his call. He wants to see me, but I don't think I can do it."

April was surprised when Violet, who was usually so guarded, opened her arms and hugged her.

A month earlier

Charlie stared at the student loan application open on his computer screen. "I don't know how I'm ever going to pay back all this debt."

"We'll just have to figure it out." April put her elbows on the kitchen table, thinking with a pang of grief about how many times her mom had sat at this same table, sifting through overdue bills and writing postdated checks. April and her mother had never had much more than the house, which was part of the divorce settlement, and each other. Their bond had been, to put it in algebraic terms, one of the few constants in an equation with many variables.

Charlie had never had to think about money, though, until now. April worried what it would do to him, to their relationship, on top of the demands that a newborn baby and the rigors of med school were sure to bring.

"Remind me again what the interest rates are for the loans," April said, picking up a cracker and piece of cheese from a plate in front of her. She'd been so hungry lately. Forgetful, too. The fact that she wasn't sleeping much and had to get up multiple times during the night to pee wasn't helping her mental clarity, either.

"Don't even try to start adding everything up in that calculator brain of yours." A smile cracked through the strain in Charlie's face. "Trust me, you don't want to know."

He rested his hand high on her thigh, and April sensed the heat of his skin through her leggings. She smiled back and said, "Let's finish filling out this application, so we can move on to more . . . *fun* activities."

He moved both hands back to the keyboard with a reluctant sigh. "I don't get why my parents can't just help me out with tuition. They have plenty of money, and all they ever spend it on is golf."

The mention of Charlie's parents killed the warm buzz that had been running through her body. "*I* know why they won't help you," April said. "Despite your mom hiring the wedding planner and all that, they still hate the fact that we're getting married."

Charlie twisted his mouth. "I don't think it has to do with you, specifically. It's just that a pregnant, eighteen-year-old girlfriend conflicts with their dream of me marrying a horse-riding, tennis-playing blueblood from Wellesley or Mount Holyoke."

April took a bite of cracker. Ordinarily, she treaded with caution on the tense topic of their different backgrounds. But today, she felt frazzled enough to push the conversation further than usual. She leaned back in her chair. "I bet if you broke up with me, your parents would write you a check for your tuition with money to spare."

"I don't care what my parents want," Charlie muttered.

"Wait, did they actually make that offer to you?" April didn't know why she asked. She was pretty sure she knew the answer.

"I don't want to talk about it. Let's just finish this form."

April knew she was stirring up the embers of a fire, but she couldn't stop. She didn't know if it was from pregnancy hormones or sleeplessness, but the filter that usually kept her from snapping seemed to have fallen away.

"Come on," she said. "We can't keep things from each other if we're going to be getting married."

Charlie shut his laptop with a click. "Fine. Yes. My parents told me they'd pay for my med school if I broke up with you. Okay? Does that somehow help you, to know that?"

It didn't, of course. Even though April had guessed that that was the case, it still stung to have her suspicion confirmed. She knew Charlie's parents were far from thrilled about their engagement, but lately it had seemed like they'd begun to accept it. She wouldn't classify her relationship with the Cabots as *warm,* exactly, but at least Judy had stopped looking like she was going to cry whenever April was around.

"Wow." April let out a loud exhale. "And to think that just last Saturday your mom and I spent the afternoon tasting cakes and picking out registry items."

"Why does that surprise you? My parents are always trying to control people with their money." Charlie shook his head. "I guess sometimes I forget how young you are. You haven't had a chance to realize yet what assholes people can be."

"Oh, I'm learning, that's for sure." April's cheeks flamed. "I know I'm young, but I've had to deal with a lot of problems you've never had to. So I don't see what age has to do with anything."

"Come on, I don't want to play the 'my problems are worse than yours' game. You win, okay?" Charlie squeezed his eyes shut and pulled at the long strands of sandy-colored hair overlapping his ears.

He needed a haircut, April thought. Both of them had been so overwhelmed lately—with plans for college, grad school, the baby, the wedding—that even ordinary obligations took immense effort.

"We're both stressed out," Charlie said, as if reading her mind. "Let's just focus on what's important here, which is for us to be together, right?"

"Yeah." April felt her shoulders relax a bit. She hadn't realized how much she'd been tensing them.

"I'll take out some student loans," he said. "Lots of people do. Someday hopefully I'll earn enough money to pay them back. It will be fine."

April nodded. "You know, I was thinking, once my mom's estate and debts are all settled and once this house sells, we could use whatever money is left over for your med school."

"What about your own tuition?"

"I've got my scholarship money."

"Yeah, but only if you go to the UW. What about when you transfer to a school out in Boston to be near me, like we've talked about? Then you'll need to take out loans, too." Charlie cocked his head to one side. "Anyway, it sounds like there won't be much left over from the sale of the house, if anything, once your mom's debts have been paid."

"Yeah, but there's a little bit of life insurance money, too."

Charlie frowned. "I don't think you should count on that money. Didn't you say the insurance company is still waiting on more documentation from the coroner?"

"Yeah. The autopsy was inconclusive." April's shoulders tensed up again. "The coroner couldn't settle on a specific cause of death because the wreck was so bad."

She knew what Charlie was implying—that maybe it was no accident that her mother's car had veered off the icy Beltline and over the guardrail. April had considered the possibility before. She couldn't help it. On nights when she couldn't sleep, it was hard not to think the worst. But thinking it was one thing. She didn't think she could stand to hear it said aloud by the one person in this world who loved her as much as her mother had.

"I just meant the insurance claim could be denied," Charlie said. "That's all."

"If you mean it *could be denied* because you think my mom killed herself, I've thought about that, too." April's voice came out sharp, defensive. "But I know she would never have done that. She may have had her problems, but there's no way she'd have gone that far."

Charlie shrugged. "Okay."

"You don't believe me, do you?"

"It doesn't matter what I think."

"It *does* matter. It matters to me." April got up from the table and paced the floor. The cold tile on her bare feet sent a shiver through her. Not knowing exactly what had happened the night of her mom's accident kept her in a holding pattern, a whirlpool of grief and questions that sucked her in and spit her out, no matter how hard she tried to swim out of it. Being four months pregnant, too, seemed to magnify every emotion.

"I shouldn't have brought it up." Charlie put his head in his hands. When he looked up again, he asked, "How can I make it better?"

See, that's the problem, April thought. Charlie came from a lush-lawned world where a signature on a check or withdrawal slip could heal most wounds. He didn't know what it was like, as a kid, to wonder if the phone was going get turned off again, or to wake up every morning wondering if it was going to be a good day or a bad day, based on his mom's mood swings.

"If you think there's an easy fix—some money or magic words that will solve all our problems—then maybe you're more like your parents than I thought," she said.

Now Charlie stood up. "I'm *nothing* like them. And anyway, just because my parents didn't struggle to pay the bills doesn't mean my family didn't have any problems. Sometimes I think growing up with money can make things worse, in a way."

"It's easy to say that when you had it. We'll see what you're saying when we're struggling to pay the rent."

"So what are you saying, exactly?" Charlie crossed his arms over his chest. "That you don't think I can hack it without Mommy and Daddy to pay the bills?"

"I'm saying that to pay for four years of med school—that's a lot of money. And, since you've never had to worry about money, I'm not sure you've *really* thought about what it means to turn down that big of a sum."

"I didn't *have* to think about it," Charlie said. "I didn't think about it for even a second."

"That's what worries me," April said. "It's all sweet and romantic right now to tell your parents to screw off. All Sonny and Cher and—what was that old song? 'I Got You Babe.' But we'll see what happens when things get harder. I don't want you to hold it against me someday."

"You know, maybe *you're* the one who is having second thoughts and that's why you brought this all up." Charlie pressed his lips together in a hard line. "You know, maybe my parents were right."

"About what?"

"Well, maybe you can't commit, just like your mom. She couldn't commit to your dad or to any of the crazy business schemes she thought up."

"She had an *illness,* Charlie," April said through a clenched jaw.

He dropped his arms to his sides. "Yeah, and how do I know you won't go crazy someday, too?"

She felt as if Charlie had just punched her in her swollen stomach. Until that point, their fight had been about their families, their circumstances. Now Charlie had made it personal. Ending up like her mom was April's worst fear, and it could still happen. Her mother's bipolar disorder didn't surface at a diagnosable level until she was in her twenties.

"You're right," she said in her iciest voice. "You *don't* know. And I suppose you don't want to stick around to find out."

"That's not what I—"

"Oh, I know what you meant," April said, her ears ringing with anger. "Hell, our baby will probably turn out crazy, too."

"*Fuck.*" Charlie slammed his hand against the table. "Can't we just reset this whole conversation? Pretend it didn't happen?" His voice bordered on desperation.

"I don't think so. Now that I know what you really think . . ." April's vision blurred as tears filled her eyes. "I can't live my life with you watching me every day, wondering if today's going to be the day I lose my mind. Maybe your parents *were* right. Maybe you should just cut your losses and get on with whatever they've got planned for you."

April expected Charlie to protest, but he didn't. Instead he just stood there, mournful and unmoving, as if he couldn't quite believe what was happening. He opened his mouth—to apologize, maybe— but no sound came out to fill the stunned space that stretched between them.

Charlie shuffled to the table and picked up his laptop. He met April's eyes with a helpless expression and held her gaze for a few long, sorrowful seconds. Then he slumped, as if in a daze, out the side door.

As soon as he was gone, April picked up her plate from the table and threw it on the floor. Jagged pieces of glass and broken cracker scattered on the tile. She realized her parents had probably fought in this very kitchen, though she'd been too small when they split to remember any details. What she did remember was growing up with the sense that family relationships were fragile and for some people, like her father, replaceable.

She kept her phone close by her bed that night as she turned beneath her blankets without sleeping. April knew, of course, that she could call Charlie. But to do so seemed like an admission that she'd been more in the wrong than he had. Sometime in the early-morning hours, before the sun came up, she resolved that no, she wouldn't call.

This was a test. A test to see if Charlie was up to the task of loving her unconditionally, despite genetics, money, and a dead mother. It was a test and she wanted more than anything for him to pass, but he had to do it on his own.

The next day, her heart nearly stopped when the doorbell rang. April couldn't conceal her disappointment when she opened the door to see a political canvasser, clutching leaflets for the Green Party candidate in the state senate primaries. She nearly slammed the door in the poor guy's face, and in the faces of the UPS driver and of the band kids selling candy bars later that week. They all smiled at her, oblivious to the fact that they were not what she wanted. What she wanted was a chance at a normal family, and with every agonizing day that passed without word from Charlie, that chance grew slimmer.

April hated waiting. She hated the powerless feeling it produced. But even more than she hated waiting, she hated the conclusion she was coming to—that Charlie was no more reliable than the other people she'd loved in her life.

April stopped waiting when, exactly two weeks after her and Charlie's fight, she checked the mailbox and found an ivory, calligraphed envelope nestled among discount-store flyers and debt-collection notices addressed to her mom. The return address on the scripted envelope read "Mr. and Mrs. Charles Cabot III." She tore it open and pulled out a thick, stiff piece of paper. There, engraved in black ink on Strathmore cotton cardstock, was the announcement that the wedding had been canceled.

Chapter 11

INVENTORY ITEM: *handbag*

APPROXIMATE DATE: *1950s*

CONDITION: *fair*

ITEM DESCRIPTION: *Straw handbag with fake-flower embellishments. Some fraying of the straw weave on bottom of bag.*

SOURCE: *purchased from a friend of Betsy Barrett*

Violet

WHEN VIOLET ARRIVED AT the store the next day, she noticed that April looked tired. Violet didn't envy the heartbreak the girl had endured. Still, she noted with a bit of jealousy that although April's belly was growing larger by the day, she continued to be one of those lucky pregnant women who didn't get bigger anywhere else.

Betsy Barrett waved at Violet from one of the orange chairs outside the dressing room, where she sat paging through a magazine.

"Hi, Betsy," Violet said. "What brings you in today?"

Betsy gripped the arms of the chair with her arthritis-knobbed hands and began to push herself up.

"No need to get up," Violet said, going over to her. "I hope you haven't been waiting long."

"Nonsense, I've been entertaining myself." Betsy pointed at a picture of a young woman in a perfume ad with an elaborate maritime tattoo spread across her shoulder blades, complete with mermaids and a multisailed vessel floating in a sea of skin marked with rippling green waves. "That ship would have sunk years ago if it were on my body."

Violet laughed and clipped a flyaway piece of black hair behind her ear with a rhinestone-studded hairpin. "So what brings you in today?"

"I've got some things for you out in the car, but I'll need some help bringing them in. April offered to help, but I told her she shouldn't be lifting heavy bags in her condition."

"Sure, I can get them," said Violet. "April, I'll be right back."

Betsy handed her the keys and said, "I'm at a meter out front."

Violet stepped outside into summer sunlight and heard the twang of dueling fiddles coming from the street musicians on the corner. A man playing the harmonica tipped his hat at her and she waved.

She spotted Betsy's silver Mercedes parked in front of the bike shop next door, Solidarity Cycles. Through the rear window of the car Violet could see several shopping bags on the backseat. She opened the door, and as she leaned over to grab the bags, she caught sight of a slip of paper on the console between the front seats. It looked like a bill, and at the top it said *Turtle Bay Cancer Treatment Center.* Her eyes watered as she grabbed the bags and set them on the sidewalk.

Violet dabbed at her eyes with her sleeve, debating whether she should confront Betsy about having seen the paper. She didn't want to seem nosy, but then again Betsy had left it out in plain view and hadn't stopped her from coming out to the car on her own. Violet wasn't sure about the etiquette in this situation. On the one hand, it would be hard to pretend she didn't know. On the other, she wanted to respect her friend's privacy.

She picked up the shopping bags and lugged them back to the store. Inside, April was dusting glassware on display shelves while Betsy chattered.

" . . . so I told them that unless they made a rule banning parents from auditions, I wasn't giving another cent to the Young Shakespeare program." Betsy shook her head. "Honest to God, you'd think it was Broadway the way these parents act."

Violet's throat constricted as she listened to her friend's voice. Betsy looked fine—a little thin, maybe, but she'd always been thin.

April set down a cranberry glass vase and placed her hands on her middle. "I'll have to try to bite my tongue when this little one starts getting involved in extracurriculars."

"Shall we see what we have here?" Violet placed Betsy's shopping bags on the counter and started going through them.

"Oh, you take your time with that," Betsy said. "I can come back later. I've got an appointment to get to."

The mention of an appointment made Violet worry about her friend even more. She hugged Betsy good-bye a little tighter than usual. "It was good to see you again."

After Betsy had gone, April came over to the register. "Hey, I might need to take a day off soon. Is that okay?"

"Sure. Any fun plans?"

"Unfortunately, no. I need to go through my mom's old stuff. I've been trying to do it after work, but lately I've been so tired when I get home I end up going to bed early. My Realtor said all the clutter is kind of off-putting for the potential buyers that have been through the house so far."

"Do you need any help?" Violet asked.

"Most of it's junk I'll probably just give to Goodwill."

"That's what my mom said when my grandma died. But it's only junk if you don't know what you're looking for. And if there's any heavier stuff you need to lift, I can do that, too."

"Look at you being all protective," April said. "You sound like my doctor."

"Yeah, well, I know you're capable of doing a lot on your own. But accepting help once in a while is okay, too."

April put her hands on her hips. "You should take your own advice, you know."

"I'm working on it."

Sam Lewis called Violet on the Fourth of July to report that the blue hat with the birdcage veil had been a hit with his students. He also asked if Violet wanted to go see the fireworks with him that night. She accepted, remembering the goose bumps she'd gotten when she and Sam had brushed hands in the shop. It had been a couple of weeks since then, and Violet had figured he wasn't going to get in touch with her. She was glad she'd been wrong.

After she closed the shop that evening, Violet ran upstairs and tried on several different outfits for her date, casting each of them aside and piling them on the bed. Miles, looking irritated at this invasion of his prime napping space, huffed out a big-jowled sigh and moved to the living room couch. Violet finally decided on an outfit that was both a little bit retro and a little bit patriotic—a blue and white striped dress with a fitted bodice and full skirt. It had short sleeves, so it showed off the tattoo on her upper arm. She finished off the look with a red leather belt to highlight her curves.

By the time Sam arrived to pick her up, Violet had worked herself into a buzzing bundle of nerves. She didn't know why she felt so anxious. She'd been on plenty of dates in the years since her divorce, most of them courtesy of Internet dating sites or a friend's setup. The setups were usually the most disappointing. Violet used to approach them with high hopes, but she'd since learned to dread the phrase "I have this single friend." Usually it meant that the man in question was the only other single person, besides Violet, that the friend knew.

Still, Violet had coffee, had drinks, and, sometimes, even had dinner or sex. She met intellectual men and international travelers. Men who were boring, boorish, or both. Men with graduate degrees, men with neuroses, men with kids. It had been a long time since she'd been truly interested in anyone, though. Since she'd felt a rush of unexpected excitement like she felt when Sam called. Still, she felt hesitant. She just wasn't sure now was the right time to be pursuing a new romance. The store needed her full attention at the moment. And, unlike other dates she'd been on, no computer algorithm or well-meaning friend had arranged this one. If it didn't go well, she had no one but herself to blame.

Miles barked and skittered to the door when someone knocked. When Violet opened it, she saw Sam standing there, wearing jeans and a soft-looking button-down shirt. He clutched a bouquet of sunflowers in one hand.

"Hey there." Sam smiled and handed her the flowers.

"Thank you. They're gorgeous." Violet hoped the sweat she could feel under her arms wasn't soaking through her cotton dress.

"You ready?"

"Yep, just let me grab my purse. You can come in."

Sam followed her into the kitchen, where Violet arranged the flowers in an antique cut-glass vase, then ran to her room to get the straw handbag she'd chosen. She dumped the contents of her regular purse into it, grabbed a cardigan, and then followed Sam down to the back lot where he'd parked his car, a Subaru wagon with a bike rack on top.

Violet preferred muscle cars, vintage roadsters, and fin-backed Caddies, but she had to admit that Sam's car fit him. It looked strong, but not too rough, and able to handle a lot of different situations.

They got in and Sam pulled the car onto Johnson Street. "So I was thinking we could stop somewhere to pick up some food to take with us to the fireworks."

"Sure," Violet replied. "That sounds great."

Sam drove downtown to Capitol Square, where music spilled out from bars and people dined at sidewalk cafés in the fading light. Violet and Sam went into a gourmet cheese shop, where they each tried half a dozen samples before deciding what to buy. Sam tended toward the fresh goat cheeses and creamy Brie, but Violet loved aged varieties, the blue-veined Stiltons and Gorgonzolas. She made sure she popped a mint after eating them. She didn't want to start out the date with bad breath.

Even though she'd lived in Wisconsin all her life, she'd never been in a specialty cheese store. It was a relief, though, to have something tangible to focus on, rather than simply staring at each other across a restaurant table and making awkward conversation. Violet laughed as Sam wrinkled his nose at the stinky Limburger and said goofy things like, "Ah, yes. I can taste the clover the sheep must have grazed on."

After an intense debate, they agreed on an aged Gruyère, a soft chèvre, and a fresh Gouda flecked with fenugreek seeds. A woman behind the counter with a French accent helped them select a bottle of wine and some crackers, olives, and a small box of handmade chocolates to go with the cheese.

By the time they got back into the car with their picnic, Violet was feeling a lot more relaxed than she'd been when Sam first picked her up.

"That was fun," she said. "I can't believe I've never been there before."

"I thought it would be good to have a mission—that it would be less awkward that way," Sam said. "It's been a while since I've been on a first date."

Violet was impressed that Sam had thought out their date so that they'd both feel comfortable. "It was a good idea. Very thoughtful."

"Oh, there's one other thing I wanted to do before we go to the fireworks."

"What's that?" she asked.

Sam leaned over to the passenger seat and kissed Violet, slowly and sweetly, before pulling away and starting the car.

For a moment, Violet couldn't speak. When her body and brain stopped humming enough for her to recover her voice, she said, "Wow. That usually doesn't come until the end of a first date."

"I couldn't wait." Sam held her gaze for a moment, then turned his eyes back to the road. "I would have called you to go out right away after I saw you in your shop, but I left the next day for a backpacking trip out west with an old buddy from college. I've been 'off the grid,' so to speak, for the last couple of weeks."

"It's okay," Violet said. "It was worth the wait."

At Winnequah Park, where the fireworks would be set off, the lawn was already quilted with blankets. Children waved sparklers and begged their parents for Popsicles from the vendors who weaved their way through the lawn chairs and coolers. As Violet and Sam walked through the grass looking for a place to sit, fireflies rose like sparks from the ground.

"How's this?" Sam asked, stopping at the top of a small hill, a few yards removed from the crowd.

"Perfect," she said. She still felt warm inside from the unexpected kiss. They sat cross-legged on a blanket Sam had brought and sipped wine while they waited for darkness.

"So you remember me from Bent Creek," Violet said. "Is it just because I hung around Jed?"

"No—well, yes. Everyone knew Jed. But there was something different about you. You didn't dress like the other popular kids, for one."

Violet laughed. "Yeah, I was the only kid who wore her grandmother's fur coat to school. I got teased a lot about the way I dressed before I started dating Jed. Then people kind of shut up about it."

"So why did you leave town?" Sam spread chèvre on a hunk of bread and handed it to Violet. "You always seemed so happy and confident in high school."

"Did I? I wasn't. I think the problem was that I wanted what I thought I was supposed to want, without thinking about what would really make me happy. I think that's why I stuck with Jed for so long. Taking care of him gave me a purpose, and I didn't know who I was without that."

"Do you know now?" Sam asked. "I mean, what makes you happy?"

"Independence. I like working for myself, having my own business. Though I wish I could be better at certain parts of it."

"Like what?"

Sam's questions were so fluid, his expression so sympathetic, that Violet forgot to be self-protective when she answered. "What I consider to be the boring stuff. Computers and records. Oh, and legal stuff. I've run into some problems with my landlord that have made my life pretty stressful lately." She stopped, nibbled on the piece of bread. "God, I'm not doing a very good job of selling myself, am I?"

"You don't need to sell me anything. I asked *you* out, remember?" Sam leaned back on his elbows and stretched his long legs in front of him.

"Violet, is that you?"

Violet turned her head and saw Karen and Tom walking toward her. Karen carried Edith across the front of her body in a cloth sling.

"Hey," Violet said, motioning for them to come over. "Karen, Tom, this is Sam."

Karen's eyes swept over Sam. "Nice to meet you. This is our daughter, Edith."

"Speaking of Edith, give me that baby," Violet said, reaching her arms up.

Karen took the baby from the sling and deposited her in Violet's arms. Edith stirred and stretched, then settled back into a slumber.

"You're brave, bringing this little one to the fireworks," Violet said. "Won't they wake her up?"

"Oh, we're on our way out," Tom said. "We just came to walk around the park a little bit. Gotta get out of the house every now and then."

Sam held up the wine bottle. "Would you like some?"

"Nah," Karen said. "We should get going before they start blowing things up and wake the beast."

Violet stroked the baby's clenched fist. "She doesn't seem like much of a beast right now."

"That's why she needs to keep sleeping." Karen scooped Edith from Violet's arms and stuck her back in the sling, all with such quick skill that the baby didn't stir. "You two have fun."

"Bye," Sam said. "Good meeting you."

After they were out of earshot, Sam asked, "You like babies, huh?"

It wasn't the type of question Violet was accustomed to hearing on a first date—most of her computer-arranged companions wanted to talk about how much money they made or how they didn't usually date people they met online, always lying on both accounts. With the baby question, Violet felt like she was being tested, but she didn't know which answer to choose, which circle to fill in with her no. 2 pencil. If she said she didn't like babies, she'd be lying. If she said she did, she feared she'd scare Sam off.

Finally, she said, "Nah. I hate puppies, too."

Sam laughed. "Yeah, and kittens are obnoxious, too."

Violet picked a handful of grass and sifted it through her fingers. "It's so crazy to see Karen with a kid. I wonder what Edith will be like once she starts walking and talking and stuff."

"I hope she has an easier time of things than I did when I was a kid."

"What do you mean?"

"If you remember me at all from high school, you'll recall that I was kind of a dork growing up. I was a sci-fi and *Star Wars* fanatic and didn't know the first thing about how to talk to girls."

She tilted her head and looked at his face, so handsome in the fading light. "Yeah, I remember," she said. "When you first came into the store, I couldn't place you, but I pulled out my yearbooks."

"Those were some rough years." Sam crossed his arms, and his eyes took on the same darkness as the July sky.

The first few fireworks—test rockets, really—popped above them and the spectators oohed and fell quiet. Violet thought about the people she'd chosen to spend her time with back in high school, and the pleasure they took in making life miserable for kids who didn't possess good looks, athletic ability, or some other inherent cool factor.

"I know Jed was part of the group that picked on you," Violet said. "I'm sorry I didn't stop them."

"It's okay," Sam said. "Anyway, I don't really remember you having any part in it. You always seemed to kind of hang back a bit from the rest of the herd."

"Yeah, but I didn't think for myself much, either. Anyway, I'm sorry things were so rough for you back then."

"Well, I turned out reasonably okay, so I don't want you to feel sorry for me," Sam said. "Unless, of course, it means you'll sleep with me, in which case, you can feel as sorry as you want."

As she sat through the rest of the fireworks display, Violet wondered if she'd ever be able to leave Bent Creek behind her. As much as she tried to move on, reminders still surfaced from time to time, like frost pushing stones through the soft dirt of a spring field. She'd be going along, living her life, when suddenly she'd trip on one.

Violet looked at Sam in the flickering light and wondered again, like she had in the store, why she hadn't noticed his kind eyes or contagious smile back in high school. She'd been too busy soaking in the validation that came along with being part of the in crowd. It had taken her years to gather up the courage to figure out who she was without it.

When the grand finale exploded its gaudy, deafening display, there was so much smoke in the sky that Violet couldn't see clearly anymore.

Sam must have noticed the shift in her mood, because as he drove her home, he asked, "Are you okay?"

Violet nodded. "I guess all the talk of Bent Creek just got me thinking about some not-so-good memories."

"Well, Bent Creek is miles—and years—away from us now," he said as he pulled his car into the lot behind her building. "Let's focus on the moment, huh?"

"How do you do it?" she asked.

"What?"

"Focus on the moment and not get caught up in thinking about all the bad stuff behind you, or worrying about the future."

Sam turned off the ignition. "Well, first, you do this." He leaned over to Violet in the passenger's seat and kissed her neck.

A warm current ran through Violet's body. "Mmm-hmm," she said. "And what else?"

"This." He kissed the other side of her neck, then lingered at her lips. The summer night was still and hot, and it was all Violet could do not to climb into the driver's seat and wrap her legs around Sam.

"I'm still having trouble focusing," she said, putting on her most inviting smile. "Do you want to come up and help me some more?"

Sam opened his door.

In her room, on top of the bold green blooms of her Marimekko bedspread, Sam unzipped the striped dress that Violet had so carefully chosen earlier that evening. She pulled at the straps of her bra, clutched at Sam's shoulders to bring him closer, so eager was she to feel him on her, in her. But Sam slowed her, kissed each freckle on her skin as he revealed it.

Violet had brought other men back to her apartment before, but never on the first date. With Sam, though, she had a sense of urgency she hadn't felt with anyone else. She sensed she had already missed out on too much time with him, too many years wasted chasing what other people thought she should want, rather than what *she* wanted. And, in this moment, she had no question about what she wanted.

Other men treated sex like an action movie they'd chosen to watch with her, attacking the experience with consumer-level hunger and hoping, as a side benefit, that Violet enjoyed it, too. Sam approached the experience more like reading a long and beautiful novel, taking as much pleasure in what was yet to be revealed as in what lay before him on the open page. And, after they'd reached the satisfying end, with Violet tangled breathless and bare in Sam's arms, they went back to the beginning and began again.

Chapter 12

INVENTORY ITEM: *blazer*

APPROXIMATE DATE: *early 1980s*

CONDITION: *excellent*

ITEM DESCRIPTION: *TWA uniform jacket. Navy blue, double-breasted blazer with shoulder pads. Wing insignia on left lapel.*

SOURCE: *retired airline attendant*

Amithi

AMITHI STOOD AT THE register, clutching a bulging garbage bag in each hand. For the last month or so, ever since the awful Chicago trip, she had been coming in to Hourglass Vintage at least once a week. Each time she came, she brought a larger haul of items to sell, as if purging her closets could purge her past of all secrets and lies.

Violet stood behind the counter, humming to herself as she arranged red roses in a crystal vase. She looked up and smiled when she saw Amithi. "Hi. Good to see you again."

"Those are beautiful flowers," Amithi said. "Did you get them from someone special?"

"Uh-huh." Violet placed the vase to one side of the counter. "It's all pretty new."

Amithi envied the soft look in Violet's eyes. She would have given anything to go back to the sense of hope she had when her relationship with Naveen was brand-new. With Violet's help, she heaved the bags onto the counter.

"I apologize for the garbage bags," she said. "But I had so many items this time, I did not have anything else to put them in. Normally I would have folded everything up a little more neatly."

In fact, since she and Naveen had come back from Chicago—she by car and he by bus, at her insistence—Amithi hadn't felt like doing anything the way she normally did. Last night she'd locked herself in the den, intending to watch television. Instead, she had ended up paging through family photo albums that, at first, made her cry, but then made her sick with anger. In every picture, no matter where it was taken—at Jayana's first birthday party, at the beach, at the celebration dinner to commemorate Naveen making tenure—Amithi saw deceit behind her husband's smile.

When Naveen had knocked on the door of the den to ask Amithi about dinner, she hadn't responded. She wasn't sure what he had done to feed himself and she didn't care. Later she had found an empty cereal bowl next to the sink and felt a stab of pleasure when she thought of him eating cornflakes for dinner.

Violet pulled out a bundle of scarves from one of the bags. Amithi helped her spread the shimmering silk out on the countertop, admiring how the colors contrasted with one another: deep purple, ochre, and emerald green. Some were embroidered with paisley patterns in gold thread, others with vines or birds.

Violet touched the smooth fabric of a red scarf. "Are these from India?"

"The silk is. But I embroidered them myself, years ago."

"By hand?" Violet ran her hands over the thread of an intricate leaf design.

"Of course. I know there are machines for that, but I don't have one, and anyway, silk is so tricky. Beautiful things often are."

"Why are you selling so many things all of a sudden? Are you cleaning out your closet?"

"Cleaning out my life."

"Is everything all right?" Violet asked.

Amithi considered herself to be a private person. She'd made a habit of never burdening other people with her troubles.

"I'm fine," she replied.

Violet raised her eyebrows. "Really? I don't believe you."

Amithi sighed. "Someone close to me betrayed me."

Once the words were out of her lips, she felt the weight of her sadness lift, just for a moment.

"I'm so sorry to hear that," Violet said. "Was it your husband?"

Amithi hesitated for a second before nodding. She was afraid that Violet would judge her for continuing to live in the same house as Naveen. Many women would have packed their things and left as soon as they found out about the affair. Amithi had thought about it. She knew that if she confided in Jayana about what was going on, her daughter would likely invite her to stay at her condo. Amithi had even gone as far as taking out her suitcase half a dozen times, only to put it back in the closet a few hours later without packing a single item.

She hated Naveen for what he'd done to her, to the life she thought they'd built together. But without that life, Amithi had no bearings. She felt like a broken kite tumbling around on a strong wind.

"Do you need to talk about it?" Violet asked.

Amithi already felt like she'd ripped open her chest for examination. Inside lived all of her deepest fears. Perhaps Naveen loved Paula in a way he'd never loved Amithi. After all, he'd chosen to date Paula on his own, whereas his parents had chosen Amithi. He'd met Paula during a time when the country was feverish with sexual and political rebellion. With that type of passion as a backdrop, his marriage to Amithi probably seemed dull, dutiful. Amithi couldn't help but wonder if Naveen wished he'd married Paula instead.

Despite the doubts and questions battling inside her head, Amithi couldn't say any more, not today. "Perhaps another time," she said.

Violet peered into one of the shopping bags. "Are you sure you want to get rid of all these things now? Do you want to wait until you're feeling more—"

"I don't need them," Amithi said. "I have so many scarves and saris—this is only a fraction of them. I still have dozens in my closet. My daughter doesn't want them, either. I pointed out that the scarves would be pretty even just with the blue jeans she likes to wear all the time, but she says it is not her style."

Violet held one of the scarves up to examine its size. "They're big enough to wear as shawls, too. The colorful ones would be gorgeous with a little black dress." She patted the side of one of the garbage bags. "It will probably take me some time to look through everything."

"That's all right. Take as long as you want," Amithi said. Any excuse to get away from the house, away from the domestic existence that now seemed so meaningless, appealed to her at the moment. What was the point of keeping a tidy house and preparing home-made meals if there was no one around to appreciate it? Jayana was grown and no longer wanted Amithi's attention. And Naveen didn't deserve it.

"You're very talented, you know that?" Violet said as she folded a scarf and set it aside. "I wish I could sew like that."

"Oh, sewing is not so hard. Like many other endeavors, you just need to have patience."

"I know some basics of sewing, like hemming and taking things in, but it takes me such a long time even to do the simplest things," Violet said. "I've got a fashion show coming up in a few weeks to raise money for the store and I know there are going to be a lot of last-minute alterations to get everything to fit the way I want it to on the models. I'm dreading doing all that sewing. I'll probably be up all night the evening before the show."

"Perhaps I could help you," Amithi said. A fashion show sounded like a good distraction from her disastrous marriage. It was also something Naveen would have thought was silly, which made her want to help out even more.

"I probably can't afford your fees," Violet said.

"I don't charge any fees. Sewing is just a hobby for me. I enjoy it."

"I'm not sure it's going to be all that enjoyable. It will probably just be a lot of measuring and small adjustments. And here's the trickiest part—all the alterations have to be temporary. We don't want to do anything to change a garment's original size. We just need it to look good on the runway."

"I think I can do that. I've had to take my own clothes in and out plenty of times because I always seem to be losing and gaining weight. I never make any cuts or do anything permanent because who knows if I will get fat again?" Amithi let out a bitter laugh. Maybe she'd let herself get fat. If she hadn't managed to hold Naveen's attention when she was young and slender and smooth skinned, why even bother trying to hold his attention now?

"If you really don't mind, I could use your help." Violet examined a blue scarf with an embroidered feather design repeated along its border. "Are these peacock feathers?"

Amithi nodded. "It's the national bird of India."

"I love peacocks," Violet said. She pointed to the wall, where a green hat hung, adorned with an iridescent peacock feather.

"Sometimes I think that India's national bird should not be a bird at all, but an airplane, because so many Indian people I know have spent a lot of time on airplanes." Amithi touched the blue scarf. "On second thought, maybe I will keep this one."

June 20, 1979

Amithi felt weary looks being cast in her direction as she hushed the howling Jayana and begged her to go to sleep. On the first leg of the flight, from Chicago to the stopover in London, the baby had been very well behaved. Now, on this final leg from Heathrow Airport to Delhi, Jayana would not stop crying, sometimes screaming so forcefully that her voice cracked and took on a machine-gun sound. Even the ever-smiling flight attendant in her tailored jacket and white blouse was beginning to look annoyed. It was as if the American-born Jayana was resisting the journey back to her roots.

Amithi had been putting off this trip since the baby was born the previous July. The phone calls and letters from her parents and Naveen's had become so incessant that she decided she could no longer put off the trip to India. The grandparents wanted to see their grandchild—they did not understand why Naveen and Amithi waited a decade to have children. They did not know that they had tried for years, that Amithi's heart had broken month after month when her cycle started, an unwelcome visitor. They did not know how difficult the birth had been, and that both mother and child had been frail afterward, at first.

The grandparents had grown beyond impatient to outright irate that Jayana was almost a year old and they still had not met her. Unable to find a time when Naveen didn't have classes to teach or conferences to attend, Amithi agreed to travel to India on her own with the baby.

Preparing for the trip with an eleven-month-old had been a challenge. She could have used her husband's help, but she knew that he had important work to do while she was gone. He had to finalize a research paper and then present it at a conference in Florida where dozens of renowned scholars would be in attendance. Though she was disappointed he wouldn't be traveling with her, Amithi couldn't fault her husband for working hard. He was, after all, the sole provider for their little family.

For Amithi, the hardest part of the trip preparations had not been the packing or the scheduling. Rather, it had been the task of getting her infant daughter's ears pierced. Amithi hadn't wanted to do it, but she predicted there would be gifts of jewelry at the *pujas,* or prayer ceremonies, that her parents and in-laws would be hosting for the child in India. She did not want people to feel badly if they showed up with pierced earrings for the baby, as she knew some of them would. Earrings were a common gift at such events.

So, a week before her scheduled flight to Delhi, Amithi went ahead with the ear piercing, although she did not hold a *karna vedha,* the traditional ceremony for the occasion. She did not want to invite a large group of people to the house to watch her daughter cry in pain. She simply asked her neighbor Lalita to come over and take care of the task. Lalita Auntie, whose own children were all grown up, had sterilized the needle and poured Amithi a glass of Naveen's scotch. Amithi had cried as the needle poked through her baby's soft skin, even though Jayana didn't utter a sound, so mesmerized was she by Lalita Auntie's kind face and soft singing.

Although Amithi had not been back to India since her wedding, she knew this trip was not about her. It would be filled with trudging through monsoons to temples and homes of distant relations Amithi either had never met or did not remember. It was so that her parents and the Singhs could show off Jayana, show off Amithi and Naveen's successes in America.

Amithi glanced down at her red-faced daughter. She leaned down and kissed Jayana's head through her black, sweaty curls. Amithi wished Naveen were there to share responsibility for the dirty looks Amithi knew were being thrown her way by other passengers on the plane. The child howled louder until, finally, after a bout of gasping sobs, she fell asleep.

Amithi draped the sleeping baby over her lap, so that her hands were free, and grabbed her sewing from her purse. She was making a shawl to wrap Jayana in during the *mundan sanskar*—the ceremony for the baby's first haircut. She was nearly finished. The final touch was to outline the feather designs in gold thread. She had chosen a peacock-feather pattern because the bird symbolized India, and she knew her relatives would be touched by the gesture. The peacock also symbolized life and love, and she could not imagine more perfect imagery for her daughter.

Amithi held up the shiny fabric and whispered to Jayana. "Look, sweetheart, look what your ma made for you."

Jayana opened her eyes and scrunched up her face. She grabbed the shawl, threw it onto the ground near her mother's feet, and wailed.

Chapter 13

INVENTORY ITEM: *boots*

APPROXIMATE DATE: *late 1970s*

CONDITION: *fair*

ITEM DESCRIPTION: *Frye boots. Calf-height, size seven. Caramel-colored leather with some scuffing at toe. Stacked heel.*

SOURCE: *Katherine Morgan's house*

Violet

ON A SATURDAY EVENING in mid-July, Violet rang the doorbell of a Craftsman-style bungalow a block away from Hourglass Vintage. While she waited, she admired the Asiatic lilies blooming in the flower beds in front of the house. Sam had dropped off a bouquet of similar flowers for Violet at the store that afternoon, along with a carton of fresh strawberries from the farmers' market. The lilies had filled the whole store with the sticky-sweet smell of summer. Violet had told Sam in a teasing voice that if he didn't stop dropping by with flowers, she was going to get accustomed to it. He'd told her to go ahead and get accustomed.

April opened the door in yoga pants and a baggy T-shirt. Dark shadows underscored her eyes.

"Thanks for coming," April said. "Enter at your own risk."

"Your flower beds are gorgeous," Violet said as she stepped into the tiled foyer.

"That's all my mom's work," April said. "She planted them ages ago."

"This place is adorable." Violet looked at the stained glass windows on either side of the door, the carved woodwork on the staircase. "And not that cluttered. You made it sound like there was stuff everywhere."

"You should have seen it before today. I've been working all afternoon. It's like an archaeology dig. How was the rest of the day at the store?"

"I called some theaters and bars about holding the fashion show. The Majestic Theatre offered me a really good price for a night in mid-August, so I think we should have it there."

"August sounds good to me. I just hope this baby doesn't come early." April patted her belly.

As April's midsection grew, so did Violet's sense of longing. She knew it was ridiculous to be jealous. April hadn't had an easy life, and wouldn't any time soon. Still, there was a luminosity about her lately, a quiet confidence. Violet had seen it in Karen's face when she was pregnant with Edith, and she feared she'd never know the feeling herself.

She looked out the window. "Places almost never go on the market in this neighborhood," Violet said. "Why are you selling it?"

"My mom left a lot of debt. Once we close, I'll use the money to pay it off. Plus, I don't need this much space and it's a lot of work and cost to take care of a whole house. Can you imagine living in this place when you were my age?" April asked.

Violet couldn't, but only because the place she'd lived in had had squirrels running around in the walls. "Honey, when I was your age I was married and renting a place behind a gas station."

"So I guess you didn't live the life of an average eighteen-year-old, either."

"Sadly, in my hometown, it was pretty average." Violet put her hands on her hips, eager to get started. She'd come to help April move forward, not to dwell on her own past. "So what do you need help with around here?"

"I've just been trying to clear things out, little by little," April said.

Violet glanced around at the framed artwork on the terra-cotta-colored walls, the mix of antique and modern furniture. They were signs of someone who'd acquired things over decades. *Kind of like me,* she thought.

"There's a lot of clothing I need to go through in my mom's room," April said.

"Are you sure you want to do this today?" Violet asked. "I'm okay with coming back another time if it's too much for you right now. I know you've been under a lot of stress lately, with your ex and everything."

April shook her head. "I need to figure out what's worth keeping and what I should just get rid of."

"I happen to be an expert at that particular task."

"Well, then, come on upstairs." April motioned for Violet to follow her.

In the corner of Katherine Morgan's slope-ceilinged bedroom, Violet spotted a two-foot-tall lamp in the shape of a goose. "I can't believe you have one of those," she said.

"What, that horrible lamp?" April asked. "I have no idea where my mom got it, but she loved that thing."

"It's Gladys the Goose." Violet kneeled on the floor to get a better look at the lamp. "It's so cute. I've never seen one in person before. These lamps have kind of a cult following, at least in my weird little vintage world. The company that designed it doesn't make them anymore."

April shot her a bewildered look. "You can have it."

"I'd love to," Violet said. "But I'm sure it meant something to your mom, so I wouldn't feel right about it. People don't buy something this unusual unless they're drawn to it."

"Yeah, well I still think it's ugly."

Violet put her hands on either side of the goose's head, as if to cover its ears. "Shhhh, she might hear you."

"I'm glad you came over because, as you can see, I have no idea what's valuable and what's not," April said.

Violet turned toward the bed, which was piled high with boxes full of clothes. "These are the things you wanted me to look through?"

"Yeah. I've had a hard time going through them because I can picture my mom wearing a lot of these things and then I get sad."

Violet began sorting through the bags of clothing, which contained mostly Lands' End sweaters, nondescript polo shirts, and khakis. She held up a long denim jumper.

"Kinda frumpy, huh?" April said. "I think she used to wear that with a turtleneck under it."

"Apparently your mom wasn't as creative about her clothes as she was with interior decorating."

"I guess not. Although I'm not even sure she was ever that into decorating, either. She just bought things she liked, even if no one else liked them and they didn't go with what was in the rest of the house. She was pretty impulsive."

From one of the bags, Violet selected two ruffled party dresses from the eighties, one in electric-blue taffeta and the other in ruched velvet. From another bag, she pulled a pair of tan stacked-heel boots. She peeked inside the shaft and set them down on the table. "Frye boots. Now *these* would sell."

"I'm pretty sure my mom had them even before I was born." April touched the scuffed leather of one of the boots. "I can remember holding her hand as a really little kid and looking over at her legs. She was almost always wearing these."

Violet pushed the boots toward her. "Do you want them?"

"My feet are too big."

"Maybe you should keep them anyway."

"What am I going to do with a pair of boots that don't fit?" April asked.

Violet glanced down at April's belly. "Give them to your daughter."

"I don't know why you're so sure I'm having a girl. Anyway, I don't want to hang on to the boots that long. The store should take them if you think they'll sell. I'd rather have someone else wear them than have them sitting in a closet for years."

"I'd pay you for them, of course," Violet said. "Are you sure?"

"Yeah, as long as they're not too beat-up for the store. I always assumed that with shoes, the less used looking, the better."

"Sometimes," Violet said. "But with sturdy-type boots, like Fryes or cowboy boots, it's nice if they look a bit worn."

As Violet sifted through the last bag of clothing, she noticed a slip of yellow paper sticking out of the pocket of a pair of jeans. She took it out and handed it to April.

"I bet it's a to-do list," April said as she unfolded the paper. "My mom was notorious for starting a list, doing one or two of the items on it, and then forgetting about it. I used to find little notes like this everywhere." She looked down. "Yep. Here it says, 'Get car washed. Put out recycling. Check on—'" April stopped and her face turned pale.

"Check on what?" Violet asked.

"I'll be right back." April rushed out of the bedroom, still holding the yellow paper.

Violet heard thumping and rustling from somewhere down the

hall, then silence. She waited a few moments, folding and refolding the items she'd taken out of the garbage bags. Then she got worried.

She stuck her head out into the hallway. "April?"

No answer. Violet walked down the hall, looking into each room. She passed two bedrooms crammed with a mix of antiques— everything from midcentury nightstands to a mission-style bed and a cuckoo clock. In a small office at the end of the hall, she found April sitting on the wood floor, surrounded by papers.

"Is everything okay?" Violet asked.

April looked up. Her face was red and wet with tears.

Violet sat down next to her. "What's going on?"

"I can't believe it." April shook her head. "Maybe Charlie was right."

"Right about what?"

April held up a document marked with green highlighter.

Violet squinted to try to read the tiny writing. "What's that?"

April wiped her eyes with the back of her hand. "It's my mom's life insurance policy. I knew she had one—I'm supposed to be getting a check in the mail any day now—but I've never actually looked at it."

Violet was confused. "Well, if you're getting some insurance money, that's good news, right?"

From the floor, April picked up the list that Violet had found. "Look at this, though. The third item."

Violet took the list. "I don't get it. It says, 'Check on life insurance policy.'"

"Right. And when I pulled out the policy—" April's voice broke as she pointed to the paper. "Look. The clause on suicide is highlighted."

Violet was confused. "You said you were getting a check, though. I always assumed that if a person committed suicide, the insurance money wouldn't be paid out."

April shook her head. "That's what I thought, too. But it doesn't work that way. What it says here is that the proceeds are paid out as long as the person didn't commit suicide within two years of when the policy was issued. This policy was issued five years ago. So the fact that the insurance company is cutting me a check doesn't rule out the possibility that she might have—" April covered her face with her hands.

Violet considered her next words carefully. "Is that really a concern? That your mom killed herself? You never mentioned that before."

"She was bipolar. She kept it under control most of the time, but every now and then she'd stop taking her medication and get all out of whack. There were times she was so depressed she wouldn't even eat. And then there's the fact that she quit her secretarial job and put all of that money into starting up her organizational consulting business or whatever it was, which she never focused on long enough to make any money from." April hugged her arms to her belly and rocked back and forth on her heels. "Charlie thinks she did it. We got into a big fight over it, and that's sort of what led us to splitting up. Although of course it's more complicated than that. We both said a lot of awful things. But I was adamant that my mom would never go that far. Now that I've seen this, I don't know."

"Okay," Violet said. "But still, all you found is a to-do list and a highlighted copy of her insurance policy. The two might not even be related."

"Why would someone highlight the suicide clause unless they were thinking about it?"

"Sure." Violet put a hand on April's shoulder. "It's a possibility. But it's also a possibility that she highlighted that section long ago, and that the list she made had nothing to do with it."

"That's the optimistic way of looking at it."

"Yeah, but it doesn't mean it might not be true."

April gathered up the papers and shoved them into a desk drawer.

Violet wished she had never found the list. She'd always felt that, when it came to the past, some things were better left buried.

Chapter 14

INVENTORY ITEM: *pantyhose*
APPROXIMATE DATE: *1945–1950*
CONDITION: *excellent*
ITEM DESCRIPTION: *Nylon, fully-fashioned stockings in sheer black with back seam.*
SOURCE: *online vintage retailer*

April

APRIL TRIED TO FOCUS on the dark-haired drag queen strutting across the stage of the Majestic Theatre downtown, a block from the capitol. The queen twirled and posed in a red, one-piece pantsuit while a Diana Ross dance remix blared from the speakers. Despite the exuberant music and the excited chatter of the auditioning models, April's mood couldn't have been darker.

"I think she's a yes," Violet said.

"Definitely," Lane added, scribbling on one of the score sheets she'd made up and brought with her to auditions.

"I'm so glad you agreed to help us," Violet said. "I was afraid you wouldn't remember who we were."

"Of course I remember," Lane said. "I get a ton of compliments whenever I wear those red shoes I bought at your shop. I've started planning entire outfits around them. Even my husband noticed them, and he doesn't notice *anything*." She smiled. "He said they make me look like one of those 'old-time pinup girls.'"

Violet turned to April. "So what do *you* think about this model?"

"Oh, um, fine," April replied, circling a number at random on her own score sheet. For once, numbers seemed meaningless. She tried to pay attention to what was going on onstage, but she couldn't stop thinking about her mom. The bright lights and chattering models in the theater only underscored her confusion and grief.

Ever since she'd seen the insurance documents and the note Violet found the other day, April had been combing through her memory, looking for some sign that would tell her, one way or the other, whether her mom's death had been intentional. When she thought of the happy times they'd spent together, like biking around the arboretum or baking carrot cake from their secret family recipe, she'd feel certain that her mom never would have left her. But then she'd recall the worst times—the days when her mom hid in bed with the lights out and the blinds closed, or the weeks when she'd stay up several nights in a row, concocting her next flawed plan for making quick money. April could often predict those bouts before they happened. Before a period of depression, she'd notice a heaviness in her mom's expression, a flatness in her voice that would tip her off. Before a manic phase, there would be a frightening, anxious energy in her eyes.

As they waited for the next model to take the stage, Violet asked, "Is everything okay?"

"Yeah," April said, glancing at Lane. She didn't want to talk about her mom in front of this woman she hardly knew. She waved a hand. "I guess I'm just moody. Must be pregnancy hormones or something."

Lane grinned. "I *thought* you were pregnant that day I came in with the costumes, but I know you're never supposed to ask. When are you due?"

"Labor Day," April said, trying to muster a smile. It was hard to be excited about bringing a new life into the world when her mother had, in all likelihood, found her own life too much to bear.

"I've got three boys at home, so if you need someone to talk to about kid stuff, you can call me," Lane said.

It was nice of Lane to offer support. April couldn't count on her high school friends for that. They'd pulled away from her since she'd gotten pregnant. While April worked, met with her mom's estate lawyer, and read baby name books, her friends were sneaking beers from their parents' refrigerators and obsessing over their latest crushes. It wasn't that April didn't get it—she'd probably have been doing those same things if her circumstances were different—but she knew she couldn't expect her classmates to understand how much her life had changed in a short period of time.

"I mean it, too. Call me anytime." Lane studied April with an earnest expression. "Here, give me your phone. I'll put my number into it."

April fished around in her purse and handed the phone to Lane.

"I remember how hard it was when the kids were babies," Lane said as she punched at the buttons. "We'd just moved here, so I didn't know many people, and my husband was working all the time. I didn't feel like I had any support system. I would hate for anyone else to have to go through that, so don't be shy about calling if you need to." She handed the phone back to April.

Violet leaned forward in her seat. "A lot of these girls are too thin," she said. "Lane, how many models on your 'yes' list are a size ten or larger?"

Lane ran her finger down her clipboard. "Two—no, three. Not counting the queens, who are all over the board in terms of sizing."

"We need more models who have some actual curves," Violet said.

"I don't want my customers coming to the show and seeing nothing but size-two college girls prancing around onstage. Not to mention that some of the best outfits April and I put together are in larger sizes."

"You got it," Lane said. She stood up on her wobbly fold-down chair and let out a two-fingered whistle. "Excuse me, models, may I have your attention?"

The chatter in the room faded within seconds.

"If you are smaller than a size ten, you may leave now. Thank you for coming, but for the rest of the evening we are looking only for size ten and larger. I repeat, if you are smaller than a size ten, you may leave. Thank you. We hope you'll still come out to watch the show."

An annoyed buzz circulated in the room as the skinnier models gathered their belongings and headed for the doors.

Impressed by Lane's ability to command attention, April thought maybe she'd judged her too harshly, had been too quick to label her as another frazzled mom. In the theater, with all eyes on her, Lane looked at home.

A few days later at the boutique, April was greeted in the morning not by Violet in her usual spot with her mug full of coffee, but by a note taped to the register that said she had a meeting, so April would need to do the opening routine.

April tore off the note, grateful to have a sign that Violet was beginning to trust her more.

She checked the mail, unlocked the doors, and counted the stacks of petty cash in the register, trying to clear her mind. Lately, whenever her thoughts weren't occupied with something immediate, April couldn't help but fixate on a mental image of her mom driving on an icy road, creeping along carefully until, with a deliberate jerk, she swiveled the steering wheel with her peach-manicured hands. Her mother, even when she would go days without showering, never ne-glected her fingernails. It was as if exercising control over that small surface area of her body made up for the lack of control she had over her mind.

To push this picture out of her head, April went about tidying up the racks of clothing, starting with rows of skirts in all lengths, from micromini to floor-length. She checked them all to make sure they were organized by size and that there were no twos where the twelves should have been. Not that she was wearing either of those sizes anymore.

Outside the shop window, a middle-aged woman stopped and ex-amined the posted hours of business on the door. April didn't recog-nize her but hoped she'd come in. Even if the lady turned out to be rude, or the type of customer who left clothes on the dressing room floor, April figured anything would be better than sitting here with the screaming silence of her own thoughts.

The woman *did* come in, and immediately said, "I'm glad to see someone in this town keeps reasonable business hours. I've been walk-ing around trying to find something open, but most of the stores don't open until eleven."

"Not us," April said. "We're open ten to seven every day of the week."

"Thank God. One of the shops had a sign on the window that said they were open until six every Tuesday, Wednesday, and Thurs-day, but only 'til four the rest of the week, except on Mondays, when they're closed. How are customers supposed to remember that?"

The woman's voice sounded slightly nasal and carried a long-voweled accent. *East Coast, maybe?* thought April. "I know what you mean," she replied. "My favorite bakery is constantly changing its hours. Sometimes I wonder if it's on purpose, like they're trying to hint to me that I don't need another chocolate chip scone."

"Well, where I'm from, the stores are open when it's convenient for the customers, not the other way around."

"You're not from Madison?"

The woman shook her head of short, tight curls. "Boston. I'm Monica, by the way."

"I'm April. Is there anything I can help you with? Are you looking for something specific?"

"I came in to look for something to wear to my nephew's graduation party this afternoon. The airline lost my luggage."

"Is your nephew graduating from high school or college?" April asked.

"College."

"Most graduation parties around here are pretty laid-back." April assessed the woman's black capri pants and blue sleeveless polo. "You could probably wear what you have on now." Realizing that her suggestion wasn't a very good sales tactic, she added, "And we could set you up with some nice accessories. Some jewelry, maybe a dressier pair of shoes."

Monica pursed her lips. "I think I need a dress. My sister and her husband are the Waspy type. The party's at their country club."

"Sure, what size are you?"

"Eight."

April walked over to a wall rack where the day dresses hung. "We just got in some adorable Lilly Pulitzer stuff that might be appropriate." She held up a white dress with little yellow and green pineapples on it. The cheery color and print seemed to mock her mood, which continued to drag, despite the distraction of this new customer.

Monica's expression went sour. "No offense, honey, but the only Pulitzers I'm into are the kind you win."

April put the dress back on the rack. "Okay, so no pineapples. What about this?" April held up a navy blue cotton shift dress. "We've got a really cool vintage necklace and earrings set that would go with it. They're gold with big green beads."

"Sounds nice," Monica said. "I'll try it on."

"The dressing rooms are right there." April pointed to the two stalls.

Monica disappeared into one of them, still chattering. "This dress is much more my style."

"To be honest, I don't like the pineapple dress either," April said. "I was just trying to picture the crowd. My ex-boyfriend's mother wears stuff like that."

"So does my sister, Judy," Monica said from behind the dressing room door. "In fact, who knows? Maybe that dress came from her closet. Wouldn't *that* be embarrassing, if I showed up in one of her cast-offs?"

April sucked in her breath so hard she almost choked on her own saliva. "I'm sorry, did you say Judy?"

"Yep, that's my sister. Miss Perfect. I'm glad my nephew is coming out to Boston for med school. I'm looking forward to spending some time with him outside his mother's grips. Don't get me wrong, I love my sister, but she can be a little much sometimes."

Monica emerged from the dressing room to examine the dress in the three-way mirror.

April stared at her, wondering why she hadn't noticed Monica's slender figure, the light brown hair, and high cheekbones, just like Charlie's mother's.

"I think this will do it." Monica put her hands on her hips as she inspected her reflection. She caught April's eye in the mirror.

"I'm sorry, is your sister's name Judy Cabot?" April asked.

"Why, yes. Do you know her?"

April felt dizzy. "Judy's son is my ex-fiancée."

Monica turned around and took in April's round stomach and raised her eyebrows. "I take it you weren't invited to the graduation party," she said.

April shook her head.

Monica frowned. "Oh, Charlie."

After Monica left, April's nerves were as tight and humming as a violin string. To calm herself, she turned to numbers. Amidst the jumbled uncertainty of her personal life, April longed to lend order to something. She opened her laptop to view the bookkeeping program she'd installed for the store. The sight of tables and cells calmed her breathing, but just barely. By the time Violet came in around lunchtime, April was desperate to talk to someone.

"Thank you for taking care of things around here this morning," Violet said.

"How was your meeting?" April asked.

"Fine, but I have another one in just a few minutes, with my landlord. Do you mind keeping an eye on things out here for a little while longer?" Violet set down her red bucket purse.

April nodded, afraid to open her mouth for fear that she'd spew out a storm of emotions.

Bells jingled, and April looked toward the shop entrance, where a man with buzz-cut hair and a belly bigger than hers pushed the door open. The space-age shapes on his tie reminded April of the patterns on movie theater carpeting.

"Hi, Ted," Violet said. She gestured toward April. "Meet my new employee, April. April, this is Ted Mortensen. His company owns our building."

The man's cologne constricted April's throat and made her nauseous, but she managed to force a smile and say, "Nice to meet you."

Ted didn't return the smile. "Violet, if you don't mind, I'd like to sit down and go over a few things with you."

"Certainly. Let's go in the back room, where we won't be disturbed by customers coming in and out," Violet said, leading the way.

April watched them go, wishing Violet had asked her to join them. After hearing that she hadn't been invited to Charlie's graduation party, she wanted nothing more than to be included in *something*.

Seconds stretched into minutes, and minutes into half an hour. In a daze, April assisted a girl a little older than she was with finding an outfit for a date. She helped a woman who looked like she could have been her mom's age find a pair of designer jeans. By the time the customers had checked out and left, almost an hour had gone by. April wondered what could possibly be taking Violet and Ted so long.

She decided to find out.

In the back room, Violet stood shuffling through papers on her worktable, looking flustered, while Ted sat in a folding chair with his arms crossed. April hovered in the door frame, trying to figure out what they were talking about.

"I know I've got my rent records in here somewhere," she heard Violet say. "But even without looking at them, I know I've never missed a payment."

"Really, it's all right," Ted said. "I believe you, but that doesn't change anything."

"I swear it was right here," Violet said, picking up a stack of papers.

April felt a rush of adrenaline and blurted out, "Maybe if you'd had all this stuff stored electronically from the beginning, you'd be able to find what you're looking for."

Both Violet and Ted turned their heads to look at her, and April knew she'd crossed a line. But she felt so unmoored, so small and discarded, that she was willing to grasp on to anything that might make her feel more significant.

April went up to the register and came back with her laptop. Ignoring the pleading looks from Violet, she sat down at the table with her and Ted.

"What is it you're looking for exactly?" April asked, setting down her computer. "Maybe I've got it entered in here already."

Ted put a hand over the laptop before April could open it. "You don't need to find the rent records. It doesn't matter." He looked at Violet. "I appreciate your efforts to be thorough and discuss this all with me, but I already told you: regardless of how diligent you've been as a tenant, it's not going to change our minds about moving forward with the eviction. The fact remains that this building is more profitable to us if we sell it."

"What eviction?" April asked.

The defeated expression on Violet's face told her all she needed to know.

Ted cleared his throat. "I'll leave you two to your work." He got up. "Think about my offer."

April followed Violet as she got up and walked with Ted to the door. She watched out the window and waited until Ted had climbed into his shiny black sedan before lashing out at Violet.

"Why didn't you say anything about an eviction?" April demanded.

"I think *I'm* the one who should be asking questions here." Violet put her hands on her hips. "For starters, why were you eavesdropping on my confidential conversation?"

April didn't have a good explanation, except that she hated secrets. Her mom had been secretive, and with her death, those secrets had turned into questions that would never have answers.

"I don't know why," April said.

"And if you were going to eavesdrop, why couldn't you at least have left it at that? You had no right to inject yourself into my meeting and undermine my authority in front of someone I really can't afford to look bad in front of right now."

"Why are we getting evicted?" April said. "Are you not paying rent?"

"I'm paying rent. I may not be good with computers, or a math genius like you, but I'm not stupid," Violet said, her voice flaring with anger. "No, they want to kick me out so they can sell the building."

April narrowed her eyes. "I can't believe you've just been coming in every day, acting like nothing is wrong. I guess it must not be a big deal to you."

Violet buttoned up the top button of her shirtdress, as if doing so would hold in her emotions. "It *is* a big deal to me. In fact, that's what I was dealing with this morning. I was meeting with Karen to talk about it."

"You could have included me. I have a right to know what's going on with the shop." April couldn't believe the things she was saying, but she couldn't stop. It was as if, for the last year, starting with her mom's death and gaining speed through her pregnancy and breakup, she'd been running from a tidal wave. She sprinted as fast as she could, but it was always inches behind her, curling over her head and threatening to wash her away. Her encounter with Monica had made her stumble just when she thought she'd earned herself a decent head start, some breathing room. The swell, always at her back, was finally catching up with her.

"April, I appreciate how you're willing to go above and beyond what I'd expect an intern to do, but it's still my store. I have a right to meet with my lawyer and my landlord on my own. And to decide what to share with you and what to keep to myself." Violet softened her voice. "Listen, I know you've been under a lot of stress lately, with dealing with your mom's house and your ex. Maybe you should take some time off."

"Are you firing me?" April asked.

"That's not what I'm saying. But I don't think it's a good idea for you to be interacting with customers when you're this emotional."

When you're this emotional, thought April. In her experience, "emotional" was code for "crazy." Like her mom.

"I'll make it easy for you and just not come back," she said.

"Are you sure that's what you want?" Violet asked.

"Yes," April said. Perhaps it was true.

She knew she'd taken things too far. Now was the time to apologize and undo some of the damage. But she was boiling with so much rage and confusion—even as the freezing tidal wave sucked her under—that her ears pounded with pressure, building and building, until no rational thought could be heard above the din.

April pushed open the door and walked out of the shop.

Chapter 15

INVENTORY ITEM: *shoes*

APPROXIMATE DATE: *late 1980s*

CONDITION: *fair*

ITEM DESCRIPTION: *Pink canvas Converse high-tops. Fabric frayed around shoelace grommets.*

SOURCE: *Amithi Singh*

Amithi

AMITHI LEANED BACK INTO the stiff leather cushions of her daughter's modern couch. Like everything else in Jayana and Jack's condo, the couch seemed to have been chosen more for aesthetics than for comfort.

"Can I put this away for you?" Jack asked, lifting the black suitcase Amithi had brought with her.

"Thank you, Jack," Amithi said, nodding.

That morning, after Naveen left for work, Amithi had taken her suitcase out from the closet, like she had done several times before. This time, though, she had packed it and had placed it next to the front door, where she passed it all day as she swept the floors, vacuumed the rugs, and carried laundry up and down the stairs. Finally, when her housework was done and the summer sun was low in the sky, she picked up the suitcase. She drove to her daughter's cramped condo on the trendy Near East Side and left behind her own spacious, spotless home.

Jack disappeared down the short hallway, toting Amithi's bag.

"Would you like anything to drink, Mom?" Jayana asked. "A cup of tea, maybe?"

Amithi glanced at the stemmed glass in Jayana's hand. "I would like a glass of that red wine you are drinking, if it is not too much trouble."

Jayana raised her eyebrows. "But you almost never drink," she said. "And you're wearing a short dress, too—well, short for you. Who are you and what have you done with my mother?"

Last time Amithi had been to Hourglass Vintage, she'd spent some of the store credit she'd amassed. Among the new clothes she purchased—well, new to her, anyway—was the sleeveless green dress she had on. Her legs seemed naked beneath its knee-length hem, but she liked how cool it felt in the summer heat.

Jayana went into the kitchen and came back with a glass of wine, which she handed to Amithi. Jack returned to the living room and sat down next to Jayana on a leather love seat, their legs touching.

Amithi winced, remembering what it was like to be newly married, before all the deception and despair. She took a drink of wine, puckering her lips at the initial bite of the alcohol. The wine tasted good, though—rich and warm in her mouth. She took another sip.

"So are you finally going to tell me what's going on?" Jayana asked, leaning forward.

Jack moved as if to get up. "If you two would like to talk in private—"

Jayana put a hand on his knee. "No, stay. It's okay, Mom, isn't it? I mean, I tell him everything anyway."

Amithi glanced at her son-in-law and found sympathy in his blue eyes. "Yes, you can stay." She lowered her voice and turned to her daughter. "Your father had an affair."

"Really? *Dad?*" Jayana's eyes grew wide. "When? Who was it?"

Amithi filled her in on what details she knew. As Jayana listened, her face grew red with anger.

"So are you moving out?" she asked when Amithi had finished.

"I do not know. I just told your father that I was coming over here to stay for a while. That is, if you and Jack do not mind."

"Of course not," Jack said. "You can stay with us as long as you want."

"What did Dad say when you told him you were leaving?"

"I don't know," Amithi said. "I left him a note, along with some dinners in the freezer and instructions for how to use the microwave."

"Jesus, the man has a PhD and can't figure out how to feed himself. It's a miracle he didn't starve all those years he lived in Chicago before he married you." Jayana sighed. "I suppose you'll need to start looking for your own apartment. And you'll need a divorce lawyer. I can ask around to see if I can find a referral for you. Jack, what was the name of that lawyer your colleague used? She was happy with the results, wasn't she?"

Amithi stared at her daughter, shocked at how methodical her reaction was. There were no tears—only crisp, productive anger.

Jack turned to Jayana. "She might not be ready to make any big decisions like that yet." To Amithi, he said, "Like I mentioned before, you're welcome here for as long as you need to stay."

"Thank you," said Amithi. "I have a lot to think about." Despite her reservations about Jack, she had to admit to herself that he was kind. And he certainly had a warmer disposition than her ever-assertive daughter.

Jayana finished her wine and poured herself another glass. "I just don't see what there is to think about."

"A great many things. Your father and I have been married for over forty years."

"Exactly. You've devoted your entire life to Dad since you were a teenager. And he went and shit on everything."

"Jayana, please. Your language."

Amithi wouldn't have phrased things the same way Jayana did, but her daughter had a point. Amithi had always put her family's happiness above all else. She had always felt that her life was fine and assumed Naveen felt the same way. Evidently, "fine" had not been good enough for Naveen. Why, then, should it be good enough for her? It had never occurred to Amithi that anything more than fine was an option.

Amithi heard a muffled ringing sound coming from her handbag. She dug out her phone and saw Naveen's number on the screen.

"Is it Dad?" Jayana asked.

Amithi nodded.

"Are you going to answer it?"

"I have nothing to say." She stared at the phone as it bleated in her hands. As soon as it fell silent, another phone began to ring—this one louder.

"Now he's calling here," Jayana said.

Jack looked from one woman to the other. "Should I answer it?"

Jayana shook her head, but Amithi said, "He's your father, Jayana."

Amithi appreciated her daughter's loyalty toward her—needed it, even—but felt torn. Honoring one's elders, even in times of disagreement, was a value ingrained in her long ago, and Amithi could not live with herself if she thought she'd failed to instill it in her daughter.

Jack picked up the phone. "Hello? . . . Yes, they're both here. Just a moment." He held the phone out to Jayana.

Jayana crossed her arms. "Tell him I'm not speaking to him. I'll start respecting him when he starts respecting Mom."

Jack put the phone back to his ear. "Naveen? Jayana says she will call you later . . . Yes, I will tell them. Good-bye." He hung up and looked at Amithi. "He wants me to tell you he is sorry and that he loves you both."

To Amithi, the words sounded emptier than the silent house she'd locked and left earlier that evening.

"Aren't there things you wanted to do, Mom, that you didn't do because of Dad? Places you wanted to go?" Jayana forced a half smile.

Amithi was grateful for it. She hated seeing her daughter upset, even on her behalf. "Of course," she said. "Relationships always involve sacrifice."

"That didn't stop Dad from cheating, so I say you should take this opportunity to do what *you* want for once and forget about Dad."

"I am getting old, Jayana. It is too late for me to be making changes."

Amithi couldn't remember the last time anyone had asked her what she wanted. She supposed there were goals she'd had when she was younger, places she'd wanted to go. It had been so long since she'd thought about them, though, that she couldn't remember what they were. Somewhere between now and her engagement all those years ago, what she wanted had shifted to what Naveen wanted, to what Jayana wanted, to what was best for the family.

Jayana shook her head. "You can't even come up with anything, can you?"

Jack reached out and touched his wife's arm. "Give your mom a break. She's been through a lot in the last couple of weeks."

Amithi gave Jack a grateful smile. She needed to change the subject. "Did I tell you I am helping out with a fashion show?"

"Oh, the one at the Indian community center?" Jayana asked. "I think I saw a poster for that."

"No, for a vintage store. I'm doing alterations. A lot of the outfits are from the nineteen forties and fifties and are very different from today's clothing, so I need to make sure the models fit into them properly."

"Well, fifties *clothing* might be making a comeback," Jayana said. "But someone needs to tell Dad that chauvinist attitudes are not."

"Good for you, Amithi," Jack said with an enthusiasm that sounded forced. "It's probably good for you to have a creative outlet."

"Doing alterations is not exactly creative," Amithi said. "But I'm glad to be getting back into sewing."

Now if only I could stitch my life back together, she thought.

December 1, 1990

Amithi bent over her embroidery frame, listening to her sister over the phone. As long as she continued to work the needle back and forth, back and forth, her mind could rest from thinking about Priya lying in a hospital bed in India, recovering from an emergency C-section. The doctors couldn't save the baby—a little girl, Priya's first child. All Priya had to show for her nine months of pregnancy was a long scar on her abdomen.

Priya could hardly articulate what happened; she just kept repeating, "The baby, the baby." Amithi obtained most of the details from her brother-in-law.

"He keeps saying everything is going to be okay," Priya said over the thousands of miles of phone line. "But it's not going to be okay, and I don't know how he can say that, so until he comes up with something else to say, I'm not talking to him."

Amithi wished she could be at the hospital with her sister. She'd crawl into the bed beside her and play with her hair like she used to do when they were little. Amithi asked if she should fly to India for a few weeks to assist Priya around the house. Jayana could come along, too. She was nearly a teenager now, and could help.

Priya said no, that seeing Amithi and her daughter together would be too painful.

"I'll come alone, then," Amithi said.

"No, *didi,* I am too jealous. Too jealous that your girl is healthy and strong and mine will soon be ashes."

All Amithi could do, then, was wait, and it was not the kind of waiting she liked. Waiting for good news was easy—the birth of a child, a job promotion. Yes, there was impatience involved, but there was also the promise of a happy event. This kind of waiting, the incremental kind, proved to be much harder. Amithi knew there would be no magic day when her sister was better. One never recovered from something like the death of a child. All Amithi could hope for was gradual, almost imperceptible improvement, for the day when her sister could laugh again, forgetting herself, even if only for a moment.

It's like when the ice melts on Lake Mendota, thought Amithi. It always started with tiny pools of water collecting on the surface of the frozen mass. The pools grew bigger as the sun grew stronger, and eventually, large chunks of ice would break apart and the living lake would consume them.

Afraid that if her hands were not busy, her mind would go crazy, Amithi worked with obsessive concentration on embroidering a blanket for her sister after she hung up the phone. On the light, soft wool, she stitched a samsara design, the Hindu wheel of life. She hoped the blanket would keep Priya warm, would provide her some comfort while she waited for her heart to emerge from winter.

Jayana came into the room, toting a thick paperback. She sat next to her mother on the couch, drew her knees to her chest, and began to read. After a few minutes, she looked up from the book and asked, "What are you making?"

"A blanket for Auntie Priya."

Jayana nodded. "To help cheer her up about the baby?"

"I don't think anything will cheer her up, but I hope to at least show her I am thinking of her."

"Why don't you just buy a blanket? It would be much faster."

"I wouldn't be able to find a blanket with this symbol on it." Amithi pointed to the circular shape outlined with thread. "See? It's an ancient Hindu symbol. The wheel stands for life, death, and rebirth. I could teach you how to embroider like this, if you'd like, *beti*."

"Nah." Jayana bent her head back down, uninterested in her mother's handiwork. After a few moments, she looked up again and said, "Why do you spend so much time sewing and making things? You never go anywhere or do anything."

"I like making things. This way, when I give someone a gift, there is a little piece of myself in it. When I was your age, I thought maybe I would like to be a fashion designer."

"Why didn't you?" Jayana asked. She stretched out her legs on the couch, so that her feet in their purple socks were just inches from touching her mother. She liked to wear her socks in layers, bunched up over her pink high-top tennis shoes. Amithi marveled at how tall her daughter was now and remembered when Jayana's legs were short and chubby sticking out of her diaper.

"Oh, it was just a childish dream," Amithi said.

Jayana frowned. "When I'm older, I'm not going to cook or sew or do any of the things you do."

A shock of hurt reverberated inside Amithi's chest. Her daughter had always been strong-willed, but when Jayana was younger, her comments toward Amithi had been benign, almost silly, usually ending in "head," such as "monkey-head" or "meanie-head." Now the insults were subtler but more pointed, and more painful.

"Cooking and sewing are useful skills, *beti,*" Amithi said, trying to keep the frustration out of her voice. If she showed her frustration, she would have lost.

"Maybe they're useful for you," Jayana replied. "But I'm not going to be a housewife like you. I'm going to work in a museum."

"What kind of museum?"

"An art museum. So I can meet famous artists, like Picasso. I learned about him in art history."

"Well, that's going to be difficult, seeing that Picasso is dead," Amithi said, happy to still be an authority on something.

Jayana rolled her eyes. "I know that. I said artists *like* Picasso."

"I see." Amithi looked down at her embroidery work. "You know, sewing is like being an artist. It involves making things. Some artists even use textiles."

"I know, Mom, but it's not the same as what you do."

"Why's that?"

"Because your work doesn't hang in a museum. No one sees it."

"You and your father see it. And the people I give it to see it."

"Yeah, but we don't count."

Amithi had always considered herself worldly, having lived on two continents. It was funny, then, how an adolescent could draw a definite boundary around Amithi's world and, with just a few sentences, make it seem small.

Chapter 16

INVENTORY ITEM: *nightgown*

APPROXIMATE DATE: *1975*

CONDITION: *excellent*

ITEM DESCRIPTION: *White nightgown with the tags still on it. Flutter sleeves. Rosebud embroidery along the square neckline.*

SOURCE: *swap meet*

April

AT DR. HONG'S OFFICE, a nurse-practitioner tightened an inflatable cuff around April's arm with a few squeezes of a hand pump.

The nurse peered down at the gauge. "Is your blood pressure usually on the high side?"

April shook her head. "I've never had any problems with it."

"And you said you've been having some cramping?"

"On and off all last night and today," April said.

"Hmmm."

This was not a noise April wanted to hear at her doctor's office. She was grateful, for the thousandth time since she found out she was pregnant, that she'd qualified for free health insurance through the state. She couldn't imagine what all these doctor visits would cost without it.

"If you'll just excuse me for a minute, I'm going to take a look at your chart and consult with Dr. Hong." The nurse's clogs squeaked against the tile floor as she left the room.

If her blood pressure had been high a minute ago, April was sure it was even higher now. She tried without success to stop the cascade of catastrophic thoughts that crowded her brain, tumbling in circles like wet clothes in a washing machine. Maybe she had preeclampsia or one of those other horrible-sounding conditions she'd read about in the pregnancy books. Come to think of it, she couldn't remember the last time she'd felt the baby move.

Instead of the nurse-practitioner, Dr. Hong came through the door with another woman in tow. Now April really began to panic. If everything were fine, the nurse-practitioner would have no reason to waste the doctor's time on a basic thing like vital signs.

"Am I having a miscarriage?" April asked.

"April, this is our radiology tech," Dr. Hong said as the other woman rolled an ultrasound machine over to the bedside. "We're going to get a look at the baby."

April noticed that Dr. Hong hadn't answered her question, which she took as another bad sign.

Dr. Hong pushed aside April's hospital gown and squirted goo on her belly. The radiology tech moved the cold wand across her skin, and April shut her eyes.

"I don't hear anything," April said. "Am I supposed to hear something?"

"We're just trying to locate the fetus," Dr. Hong said.

April didn't remember it taking this long the last time she had an ultrasound. "Is my baby okay?"

Please, please let my baby be okay.

"That's what we're trying to find out," Dr. Hong said. "And from the looks of it, he or she is doing just fine. Why don't you open your eyes? I think you'll want to see this."

April looked at the ultrasound screen, where a little sprout-looking thing with a big head waved two tiny arms and two tiny legs.

"Oh, thank God," April whispered.

The tech tapped at some buttons on the machine. "I'm just taking some measurements," she said. "But so far everything looks normal."

April stared in wonderment at the baby—*her* baby—wishing Charlie were there for this moment. Her mom, too.

"I see from my nurse's notes that your blood pressure numbers are high," said the doctor. "Have you been dealing with a lot of stress lately?"

"I guess you could say that."

The tech finished taking her measurements and printed out a black and white picture. She handed it to April and said, "You take it easy, now."

The tech left the room and Dr. Hong sat down at a small computer desk. She hit a few keys and pulled up a screen full of data. Normally, April would have been comforted at the sight of all those numbers, but today they just looked ominous and incomprehensible, like a language she didn't know how to read. It had been a relief to see that the baby was okay, but there were still all sorts of things that could go wrong.

"Do I have preeclampsia?" she asked.

"I don't think so, but we can't rule it out yet," the doctor replied. "The protein levels in your urine sample came back normal, and you don't have any swelling—"

"Are you kidding me?" April gestured toward her middle.

Dr. Hong laughed. "I mean abnormal swelling, like in your face or your arms and legs. Swelling of the abdomen is, as you know, perfectly normal. Anyway, besides the high blood pressure, you don't have any of the telltale signs of preeclampsia. But just to be on the safe side, I'm going to order you on modified bed rest. I suspect the slight rise in your blood pressure is stress related and will go down on its own, but the bed rest will help that happen faster."

"What do you mean by modified bed rest?" April asked. "Do I have to be in bed all the time?" She pictured herself lying around, her muscles and mind atrophying as her pregnancy wore on.

"No. You can sit on the couch with your feet elevated, and you can get up to go to the bathroom or shower, but I don't want you lifting anything heavier than five pounds. I don't want you going out and running errands or going to work or anything. And no sex."

"Well, the work and the sex won't be a problem," April said. "But my mom's house is on the market and I've gotta get it cleaned out."

"Then you'll have to ask someone or hire someone to do that for you. Do you need a note for your employer?"

"That won't be necessary. I lost my summer internship because I kind of blew up at my boss."

"Mmm-hmm." Dr. Hong typed something. "And how would you describe your mood lately?"

April didn't want to answer the question.

"There's no right or wrong answer here." Dr. Hong's eyes crinkled at the edges as she put on a sympathetic expression. "Just answer honestly."

April knew what was going on. She was being screened for depression, or some other mental health issue. Like her mom. She got the same series of questions at every office visit. Usually, she answered with a benign response like "a little tired, but otherwise okay." Lately, though, April felt as though her life were a balloon she'd been holding by a string and, despite her careful calculations, she'd somehow lost her grip on it. She could see it floating away and she needed to jump up and grab it before it drifted too far.

"April?"

She focused on Dr. Hong's face, but her voice sounded distant.

April hugged the thin cotton gown to her body. She shivered, feeling exposed.

"I'm going to take your response to mean 'not good,'" Dr. Hong said. She removed her glasses. "All women are at risk of postpartum depression, but as you know, with your family history, you're at greater risk, so I want to make sure we monitor you, not just after the birth, but now, too. Just to be extra cautious."

April thought about the note Violet had found in her mom's pocket. "How am I supposed to know if something is actually wrong or I'm just being hormonal?" she asked.

"It's a good question. Your hormones are certainly on overdrive during pregnancy, so some emotional swings are to be expected. But if you start to feel like your moods are affecting your ability to go about living your daily life, then please let me know."

"Like freaking out at my boss, you mean?"

"Let's not jump to any conclusions over a single incident." Dr. Hong gave April a small smile. "Don't beat yourself up too much about what happened. A lot of pregnant women have moments where they don't feel quite like themselves. It might be worth it to talk to your boss."

April respected Dr. Hong, but she doubted talking to Violet would do much good. If she was going to get her internship back, then she would need to perform some sort of penance to make up for the trust she'd destroyed. A mere apology wouldn't cut it.

When she got home, April rummaged through the kitchen for some snacks to keep within arm's reach to avoid having to get up for multiple trips. She put on one of her mom's loose-fitting nightgown-

and-robe sets, since her own pajamas no longer fit her, and settled into the couch with her laptop, trying not to think about how many hours she'd be spending in this same spot.

She checked her e-mail and saw another new message from Charlie sitting in her inbox. All she had to do was ask and she knew he would come over. He'd probably feel sorry for her and she was pretty sure she could take advantage of that. It would be nice to see him, and even nicer to have him wait on her. But having Charlie around for a little while would only make it all the harder when he left for Boston in the fall, and anyway, she wasn't ready to forgive him for the things he'd said and for calling off the wedding without so much as a phone call to let her know that cancellation cards were in the mail. Remembering Dr. Hong's advice to avoid stress as much as possible, she hit delete without opening the message.

The next several days passed in a groggy fog. April quickly grew tired of surfing the Internet and watching TV, and she didn't have any good books to read. She spent her time either sleeping out of sheer boredom or examining her problems like they were wriggling specimens on a lab slide. All of the plans she'd made in the last several months had fallen apart. The wedding, her ideas for the store . . . she couldn't help feeling like she'd even failed her child in some way. She knew how hard it had been for her mom to support and raise her as a single parent. Now she would have to face the same challenges, at an even younger age than her mother had.

She hoped Charlie would be a part of their child's life. She even hoped, when she allowed herself to admit it, that there was still a chance for the three of them to be together, as a family. But she knew that after Charlie moved to Boston, it wouldn't be long before he built a life independent of hers. She'd seen it happen with her own father. The way that his contact became less frequent over the years, until he finally cut her off completely.

Maybe Charlie would visit them on breaks from school, at first. He'd probably come to their baby's first birthday party. And, of course, he'd be legally obligated to send child support, though she imagined it wouldn't be much, given his student status. But for the everyday events—the doctor's appointments, the bedtime stories, the first steps—Charlie would be hundreds of miles away. And it broke her heart.

So slow and uneventful was her time on bed rest that April didn't even know what day of the week it was when she got a call from Lane Lawton. She stared down at the name on the caller ID, debating whether or not to answer. She didn't want to have to explain to Lane that, since they'd last spoken, she'd not only lost her job, but possibly was losing her mind as well. Then she thought of her mother, and how she used to shut people out when she needed them most.

April picked up the phone.

Lane's voice sounded worried. "April? I haven't seen you at rehearsals for the revue, and when I asked Violet about it, she said you were no longer interning at the store. Is everything okay? How's the baby?"

"The baby is fine, but I'm on bed rest."

"Oh, you poor—Danny, you get off that right now—sorry, what I meant to say is you poor thing. I had to be on bed rest for a while with my third, so I know it's no picnic. Can I come over with a meal or something?"

April looked down at her unwashed nightgown and was about to refuse, but again she thought of her mom and said, "That would be amazing."

"I can come over tonight after the kids—hands *out* of the butter dish, thank you, now go over to the sink and wash your hands."

"If this is a bad time, I can call you back."

"It's not a bad time, just a regular old afternoon. Listen, I'll come by after the kids are in bed tonight."

That evening, Lane let herself in, despite the fact that she'd never been to April's house. She showed up with a Tupperware and handed April a stack of shiny gossip magazines.

"Oh, my God," April said as she looked at the feuding celebrity couple on the cover of one of the magazines. "How did you know what I needed without me even asking?"

"Like I said, I was laid up during my last pregnancy, too. The only thing that kept me from being miserable was reading about other people's miseries," Lane said. "Do you mind if I open your cupboards to look for dishes? I brought you some dinner."

"Sure, dishes are in the cabinet next to the refrigerator."

April heard some clanging from the kitchen, and Lane came back with a bowl full of pasta salad and a fork. She handed them to April. "I don't care if you're not hungry. I can guarantee you that baby is hungry."

"Thanks." April took a bite of pasta. "This is the only thing I've eaten all week that isn't some variation of a peanut butter sandwich."

"I have to make a ton of food for my boys, anyway, so it's no trouble to make a little more," said Lane. "Now, tell me what's going on."

Just having Lane in the room made April feel more relaxed than she had in weeks.

In between big bites of pasta salad, she spewed out her story, starting with her mom's possible suicide and ending at Dr. Hong's office.

"If my mom killed herself, it makes me wonder if any of the times we had together were ever really happy, or if I just remember them that way because I didn't know what was going on with her," she said.

Lane reached over and patted April's arm. "I'm sure they were happy times for her, too."

"My mind is going in circles, trying to figure out what really happened. And the only conclusion I keep coming to is that I'll never really know, which isn't much of a conclusion at all."

Lane took a rubber band from around her wrist and pulled her highlighted hair into a ponytail. "You've gotta let it go then," she said.

"But how? If my mom killed herself, then—"

"Then what? It doesn't mean she didn't love you. It doesn't change any of the good times you shared. Even if the worst is true, which is a big 'if' since you don't have any proof one way or the other, your mom was still the person you remember her to be. How she died isn't as important as how she lived."

"Yeah, but she didn't exactly live the perfect life."

"None of us do. That's not the point. God, I hope my kids never judge me by whether or not I was perfect. All I want is for them to know I love them."

That, at least, April knew. Realizing that fact gave her a sense of comfort she hadn't felt in a long time.

"So is my body ever going to feel normal again?" she asked after she'd chewed the last bite of pasta.

Lane laughed. "Yes. And you're in your third trimester already, so it's all downhill from here."

"I've never understood that expression," April said. "Is it supposed to mean that things are going to get better, or worse?"

"In this case, better."

"But I'm so worried that I'm going to have the same problems my mom did. Mental-health-wise, I mean."

"You won't." Lane shook her head. "You won't because you're aware of what your mom went through, so you would never let yourself get to that point."

"Yeah, but I haven't been feeling like myself. I haven't felt like doing anything. How do I know I'm not two steps away from sinking into some awful hole?"

"Honey, you're on bed rest. Bed rest would make anyone feel depressed," Lane said. "I'm no shrink, but I think the fact that you got through your mom's death and most of your pregnancy without having a complete nervous breakdown says a lot for your sanity. You've had a rough few months, but that baby is strong and so are you."

"Thanks." April missed her mom in that moment with a suffocating ache in her chest, but she was glad someone else cared.

"And just to make sure of it, I'll come over as often as I can until your doctor says it's okay for you to be off bed rest," Lane said. "How does that sound?"

April nodded. She didn't even try to object. She just said, "Thank you."

"It will need to be in the evenings, after my kids' bedtime. If you need anything, you just call me and let me know what it is and I'll get it for you."

After Lane had gone home, April thought about how quick she'd been to write her off as just another harried Midwestern mom. She had assumed Lane had taken the easy way out by setting her acting dreams aside to wipe drool off chins and fingerprints off furniture. Now April could see that there was a lot more to Lane than she'd suspected. It occurred to April that Lane's leaving the theater to focus on her kids was not the result of Lane giving up on what she wanted but had likely been a choice, one that was thought out and desired just as much as a starring role.

Chapter 17

INVENTORY ITEM: *teapot*
APPROXIMATE DATE: *1950s*
CONDITION: *excellent*
ITEM DESCRIPTION: *Royal Doulton china teapot, ivory with pink roses.*
SOURCE: *Betsy Barrett*

Violet

VIOLET PARKED HER CAR in Betsy's semicircular driveway, then climbed the concrete path that wound through the August wildflowers in the front yard. Betsy's house was the only place Violet had ever been where an employee always answered the door. A housekeeper showed her into the living room and gave her chamomile tea in a china cup. Violet sat back on the brocade sofa and looked out at Lake Mendota through the velvet-curtained windows. She tried to relax. Violet still hadn't told Betsy she knew about her illness, and she feared her friend might have more bad news.

Betsy walked into the room holding her own cup of tea. She looked bone thin in her gray linen dress but otherwise in good spirits. Violet stood up.

"Oh, sit down, please," Betsy said. "I see you have some tea. Can I get you anything else?"

"No, I'm fine, thanks."

Betsy sat down in a chair across from the sofa, and Violet noticed the older woman's impeccable posture. Even though she was tall, Betsy sat up straight to appear even taller and held her chin high. She was a woman who didn't apologize for being who she was—a quality Violet remembered about her own grandmother.

Violet smiled as she recalled how, when she was a child, she would sit on the piano bench while Grandma Lou played. Her grandmother's fingers, with their smooth, red nails, would fly across the keys and she'd rock back and forth, singing, *Would you like to swing on a star?* Violet would join in, reveling in how good it felt to belt out a song, deep from the diaphragm. In the safety of Grandma Lou's living room, she never had to apologize for being herself.

Betsy blew on the top of her tea, sending a puff of steam into the air. "Thanks for agreeing to meet me," she said. "I wanted to say I'm so sorry to hear things didn't work out with April. I want you to know I don't hold you responsible. She's been through a lot, that girl."

"Have you talked to her lately?" Violet asked.

"Not since the day she called to tell me she'd quit. I tried to talk her out of it, but she's got a mind of her own. I talked to her adviser at the university and they said they'd be willing to give partial credit for the internship." Betsy sipped her tea. "Have you heard from her?"

Violet shook her head.

"How about you? Is everything all right?" Betsy asked. "You seem stressed."

Leave it to Betsy to be concerned about me when she's the one who's sick, Violet thought. "I've been fine," she replied. "We've got the runway show coming up, and then there's . . . well, things have been a bit complicated lately."

Betsy sighed. "Okay, I'll come clean."

"Thank God," Violet said. "I've been trying to figure out whether to say something."

"I've been wanting to tell you, too, but you have to understand that I'm in an awkward position. On the one hand, you're a dear friend and I want your shop to succeed. On the other hand, I've got a lot of business connections I have to think about. The owner of the development group that's been negotiating with your landlord is the president of my husband's old company. Even though I sold out my interest after Walt died, I still feel like I have to keep up a good relationship."

Violet blinked. "I'm sorry, what are you talking about?"

"The developer who's buying your building," Betsy said. "To turn it into condos? I thought that's what we were talking about."

"No," Violet said. "All my landlord told me was that they're putting the building on the market, so they want me out."

"It doesn't need to go on the market," Betsy said. "The developer already had the plans approved by the city council to gut the building, put an addition on the back of it, and turn it into a four-unit luxury condo complex."

"So it's a done deal?"

"Well, nothing in real estate is really done until the ink on the deed is dry. But all signs point toward it happening. I thought you knew."

"I didn't," Violet said, feeling betrayed that Betsy hadn't said anything earlier. Perhaps she and Betsy weren't as close as she'd thought. But then she felt guilty for holding anything against Betsy, since she was sick. And Violet also felt like a hypocrite, because she was guilty of keeping quiet about certain important matters, too.

What bothered Violet the most about the news of the development project was that it meant her landlord assumed that Violet wouldn't—no, couldn't *afford*—to exercise her right of first refusal on the building. They weren't even waiting for her to decide what she was going to do before moving ahead with their plans. It was as if the chance of her buying the building was too remote to even worry about. It *was* remote, but Violet still clung to the possibility that, between the revue and maybe a miracle, she'd scrounge up enough money to make a down payment and qualify for a loan. Because if that didn't happen, she didn't know what she was going to do. She'd been poring over the classifieds every week, and the prospect of finding another affordable shop space in the neighborhood was looking grim.

Betsy set down her teacup. "So if you weren't referring to the plans for the building, then what is it you wanted to bring up?"

Violet tried to think about how best to phrase what she had to say about the information she'd found in Betsy's car. Concluding that there was no good way, she just blurted out, "I know about your cancer, Betsy. I'm sorry. I saw an insurance form or a bill or something in your front seat when I went out to get the clothes last time you came into the shop."

Betsy didn't say anything. The words seemed to hover in the air, above the lacquered coffee table.

"Oh, no," Betsy finally said. She reached over and patted Violet's shoulder. "I didn't realize I had left that piece of paper sitting out."

Violet set down her tea and hugged her arms to her chest, feeling chilled in the air-conditioned room. "I know it's none of my business, but I'm just so worried about you. I don't have any family in Madison, so you've become kind of like my family here."

Betsy's expression changed from one of sympathy to a smile. "That's very sweet of you to say, and I can tell you the feeling is quite mutual, but there's nothing to worry about. I kicked that cancer in the butt. That paper is months and months old. I just haven't cleaned out the car in a while. I really should keep it tidier. If Walt were still around, he wouldn't stand for all the clutter I keep in there."

Violet sniffled, feeling skeptical. "Really?"

"Yes, I'm happy to say." Betsy smiled. "The doctors found a lump in my breast, and I went through radiation treatment and had a double mastectomy. I've been cancer-free for over a year."

"You were going through all of that and you never told me?"

"It never came up, and anyway, I didn't want people to know I was sick because then they'd insist on me taking it easy, and I've never been good at that. And, to be perfectly honest, I didn't want people thinking I was going to die. As you know, I'm involved with several charitable organizations and all of them, naturally, hope I'll leave them a little something in my will someday. You can bet that if any of them got a whiff of a rumor that I might be kicking the bucket soon, they'd be lined up to kiss my ass, bless their hearts."

Violet laughed. "You're probably right." She shook her head. "I can't believe you had a double mastectomy. Jesus."

"I'm seventy-six years old. What use do I have for these anymore?" She cupped her hands under her bra line. "I wear falsies now so my clothes still fit properly."

"I'm so glad you're okay," Violet said.

"Oh, stop fussing over me. Cancer was no picnic, but it did teach me a thing or two. I learned that there's no point in mulling over what could have been or what should have been. If you do, you miss out on what's going on right in front of you, and that's all there is, really."

As Violet drove home that night, her thoughts reverberated inside her skull like it was a kettledrum, and a muddle of emotions fought for space in her heart. There was the shock of learning about the plan for her building, hurt as to why Betsy wouldn't have told her about it, and relief about Betsy's being in remission.

Betsy's comments about letting go of what "could have" and "should have" been reminded Violet of something Sam had said to her on their first date. She phoned him on her way home.

"Hi," he said. "I'm glad you called. What are you up to?"

"I just had tea with my friend Betsy who's battled cancer. She said something about living in the moment that sounded familiar. So I'm calling to tell you that, at this moment, I want to be with you."

"Exactly what I was thinking," Sam said.

"If you want, you can come to my place. It's probably the last night I'll be able to really relax this week, since I've got the revue coming up in a few days. I've got some wine in the fridge for us and a whole lot of musicals on DVD."

"I'll take you up on the wine, but I'll have to skip the musicals."

Violet let out an exaggerated sigh. "I knew you weren't perfect."

"Are you home right now?" Sam asked.

"I'm on my way. I'll meet you there."

Violet rolled along Johnson Street in her old, wood-paneled Wagoneer. She passed two cars with dripping kayaks strapped to their roofs, probably coming home from an evening paddle in one of the lakes. A Led Zeppelin song played on the radio. The anticipation of seeing Sam put her in a singing kind of mood, and she crooned along with Robert Plant. She parked behind her building and hurried to the back entrance, hoping she'd have enough time to light candles and pour some wine before Sam arrived. Her heels sounded on the worn wood as she ascended the back staircase. When she opened the door, Miles didn't run to greet her.

That's odd, she thought, beginning to worry that something had happened to him.

"Miles," she called, reaching for the light switch.

"Hey, babe," said a low voice.

Violet jumped a mile and flicked the kitchen light on to reveal a drunk and drooping—but still formidable—Jed, sitting on the floor against the refrigerator. And petting her dog.

"What the *fuck* are you doing here?" she asked. She had thought she was done with having to deal with Jed and his benders.

At the sound of Violet's shouting, Miles raised his ears but stayed put at Jed's side. *So much for loyalty,* Violet thought. Back when they'd adopted Miles together from a rescue shelter, Jed had done little to care for the dog. Walking him, feeding him, and bathing him fell to Violet. Apparently Miles had forgotten all that.

"I'm just passing through town." Jed grinned at her, not looking convinced of his own lie. He tried to get to his feet but stumbled. He grabbed on to the counter and pulled himself up.

"You're drunk," Violet said, seething with rage. "Get out of here or I'm going to call the police and report you for breaking in."

"The door was unlocked," Jed said. "I didn't break in."

Shit, Violet thought. She'd been distracted as she left for Betsy's house. She must have forgotten to lock up. It was easy to forget, in a relatively safe Midwestern city like Madison.

Jed took a swig from a green, shapely bottle. Violet recognized it as the white wine she'd bought for her and Sam to drink.

"That's my fucking wine."

"Saving it for something special?" He glanced at the bottle in one hand and, with the other, reached out and grabbed her waist.

Violet jerked away. He came forward and tried again to grab her, but Violet reached down and slipped off one of her shoes, a leopard-print flat. She hurled it in Jed's direction. It missed him and clunked against the refrigerator. It was more of a gesture of sheer frustration than anything. Jed had never hurt her, physically anyway, and even if he wanted to, he was too inebriated to pull it off.

Jed picked up the shoe and examined it with blurry-eyed wonder. "You've always had such tiny little feet. Do you remember, Vi? How I used to rub your feet when you were done working double shifts at the Sunshine Café?"

Violet reached down and took off the other shoe, advancing toward him with it. "Get. The fuck. Out of. My apartment. I've got someone coming over, and you better not be here when he arrives."

"Ooooh, a boyfriend? He gonna beat me up?" Jed took a couple of wobbly steps forward and collapsed in a liquid heap of loose muscle and spilled wine.

"You don't have my permission to be here. I can still call the police," Violet said. "So you'd better get out."

"You won't call the police."

"Try me." She walked over to the phone on the counter.

"Okay, okay." Jed held his hands up. "I'll go."

When he didn't move, Violet asked, "Where's your truck?"

Jed sat up on the wood floor with his knees to his chest. "Wrecked it."

"Jesus. *Tonight?*"

"Nah, a few months ago."

"How did you get here?"

"Lenny sold me his van."

Violet sighed. The patience she'd once had for this man had run out years earlier, when she finally realized that, for all of his luminescent charm and fame in high school, things like ambition and happiness died within a mile of Jed Cline.

"So where's your *van,* then?" Violet asked.

"It's parked just down the street."

"Probably not anymore. It's a street-cleaning night. The city starts towing cars after seven o'clock," said Violet.

"So maybe I should just stay here tonight then." Jed looked up at her with an expression that was probably intended to be sexy but instead just looked desperate, defeated—the expression of a man holding on to a tiny spiderweb's thread of hope.

"No way." Letting him stay the night was out of the question, but so was letting him drive anywhere. Violet paced the kitchen, not sure what to do. She didn't know what had spurred him to make the four-hour trip from Bent Creek to see her, but she didn't have time to find out. She needed to get him out of there before Sam arrived.

"Get up," she said. "I'm taking you to the Super 8 on East Washington."

"But I need to talk to you. I lost my job." Jed struggled to stand in his ancient steel-toed boots. "You always used to help me figure out what to do."

"I thought you were done making these surprise visits. For that matter, I thought you'd stopped drinking. What happened to rehab?"

"Fuck rehab." Jed shook his head like there was a scorpion in his hair. When he stopped, his eyes looked resigned and sad. "Don't you miss me, Vi? Sometimes I think about when we were first together. We had a lot of fun."

Violet did miss some things about their time together but it wasn't Jed she missed. It was the innocence and hope she'd had in the beginning of their relationship. Rarely had she allowed herself to feel hopeful since. She suspected hope was what Jed was missing, too.

"Come on. I'll drive you to the motel," she said.

Clutching on to the counter, Jed managed to hoist himself up. As soon as he got to his feet, Miles started barking again.

"It's okay, boy," said Violet. "He's leaving."

Violet heard Jed shuffling behind her as she went out the door. At the top of the back steps, she looked down and saw Sam standing at the bottom.

"Get back inside," she hissed to Jed, but he had already spotted Sam.

"Hey, do I know you?" Jed asked.

Sam shot Violet a bewildered look, and she held up her hands to show that she was just as surprised as he was.

"Dude, I asked you a question," said Jed, louder this time.

"It's possible," Sam replied.

"You from Bent Creek?"

"Unfortunately."

"I was just about to drop him off at a motel," Violet said. "Please come up and help yourself to anything until I get back. There *was* some wine"—she glared at Jed—"but that's all gone now."

Sam came up the stairs and Jed grabbed his shoulder. "I want to catch up with my buddy here from Bent Creek. Can't we stay for just a little while?"

"Listen, man." Jed leaned toward Sam and, in doing so, wavered on his feet. For a moment, Violet thought he was going to tumble down the stairs. He grabbed the railing. "Have your fun now," he said. "It's only a matter of time before this bitch thinks she's too good for you."

Sam wound back his fist, about to take a swing, but Violet grabbed his arm. "Please don't."

Sam clenched his jaw.

"Aw, you still care about me, don't you, Vi?" said Jed.

"No," she said in his direction, then looked again at Sam. "He's not worth it. One punch and his drunk ass will probably fall down the stairs and we'll all end up at the police station. That's not how I wanted to spend this evening." She gave him the sexiest smile she could get away with while her ex-husband stood behind her.

Sam dropped his fist and gave Jed a murderous look. "Okay," he said. He turned to Violet. "You want me to ride with you there? I don't want you alone with this guy."

"Sure, you can come along," she said. She didn't want the two men in the car together, but she also didn't want any more time alone with Jed.

The three-mile drive to the Super 8 on the east side of town felt like it took hours. Jed babbled in the backseat.

"I'd been doing real good, going to AA meetings and everything, until I got into a fight with my boss at the factory," he said. "Man, that guy is a dick."

Sam stared straight ahead, looking as though he might jump back there and strangle Jed at any moment.

"So you came down here after getting fired?" asked Violet.

"I'm not real sure, exactly. I remember going out afterward, to blow off steam, and then everything is sorta fuzzy after that until I woke up in my car in a rest station parking lot near Eau Claire. I figured I was almost halfway to Madison so I kept on driving."

"Jesus, you could have killed someone."

"It's not my fault," Jed said. "It runs in families, you know."

"Right," said Sam. He leaned a muscular forearm on the armrest and whipped his head around to look at Jed. "Nothing is your fault. You couldn't stop yourself from driving drunk, or breaking into Violet's apartment—"

"Or spending my tuition money on booze," Violet added.

"Right. You couldn't help any of it. You're just genetically predisposed to being an asshole," Sam said.

Violet glanced in the rearview mirror as she pulled into the parking lot of the motel.

A look of recognition crossed Jed's face. "Hey, I remember you now. Sam. Sam Lewis. You were all weird and skinny back then. You turned out a lot better than I would've thought."

"Sorry I can't say the same for you," Sam said.

Jed got out of the car.

Sam rolled down his window. "You better not come by Violet's tomorrow or any other day, you hear me?"

"What am I supposed to do?" Jed asked. He looked at Violet with the same lost look that, years ago, would have hooked her. She had a weakness for anything worn and broken, and she had to fight it constantly in running the shop—curbing the impulse to buy a coat with a torn lining that would cost more to replace than she could ever get for it on the sales floor. But she'd learned, over the years, that some things were beyond repair. Her relationship with Jed was one of them.

"Go back to Bent Creek, Jed," she said. "I can't help you anymore."

Jed walked toward the motel entrance with his shoulders slumped. He no longer carried himself with the swagger Violet remembered. Life must have beat it out of him.

"You okay?" Sam asked as Violet pulled out of the parking lot.

"I think so," she said. "Can I stay at your place tonight, though? I'm way too freaked out to go back home right now."

"Of course." Sam reached over and touched her arm at the exact spot her tattoo emerged from the short sleeve of her cotton eyelet blouse.

Violet glanced down at the open-winged phoenix on her bicep. She'd gotten the tattoo on the day she arrived in Madison five years earlier. Before she even unloaded the boxes from her Jeep into her apartment, she had stopped at Gary's Tattoo Artistry on Williamson Street and shown the eponymous owner a page in a vintage mythology book she'd always loved. Though her marriage had gone up in flames, she was determined to use her newfound freedom in order to fly.

"I'm sorry you got dragged into that," Violet said to Sam. "Thank you for not escalating things into a fight back at my place."

"It's not often I want to hit someone," he said. "And I really wanted to."

"I wouldn't have blamed you if you did. But I'm glad you didn't. It would have just made everything messier, and I wanted to get him out of my place as soon as possible."

Sam ran his hands through his gray-speckled hair. "When he called you a bitch—"

"It's not like I've never been called that before," Violet said. "I figure any woman who's not a total pushover has been called a bitch once or twice in her life. I can take it."

They rode in silence for a few moments.

"Is there still something going on there?" Sam asked.

At a stoplight, she turned her face toward Sam. "What, between Jed and me?"

"Yeah. I mean, why would he drive all that way if he didn't think—"

Violet squeezed Sam's hand. "There's nothing going on."

"I don't know why you don't just cut him out for good."

"I've tried, but every time something happens I think it's going to be the last time. Karen is always telling me I should get a restraining order, and she's probably right."

Sam let out a loud, frustrated breath. "People like that are the reason I never want to have kids. It was bad enough to live through getting made fun of growing up. I imagine it was even harder for my parents to watch me get picked on by guys like him."

The light turned green and Violet knew she needed to go, but her brain was stuck on what Sam had just said. He hadn't said *I might not want to have kids* or *I'm not sure.* He'd said "never."

Someone behind her honked and she moved her foot to the gas pedal.

"I thought you said you've moved past all that," she said.

"Yeah, well, not enough to want to put an innocent kid through it."

"But your kid might not get bullied."

"Don't they all? And if they don't, then they're the ones doing the bullying, which is even worse."

"That's kind of a cynical outlook, don't you think?"

Sam shrugged. "Maybe, but with the world population breaking seven billion, it's not like anybody is missing out by me deciding not to father children."

Violet glanced at Sam's face in the glow of the streetlights and thought, *That's not necessarily true.*

They were silent for a few moments.

Sam cleared his throat. "I probably shouldn't have said anything."

"Why not? I'm glad you're honest with me."

"I guess all I'm saying is that I'm sorry I brought it up today, with everything else you had to deal with."

"It's okay. It was going to come up eventually, don't you think?" Violet asked.

"Yeah, it always does," said Sam. "I really like you. I think—no, I'm positive I'm falling in love with you. I understand if this changes things, though."

Violet grew quiet. The joy of Sam's saying he loved her was tempered by the shock of his admission that he didn't want to have children. She wished she didn't feel this way. After all, she wasn't even sure she ever wanted to get married again. She loved the freedom of being on her own and wasn't sure she'd be willing to give it up, even for someone as special as Sam. It seemed premature to be talking about a family. Still, she couldn't help feeling like something precious was being taken away from her. She knew it was silly. She knew that, at her age, it probably wouldn't be easy, if it were even possible, for her to have children of her own.

"I probably should have brought this up sooner," Sam said. "But I guess I was enjoying getting to know you too much, and I was afraid I'd lose the chance to continue getting to know you. Plus, I didn't want to bring up such a serious topic so soon."

"It's still soon," Violet said. "We've been dating less than two months."

"Yeah, but I feel more for you than for people I've dated for years. I can see myself with you for a long time, you know?"

"Yeah," said Violet. "I do."

"So, is the kids thing a deal breaker for you?"

Violet didn't know. She loved babies, and she supposed she'd always imagined that children would be part of her life. But it had been a very long day, and she needed time to think.

"Do I have to answer that?" Violet asked. "Because, to be honest, I don't know what I'd say. In response to the other thing you said, though, it's mutual. I'm falling in love with you, too. So can we just leave it at that for now, and revisit the kids topic some other time?"

"Absolutely." Sam leaned over and kissed her. "I just wanted to be fair and give you an easy out if you want one."

"I don't want one," Violet said.

And that, at least, she was sure of.

Chapter 18

INVENTORY ITEM: *lamp*
APPROXIMATE DATE: *1980*
CONDITION: *good*
ITEM DESCRIPTION: *Polychrome goose lamp manufactured by Kaplanheller Inc.*
SOURCE: *estate of Katherine Morgan; not for sale*

April

AFTER TWO WEEKS OF bed rest, April couldn't wait to get out of the house, even if only to go to the doctor. Lane picked her up for her appointment, and when April got inside the Volvo station wagon, everything she touched felt sticky—the door handles, the dashboard, even the leather seats. She folded her hands in her lap and tried to touch as few surfaces as possible.

"Thanks for coming to get me. I know it's early," April said.

"Eight o'clock isn't early for me. I'm up at six every morning so I can have half an hour of peace before my kids get up," Lane said from behind the steering wheel. "And don't think I don't see you squirming over there. Just wait—your car will look like this someday, too. And your house. And pretty much anything your kids touch."

"Kids touch, kids touch," said Lane's youngest son from the backseat.

"Whoa," April said. "Who said anything about kids? When I had the ultrasounds, there was only one in there. That better still be the case."

"Don't underestimate what just one can do," Lane said.

"Stop pinching me," one of the boys cried from the backseat. "Mom!"

"Pipe down. All three of you." Lane made a stern face in the rearview mirror.

"I have no idea what you're talking about," April said. "My baby is going to be perfect. I showed you the ultrasound photo, right? Perfect."

"You're right." Lane smiled as she pulled into the clinic lot and drove up to the front door. "I'm just gonna take these guys to McDonald's for some pancakes."

A chant started in the backseat. "PlayPlace! PlayPlace!"

"Don't tell my husband I'm feeding my kids fast food." Lane winked. "He thinks they should be eating quinoa and organic carrots."

"I've never even met the elusive professor," April said. "So I think your secret is safe."

"Mommy, she said a bad word," said the oldest child.

"'Elusive' is not a bad word, honey," Lane said. She turned to April. "He thinks any word he hasn't heard of is a bad word. So you'll call me when you're done? I'll come pick you up."

"Yep." April unbuckled her seat belt. "Thanks so much, Lane."

In Dr. Hong's examining room, April's heart raced as the nurse took her blood pressure. She knew she should relax to get the best chance of an accurate reading, but she couldn't. Her freedom lay in what the blood pressure gauge said. The nurse left the room to get the doctor, and April waited for the verdict, thinking about how everything always seemed to come down to numbers.

*A*fter the happy announcement that Dr. Hong was lifting her bed rest order, April went home and heaved open the barn-style doors of the un-attached garage behind the house. Sunlight flooded into the space and shone on the dusty hood of the Toyota. She hadn't gotten behind the wheel of a vehicle since before her mom's accident. She was pretty sure that her fear of driving qualified as the kind of anxiety that Dr. Hong had warned her to watch for—the kind that interfered with her daily life. As if to prove to herself and to the doctor that she was perfectly fine, mental-health-wise, April got in and settled into the driver's seat, taking slow breaths to keep panic from paralyzing her. The car still smelled the same inside as she remembered it, stuffy and slightly sweet from the air freshener hanging from the rearview mirror.

She'd driven the car hundreds of times before. It had been the car her mom let her use to drive to school.

You can do this, she thought.

She turned the key in the ignition and adjusted the mirrors before easing out of the garage and, very cautiously, backing onto the street. Since it was the middle of the day, there wasn't much traffic as she crawled along, gripping the steering wheel with sweaty hands.

She stopped at the light at the end of her block. As she waited at the intersection watching cars whiz by, her heart pounded. Being stopped made her think about everything that could go wrong, and she considered going back.

Then the light turned and, reflexively, she put her foot on the gas. She felt nothing less than triumphant when she cleared the inter-section and parked in the lot behind Hourglass Vintage on the next block. She got out of the car and opened the hatchback. The plastic goose lamp she'd brought from her mom's house sat patiently on a nest of blankets in the trunk.

As she carried the lamp toward the store, April couldn't help laughing at herself. She must have looked ridiculous, waddling across the parking lot with a giant goose.

A middle-aged woman called out from the coffee shop parking lot next door. "That looks awfully big. Do you need some help with that?"

"I know it looks heavy, but it's just hollow plastic," April said.

"But you can hardly see over the top of it," the woman said. "Please, let me do it."

April thought about the weeks she'd spent on bed rest and realized she needed to get better at accepting help. "Okay," she said. "That would be great."

The woman hurried over and took the lamp. "You shouldn't be lifting large things."

The woman eyed the lamp with a curious expression. "What an interesting piece. Are you going to sell it to the shop? Because I'm not sure they're open yet."

"No. It's a gift."

April figured the woman probably thought she was crazy, but for once that didn't bother her. Violet had taken a risk by taking her on as an intern. Now it was April's turn to risk something—her pride, by apologizing.

"Where do you want to put it?" the woman asked.

"Let's go around to the front door. The owner always checks the mailbox out front in the morning. This way, she'll be sure to see it."

They walked around to the street side of the building, and as soon as they rounded the corner, April clapped her hand to her mouth.

The store's display window was shattered, and glass littered the sidewalk. That wasn't the worst of it, though. Across the building's beautiful brick façade, someone had spray-painted "CUNT" in fluorescent orange letters.

"Oh, dear," the woman said.

April dug in her purse for her phone and dialed.

"Violet?" she said. "You need to come down here right away."

Chapter 19

INVENTORY ITEM: *corset*

APPROXIMATE DATE: *2009*

CONDITION: *excellent*

ITEM DESCRIPTION: *New strapless corset in black spandex with lace-up back, for wear under vintage garments.*

SOURCE: *eBay*

Violet

SAM PULLED UP IN front of the store. The car hadn't even come to a complete stop when Violet jumped out and ran over to April, who was standing on the sidewalk surrounded by broken glass.

"I'll pull around back to park," Sam called out the window. "I'll be right there."

"I can't believe this," Violet said. She hugged April and then let go and held her by both shoulders. "Are you okay?"

"I'm fine," April said. "I'm glad *you're* okay. The first thing I thought when I saw the damage was that I hoped you weren't inside."

"I stayed at Sam's," Violet said. "My ex showed up last night."

"Do you think it was him that did this?" April asked.

"It was definitely him," Sam said, coming up next to them. "We should probably call your landlord, Violet. And your insurance company . . ."

Violet didn't hear the rest of what Sam said because she'd already unlocked the door and flicked on the overhead lights inside the shop.

"Violet, no," Sam said, following her. "The police said to wait for them."

She held her breath as she surveyed her store. The size-six mannequin had tipped over, and its head and one arm had fallen off. Its 1940s sundress lay askew and covered with glass. A brick lay on the wood floor next to a shelf full of tableware, and several pieces of china lay shattered on the floor.

Seeing the damage to her store, the only achievement she'd ever really been proud of, sent rage racing through Violet's body. She crouched on the floor and started picking up pieces of a Wedgwood tureen with shaking hands.

"Hey, let's wait until the police get here, so they can see everything exactly as we found it and get it all in their report," Sam said. He helped Violet up and put his arms around her. "They should be here any minute. They're sending someone over to the motel, too, to look for Jed. If he's still there, they'll take him in for questioning."

"This can't be happening," Violet said. "The revue is in three days. We've got the rehearsal tonight. How am I supposed to pull off the show *and* get the store put back together?"

"I'll help," Sam said.

"Me too," April said, peeking through the open door. "I mean, if you'll let me after the way I acted the last time I was here."

Violet gave both of them a grateful look. "Okay, so what do we do first?"

"I'll need to get a tarp to tape up that window for now," Sam said. "And I'm gonna call around about renting a power washer to get that spray paint off the building."

"Good thinking. I need all the good PR I can muster, with the show coming up, and I'm pretty sure having an obscenity sprayed on the front of the store is not good PR." She put her head in her hands. "I can't believe Jed went this far."

"I can," Sam said. "I'm just pissed I didn't teach that asshole a lesson last night when I had the chance."

Five years since I left him, Violet thought as she stared at the brick lying on the floor. *And still Jed manages to destroy anything that's important to me.*

"Come on, let's go back outside," Sam said, putting a hand on Violet's shoulder and leading her toward the door. "The cops are gonna be here any minute."

As Violet stepped outside, she noticed the goose lamp standing next to the front door.

She looked at April, bewildered. "Was that here before? Or am I so stressed out I'm seeing things?"

April's face flushed. "That's why I came this morning. I meant to bring it for you as an apology—a sort of peace offering."

"I love it." Violet put a hand to her chest. "And thank you for the way you handled things today."

"I know you'll probably need to give it some thought, and you've got a lot on your mind right now," April said. "But I was hoping you'd at least consider letting me have my position at the store back."

Violet was truly touched by April's gift, and impressed by how calm she'd kept in discovering the vandalism. But April was right. Violet had a lot on her mind, and she wasn't sure she needed the added worry of taking an intern back on at the moment.

"I'll think about it," she promised.

April nodded. "Okay, but in the meantime I'm gonna help you guys clean all this up."

$\mathcal{D}$espite all that she'd been through, Violet still had to run the dress rehearsal for the revue that evening. April and Sam stayed behind at the shop, putting things back into as good of a shape as was possible with a tarp and pieces of plywood covering the window.

From the front row of seats at the Majestic Theatre, Violet clapped her hands to try to get the attention of the models, who seemed to be more interested in talking than rehearsing.

"Everyone, please," Violet yelled with her last ounce of energy. She'd been on the phone off and on all day with the police. They still hadn't found Jed. By the time they arrived at the motel, he had already checked out. Local police radioed the state patrol near Bent Creek to be on the lookout, but so far no one had spotted him. It didn't help that Violet wasn't sure what vehicle he was driving. In the meantime, the officer who'd shown up at the store had helped Violet fill out a restraining order.

Violet had also spoken with Ted Mortensen, who had been surprisingly friendly about the whole thing. He informed her that she'd need to use her renter's insurance to cover her losses for what was damaged inside the shop, but that Mortensen & Son would work with its own insurer to deal with the damage to the building itself.

"Don't you worry," Ted had said. "We'll handle the claims for the structural damage and so forth. You just focus on running your business. Don't you have some big production coming up? I've seen the posters all over town."

"Yeah," Violet had told him. "I know about your plans to sell my building to the condo developer, and all I've got to say is, don't sign any contracts in blood just yet. I'm doing everything I can to come up with the money."

Ted had laughed, which irritated Violet. She knew the chance that she'd be able to raise enough funds to exercise her option to purchase the building was slim to none. But she didn't need to be reminded of that fact by Ted.

Now, in the theater, the chatter of the models got louder, and Violet shot Amithi and Lane a desperate look. Lane stood up, blew on her fingers, and whistled. The shrill sound shocked everybody on-stage into silence.

"Thanks," said Violet.

Lane shrugged. "I'm glad to see someone listens to me. My kids certainly don't."

"Okay, so we're going to do a full run-through," Violet said. "Does everyone know what they're supposed to wear? There should be a list on your hanger of everything you'll need for your outfit—all of your accessories and everything."

"I didn't see a list," said one of the younger models.

"I'm gonna speak for myself here," said the man—Violet's hair-dresser, in fact—who'd soon be transforming into the vivacious Ivanna Martini and would be emceeing the show. "But I'm pretty sure I'll need some things that aren't on that list that I don't really want to discuss in mixed company, if you know what I mean."

The other men onstage piped up. Some of them wore street clothes and some had shown up at the rehearsal already in drag.

Violet held up her hands. "Okay, okay. What I meant was that the list has everything on it *from the store* that we want you to wear. But obviously you need to bring your own undergarments and nylons and what have you. You are welcome to add whatever, um, enhancements you need to make yourself look beautiful on the big day."

This seemed to clarify things, because several of the models on-stage nodded.

One of the curvier women, a thirtysomething burlesque dancer, said, "Thank God, because I need my corset and my Spanx."

"Oh, I'll give you Spanx, honey, don't you worry," said the man next to her. He was wearing what Violet thought of as "half drag"—false eyelashes and a wig, but jeans and a button-down oxford with the sleeves rolled up. He whacked the burlesque dancer on her round backside and she giggled.

"Where did you find a corset?" one of the other girls asked. "I've been looking for one, too."

"We have some in the shop if anyone needs one," Violet said. "And don't worry, they're new, not used, but they're made specially to go under vintage garments. Does anyone have any more questions on wardrobe?" When no one spoke up, she continued. "All right, so you all have about half an hour to get backstage and get in costume, and then we'll do the run-through. Ready? Go."

The models scattered off the stage.

Amithi turned to Violet and said, "Did I tell you my daughter and her husband are coming to the revue? I've been staying with them for the past few weeks."

"You didn't tell me you were staying with them," Violet said. "I take it things are still uncertain with your husband, then."

Amithi's voice cracked as she said, "Yes."

Violet opened up her arms for a hug. When Amithi didn't react, Violet went ahead and embraced her anyway. At first, Amithi's body felt stiff, but then she dropped her shoulders and relaxed.

Amithi had tears in her eyes when Violet pulled away. "I am sorry to bother you with my troubles. I know you are very busy today."

"I've got quite a few troubles of my own, so at least I know I'm not the only one," said Violet.

"I am glad you will have a chance to meet my daughter."

"I can't wait," Violet said.

Seeing the pride in Amithi's face when she talked about her daughter reminded Violet of the question Sam had asked her the night before, about whether or not she wanted kids. She hated that the conversation came to mind now, after everything Sam had done for her in the past twenty-four hours. He had been such an incredible support, making calls for her and running errands to get clean-up supplies for the store. Even as she was grateful for his help, she sensed something had shifted between them since the previous night. She willed herself not to worry about it, but nevertheless, Sam's confession about not wanting a family changed the way she saw their future, if they had one. Between Sam, the incident with Jed, the eviction action, and the revue, Violet felt like she was standing on a suspension bridge ready to snap and send her plunging into unknown currents.

Lane came over and checked something off on her clipboard. "So, Violet, have you thought about how you want to do the auction part?"

"I'm sorta stuck on it," Violet said. "I think I've ruled out a live auction because it would just be too much going on onstage, with the fashion show and everything. And anyway, I don't have an auctioneer lined up. So I was thinking of doing a silent auction and opening it up for bidding after the show, but I need to get programs printed so people can take notes while they watch the models and mark off things they're interested in, so they know what to bid on later."

"That makes sense," Lane said. "We need to get those programs printed quickly, though. The revue's only a couple of days away."

"I know. I kept meaning to get to it, but between cleaning up after the vandalism and all the other last-minute stuff, I don't know how I'm going to find time."

Lane shook her head. "I still can't believe what happened at the store."

"It looks awful," Violet said. "You haven't even seen it, and hopefully you won't have to. Sam is already working on getting rid of the graffiti. What I'm most worried about, though, is my ex coming back and doing something worse. I've got a restraining order in the works, but it's only helpful if someone *catches* him near my property."

Two models came out onto the stage, bickering about the order of the lineup.

Violet had lost her patience. She shouted, "There will be no more changes to the order of the show. Please let everybody else know."

One of the models, a leggy drag queen in a purple seventies jump-suit, stomped off through the wing at stage left. The other model, a petite girl with dyed red hair and a nose ring, gave Violet and Lane an apologetic look and followed her cast mate off the stage.

"Is there anyone you could delegate the program project to?" Lane asked after they'd gone.

Violet thought about it. April was good at computer stuff—she could probably design and print out the programs in plenty of time. And there was still the auction to organize. Violet still thought April had overstepped her bounds. But she'd been so sincere in her apology about how she'd acted that Violet felt she deserved another chance.

Violet called her at the shop. "Hi, April? It's Violet. How are things going over there?"

"Pretty good," April said. "Sam got the mannequin put back to-gether."

Violet smiled, thinking about Sam fussing with the sundress-clad mannequin. It made her love him even more.

"Hey, Lane said you've been on bed rest for the last two weeks. Why didn't you tell me?"

"I figured you had enough to worry about."

"Next time something important is going on in your life, good *or* bad, keep me in the loop, promise?"

"Promise," April said. "How's the rehearsal going?"

"Okay," Violet replied. "Can I entrust you with an important task?"

"Absolutely. What do you want me to do?"

"The whole auction component of the revue."

"Really?" April sounded excited.

"Yes, really. I was thinking we'd do a silent auction, and take bids for about an hour or so after the runway show while people have cocktails and things. I need you to work with someone to get the programs printed, and organize and make all of the bidding materials. You can hire someone to help you with it if you want, but I can only give you a budget of a couple hundred dollars to do it."

"Oh, that's no problem. I'm good at working within a budget."

"Great. Do you think you could have a mock-up for me to look at by the end of the day tomorrow? I want to take a look at it before it goes to print."

"Sure. I'll have to make some calls, but don't worry. I'll get it done."

"Thank you for doing this on such short notice."

"No, thank *you*. I was really hoping I could still be involved with the revue somehow."

"In case you didn't figure it out, this also means you can have your internship back."

"Really?"

"Yeah," Violet said. "What kind of boss lets a teenage mother work for no pay *and* no college credit?"

"You joke, but I know it's really because you love me," April teased.

When they hung up, Violet realized how much she'd missed April in the weeks she'd been away. Not just her head for numbers and way with technology, but also her friendship.

On Wednesday, the day before the revue, the store was busier than usual. The line for the checkout counter stretched from wall to wall, with people waiting to purchase outfits to wear to the show. Violet should have been ecstatic about the constant stream of sales, but she felt on edge as she stood behind the counter ringing up customers. Every time she saw a male figure on the sidewalk outside, her heart pounded and her body froze. The police still hadn't found Jed, and as the days went by, she was starting to lose hope that they ever would.

As Violet rang up customers' purchases, she reminded them to come to the show and bring a friend or two. When the line finally died down, she noticed a blond boy she didn't recognize standing inside the doorway of the store, shifting his feet in his leather flip-flops. He looked no older than twenty-one or twenty-two.

Violet walked over to him. "May I help you with something?"

The boy gave her an apologetic smile and said, "My name's Charlie Cabot. I'm actually looking for April."

Violet surveyed his pastel polo shirt, crisp khaki shorts, and tanned skin. The only way he could have looked more like the picture she had of him in her imagination would have been if he were carrying a tennis racket.

"April's not here right now." Violet wasn't sure how much to reveal to him. She knew that if her own ex showed up at her workplace asking questions about her whereabouts, she wouldn't want him to walk away with any information. Unfortunately, Jed knew all too well where Violet worked.

"When do you expect her in next?" Charlie asked.

"I'm sorry, I can't tell you that." Violet thought quickly for an excuse. "It's our store policy not to give out employees' personal information." She figured it wasn't exactly a lie. It was a good idea and probably a policy she should implement.

"Can I maybe talk to you about something?" he asked.

"Sure, let's have a seat."

They sat down in the orange lounge chairs, and Charlie leaned forward and put his elbows on his knees.

"I don't know how much April told you, but I guess you probably think I'm a pretty shitty human being," he said.

Violet didn't say anything, so Charlie continued. "I know I am. I made a mistake. I let my parents make my decisions for me instead of doing what I knew was right—and what I wanted to do."

Violet leaned back in her chair. "Why are you telling me this? You should tell April."

"I've tried. I've been calling her and e-mailing her all summer, but she's been shutting me out. I even went to her house once and rang the doorbell, but no one answered, and I felt kind of stalker-ish just lurking outside her door, so I left. My aunt told me April was working here. I guess she came here when she was in town for my graduation party."

"It sounds like April doesn't want to talk to you, though." Violet had just met Charlie, but she could tell from the look on his face that he was hurting.

"That's why I need your help," Charlie said. "I just need to talk to her once, so I can tell her I want to be with her and the baby. If, after I've had a chance to apologize, she still doesn't want to be with me, then fine. I'll back off, and maybe we can work something out so I can have time with the baby. But I need to at least try to get her back. I won't be able to live with myself if I don't give it a shot."

"That's no small feat. Especially since she won't even talk to you."

"I know," said Charlie. "But I'm up for it."

The earnestness in Charlie's eyes dissipated some of the distrust Violet had been feeling.

"Do you think you can help me?" he asked.

"How?"

"Well, since she won't pick up her phone or return my e-mails, it has to be something big. Something really special, like in the movies. You know, like in *Once,* when that guy buys his girl a piano. Or in *Love Actually* when that British dude learns Portuguese so he can ask his housekeeper to marry him."

"You've seen *Love Actually*?"

Charlie's face turned red. "April made me watch it."

"Well, I don't have any connections to people who can teach you Portuguese, sorry," Violet said. "And I don't think April knows how to play the piano."

"It doesn't have to be *that,* exactly. It just needs to be something she would love, something that would surprise her."

"Like what?"

"I don't know. See, that's where I need you. I'm a science guy. I'm no good at creative stuff."

Violet knew April and Charlie's relationship, or lack thereof, was none of her business. She also knew that April had guarded herself against him for the last few months and that his efforts would probably be rebuffed. Still, she'd always been a romantic, and she knew how hard it was to find someone to care for, someone to count on. If April and Charlie had even a chance at achieving that, she wanted to help.

"Well," she said, "give me a few days to think about it. The store is putting on a big fashion show in a few days, so I probably won't be able to get back to you until after that. I'll try to come up with a few ideas to give you a place to start, but it still needs to be your thing. You're the one who needs to win her over, not me. And if your plan flops, I don't want to be blamed for it."

"I won't, don't worry," he said. "Hey, the show you're talking about, is that the one I keep seeing posters for? The Hourglass Revue?"

As soon as she mentioned it, Violet felt a pang of regret. She knew what Charlie was thinking—that April would be there. Now he would probably show up, with the hopes of seeing her. And Violet wasn't sure April would be happy about that.

Violet didn't know why, but the Majestic Theatre seemed bigger on Thursday evening than it had during the auditions and rehearsals. The stage—framed in gilt and red plasterwork—looked so official, so professional. As the hours crept closer to curtain time, Violet grew more and more anxious, wondering what she had gotten herself into. What if the place was empty? What if she didn't make enough money from the auction even to cover the rental fee for the theater?

As if Violet weren't stressed enough, some of the drag queens and more demanding women in the cast kept coming up to her and asking ridiculous questions like, "Are you sure 'I Believe in Miracles' is the right music for when I walk down the runway?" or "Can I be moved up sooner in the lineup?"

Lane did her best to handle all the cast-related questions, but some of the models' complaints still overflowed to Violet. While Violet ran around making sure that everyone knew where they were supposed to be and what they needed to do, Amithi took care of last-minute wardrobe mishaps backstage.

When April arrived with a box full of programs, Violet felt a wave of relief. "Oh, thank God. Another pair of hands. How were things at the store this afternoon?" She hugged April.

"It was a pretty good afternoon," April said. "We made a ton of sales. Everyone was asking about the revue tonight, and some people were even shopping for outfits to wear to it. I think we're going to have a lot of people."

"I hope so." Violet pulled back. "I was too distracted earlier to notice that you've gotten bigger in the last couple of weeks. In a good way, I mean. I hope I look half as cute as you if I ever get pregnant, which is a big 'if.'"

Violet didn't mention how much she'd been wrestling with that question ever since Sam told her he didn't want kids. She had way too much to worry about with the revue to delve into such a complicated decision, so she'd been trying not to think about it.

"I feel huge, but thanks." April patted her belly. "So what can I do to help?"

"The theater crew set up some tables in the back for the silent auction. Do you think you could arrange all the bidding forms and the raffle stuff?"

"Are the auction items actually going to be on the tables? You know, the clothes and things?"

"Yep," Violet said. "The girls—and queens—have been instructed to bring their wardrobe items back there after they've changed and to place them in the same order they came down the runway. If you could set up some numbered signs or something, so they know where the items are supposed to go, it will make your life easier later, so you don't have to answer a thousand questions."

"Sounds good. What time do the doors open?"

"Eight."

"I'd better get working, then."

As April walked toward the auction tables, Violet noticed that her gait was slower and more deliberate than it had been a few weeks ago. She imagined it was getting difficult for her to move around.

Amithi came rushing up the middle aisle wearing a sari. A round, red bindi sparkled on her forehead. A younger version of herself trailed behind her.

"Violet, I would like you to meet my daughter, Jayana." Amithi gestured toward the girl, who looked to be in her early thirties and had the same dark hair and vivid eyes as Amithi. That was where the similarities ended, though. Jayana wore jeans and a tank top, with no jewelry except for a plain gold wedding band.

"Nice to meet you. My mom talks about you all the time," Jayana said. "I can't believe you got her to help you with this."

"She's a talented seamstress," Violet said. "I couldn't have gotten all the clothing ready for the show without her."

"I guess I just never pictured my mom sewing drag queens into their bustiers." Jayana turned to Violet. "I don't get it. My mom freaked out about me not wanting an Indian wedding, but she has no problem with gender ambiguity."

"They are nice people, those drag queens. They make me laugh." Amithi's smile lit up her whole face, so that the red circle on her forehead was the rising sun and her cheeks were round hills bathed in pink light.

"I haven't seen you in a sari since the day you first came into the shop," Violet said.

"I couldn't imagine a big event like this without one."

"How are things going backstage?"

Amithi's face turned serious. "Fine, but have you seen the man who is supposed to be running the lights and the sound system? Shouldn't there be some kind of testing going on?"

"What?" Violet felt panic rise in her chest. "The tech guy should have been here hours ago. He's not backstage?"

Amithi shook her head. "I thought he would be out here."

Violet balled up her fists. "Fuck." Then she realized that the elegant and composed Amithi would never say such a thing and added, "Sorry."

"No, you're right," Amithi said. "Fuck."

Jayana giggled, then said, "I know it's not funny, but it's just that I've never heard my mom swear. Okay, so what can we do? Do you have the tech guy's number?"

Violet dug her phone out of the pocket of her red, bubble-hemmed dress—something she'd found in the store's collection of 1980s prom dresses. Amithi had added the pockets for her. "I'll call him," she said. "But we only have forty-five minutes before the doors open, and an hour and fifteen before the curtain goes up. We need a backup plan in case he can't get here. Do you know anybody else who knows how to do sound and lights for a theater?"

Jayana and Amithi stared back at her with blank expressions.

"Maybe Lane knows someone," Amithi said.

"Good idea. Will you go talk to her while I make this call? And, Jayana, see that blond girl over by the tables?" Violet pointed at April.

Jayana nodded.

"Would you go ask her if she's seen the tech guy and, if not, if she knows anyone who can help us out?"

"Sure."

While Jayana hurried over to April, Violet dialed the number she had for the guy she'd hired to do the sound and lights. As the phone rang and rang, she chided herself for not having gone with the theater's recommendation of whom to use. Instead, she'd hired a student to save a few bucks. She should have known that, like buying a vintage Burberry trench coat, sometimes it was better to spend a little more for the real deal.

Violet left an angry voice mail for the student. She stuck her phone back in her pocket and saw Lane, looking glamorous in a black shift dress, running across the stage. Her silver flats tapped against the wood floors, and to Violet's amazement, she jumped off the stage's edge instead of taking the stairs.

"You needed me for something?" Lane stood in front of Violet, breathless.

"Doesn't that kill your knees?" Violet asked.

"Nah, I spend my days chasing after three little boys. They keep me pretty limber. What's going on?"

"The tech guy isn't here. I know, I know. I should have hired the professional that the theater manager recommended but I was a cheapskate and now I'm screwed because the student I hired hasn't shown up and he isn't answering his phone. Do you know anyone from your theater contacts who can run the lights and sound board?"

"It's been so long. I honestly don't remember any names." Lane crossed her arms and appeared to think about it. "I used to know how to do the tech stuff, but it's been years—I mean, decades."

Violet perked up. "What?"

"When I was in the drama club in high school, I dated our stage manager. We used to, uh, hang out in the sound booth." Lane blushed. "Anyway, I got him to show me how to work the sound and lights. I was curious."

"That is so badass," Violet said. "I've never seen a woman manning—or, sorry, operating a sound board."

"I wanted to know everything there was to know about theater."

"Do you think you can still do it?"

"I don't know. I'm sure a lot has changed, technology-wise, since back then. I don't know if I'd be able to figure it out."

"Okay." Violet went into director mode. "Lane, you go find the theater manager and ask him to show you the sound and light equipment. Take a look at it and see if you're comfortable with it. Also ask him if he knows anyone else he can call at the last minute."

"Okay."

As Lane ran off in her shiny shoes, Violet's phone rang. She answered right away, hoping it was the tech guy calling her back. "Hello?"

"Is this Violet Turner?" asked a man's voice.

"Yes."

"Violet, this is Officer O'Malley. We met at your store a couple of days ago."

"Yes?" Violet gripped the phone with an unsteady hand. "Did you find Jed?"

"We received word from police in northern Wisconsin that they located the suspect and he's being held on probable cause to arrest."

"Really? Where did they find him?"

"He was picked up at a gas station twenty miles from Bent Creek. Must have been making his way back home."

"So what happens now?" she asked.

"He's at the police station up there. The DA's office here in Madison will need to get him transported back here before we can pursue a criminal complaint locally. So we need to know if you want to press charges."

"What happens if I don't?" she asked.

"Well, without testimony or a statement from you, as the property owner, it would be pretty hard for the DA to make a winnable case, so he'd probably drop it."

As Violet listened to the officer explain the process, conflicting concerns battled in her brain. She was glad Jed had been caught. She wanted him to be held accountable for what he'd done, but she also didn't want him anywhere near Madison ever again.

"Would he have to go to jail?" Violet asked.

"Possibly. Vandalism convictions range from just a misdemeanor and a fine to a felony conviction with a prison sentence. It all depends on what the DA's office charges him with and what they're able to prove. And you can bet your insurance company or your landlord's insurance will go after him with a subrogation lawsuit, too, to recover any money they'll be paying out in claims to get the property repaired."

"Do you need an answer from me right this minute? I'm kind of in the middle of something I can't get away from."

"You can think about it for a few hours or so, but don't wait too long. Without any direction from the DA, the police in Bent Creek won't be able to justify holding the suspect much longer than over-night." He gave her the number of one of the assistant district attor-neys so she could call when she'd made up her mind.

Violet thanked him and hung up. Before she could think about what the officer had said, Lane returned. Violet didn't have time to explain what was going on with the police, so she tried to look as nonchalant as was possible with less than an hour left before the show.

"I have good news and bad news," Lane said. "The bad news is that the theater manager called a couple of people and no one can do the tech stuff on such short notice. The good news, though, is that he showed me the sound board and it's pretty old. It actually looks similar to what I used in high school. There are a few differences, of course, but I think I can figure out the basics."

Violet looked at her watch—she'd chosen to wear her leather-strapped, 1950s Wyler because it looked so serious and official with its large gold numerals. It was quarter to eight. Apparently tonight was a night for quick decisions.

"Okay, Lane, barring any last-minute appearance from our tech guy, I think you're it," she said. "Get in there and run some tests. We don't need anything fancy. We just need the microphones on and the spotlights functioning so the audience can see our models and, more importantly, their clothes."

"I think I can do that."

"I'm gonna need a better answer than that."

"Okay, I know I can do it. If there's anything I've learned from theater and motherhood, it's that I can improvise."

As Lane headed toward the sound booth, Violet climbed the stairs to the stage and poked her head through the curtain. A flurry of models and clothes swirled around backstage, and a pungent cloud of hairspray lingered in the air.

"Less than forty-five minutes 'til curtain," she said. "How are we doing back here?"

Amithi looked up from sewing a button onto a blouse.

"Everything under control?" Violet asked.

Amithi took a safety pin out of the corner of her mouth. "Yes. Just a few final adjustments."

A thin, panicked model wandered over to Amithi. "Do you think you can fix my dress?" she asked. A broken spaghetti strap dangled from the bodice of the black, 1930s trumpet gown the girl was wearing. She had to hold the dress with crisscrossed arms to keep it from falling down.

"Sure," Amithi said. "Hold still, please."

Violet saw Jayana sitting in a nearby chair, looking like an outsider amidst the hustle of activity around her. When she noticed

Violet looking at her, Jayana said, "I wish I could sew. Or do hair or something so I could be helpful."

"I tried to teach you, all those years ago," Amithi said. "But you swore you'd never need to know how."

"Yeah, when I was a kid, sewing seemed so antifeminist, so *retro*." Jayana made a face.

"Who's calling who antifeminist?" A black-haired model with nose and lip piercings, wearing nothing but frilly underwear and a pointy bra, turned to Jayana with her hands on her hips. "You say 'retro' like it's a bad thing."

"Yeah, what's wrong with retro?" Violet asked, realizing that she should be insulted. This show—really, her entire career—was all *about* retro.

Jayana turned pink as she tried to recover from her blunder. "Oh, you know what I mean."

"No," Amithi said. "We don't."

"Well, it's just—well, when I was kid, sewing seemed to be such women's work. Now it's getting cool again."

"Maybe it always *was* cool, and you just didn't realize it." Amithi snipped the thread she was working with and tied it off.

Chapter 20

INVENTORY ITEM: *cocktail dress*

APPROXIMATE DATE: *1960s*

CONDITION: *excellent*

ITEM DESCRIPTION: *Gold micromini dress with long sleeves.*

SOURCE: *estate sale*

April

"LADIES AND GENTLEMEN AND everyone in between, welcome to the Hourglass Revue."

April stood behind one of the auction tables in the back of the theater and watched the busty and big-haired Ivanna Martini take to the microphone, gripping it with a white-gloved hand.

"We have a lovely show for you this evening featuring rare and beautiful clothing and accessories from Hourglass Vintage. All of the items you'll see onstage tonight are for sale—well, except me, of course, but if you happen to be a millionaire, then maybe we can talk later." Ivanna batted her fake eyelashes and shimmied her hips in her blue sequined gown. "Any millionaires out there?"

The audience laughed.

"You'll do." Ivanna pointed at Betsy Barrett, who was sitting in the front row. "I'm not opposed to a sugar mama, you know. I'm a modern girl."

April panicked for a moment, hoping Betsy wasn't embarrassed. Though she knew Betsy often spoke her mind and even swore, she was also a well-respected philanthropist in the community and might not appreciate being hit on by a drag queen.

To April's great relief, Betsy blew a kiss to Ivanna Martini, who pretended to catch it and hold it to her heart. "Other than yours truly, everything you'll see on the runway tonight is listed in your catalog along with the starting bidding price, in order of appearance," said Ivanna. "If you see something you like, you can bid on it during the silent-auction part of the evening immediately following the show. There will also be a raffle for a very special item. My friend Amanda is going to come out here to show it to you."

A long-legged queen in a gold minidress traipsed onto the stage with the boutique's prized Hermès bag slung over her arm. The purse's buckles gleamed under the stage lights.

"Ladies and gentlemen," Ivanna said, "give a big warm welcome to Amanda Reckenwith."

The audience clapped and murmured to one another.

"Remember," said Ivanna, "the more tickets you buy, the more chances you have of winning this fabulous handbag. But let's get on with the runway show, shall we? Please sit back and open your minds, open your hearts, and, most importantly, open your wallets. Enjoy the show!"

The music started—Lena Horne sampled with a hip-hop beat—and a woman pranced across the stage in a coral-colored 1940s suit by Elsa Schiaparelli. The jacket had a nipped-in waist that flattered the model's hourglass shape. She unbuttoned the military-style buttons and took off the jacket to reveal a matching silk shell and arms inked with colorful tattoos. April happened to know that the suit was quite rare and valuable. She'd written a little bit about its history in the program: A customer had found it in her Italian grandmother's basement. The grandmother had bought it on a trip to New York during the war years. It had been a splurge, but she'd been so thrilled to see an Italian designer making it big in New York that she just had to own something made by Schiaparelli. She'd offered to give the outfit to her granddaughter, but the tiny suit didn't fit the girl's figure without the bondage of heavy-duty undergarments. Instead, grandmother and granddaughter had come into the store together and sold it. With the money, they'd driven down to Chicago to view Italian paintings at the Art Institute and have a fancy lunch together at the Drake Hotel.

Before starting her internship, April didn't even know who Elsa Schiaparelli was. In the short time she'd been working at Hourglass Vintage, April had learned so much from Violet—how to tell if a designer garment was authentic or fake, how to tie a silk scarf, how to remove stains from vintage fabric with a Q-tip and dish soap. Most of all, she'd learned that just because something wasn't perfect didn't mean it wasn't valuable.

A new model appeared onstage, this one wearing a pink 1950s dress with a frilly skirt that stood nearly straight out from her hips, supported by layers upon layers of crinoline. She wore a white mink stole over her shoulders and smiled at the audience with painted red lips.

As the show continued, every ensemble was more elaborate, more breathtaking than the last. When the final model on the program—a dark-skinned drag queen wearing a silver one-piece pantsuit with a halter neck—strutted onto the stage, the audience cheered. Amithi, looking demure in her silk sari, stood up and yelled. Even Sam, who looked a little out of place among the dressed-up crowd in his plaid shirt and jeans, got out of his seat and whistled.

April straightened out the bid forms and made sure there were plenty of pens, preparing herself for the rush of people she hoped would make their way to the silent-auction tables as soon as the curtain closed. Just when she was about to sit down, she heard an announcement from the stage.

"In just a few moments, ladies and gentlemen, the bidding will start for all the wonderful auction items you've seen in your catalog and onstage. But please sit tight. We have one more special guest for you this evening." Ivanna left the stage to blaring disco music.

A blond drag queen appeared on the runway dressed in a nurse's outfit, complete with thigh-high white patent boots and a hat with a sparkly red cross. She grabbed the microphone from its stand. "Ladies and gentlemen, I am here tonight as the assistant and humble servant to a very important doctor. His name is Doctor Love. Let's give him a warm welcome so he'll come out and show us his bedside manner." The nurse held her thin, muscular arms in the air and the audience cheered.

April looked toward the stage wings to see if she could catch a glimpse of Violet's expression. Was this planned? It wasn't in the program. Then again, April had missed the dress rehearsal, so they could have gone over it then. With the bright lights, she couldn't see Violet's face clearly.

"Would you all like the good Doctor Love to pay us a house call?" the nurse yelled.

April didn't know what to do. Had the queens gotten out of control? Taken the show in a different direction? For all she knew, Doctor Love might be a stripper.

As the audience grew louder, April closed her eyes, afraid to see what might come next. She heard the nurse say, "Well, hello, handsome doctor. Will you be performing any examinations today?"

The audience laughed and April opened her eyes.

Onstage, in a white lab coat trimmed with silver sequins, stood Charlie.

April felt light-headed and dropped into one of the chairs behind the auction tables. How did Charlie get onstage?

"Sorry, nurse," he said. "I won't be performing any examinations today. But I do have an important operation to do."

"Oh?" The nurse batted her fake, glitter-crusted eyelashes.

"I botched something up and I need to fix it."

April felt the baby moving around in her belly like an acrobat.

"What, did you sew a scalpel inside someone's chest? Amputate the wrong . . . appendage?" The nurse grabbed the air right in front of Charlie's crotch.

Charlie blushed as red as the cross on the nurse's hat. "No," he said. "All appendages that are supposed to be intact are intact."

The nurse wiped her hand across her forehead in mock relief. "Whew. Because that would be a shame, doctor. A real shame." She shifted her weight from one platform boot to the other and put a long-nailed hand on her hip. "So what is it, Doctor Love? What did you come here to do?"

"I came here to let my girlfriend know—well, my ex-girlfriend— that I'm sorry for what I did. I've been a real jerk. And a coward."

The nurse wagged a finger. "Oh, Doctor Love, here at the Hour-glass Revue we don't tolerate that sort of thing, do we?"

The audience booed at Charlie, who held up his hands. "I know I deserve it," he said. "I made a mistake. And now I need to make it right."

April couldn't believe that Charlie Cabot, who'd practically been raised at his parents' country club, was standing onstage with a drag queen. For her.

"Is your ex out there in the audience today?" The nurse put her hand over her eyes like she was giving a sailor's salute and looked from side to side.

"Yeah, but I don't want to embarrass her. She knows who she is."

The audience groaned. They'd clearly been hoping for some on-stage drama.

April felt relieved. She wasn't yet sure how she felt about this routine.

"So what do you need to tell her, Doctor Love?" the nurse asked.

Charlie stood with his shoulders square to the crowd and said, "I'm sorry. I'm sorry that we fought and even sorrier that I canceled the wedding without talking to you about it. I will never, ever hurt you like that again."

People in the audience murmured to one another, and April bit her lip to keep from crying. She didn't want to draw attention to herself. And anyway, she still couldn't decide if she was flattered or pissed off.

"Doctor, you've been a bad boy, haven't you? I think you need a spanking," the nurse shouted. "Does everyone else think he needs a spanking?"

The crowd cheered. The nurse stood behind Charlie and whacked his butt several times. The audience laughed, and Charlie's face flamed.

April smiled in spite of her shock. Just as she'd done penance for Violet by dropping off a plastic goose at her door, Charlie was doing penance for her in a very public way. And she had to admit it was funny, though painful to watch.

"That's fair," Charlie said when the spanking stopped. "I absolutely deserved that."

"Oh, I'm not done with you yet," the nurse said. She leaned in again and pinched his behind. "A pinch to grow an inch. Or eight or ten, if your girl is lucky." She flung back her head, showing her Adam's apple, and let out a throaty laugh. The audience joined in. "So is there anything else you want to say to your ex?"

"Just one more thing." Charlie stuck his hands in the pockets of his lab coat. "I got in off the wait list at UW."

April gasped. A few people in the back row turned around to look at her, and they nudged one another at the realization that she was the girl Doctor Love was talking about.

From onstage, Charlie continued. "I'm staying here in Madison with the hopes that someday, maybe not today—and that's understandable—but someday maybe you'll take me back and we can be together." He pulled a hand out of his pocket and held up a tiny object that shone under the spotlights. "I got a ring this time. It's yours if you want it."

The audience oohed and clapped. Everyone squirmed and looked around for the girl on the other end of the proposal. The people in the back row who'd noticed her before turned and looked but didn't say anything.

"Where is she?" the nurse said into the microphone. "Come on up here, girl. We want to see you."

"No," Charlie said. "Only if she wants to. Like I said, I don't want to embarrass her. I just want her to know how much she means to me."

"Oh, pooh," said the nurse. "Get her up here. Come on, audience, help me out. We want the girl! We want the girl!"

The audience chanted along, stomping and clapping. Now not just the back row but the last eight or ten rows had figured out April's identity and twisted around in their seats to stare at her. Part of her wanted to run up there and throw her arms around Charlie. She'd missed him so much, and she really wanted to believe that he had changed his mind. But her cautious, protective side held her back.

The crowd's chant grew louder. April saw Amithi hurrying toward her up the side aisle, as fast as her tightly wrapped sari would let her go. Amithi leaned over the auction table and put her soft, small hands on either side of April's cheeks.

"How are you doing, dear?" she asked. "Violet asked me to come back here and check on you. She was worried this might be too stressful for you."

"Oh, I'm doing fine." April brushed a tear from her cheek after Amithi took her hands away. "Just really surprised. Charlie was the last person I expected to see onstage."

"You don't have to go to him if you don't want to," Amithi said. "I can take you out of here and we can go somewhere quiet to talk."

April shook her head. "I want to be here to work the auction. I've been looking forward to it." She also looked forward to adding up all the cash after the show and, hopefully, figuring out how much they'd made in profit. It wasn't every day she got to play around with numbers and calculations in such a tangible way.

"Well, we can leave for just a few minutes if you'd like, until the curtain closes," Amithi said.

April peered up at the stage, where Charlie stood looking forlorn.

The nurse yelled, "Have you no heart, girl? Look at this man. He's put himself through all of this for you. Come on up here and show him some love."

Amithi studied April's face in the dark. "You want to go, don't you? Maybe just a little bit?"

"Maybe a little," April whispered. "But I'm afraid of what will happen if I do. I think he really cares for me, but how can I be sure? We've hurt each other so much."

Amithi put her hand on April's arm. "You remind me a little of myself long ago. I was young, like you, when I got married."

April had overheard Amithi talking to Violet at the store about her marital troubles. "Yeah, but he—"

"My husband broke my heart, yes. There is always that chance, with love. But to not even try—well, you might as well just not live, because nothing is certain. Sometimes you just have to take a chance."

It was what April's mother used to say.

She turned her eyes again to Charlie, standing onstage in his glittery lab coat, something he wouldn't have been caught dead in if he didn't think it would amuse her. She was pretty sure his mother, ever appropriate, would die if she could see her son now, getting harassed by a slutty nurse for April's sake.

She got up, and although it usually took some effort to raise her pregnant belly out of a chair, she felt light. She made her way up the aisle toward the stage and broke into a clumsy run for the last few steps, being careful not to trip over the folds of the vintage maxidress she was wearing.

Charlie saw her and ran down the staircase from the stage to throw his arms around her. They kissed, and April felt as if no time had passed since their last kiss—it was warm, familiar. He was the same Charlie, still smelling of Ivory soap.

She realized she must have looked quite different to him, though, because he put his hand on her bulging stomach and looked into her eyes with wonderment.

"That's our baby," she said.

"Do you know if it's a boy or a girl?" he asked.

She shook her head. "Not yet."

"Good. I want to be there when you find out. I want to be there for everything."

"I'm not sure yet about the ring," April said. "I still need some time to think about getting married and all of that. I don't want to rush into things this time."

"It's okay. Take as much time as you need. I'm so sorry, April. I never should have said that stuff about your mom, and you. You're not crazy, and even if you were, I'd love you anyway."

"I might be someday," April said. "Time will tell."

"I won't let that happen if I can help it." Charlie looked down at his shiny lab coat. "Anyway, who's the crazy one now? I'm standing here with a drag queen, pouring my heart out in front of a few hundred people."

April laughed, choking back tears. "I'm sorry, too. Some of the things I said were terrible."

"Yeah, but what I said was worse. And I never should have canceled the wedding. I was upset about our fight, and I let my parents pressure me into it. It seemed like the right thing for about a second, but I realized pretty quickly that it was a huge mistake. That's why I've been trying to get in touch with you. My mom was the one who sent out the cancellations. I didn't know until after the fact that they'd gone out, and I hate that I was too big of a wimp to do anything about it until now."

Above them on the stage, the nurse said, "Okay, okay. You've had your little moment. Now get up here so the rest of us can see you."

Charlie took April's hand and helped her climb the stairs. When they reached the top, the audience cheered.

"Well, there you go, ladies and gentlemen," said the nurse. "Happy endings aren't just for fairy tales and massage parlors."

April felt her body radiating heat, from the excitement and the burn of the spotlights.

It only took the nurse a moment to figure out that April was pregnant. "Oh, Doctor Love," she said. "You're lucky you made the right choice, because if you hadn't, me and the other queens would have run you out of town and kicked your skinny little ass with our high heels."

"I know I'm lucky." Charlie gripped April's hand like it was his lifeline. "And I won't forget it again."

Chapter 21

INVENTORY ITEM: *dress*

APPROXIMATE DATE: *1982*

CONDITION: *excellent*

ITEM DESCRIPTION: *Red silk taffeta dress with bubble hem and ruffled neckline.*

SOURCE: *Ragstock store on State Street*

Violet

VIOLET TAPPED HER STOCKING feet on the floor as April counted the stack of money for the second time. Both of them had kicked off their shoes and now sat, still in their dress clothes, at a table in the back of the theater.

April set down the last few bills on the table, moving her lips as she counted.

"So?" Violet said. She stuck her hands into the pockets of her red dress to keep from picking at her fingernails, a nervous habit.

"Same as last time. I told you, I don't miscount."

A knot of disappointment settled into Violet's stomach. "I was hoping you did just this once."

"It's still a ton of money," April said. "The raffle was a big hit."

"Yeah, but it's not nearly enough for a down payment on a million-dollar building," Violet said. Perhaps she'd been naïve, she thought, in hoping she could make enough money in one night to solve all of her problems.

"Did I tell you I ran into Karen and Tom?" April asked. "They were looking for you after the show."

"No, I didn't know they were here."

"I tried to find you. Karen said they had to get home to relieve their babysitter but told me to tell you congratulations on the show."

Violet thought about what Karen had said to her when she first told her about the eviction—that maybe she should consider taking the Mortensens' settlement offer. Karen had probably been right when she said that accepting the offer would be the least risky option. But Violet had learned from experience that some risks were worth taking. She'd settled once before, back when she was young. When she married Jed, she'd loved him, in her own childish way—something she couldn't even fathom now. But she'd let her compulsion to take care of him overshadow her own dreams of going off to college, thinking she couldn't have both. She'd been afraid that if she set her sights too high, if she wanted too much, she surely couldn't succeed, so she never bothered striving.

The thought of Jed brought Violet's mind back around to the question of what to do about the vandalism charges. She hadn't yet told April that the police had found him. She knew April would tell her to go ahead with pressing charges, and Violet needed to make that decision on her own.

"I can't believe you were in on Charlie's surprise appearance tonight," April said.

"I'm good at keeping secrets," Violet said. "*I* can't believe he proposed. I didn't know he was going to do that."

"I'm not sure if I'm going to say yes. I have to give it some time." April zipped the cash into a padded vinyl deposit envelope.

"I helped him pull it off, but it was Charlie's idea, really," Violet said. "As soon as he heard about the show, he asked if he could get onstage for part of it. He thought it was the only way to get through to you, since you weren't taking his calls or anything. I wasn't sure how you'd feel about it, honestly. But he looked so damned sad I had to let him do it. And I thought his whole Doctor Love thing was pretty genius. Not to mention it was sweet that he was willing to make a complete ass out of himself for you." Violet held out her hand. "Here, why don't you give me that deposit envelope? I can drop it off in the bank slot on my way home. I'm sure you and Charlie have a lot to catch up on."

April handed her the zippered case. "Is Sam picking you up? I saw him hanging around after the show."

Violet shook her head. "I told him not to wait for me, since I didn't know how much time it would take to wrap everything up. Besides, we have dinner reservations for tomorrow night, so I'll see him then, anyway."

Not wanting Sam to have to wait for her wasn't the real reason Violet had sent him home. She felt certain that, after everything that had happened with Charlie and April onstage, the topic of the future—and whether she and Sam had one together—would come up. And that was one conversation she couldn't handle tonight, mostly because she wasn't sure what she would say.

"Okay," April said. "Well, if you're sure you don't need me, I'll see you tomorrow at the store." She got up and went out the door, leaving Violet in the empty theater.

After the last few days of surprises and commotion, Violet looked forward to going back to the quiet of her apartment. She still wasn't entirely sure what she was going to tell the DA's office about pressing charges, but she decided that whatever answer she was going to give them could wait until the next morning. As long as she knew Jed was locked up, at least for the next several hours, Violet could get a decent night's sleep in her own bed. *After everything he's done,* she thought, *he owes me at least that much.*

The next morning Violet awoke early with a clear mind. She made coffee and went down to the shop before the sun was even up. The first thing she did was call the number of the assistant DA that the police officer had given to her. The attorney wasn't in the office yet, but Violet left a message saying she wanted to go ahead with the charges against Jed. She'd made too many excuses for him over the years, gotten him out of too many debacles. And her sympathy hadn't helped him at all; in fact, all it had done was hurt *her.*

April came in just before the store opened at ten, looking happy and relaxed.

"I take it you had a good night?" Violet asked.

April nodded. "Charlie and I spent a lot of time talking last night. He wants to get back together right away—well, I'm sure you could tell that from last night. I'm not so sure. I have no doubt he loves me, though, and wants it to work, so that's a step. I need some time to learn how to trust him again before I can decide whether I want to get married."

"You're young. You've got time to figure that out," Violet said. *I, on the other hand, do not have quite as much time,* she thought. She knew she needed to make a decision about Sam and whether she could live with the fact that they'd never have a family together, even if things continued to go well between them.

Violet was well aware that at her age there was no guarantee she'd have an easy time getting pregnant, if that's what she decided she wanted, but there were other options. She could adopt a baby, even if there was no man in the picture. She'd thought about it before. She didn't know what would make her happier, though: having Sam and no baby, or having a baby and no Sam. Until she was able to answer that question, Violet was afraid to spend too much time with him because she knew it would just make the decision harder. She made a mental note to call him later to cancel their date for that night.

The loud sound of plastic flapping in the wind startled Violet out of her thoughts.

"When is your landlord gonna get that broken glass fixed?" April asked, pointing to the window. "I thought they were supposed to take care of it."

"You know what? I'm gonna go down to his office and talk to him," Violet said. Sometimes she felt her own fate was like that tarp, just being tossed around by forces beyond her control. And she was tired of it. "Do you think you can keep an eye on things here for an hour or so while I go down to Ted's office?" Violet asked.

"Yeah, sure," April said. "That's what I'm here for."

When Violet arrived at the offices of Mortensen & Son Inc., the receptionist asked if she had an appointment.

"No," Violet said. "But I have some information pertinent to the sale for the new condo development. On Johnson Street?"

The receptionist picked up the phone and, after a hushed conversation, showed Violet into Ted's office.

"Violet," he said when he saw her. "Please have a seat. Are you here to talk about the offer we made?"

"No, I'm here to talk about when you're going to fix the window. I know you're planning to sell the building to a development firm, and I know someone with connections to its president," she said. "He'd probably be interested to know that you're neglecting repairs that, ultimately, will affect the value of the building."

"Right." Ted cleared his throat. "About that. See, I've talked some more with our insurance company, and given that the developer is planning to demolish the building, the insurer doesn't think it's worth it to make those repairs. Especially since we're just a few weeks away from securing an eviction order from the court, assuming you don't move out voluntarily before then."

"Wait, I thought the condo project was supposed to be a rehab, not a demolition," Violet said.

"Plans have changed."

"So you're just planning on letting the store keep on operating out of a building with plywood and plastic covering the windows."

"You're welcome to pay for the repairs yourself, though I hardly think it's worth it," Ted said. He folded his hands and placed them on top of his desk. "The offer still stands for you to move out voluntarily without a court order."

"I need to speak with my lawyer," Violet said.

She returned to Hourglass Vintage, seething. It must have shown on her face because April said, "I take it the conversation didn't go well."

"They're not fixing anything," Violet said. "The developer who's set to buy the building as soon as we're out of here has got a wrecking ball in the works. I wish I could tell everybody to fuck off and just buy the building out from under the developer. But we both know I don't have the money for that."

April shook her head. "How can this possibly all be legal?"

"I've gotta call Karen, but she already looked at all the paperwork a couple months ago and pretty much said we were screwed. That the most she could do was buy me a little bit of time to come up with some money to have a shot at buying the place. But that's not happening. I can't believe I even thought it was a possibility. We didn't make enough from the revue to even come close. And there's nothing for rent in the neighborhood that would work as another shop space."

April's eyes grew wide and she let out a little gasp.

"What?" Violet said. "Is it the baby? Do you need me to take you to the hospital?"

April shook her head and grabbed a piece of paper. She wrote down some numbers, biting her lip.

"What are you doing?" Violet asked. "You're freaking me out."

"Just a second—let me think." April scribbled some more on the paper, then picked it up and held it in the air.

"Did you just figure out the secret to time travel or something? Can we go back in time to before any of this eviction stuff started?"

"Not quite." April tilted her head to one side. "But what if you bought my mom's house? I'm not asking anywhere near as much as your landlord is for this place."

"Seriously?" Violet thought about the green stucco bungalow just a block down the street. "You'd be willing to sell it to me?"

"Why not? Dozens of people have looked at it, but not a single one has made an offer, even after the Realtor convinced me to drop the price. The way the neighborhood has shifted, with so many restaurants and retail stores now, a lot of people have said the street is too busy. Or that the house needs too much updating."

"Is it even possible—I mean, would the city allow the house to be used as a retail store?"

April nodded. "I know it's possible because my mom looked into turning it into commercial space when she was thinking about starting her organization company. There are plenty of other businesses in the neighborhood that operate out of houses. There's that spa and salon in the blue Victorian on the other side of the street. And there's that sushi restaurant in the white farmhouse on the corner. I can't believe I didn't think of this option before."

"Are you sure you'd be okay with selling it to me, though?" Violet softened her voice. "I know the place holds a lot of memories for you."

"You'd be doing me a favor, actually. I'm pretty eager to get it sold before the baby comes and school starts." April pushed the pencil and paper aside. "Anyway, no pressure or anything. It's just an idea."

Violet thought aloud. "The house is in a great location, probably even better than this one. It's right next to the grocery co-op, so it would get a ton of foot traffic." She pictured hanging her shop sign above the double French doors of the bungalow and putting Adirondack chairs on the front porch so that customers could hang out and linger awhile.

They were silent for a moment, letting the idea take shape.

"How do you think your mom would feel about it?" Violet asked.

"I think it would honor her memory, actually. She always had an entrepreneurial spirit." April gave her a shy smile. "And besides, this is the closest thing I can think of to keeping the house in the family."

Chapter 22

INVENTORY ITEM: *apron*

APPROXIMATE DATE: *1950s*

CONDITION: *fair*

ITEM DESCRIPTION: *Blue cotton apron with a daisy print, somewhat faded.*

SOURCE: *VFW flea market*

Amithi

AMITHI PUSHED THROUGH THE door of Hourglass Vintage, clutching a small shopping bag.

Inside the store, Violet was packing vintage gowns into a plastic crate between layers of acid-free paper. When she saw Amithi, she set aside the container and wiped her hands on her ruffled apron. "Hello there, stranger," she said. "I haven't seen you since the revue. You look great."

Amithi glanced down at the paisley Indian blouse she'd paired with loose linen pants, wedge sandals, and a turquoise necklace. After years of worrying about what to wear and when, she felt like she'd finally settled on a style that was neither fully Indian nor fully American; rather, it was hers.

"Thank you," Amithi said, setting the shopping bag on the counter. "What are you doing with all the boxes?" She gestured around to the moving crates piled everywhere.

"I'm buying April's mother's house," Violet said. "She was having a tough time selling it because it needs some work, but that's what makes it affordable for me. Well, that and the fact that she cut me a good deal. But anyway, some of the quirky stuff that bothered other buyers, like the short door frames or the fact that the kitchen and bathrooms haven't been updated since the 1950s—well, that stuff just gives it more character, in my opinion."

"Congratulations, that is wonderful news," Amithi said. "And how is April? Has she had her baby yet?"

"Not yet. She's actually at the doctor right now. She has to go in every week, now that she's in her final month of pregnancy. But I will be sure to tell you when her son or daughter arrives."

"Speaking of daughters, you will never believe what Jayana asked me," Amithi said. "After she came to the revue, she told me she wanted to learn how to sew."

"Wow. The work you did must have really made an impression on her."

"I said I could give her some lessons, but she came up with a better idea. She said we should go to India together to buy textiles and to visit my family." Amithi grinned. She still could hardly believe Jayana had suggested it. "So we will be making the trip in October. While we are there, my mother, sister, and I will all teach Jayana about sewing. And after I go to India with her, I am thinking I will go somewhere else by myself, too. I have never traveled on my own before, and I think it is time."

"That's wonderful." Violet reached behind her back to untie her apron. She took it off and set it down on the counter. "Where are you thinking of going?"

"I am not sure yet. Oh, I almost forgot." Amithi pulled a stack of business cards from her purse and handed them to Violet.

"'Amithi Singh Custom Tailoring,'" Violet read. Her face lit up. "You're starting your own business? Welcome to the club. Lord knows it's got its ups and downs, but I can tell you that nothing beats being your own boss."

Pride filled Amithi's chest. It was a different sensation than the pride she'd felt for Jayana as a mother, or for Naveen's career successes as a wife. This was a pride in herself, and it felt both unfamiliar and wonderful.

"I've never had a boss," she said. "I've never worked before—well, for money, anyway."

She'd never had to. Even now, Amithi continued to use her and Naveen's joint checking account and credit cards, just as she'd always done. So far, she hadn't encountered any resistance, even though it had been weeks since she'd started staying at Jayana and Jack's condo. Still, just knowing that she *could* earn some money of her own, if she needed to, was a comfort.

"People are constantly asking me if I know of a good tailor," Violet said. "Now I can give them your information." She propped up the stack of Amithi's business cards in front of her cash register.

"And one more thing." Amithi reached into the shopping bag she'd brought with her and held up a pink silk shift dress. "I made a sample dress out of some silk from one of my old saris."

Violet touched a seam along the side. "This is gorgeous. I would wear this."

Amithi beamed. "I started off with a simple design, but I am hoping to learn how to do some more complicated patterns, too."

"Were you bringing this in to sell?" Violet asked.

Amithi shook her head. "Maybe someday I will have a whole line of clothing to sell, but for now I am just experimenting. I suppose I will need to think about finding a space to do all my work. My projects are starting to take over Jayana and Jack's condo. I'm still staying there for now, and I don't think they appreciate my piles of fabric everywhere."

"You know, once I get settled into the new house, maybe I could rent some space to you. There's a lovely sunroom on the second floor that would be perfect for a sewing room. I'll be living on the second floor, too, but I don't need all that space."

"I will have to keep that in mind," Amithi said.

"What does your husband think about all this?"

"It does not matter. Whatever happens with Naveen, the tailoring business was something I had to do. When I was working on the revue, I felt *useful*. I liked that feeling."

Amithi didn't mention the other thing she had realized at the revue, which was that she wasn't ready to forgive Naveen, and she wasn't sure if she ever would be. She'd been glad to see Charlie and April reconnect, but seeing the two of them onstage, so young and full of hope, had only made Amithi angrier with Naveen. From where Amithi stood now, her own youth and the hopefulness she'd once felt just looked like naïveté. April and Charlie had plenty of time to rebuild the trust that had been lost between them. Amithi still had time, too, but less of it. She'd already spent enough years being a wife and mother. It was time to just be herself. First, though, she had to figure out who that was.

Not since she was a little girl had she felt such a sense of possibility, and it both thrilled and terrified her.

August 12, 1956

Six-year-old Amithi stood before the massive Hawa Mahal, gaping. Never had she seen a building so large, so elaborate. It must have had a thousand windows peeking out from its pink façade. She could not believe that this palace existed in the same city where she lived. Why had no one shown it to her before?

Her mother held both Amithi and Priya by the hand. Amithi felt her fingers throbbing, so strong was her mother's grip.

"Ma, you're hurting me," she said.

"All right, but promise me you'll stay close." Her mother released Amithi but kept holding on to Priya, who was still a toddler.

Amithi nodded as they went into the palace. She stayed by her mother's side as they wandered the spacious rooms, each one more opulent than the next. Amithi paused in one of the wide hallways, mesmerized by a rainbow-colored stained glass window. The sunlight coming through the faceted panes made them look like jewels.

"Isn't it beautiful, Ma?" she asked.

She turned to look at her mother, but her mother was no longer there. The mass of tourists snaking through the hallway pressed up against Amithi. She looked in front of her and behind her but recognized no one.

Panicked, she passed through an arched doorway into the next room. This room, too, was crowded. The other visitors towered over her, blocking her view. She followed a narrow corridor, calling for her mother. People passed her but did not stop.

She climbed one staircase, then another, until she reached the top floor, five stories above the ground. She peered out one of the latticed windows, hoping that perhaps she'd be able to see her mother and sister in one of the palace's courtyards below.

Goose bumps prickled her skin as she looked beyond the window. All of Jaipur was laid out before her—turreted temples, vast gardens, and sparkling lakes, with the Aravalli Mountains rising above it all. With so much beauty in front of her, Amithi forgot she was lost.

Chapter 23

INVENTORY ITEM: *suit*

APPROXIMATE DATE: *1999*

CONDITION: *excellent*

ITEM DESCRIPTION: *Skirt and jacket by St. John Sportswear. Royal blue, wool jersey knit with white piping. Like new.*

SOURCE: *Junior League charity auction*

April

CHARLIE CLOSED THE DOOR of the moving truck.

"Want to take one last look around to make sure you didn't forget anything?" he asked.

"I'm sure if I forgot anything, Violet will let me know," April said.

"Yeah, but don't you want to sort of . . . say good-bye?" Charlie squeezed her hand. "It's gonna look a lot different next time you're here."

April nodded and entered her mother's house. She walked through the foyer and into the living room and kitchen, marveling at how big the house looked without anything in it. She climbed the stairs and passed through the bedrooms. Her room, which until a few days ago had been stuffed with eighteen years' worth of clothing, picture frames, and a few favorite dolls saved from childhood, felt like someone else's space. The walls were now painted white and the only object in sight was the heating register. She walked back downstairs, expecting to feel at least a little bit sad that, even though it was being bought by a dear friend, the place would no longer be hers, no longer her mother's. But without the quirky mix of art and furniture, the place didn't feel like her mom's house at all, which made it much easier to shut the door, lock it, and slip the keys in her pocket to bring to the closing later that day.

Charlie stuck out his hand and helped April hoist herself into the truck on the passenger's side. "You sure you don't want to drive this thing?" he asked.

"Driving my mom's car was bad enough after not driving for a year. I think I'll leave the truck driving up to you."

Charlie got in and put the keys in the ignition. Before starting the truck, he asked, "You doing okay?"

April stared out the window at the house. "When we were packing things up, Violet found a note my mom had written herself about checking on some things in her life insurance policy. It looks like you might have been right. That my mom—" She forced herself to say the words. "Killed herself."

Charlie didn't say anything. He scooted over on the bench seat and held April while she wept with the sort of unrestrained, body-quaking grief she could only share with him. He continued to hold her, there in the rental truck, in the driveway of her mother's house, until her breathing slowed.

When April pulled back, she said, "I've been wanting to tell you, but I didn't know when to bring it up. I've been enjoying just being with you again and didn't want to spoil that with more bad news. It seems like, since we met, that's all we've been dealing with. One hard thing after another."

"Really? That's not how I see it at all," Charlie said. "I see it as incredibly lucky that we met. And all the hard stuff—well, every couple has to deal with it sooner or later, right? I figure our relationship has just been sort of front-loaded with a bunch of challenges, so that we've got more of the good times to look forward to."

April nodded. "And we'll be stronger for it."

"Exactly," Charlie said. Then he added, quietly, "I do wish I'd had more time to get to know your mom better, though."

"I wish I'd known her better, too." April wiped her tears with the back of her hand and looked at the house again with clear eyes. Then she thumped the vinyl seat and smiled at Charlie. "Let's go."

They drove half a mile to their new apartment. April had deliberated a lot about whether or not they should live together. Charlie was the one who'd brought it up. His lease with his senior-year roommate was about to end, and he needed to find a new place to live, now that he was going to be attending medical school in Madison. Part of April hesitated, realizing that if things didn't work out with Charlie, living together would make it all the harder to break up a second time. But the truth was that, even if their future was uncertain, she wanted to be with Charlie now, and Lord knew she'd need help when the baby came in just over a month—*if* the kid didn't decide to come early. So they'd signed a lease on a two-bedroom flat on the first floor of an old house that was close to campus and right on the bus line. Charlie still hadn't told his parents, though.

Charlie walked in and out of the apartment with boxes while April sat on the wood floor and unpacked. She unwrapped plates and mugs from wads of newspaper and placed them into the built-in china cabinet. She suspected she had nicer dishes than most eighteen-year-olds. There were large earthenware bowls made by artist friends of her mom, pewter platters from her parents' wedding two decades ago, and etched wineglasses passed down from her maternal grandparents, who had both died when April was little. The china cabinet, with its leaded glass doors, had been one of the selling points of this apartment for April. Even though she and Charlie were only two people and would probably never use a lot of the tableware she'd inherited, it made her feel better about having all of this beautiful stuff if she could at least look at it. This was her way of preempting pity—by putting pieces of her past on display, where they'd be admired, instead of tucked away in a box.

April stopped Charlie, who had an armload of clothes still on hangers.

"We need to tell your parents about us living together," she said.

"I know." He disappeared into the bedroom, then came out with his hands free.

"No, I mean we need to tell them *now*."

"Right now? We only have the moving truck until three, and then I've got to get you to the closing."

"Okay, maybe not this minute, but soon. This week, at least. The baby and I shouldn't be something you have to hide."

Charlie crouched down beside her. "You're not. They already know we're back together."

"Yes, but they haven't seen me since spring, so it's probably not real for them. I bet they're hoping we'll break up any day. In order for this to be real, for them and even for us, it needs to be out in the open. Completely."

Charlie put a hand on the small of her back. "I know you're right. We'll tell them."

"When?"

"I'll call them tonight and set something up."

The next evening, Charlie and April walked hand in hand up the stone walkway to the Cabots' sprawling, Tudor-style house. White rosebushes bloomed on either side of the varnished front door. Charlie rang the bell, and a high-pitched barking sound greeted them from inside.

Judy Cabot cracked the door and said, "Careful for the dogs."

Charlie and April squeezed through the barely open door, which was tough for April with her protruding stomach. As soon as they were over the threshold, two white, hypoallergenic balls of fluff jumped at their ankles. Their tiny claws scratched against April's bare skin—she was wearing a skirt and flip-flops. The shoes, she knew, were probably not up to Judy's standards, but she was eight months pregnant and the thought of stuffing her bulging feet into a pump or even a wedge sandal was not something she could tolerate.

"Oh, my, look at you," Judy said when her eyes landed on April's belly. That was all she said. No knowing glances from one mother to another, no mention of "that glow" so many women told April she had.

"Doesn't she look great?" Charlie said, putting his arm around April's wide waist.

Seeing Judy, April thought immediately of the day she'd gotten the wedding cancellation card in the mail, and the memory still stung. But Charlie's proud smile made her realize how far they'd come as a couple since then, and she had the strength to say, "Hello, Judy."

Charlie gave his mother a terse kiss on the cheek. "Where's Dad?"

"He's on the patio. Come on out."

They followed Judy through the kitchen, where she paused and asked, "Would you care for a gin and tonic? I just made some for your father and me."

"Sure," Charlie said.

April watched in astonishment as Judy mixed her son a drink and didn't bother to offer her anything nonalcoholic, which seemed like an obvious courtesy, given that April was both underage and pregnant with her grandchild. Charlie, thank God, was a little more observant. He walked over to the fridge and opened it.

"Do you want some lemonade, April, or maybe some San Pellegrino?" he asked.

"Lemonade would be great, thanks," she said. While Charlie poured her some, April glanced at Judy, who was squeezing lime into a rocks glass with singular concentration.

Judy took the stirring spoon out of the glass. "There we are. Let's go outside, shall we?"

On the back patio, Trip sat at a table, swirling a near-empty glass and gazing out at his dazzling green, chemically enhanced lawn.

"Hi, Dad." Charlie sat down across from his father and motioned for April to join him.

April grabbed both handles of the low patio chair and eased herself down onto the cushion. All her life she'd taken for granted the ability to get in and out of chairs without trouble.

"Well, hi there," Trip said. "What brings you over tonight?"

April thought it odd that Charlie lived in the same city as his parents but had to have a reason for coming over.

"Oh, just wanted to catch up on some things before school starts, and the baby comes, and things get hectic as all hell," Charlie said.

Judy frowned. "Charlie. Language."

"I'm an adult, Mom. I can say 'hell.' It's not like I said 'fuck.'"

Judy's mouth dropped open. "Charles!"

April elbowed Charlie under the table. They had enough of a challenge in front of them. He didn't need to start early by getting his mother riled up.

"Yep, you've definitely got your work cut out for you," Trip said. "I'm sure medical school is hard enough, without worrying about caring for a child, too."

"I think I can handle it," Charlie said. "April and I are going to share responsibilities for the baby, which is why we've decided to live together."

"Is the engagement back on, then?" Judy asked, not looking pleased.

"Maybe someday," Charlie said. "I hope so. But we've got time to figure that out. For now, we're just going to see how things go."

"'See how things go'?" Judy didn't even try to keep the disapproval out of her voice. "This isn't a high school romance, Charles."

"I'm not in high school anymore," said April. "I'm starting college in a few weeks."

"You're still a *teenager*." Judy crossed her tennis-toned arms in front of her chest. She turned her gaze to her son. "Go ahead and do what you want, Charles. I won't try anymore to talk you out of it. But you're not getting one cent from us."

"Oh, you've made that quite clear already, that I can only have your money if I do things your way. Don't worry. I've already had my student loans approved, so I won't need anything from you."

"Fine." Judy slammed her drink down on the table. The ice cubes clanked around and sloshed some gin and tonic over the side. "Because you haven't shown us that you're responsible enough to make a plan and execute it. First you were getting married, then you weren't. You were set to go to school in Boston, now you're here. We will not finance that sort of bouncing around, will we, Trip?"

"Mmmmm," said her husband.

Now Charlie slammed his drink down. "I have a *plan*. It's the same plan I've wanted since the beginning, to go to school here and be with April and the baby. Just because it's not *your* plan doesn't mean it's not responsible."

"We wanted to tell you because we hope you'll be a part of the baby's life, and ours." April spoke up, even though she was thinking that her life would be a hell of a lot easier if Judy and Trip lived halfway across the country. She knew, though, that it was the right thing to say. Charlie's parents had lived in Madison for over thirty years and they weren't going anywhere, except maybe on the occasional golf trip or Mediterranean cruise.

Judy sighed. "I just wish you'd think things through before making such big decisions, that's all."

"I have thought it through, Mom. And if you're going to keep questioning my judgment, I'm not going to sit here anymore and listen to it."

"I'm sorry, but we just can't watch you ruin your life, can we?" Judy said. She turned to her husband.

Trip fidgeted in his seat. "Er, yes," he said. "I mean no."

April felt a surge of emotion run through her—a river of rage that threatened to spill over in an outburst similar to the one she'd had at the store on the day she stormed out of Hourglass Vintage. She pictured Judy putting botanical stamps on all those cancellation cards, and in particular, the one that was addressed to April.

Charlie jumped to his feet, extending a hand to April to help her out of her chair.

"Where are you going?" Judy asked.

"We're going home," he replied. "I don't have to sit here and take your insults and condescension. I don't *need* you."

That, perhaps, may have been the most hurtful thing Charlie could have said to his mother. April watched Judy's berry-tinted lips turn downward and the fire go out of her eyes. Charlie was an only child, like April (she didn't really count her half siblings in Ohio, whom she barely knew). For him to say he didn't need his mother was to extinguish her purpose in this world. April wasn't fooled by Judy's luncheons and charity events. They were nothing more than a way to fill up her otherwise long days, and an excuse to show off her latest St. John suit. Her true vocation was fretting over her golden-haired son, and without that outlet for her boundless nervous energy, she appeared, all of a sudden, to be lost.

Charlie left his still-full drink on the table. He walked over to his father, patted him on the shoulder, and then went with April into the house.

"I can't believe her," Charlie said as soon as he'd closed the French doors behind them. "I'm just trying to be honest, so that maybe we can get to a point where they're not constantly disapproving of us, but man, she makes it really hard."

"It'll blow over," April said, hoping it was true.

Charlie headed toward the front door. "Let's go."

"Hang on, I have to use the bathroom. Sorry." Being pregnant was a real pain in the ass sometimes.

Charlie looked impatient. "Okay, I'll wait for you out in the car."

April padded through the foyer and let herself into the marble-tiled guest bathroom. On her way out, she almost ran into Trip.

"Oh, good. You haven't left yet," he said.

"We're just about to."

Trip scratched his head of thick, gray hair. "Sorry about all the quarreling."

April shrugged. "It's okay."

He glanced at her midsection and asked, "Are you feeling well? I mean, everything is going all right with the baby?"

April put a protective hand on her belly, remembering her blood pressure scare and the bed rest. "Things were a little rough for a while, but I've been feeling good lately. Thanks for asking."

Trip cleared his throat and continued. "My wife loves Charlie and she means well, but it doesn't always come across that way." He stuck his hand in his pocket and produced a piece of paper, which he pressed into April's hand. She looked down at it and, from the signature line on the back, could see that it was a check.

"Don't tell Judy," Trip said.

April handed the check back to him without looking at the sum written on it. "I can't accept this."

"Please, I feel so terrible about everything. About the way we've handled the"—he cleared his throat and glanced at April's stomach—"situation."

April couldn't take the money, even though it would be nice to start a college fund for the little one. She knew, though, that Charlie would be hurt if she cashed the check, especially after his speech today about not needing his parents anymore. Still, April was touched that Trip wanted to help.

"Please, take it," he said.

April shook her head. "Save it for one of the baby's birthdays or graduation. I hope you'll be there. You and Judy both."

Trip didn't hug her—the Cabots weren't big on physical affection—but he did lock eyes with April for a long moment, and she could have sworn she saw him blink back a tear.

Chapter 24

INVENTORY ITEM: *coat*
APPROXIMATE DATE: *1962*
CONDITION: *good*
ITEM DESCRIPTION: *White cashmere coat with three-quarter-length sleeves. Matching elbow-length kid gloves.*
SOURCE: *Betsy Barrett. Worn to the White House for a luncheon in support of the arts.*

Violet

ON A LATE-AUGUST EVENING, Violet hummed along to a Dolly Parton album as she painted an orange accent wall in her new store. She smiled as she recalled the look on Ted Mortensen's face when she told him she would, after all, be taking his offer to give her two months' worth of rent to sign away her right of first refusal and move out voluntarily—except that she'd demanded six months' rent instead. With Karen's prompting, she'd told Ted that it was a "small amount of money" to avoid the hassle of having to go to court over her lease, when the development firm was so eager to close and get started on its condo project before cold weather set in.

To her surprise, Ted had agreed. Violet used the money, along with her earnings from the Hourglass Revue, as part of her down payment on April's mother's bungalow.

Violet was reaching for a high corner with a paint roller when the phone rang and she nearly fell off her ladder. She climbed down and turned down the music before answering.

"May I please speak with Ms. Violet Turner?" said a woman's voice on the other end.

Violet gripped the curly cord of her rotary phone. "Speaking."

"My name is Ellen and I'm a caseworker at Agrace Hospice. I understand you're a friend of Betsy Barrett?"

"Yes." Violet almost lost her balance. She leaned on the counter. *Hospice? Isn't that for dying people?*

"We're organizing a spiritual service at the chapel here for her, and she asked me to contact you to see if you'd like to be a part of it."

Violet felt a tightness rise in her throat. She didn't want to hear what she feared was next. "Is—is she dead?"

"Oh, no. I'm sorry. I should have made that clear. Mrs. Barrett has been moved to the inpatient unit here at the hospice. Our nursing staff had been treating her at home for a while, but there are lots of limitations on in-home care. Last week she came down with pneumonia, so her nurses recommended that it was time for her to be moved to the inpatient unit, and she agreed."

"But pneumonia's curable, right?" Violet asked.

"For healthy people, yes. It often is. But for a cancer patient, like Mrs. Barrett, whose immune system is compromised . . . well, it's very difficult to recover."

Violet let this information sink in. "But that can't be," she said. "I just saw her a few weeks ago. She came to a fashion auction that our store put on, and she looked fine. Skinny, I guess, but she's always been thin."

"Things can change drastically for someone with a terminal illness, especially at her age."

The words "terminal illness" clattered around inside Violet's head.

"I'm sorry if this is a shock to you," Ellen said. "But please know that the reason I'm calling is that Mrs. Barrett wants to see you. She has asked for a spiritual ceremony, sort of a living memorial to help her prepare for her next journey. She'd like to ask if you're willing to do a reading or a reflection. She would have called herself, but she's been very tired and in and out of sleep all day, so I said I'd take care of it for her."

"Of course I'll do it," Violet said. "Did she have a particular prayer or something in mind?"

"No. Mrs. Barrett wants people to use their creativity to share whatever they feel moved to share. She *did* say she doesn't want anything too religious or preachy. She doesn't want anyone to feel left out if they don't adhere to a particular faith."

"That sounds like Betsy. So when is the ceremony going to be?"

"Tomorrow evening, at our chapel starting at six o'clock. I apologize for the short notice, but here we take things one day at a time, and to be honest I don't know how much longer Mrs. Barrett will be with us. I think she knows it, too, which is why she wants to do this."

"Okay, I'll be there."

Violet hung up the phone and sat down on the drop cloth she'd been using for painting. She didn't cry; she was too shocked.

Amithi came downstairs from where she'd been working on alterations in the sunroom. Violet had been letting her try out the space, to see if she'd like to rent it for her tailoring business when she returned from her travels with Jayana.

Amithi touched Violet's shoulder. "I heard you talking down here and you sounded upset. Is anything wrong?"

"I just found out that Betsy's been admitted to hospice."

"That's terrible." Amithi frowned. "I have only met her a couple of times, but she seems to be a lovely woman. She has done so much for the community."

"Come to think of it, it's been a while since she's come into the store. I should have known something was wrong and checked in on her. She doesn't have anyone—no kids or anything." Violet's stomach churned with guilt. "I need to call April and let her know about the service."

"Wouldn't Betsy have reached out to you if she wanted help?"

"No, she wouldn't. She's too proud. And now it's too late."

"It is not too late. You can still see her, can you not?" Amithi asked.

"She wants me to be a part of a spiritual service they're doing tomorrow. I'm supposed to come up with something to read. I have no idea what to do."

"Does she have a favorite poem? A scripture?"

"She loves music and art and dance," Violet said. "But I'm no ballerina. That requires balance, and I'm barely staying on my feet."

As Violet drove to the hospice facility the next evening, past the new, monochromatic subdivisions on the far southwest side of town, she couldn't help thinking what she could have done differently. She wondered if she should have asked more questions about Betsy's cancer when she'd gone over to her house earlier in the summer. Violet had wanted so badly to believe Betsy when she insisted that she was in remission; maybe she'd missed some important signals that everything was not, after all, fine.

When she arrived, Violet asked the hospice receptionist if she could see Betsy before the service, but the receptionist said no. All guests were to be directed to the chapel.

Violet walked into the dim, candlelit space. The smell of musky incense, sandalwood maybe, permeated the room. What struck her most of all, though, were all the flowers. They weren't the type of fan-shaped, muted arrangements she typically associated with church services. There were armloads of orange, purple, and yellow dahlias the size of dinner plates, towering stems of bright pink gladiolas, bunches of sunflowers that looked like they'd been gathered from someone's garden.

The small space was crowded with guests, even though the ceremony wouldn't start for another twenty minutes. All the seats looked full except for two rows roped off in the front. Several people stood around the perimeter of the room with nowhere to sit.

A woman in a skirt suit came up to Violet. "I'm Ellen," she said. "Are you part of the program tonight?"

"Yes. I think we spoke on the phone. I'm Violet Turner."

"I've reserved some spots for Betsy's honored guests."

"Honored guests?"

"Yes. Follow me."

Ellen moved aside one of the ropes and let Violet into the front row. "The ceremony tonight will be pretty laid-back, so there's no need to be nervous. I'll be directing things up front, and I'll call your name when it's time for you to come up and share. Now, if you'll excuse me, I need to take care of a few last-minute things."

Violet didn't recognize any of the other guests. She wondered if April would be coming. She'd left her a message with information about the service.

A young woman sitting next to Violet turned to her. "How do you know Betsy?" she asked. Violet guessed the girl was about April's age.

"I own a vintage boutique and Betsy has been coming in there for years," Violet replied. "How do you know her?"

"She set up a music scholarship at the university a few years ago, and I got it. The scholarship pays half my tuition for all four years.

Without it, I would have had to take out a bunch of loans that would have taken me forever to pay back." The girl tucked her long hair behind her ears. "Most musicians don't make a ton of money, so it's nice to know I'll have a little more financial freedom when I graduate."

"What do you play?" Violet asked.

"Oh, lots of things, but mostly I love violin and anything with strings." The girl's eyes lit up as she talked about her favorite composers and performers, most of whom Violet had never heard.

Ellen wheeled Betsy into the chapel and positioned her wheelchair next to the front row. Violet was shocked at how frail her friend looked. She'd put on a thick, ethnic-looking wrap sweater for the occasion, but underneath the brightly colored wool, her elbows and waist were all straight lines and sharp angles. One sleeve of the sweater was rolled up to make room for the IV needles taped into her pale flesh. A drip bag hung from a pole on her chair.

Violet waved at Betsy and she smiled back, looking tired. Several people came up to Betsy to say hello, and Ellen allowed them to chat for a moment before shooing them away.

Ellen took the stage and welcomed everyone, explaining that the idea for the night's program had stemmed from a conversation she'd had with Betsy.

"Mrs. Barrett and I were planning her funeral and burial services, and I think she was getting quite frustrated," Ellen said. "After over an hour of discussing flowers and music, she said 'What's the point of personalizing all of this stuff if I'm not even going to be there? The hell with it. Why not have a ceremony while I'm still alive and can see all my friends?' So that is why each of you was invited tonight: because Mrs. Barrett wanted to celebrate her life with you now, while she's here. She wants you to remember her for who she is, and not 'as some body in a casket, pumped full of chemicals.'" Ellen smiled. "Those are her words, not mine."

The audience laughed with some hesitation.

The program that followed was a testament to things that Betsy loved and the lives she'd touched. A jazz trio performed a medley of swing tunes that got everyone, including Betsy, tapping their feet. A young man and woman performed a modern dance routine with gravity-defying lifts and leaps. Several people took to the microphone to share stories, literary excerpts, or songs.

And then it was Violet's turn. Violet didn't usually think of herself as ordinary. She prided herself on being a little bit different, in her clothing and tastes and mannerisms. But amidst this crowd of performers and artists, she felt self-conscious and bland. The outfit she'd chosen the night before, a 1940s short-sleeved suit with a nipped waist and shiny brass buttons, had seemed perfect when she put it on—a nod to Betsy's younger days. Now it seemed boring, conservative even.

Violet stepped up to the podium, where she had a view of all the guests gathered. She spotted April in the back row and met her gaze for a moment, then looked down at the piece of paper in her hands. Violet had spent hours writing the reflection she was about to read, and now she worried that it would sound pedestrian. There was nothing she could do about it now, though, so she cleared her throat and began to read.

"'A thing of beauty is a joy forever.' The poet John Keats wrote that, and Betsy Barrett, more than anyone else I know, understands it. Betsy loves beauty, and has an eye for it. She displays it in her home and channels it in the way she dresses, but most importantly, she fosters beauty in the world around her." Violet looked up and caught Betsy smiling, her eyes wet and shining. This gave Violet the confidence to stray a bit from her script. "You've seen dancers, singers, and musicians tonight. All of them are here because of Betsy's unfaltering support of the arts and local businesses. My vintage shop would not exist without her help. Fortunately, her legacy will live on with the many garments that came from her closet. Each one has a story from Betsy's incredible life to go with it. The white wool coat? She told me she wore it when she met Jackie Kennedy at the White House—a kindred spirit and fellow patron of the arts. The silver evening dress? She'd bought it in Paris in the 1950s, when she finally convinced her husband to take her to Europe, where he'd been stationed during World War II. When I asked Betsy why she was getting rid of these beautiful items, she said, 'I've had my time with them. It's someone else's turn to enjoy them.' Betsy doesn't keep beautiful things to herself. I've learned from her that a pretty thing isn't worth much if you can't share it with anyone. It's just a thing. Only when you let others enjoy it, too, does it become truly beautiful."

Violet swallowed the swelling in her throat and stepped down from the podium. Only when she was back at her seat did she allow herself to shed a few quiet tears. She looked over at Betsy, who nodded at her and mouthed "thank you."

After the ceremony, everyone seemed to want to have a few minutes with Betsy. Violet hovered near the edge of the room, waiting, and April joined her.

"That was beautiful," April said.

"Thanks," Violet said. "I'm glad you made it."

"Of course. Betsy has done so much for me. I didn't even know she was sick, though, did you?"

"No. Well, sort of. It's complicated."

Betsy waved at them and motioned for them to come over.

"You go," April said. "I'll talk to her in a little bit. You should have her to yourself for a few minutes. You've known her longer."

"Okay." Violet managed a small smile. "Thanks."

Violet hugged Betsy, being careful not to disrupt the IV needles. Her friend's body felt just as frail and angular as it looked. Violet settled into the seat next to the wheelchair.

"Thank you for coming," Betsy said. "I know it must have been a surprise."

"Why didn't you let me know you were sick again?" Violet asked.

"It happened quickly. By the time I realized it wasn't just a virus, but that the cancer was back, I was laid up with pneumonia with nurses around me day and night. I knew you had a lot going on at the store. I didn't want to worry you if it didn't end up being serious."

"But it *was* serious. And now I feel terrible that I didn't know what was going on. How long has the cancer been back?"

"I know what you're thinking. When you came to my house that day, I told you the truth. I really was in remission. Everything was going fine for a while there. And I'm grateful for it." Betsy coughed—a labored, wheezing sound that made Violet shudder.

"Is there anything I can do for you to make things more comfortable here?" Violet asked.

"Oh, the staff's been great. And I'll let you in on a little hospice secret." She leaned forward and put her blue-veined hand on Violet's arm. "They give really good drugs here."

Violet laughed. "There are probably easier ways to get drugs, Betsy."

"Sure, you tell me that now. It's a relief, though. I'm not in any pain."

Violet stopped smiling and said in a serious voice, "If there's anything you need, just let me know. If you want anything from your house, or are craving a certain kind of food, I'd be happy to pick it up for you."

"The food I crave these days is whatever will stay down."

"Oh, I'm so sorry to hear that."

"Stop saying you're sorry," Betsy said. "There's nothing worse than having a bunch of people feel sorry for you, and really, there's no reason to pity me. I've been luckier than most people in life. And just look around this room—all these people are friends, not family. Some people probably think it's sad that I don't have any children, or any family left. But what they don't realize is that family *has* to come to something like this. Friends don't. They choose to come. So I'm lucky in that way. These people want to be here."

"Well, we wish we were here for another reason."

"Oh, pooh. I'll take whatever reason I can get. Promise me that when you leave here you won't feel sorry for me."

"I promise. You are many things, Betsy, but someone to pity is not one of them."

"Will you promise me something else, too?"

Violet nodded.

"Don't make the same mistake I did and wait for the perfect time to do the things you want to do in life. For so long, I sat on my hands because I was afraid of what people would think of me—my husband, his colleagues, our friends. I was afraid to put my heart into the things I really cared about because I didn't want to be controversial, or for people to disagree with me. Don't do that."

The line of people waiting to talk to Betsy had doubled in size since Violet had been chatting with her, and April was up next.

"Okay." Violet stood up. "I better let some of the other guests say hi. You're quite popular." She bent down and kissed Betsy's cheek. "Can I come visit you?"

Betsy nodded. "My schedule's pretty full for the next few days, but next week would be good."

Violet had visited very few people in hospital settings—her grandmother just before she died, lying on the propped-up pillows in her silk kimono; Karen after her labor with Edith, clutching the wrinkled little baby to her breast; and Jed when he had alcohol poisoning, his face pink and bloated. In none of those instances did she have to compete with other visitors for time slots.

As the crowd began to thin out, Violet walked to her car, feeling like she should be mournful. But then she remembered what Betsy had said about not feeling sorry for her and tried her best to honor her promise. She thought, too, about Betsy's other advice—about not waiting to go after what her heart desired.

She drove to Sam's house.

He answered the door wearing plaid pajama pants and a worn gray T-shirt.

"Hi," he said, leaning in to kiss her. "Good to see you. Come on in. Can I get you something? A beer? A cup of tea?"

Violet stepped inside. "A beer sounds great, thanks. I just came from Betsy's memorial service."

"I'm sorry." Sam enveloped her in a tight hug, and she breathed him in. He smelled like he'd just showered, and his hair was still damp.

Violet pulled away. "No, it was good, actually. And it got me thinking."

"Do you want to talk about it?" he asked. "Here, let me get you that beer and we can sit outside. Have you seen the moon out there? It's a beautiful night."

Sam went to the kitchen and came back with two bottles of some sort of microbrew.

They settled onto the steps of his wide front porch, lit by paper lanterns under the August moon, and Violet told him that she wanted a baby.

"I realize it might sound kind of ridiculous," she said. "To end a perfectly good—no, better than good—relationship because I want to have a child in my life someday. I mean, I'm almost forty. There's not a lot of time left for 'someday.' And it's not as if there's anyone else out there I want to have a family with. But I guess what I'm saying is that I'm not ready to close that door. There are other options, even if the traditional family scenario doesn't work out for me. And I'd be lying if I said I'm not considering them."

The sound of crickets filled the silence that followed. There was just enough moonlight for Violet to see the look of disappointment on Sam's face.

"It's not ridiculous," he said. "You should get what you want out of life. I would never ask you to give up something you want."

"And I can't ask you to change your mind, either," said Violet, hoping he'd tell her she was wrong. "Are you surprised at my decision?"

"No," Sam said. "I could have predicted it on our first date, from the way your face lit up when you held Karen's baby."

Violet took a sip of the beer he'd given her—it was rich and tasted a little bit like chocolate. Unlike Jed, who consumed whatever was on sale by the caseload, Sam stuck to small-batch bottles from local breweries and sometimes even home brews from his buddies. Violet liked that Sam would rather have a little bit of something exceptional than a lot of something mediocre. She told him so.

"*You're* exceptional," he said, brushing a stray black curl away from Violet's face. "But I don't want to have to settle for just a little bit of you." He dropped his hand to his lap. "Unfortunately, it's usually a deal breaker, the kids thing."

Violet wondered how many women Sam had had this same conversation with. She hated having to end things with him when, other than the kids issue, everything had been going so well. What Violet was doing went against Sam's entire philosophy of living in the moment. She wasn't living in the moment. She was sacrificing happiness in the moment for the hope of a different kind of happiness in the future.

"I wish I could give you a different answer." Violet reached for Sam's hand and held it in both of hers.

"Me too," he said. His voice carried no trace of sarcasm, just sadness. Violet could tell he meant it.

She knew it was childish, but she felt hurt that she wasn't able to change his mind, that she didn't have some special quality that the other women hadn't possessed. Thinking she could change people, though, had always been a problem for Violet. And it was time to stop making the same mistakes.

Chapter 25

INVENTORY ITEM: *pants*
APPROXIMATE DATE: *early 1990s*
CONDITION: *good*
ITEM DESCRIPTION: *Capri pants by Brooks Brothers. Pink cotton with green embroidered turtle design.*
SOURCE: *Dig & Save thrift outlet*

April

APRIL HEAVED HERSELF TO a seated position in bed and tried to remember what day it was. At this late stage in her pregnancy, she was ticking off the days until her due date. The days seemed to stretch on forever because she could barely sleep at night. No matter what way she turned, there was some lumpy piece of her body or the baby's body in the way. And the kid wouldn't stop moving. This morning, she had a consistent ache low in her stomach.

She remembered it was August thirty-first—six days from Labor Day, her aptly named due date.

"You sure seem excited to get a start on things," April said, putting her hands on her belly. "I have to warn you, though, kid, it's not all sunshine and rainbows. It's a crazy world out here some-times."

Charlie rolled over and rubbed April's thigh. "What time is it?"

"Six."

"Go back to bed."

"Can't. I hardly slept. I've been lying here for an hour already waiting for it to get light outside so I could get up and feel somewhat normal about it."

"Oh, I can make you feel much, much better than normal," Charlie said with a delicious grin. He reached for her.

She squirmed. "No, I feel disgusting."

"I don't think you look disgusting. I think you look beautiful."

After so many months of being alone during her pregnancy, she reveled in the soft luxury of the compliment, as if she were lying wrapped in a fur blanket. This time, when Charlie reached for her, she didn't squirm away.

Later that morning, when April came in to work at the shop, she paused inside the front door to admire what Violet had done with her mom's place since the closing. She'd painted the walls her signature blue, except for a bright orange accent wall behind the register. Violet had also organized the shop into sections, with clothing in the main room up front, dishes and housewares in the formal dining room, and linens tucked on shelves in the open closets. It was like walking into someone's beautiful home, where everything was for sale. Gladys the Goose stood on a pedestal table in the foyer, casting a friendly glow upon anyone who walked through the door. Most impressive of all, though, at least by April's standards, was the fact that Violet had set up a shiny new computer at the register counter and, with April's help, was now implementing a bar code system to keep track of all her merchandise.

Violet sat on the white shag rug in the dining room, pulling glassware out of boxes and dusting each champagne flute and dessert bowl before sticking a coded price tag on it and placing it on a shelf.

Violet looked up when April came in. "Good morning."

"Still unpacking, I see," April said.

"Yep. I can't believe how much stuff I have."

"Can I help?"

"Sure," Violet said. "I could use a hand switching out the summer stock. The students have already started to come back from break, and they're looking for fall clothes."

"Sounds good," April said. "I still can't lift anything heavy, though."

"That won't be a problem. I can take care of bringing out the boxes of inventory from where I stuck them in the basement. I'll just have you arrange the clothes on hangers and on the racks. Actually, why don't you start by taking down some of the summer items? If you put them in boxes, I'll carry them downstairs when you're done."

April removed gauzy sundresses, cotton Bermuda shorts, and strappy tank tops from hangers. She couldn't believe how quickly the summer had passed. This year, even more than in other years, she felt a sense of loss as the days shortened. Not only was she leaving the summer behind, but soon she'd be leaving behind her life as she knew it. April felt like her childhood had ended, for the most part, when her mom died. Now that she was just days from her due date, she felt like she was being catapulted into yet another level of the adult world. The fact that she had Charlie to help her made the concept only slightly less scary.

After she'd cleared an entire rack of summer clothing, April sat cross-legged on the floor, folding the items into boxes. She felt a wet sensation in the seat of her pants. Her pulse quickened. Was her water breaking? She shifted to look at the floor. When she saw nothing, she got up. She felt a trickle down the inside of her legs and hurried to the bathroom in the back hall, covering her rear end with her hands. Once she'd shut the door, she inspected her pants and underwear, which were soaked with clear fluid. She stuffed a wad of paper towels into her underwear. She needed to call her doctor. But first she needed to change her pants, and she didn't have an extra pair.

April darted out of the lavatory and dug through one of the boxes she'd just packed until she found a pair of pants large enough to fit her—a pair of plus-sized pink capris embroidered with dozens of little green turtles. They would have to do. She grabbed a long scarf from one of the racks to use as a belt and went back into the bathroom to change out of her wet clothing.

When she returned to the dining room wearing the pink pants, Violet gave her a curious look.

"I think my water broke," April said. "I hope it's okay that I put these on."

Violet's eyes grew wide. "Sure, whatever you need. Is there anything I can do?"

"I don't know. I've gotta call my doctor." April grabbed her cell phone from her purse and dialed Dr. Hong's office. One of her nurses answered the phone and, upon hearing that April's water had probably broken, instructed her to go to the hospital right away.

"I've gotta go," April said after she'd hung up. She looked around at the boxes strewn everywhere. "I'm sorry to leave you with all this chaos."

"Oh, you're not leaving me," Violet said. "I'm taking you to the hospital."

"I can call Charlie."

"No way. Tell him to meet us there."

Violet pulled the Jeep out of the garage and helped April get into the passenger seat. They took the fastest way to the hospital, following John Nolen Drive along the shore of Lake Monona. April watched the bikers and Rollerbladers cruising along the lakefront path, astonished that today was just an ordinary day for them.

"Are you doing okay?" Violet asked, glancing over at April. "Should we be, like, timing your contractions or something?"

April shrugged. "Your guess is as good as mine. I'm not really feeling anything, though, so I don't know what we would time."

"Are you nervous?" Violet asked. "Excited?"

April laughed. "*You* sound excited."

"Sorry, I guess maybe I'm living a little vicariously."

"Okay, yes, I'm excited," April said. "And scared, too."

At the hospital, Violet insisted that they get out at the emergency room entrance. Violet handed her keys to an attendant near the door.

"We can just park the car in the lot and go in the regular doors," April said. "I'm pretty sure I can manage walking a few hundred feet."

"No way," Violet said, finding a wheelchair near the doors and helping April into it. She wheeled April into the elevator and up to the labor and delivery floor.

While April checked in at the reception desk, she looked around and noticed that she was the youngest person in the waiting area by at least ten years. All the other women around her were dressed in cute maternity clothes. One of the women clutched a binder labeled "Birth Plan" to her chest and barked orders at the man sitting with her, who April guessed was her very obedient husband. Another lady sat with her belly popping out of a black suit blazer, tapping away at her Black-Berry and appearing as if she were negotiating a multimillion-dollar deal from her waiting room chair.

Where are all the teenage mothers I'm always hearing about on the news? April wondered. She would have liked to see at least one person who looked as clueless as she felt.

Charlie arrived ten minutes later, bursting through the doors of the waiting area, where April was still waiting to be put into a triage room. "Do you really think the baby's coming?" he asked.

April shrugged. "That's what the water breaking always means on TV. You don't need to panic, though. The nurse said I probably have a little bit of time, since I'm not having contractions yet. At least I don't think so. Anyway, she said they can do a test to tell if my water really broke or if I just peed my pants without knowing it."

"Can that happen?" Charlie asked.

"I guess so. The nurse acted like it happens all the time."

Once April was settled into a tiny triage room, shielded from the open door by a mint-green curtain, she insisted that Violet go home.

"It could be a long time," April said. "And anyway, Charlie's here now."

"Okay, but only if you promise you'll call me as soon as the baby is here," Violet said. "Or if there's anything I can do in the meantime."

"We will," April said. "Thank you for everything."

After Violet had gone, Charlie stood next to April's bed, looking anxious as the nurse made April spread her legs so she could conduct some sort of litmus test with a strip of colored paper, sort of like chemistry class.

"Yep, your water broke," the nurse said.

"Good, I'm glad to hear I didn't pee my pants. I've lost control of a lot of my body over the last nine months, and my bladder is one of my last strongholds."

April was trying to lighten the mood by making a joke, but the nurse didn't catch it. She just asked, "How far apart are your contractions? And how long are they lasting?"

"I don't know. I've had some pain, but nothing regular that I could time." She thought back to the events of the morning and blushed. "I did, um, have sex this morning, though. Do you think that could have brought this on?"

To April's embarrassment, the nurse typed that information into her patient chart on the computer.

"Orgasm can stimulate the uterus into action," the nurse said. "Especially at this late stage of pregnancy. So, yes, it might have helped you along a little, but sex or none, this baby is ready to come out. Since you don't seem to be having regular contractions yet, it may be a while, though."

"A while? Like hours?"

"Hours or, in some cases, days."

Days? April prayed it wouldn't be days. "So can I go home and come back later?" she asked.

The nurse shook her head. "Once your water has broken, you're at higher risk of infection. And since you had some complications earlier in your pregnancy, we'd like to keep you here to monitor you."

The nurse set April up in a bigger room that she referred to as a "birthing suite." It was really just a regular hospital room with the walls painted mauve and more comfortable chairs, but April was just glad not to have to share it with anyone, especially BlackBerry Mom or Birth Plan Binder Lady.

Charlie settled into one of the cushy chairs next to April's bed. He squeezed her hand. "You ready for this?"

April thought about it. "I don't think I'll ever be ready. I'm pretty sure that's why pregnancy is the way it is. You've got nine months to get used to the idea of having this thing inside of you, and by the time you come to the end, you're so damn uncomfortable that you just want it out, even if the thought of taking care of a baby terrifies you."

"Are you terrified?" Charlie asked.

"All those other women in the waiting room freaked me out. They seem to have everything planned."

"Well, if there's one thing I've learned from my premed studies, it's that the human body can do some pretty weird things. Even with all their planning, there's no guarantee that everything will go the way those women want it to. The body is unpredictable."

April settled back onto the pillows and said, "*Life* is unpredictable."

Chapter 26

INVENTORY ITEM: *baby bonnet*
APPROXIMATE DATE: *1940s*
CONDITION: *excellent*
ITEM DESCRIPTION: *White linen baby bonnet with embroidered yellow ducks; trimmed with silk ribbon and white lace.*
SOURCE: *farmstead estate sale*

Violet

VIOLET WAITED FOR A phone call while she hung fur-collared wool coats on racks. She waited while she folded angora sweaters and arranged them on display tables. And she waited some more as she went through her closing routine that evening and locked up the double front doors of the bungalow.

She needed some good news. The last few months had brought their share of bad news, and Violet figured it was about time she had something to celebrate. April and Charlie's baby seemed like a perfect reason to do so. Waiting for the news, though, was making her crazy.

She left the house, where she'd been working what felt like non-stop to get things set up the way she wanted them. Just for something else to do, she wandered over to Pinkus McBride's, the neighborhood corner store, to buy a card for April. The convenience store only had a few baby-themed cards, and all of them were either pink or blue. Not knowing which to get, she picked out a plain white card that had *Congratulations* scripted across the front in shiny gold letters.

"Celebrating something special?" asked the teenage clerk as he scanned the bar code on the card.

"My intern—I mean friend—is at the hospital right now having a baby." Violet dug in her wallet and produced a few crumpled bills.

"Cool. You got kids?" he asked.

Violet shook her head. "Maybe someday."

The clerk sized her up and gave her a skeptical look. Violet grabbed the card and left the store. She walked past James Madison Park on the way home, where barefoot, college-age kids played Frisbee in the dusk and lounged on blankets near the lakeshore. She wished she could share in their carefree enjoyment of the warm evening, probably one of the last of the year, but she had far too much on her mind.

She walked down to the small beach at the park and stood with her toes in the pebbly sand watching a group of sailboats round a buoy halfway across Lake Mendota. A man selling ice cream bars from a pushcart yelled, "Cold treats for a hot day!" A little girl bought a red, white, and blue bomb pop, which reminded Violet of the Fourth of July, and with a pang of sadness, she thought of her and Sam's first date. She headed home.

When she returned to the green bungalow, Miles greeted her at the door. As she bent down to pet him, the phone rang. She answered it, full of hope that April and Charlie's baby was finally here.

"Hello?"

"Is this Violet Turner?" asked a vaguely familiar voice.

Violet sucked in her breath. "Yes."

"This is Ellen from Agrace Hospice, and I'm afraid I have some bad news."

Violet leaned on the countertop. "Yes?"

"Betsy passed on this afternoon."

Violet heard a whooshing sound in her ears and felt light-headed. She realized she'd been holding her breath since she picked up the phone. She let it out and, as she did, tears ran down her face and splattered on the wood floor.

"I'm sorry to have to tell you such awful news," Ellen said. "But I think you should know that she went peacefully and without pain."

This information didn't stop the flow of tears. Violet asked, "Will there be a funeral?"

"Betsy didn't want a funeral. She donated most of her estate to a charitable trust that will turn her home into an artists' residence, a place that people can apply for scholarships to go to and have a quiet, supportive place to work. She said that will be her memorial—the Barrett Center for the Arts. She didn't want a casket or a ceremony or anything."

"So, she'll be buried, then?"

"Cremated," Ellen said. "Violet, I usually don't share these kinds of details with non–family members, but Betsy made it clear in her directives that she wanted you to be informed when she passed."

Violet forced herself to say, "Thank you. I appreciate you letting me know."

"Do you have any questions?"

Violet sniffled. "Just—is there anything I can do?"

"Everything's already being taken care of," Ellen replied. "Her estate attorney has been notified, so that he can get working on the trust, and hospice has already contacted the cremation service. Betsy left very detailed instructions as to what was to happen when she died. She did not want to inconvenience anyone."

It amazed and inspired Violet that even on her deathbed, Betsy was thinking of other people before herself. Still, after she and Ellen hung up, Violet couldn't help feeling not only sad but also unsettled. She'd been expecting Betsy's death any day now, but she also thought she'd get a little more notice, another chance to visit and say good-bye. Now there wouldn't even be a funeral, and Violet wondered how she'd ever be able to feel any sense of closure.

She sat down, and as if he sensed her sadness, Miles rested his snout on her lap. She leaned down and patted his wrinkly head, glad to have his company. She knew Betsy had said not to feel sorry for her, but Violet couldn't help wondering if her friend had died alone. Certainly hospice staff would have been at her side, but had any loved one been there to hold her hand? To tell her not to be afraid?

Violet thought about April, in another hospital bed, going through a very different experience. She envied April a little—not the fact that she was in labor, of course, but the fact that she would soon have a family of her own. When she and April had first met, they'd had a lot in common. They were both single and without family, and Violet suspected that fact had something to do with why, despite their differences, they'd formed a connection. Now April had Charlie, and very soon they'd have a child. Violet was happy for them, but their situation also had the uncomfortable effect of highlighting what Violet *didn't* have, especially now that she was no longer even in a relationship.

Since she'd broken up with Sam, the days had been dragging. Violet tried to distract herself with work, but even tasks she normally enjoyed, like going through boxes of treasures that customers brought in to sell or helping a college girl pick out a dress for a date, held little appeal. It had been a long time since she'd allowed herself to care for anyone like she'd cared for Sam, and now she knew why. It hurt too much when things ended.

Before she met Sam, Violet had almost resigned herself to the fact that she wouldn't find love again. She dutifully went on dates, mostly at Karen's urging that she had to get herself "back out there." Mostly, though, Violet wanted only to be at peace with herself and her own past, and she tried everything that might help her do that. She'd done tai chi and yoga, which only made her antsy and gave her mind too much unoccupied time to dwell on regrets. She'd had her energy work done by a Reiki master, been poked by the needles of an acupuncturist. She'd even, at the suggestion of Erma, the neighborhood witch, sat in the middle of a chalked circle with a shaman and gone on a mental journey to meet her animal spirit guide. Hers was a starfish. The shaman had told her it was because starfish regenerate. They can suffer an accident, lose a limb, and grow whole again even after great trauma. Violet liked to think she was like the starfish in that way, but she feared she still wasn't whole.

She distracted herself from her sadness and longing by continuing to organize things in her new space. She fiddled with the arrangement of the clothing racks and the layout of the furniture. She was so engrossed in her work and her grief that she jumped when the phone rang again just after ten thirty. She picked it up.

"Hello?"

"It's a girl!" cried Charlie's voice on the other end. "I hope it's not too late to call. We just thought you'd like to know, since April left work so suddenly today."

"It's never too late for good news. I've been thinking about April all day, hoping everything was going okay. Does the little one have a name?"

"Katherine, after April's mom. But we're going to call her Kate."

"Baby Kate." Violet smiled. "It's perfect. How's April doing?"

"She's sleeping at the moment, but she's great. She can't wait to show off the baby."

"So when can she do that? I mean, when can I come see you guys?"

"We're going home the day after tomorrow, hopefully, so maybe you can come by our place then."

"Sure. I can come over after work that night, but are you sure it won't be too much? I mean, won't April be exhausted?"

"Maybe, but she's dying for you to meet Kate. You're the first person April mentioned, once everything settled down after the delivery. She said, 'I can't wait for Violet to see her.'"

Violet felt a surge of pride. She may not have had a family of her own, but this was almost as good.

Two nights later, Violet sat in a rocking chair at April and Charlie's apartment, holding little Kate in her arms. Through losing her grandmother and Betsy, she had become more acquainted with death than she cared to be. It felt wonderful, then, to have this new, warm bundle curled up against her. The baby had been sleeping since Violet arrived, so she hadn't caught a glimpse of her eyes yet, but her pudgy cheeks, wrinkled hands, and long eyelashes were pure perfection.

"She's gorgeous," Violet declared.

"I'm glad you think so because I do, too." Dark circles outlined April's eyes, and her hair was pulled into a messy ponytail. Still, she looked less weighed down than Violet had ever seen her, not just in the sense that she was no longer carrying around a baby inside of her, but also on a deeper level. April seemed content.

Violet nodded toward a package on the table, wrapped in an old map and tied with twine. "I brought a little something for Kate."

"That's sweet," April said. "You didn't have to."

"Are you kidding? And pass up the opportunity to pick out something tiny and cute?" Violet tucked in a loose end of Kate's swaddle blanket. "Open it."

April picked up the package and opened it, being careful not to tear the paper. Inside was a small box, and she lifted the lid and held up a white bonnet adorned with embroidered yellow ducks and hand-looped lace.

"It's gorgeous," April said. "I've never seen anything like it."

"It's from the nineteen forties. While you were—" Violet paused, not wanting to bring up their rift during such a happy time. "When you were gone and I was going through stuff for the revue, I came across it in one of my boxes in the back room of the old building. I bought it years ago at an estate sale on an old farmstead."

"I didn't know you had baby stuff in your inventory," April said.

"Yeah, a few things. For a while, I started collecting baby items because—" Violet stopped, embarrassed to admit the truth, which was that, for a time, she had compiled a small stock of infant clothes in the hopes of someday having a child of her own. "I, um, used to think about carrying some baby items in the store, but never got around to it," she said. "Anyway, when I saw this, I set it aside for you."

"You were thinking of me even after I'd been such a pain in your ass?" April asked.

"Sure. Even though you weren't interning anymore, I was hoping I'd still have a chance to give it to you and meet the baby."

Kate opened her eyes and stretched her arms above her head with a peaceful sigh.

"Aw, she likes it," April said. "That's the first time she's opened her eyes in hours."

Violet leaned down so that her face was just inches from the baby's. "Hi, Kate. I'm Violet. I'm so happy to meet you."

April smiled and ran a finger along the yellow ribbon on the bonnet. "Thank you for this."

Crickets sang outside, and two girls on bikes chattered as they pedaled past the open window.

"I like your new apartment," Violet said, noticing the built-in cabinets and crown moldings. "It's got some great old details."

"Yeah, it reminds me of my mom's house—er, your house—a little bit. It's closer to the med school, though, so it will be a lot easier for Charlie. His first-semester schedule is pretty busy, and he doesn't have much flexibility with it. I planned my own classes around when he's free, so we can switch on and off being home with Kate. But there's a seminar I really want to take with a visiting math professor that conflicts with something in Charlie's schedule, so I don't know what we're gonna to do about that. It's only one evening a week. I guess we'll just have to find someone to watch the baby that one night."

"I'll do it," Violet offered. She didn't even think about it. She just said it, and when it came out, it sounded right.

April's face perked up. "Really? It wouldn't be too much work, with the store and everything?"

"Not at all. I love babies, and the way things are going for me, it's looking like there's less and less of a chance I'll ever have my own, so I'll take my baby time when I can get it."

"Yeah, but what about all the stuff you have to do to close up at night?"

"I can just leave all of the more complicated closing stuff for other nights, and if no customers are there at the end of the evening, I can always just shut down a few minutes early."

"Oh, my God, that would be wonderful," April said. "I can't wait to tell Charlie. He'll be so relieved. He was planning on talking to one of his professors to see if he could cut out of class fifteen minutes early every Wednesday, but now he won't have to."

"Where is Charlie, by the way?"

"Oh, he's at the store getting diapers and onesies and a whole bunch of other stuff we need. We have a few things, but I don't think we had any idea how many changes of clothes this kid would need. I've changed her outfit three times already today because of some, um, accidents."

"Well, you must have cleaned her up well because she smells heavenly right now." Violet felt her arm falling asleep, so she shifted Kate in her lap.

"Hey, you said you've thought before about carrying vintage baby items in the shop," April said. "We should do that."

Violet thought about it. "Sure, we could try it out. I mean, I wouldn't want to carry a ton of that stuff. I still want the emphasis to be on regular women's fashion. But if it means people would buy more when they came in, maybe something for themselves, something for their kids . . ."

"Exactly."

Kate started crying, and Violet got up and walked her around the room, bouncing her gently.

"I need to get one of those baby swings, I think," April said. "She loves being rocked or bounced, and it would be nice to have my hands free for a little while sometimes."

An idea occurred to Violet. "I'm gonna throw you a shower," she said. "You can register for whatever stuff you need but don't have yet."

"Isn't that supposed to happen *before* the baby?"

"Yeah, but who says I can't throw you one now? I've never been big on convention, anyway. Talk to Charlie and figure out a date that works for both of you and I'll get planning."

A smile spread across April's face. Violet didn't want to tell her about Betsy—she didn't want to do anything to break up the happy feel to this evening—but she knew she had to tell her. April would find out eventually.

Violet sat back down, making soft shushing noises. As Kate quieted down, she said, "Betsy passed away two days ago."

"No." April put a hand to her mouth. "Were you there, when she . . . ?"

Violet shook her head. "I got the news just a couple of hours before Charlie called me."

"Bad news followed by good news."

Violet kept her other bad news—her breakup with Sam—to herself for the time being. She didn't want anything else to shift the focus away from perfect little Kate, who was now settling back to sleep in her arms.

Chapter 27

INVENTORY ITEM: *passport holder*

APPROXIMATE DATE: *1975*

CONDITION: *fair*

ITEM DESCRIPTION: *Tan and white pony-skin passport holder. Leather lined. Some general wear and tear.*

SOURCE: *flea market*

Amithi

AMITHI PUSHED OPEN THE front door of the house she'd entered thousands of times. The hinges squeaked, and she noted with irritation that Naveen must not have fixed them. She shut the door behind her. Despite the fact that it was a beautiful September day, warm and golden, the windows were shut and the house smelled stuffy, stale.

If she had her timing right, she guessed Naveen was teaching a class this afternoon. Amithi passed the kitchen and looked inside to see dirty dishes covering the countertops. A few brown bananas and a wrinkled apple moldered in the fruit bowl, and half of a Taste of India microwave dinner sat in a box on the table. It took all of Amithi's willpower not to go into the kitchen and start cleaning. She reminded herself she was just there to get her passport and kept walking.

In the office, she opened up the file cabinet and retrieved the folder where she and Naveen kept all of their important documents, like their naturalization papers and social security cards. She riffled through the file and found her passport underneath a certified copy of Jayana's birth certificate. Seeing her signature and Naveen's next to one another on the certificate, signed so many years ago, reminded Amithi of just how much her life was intertwined with his.

All the more reason why I need to leave for a while, she thought, and snapped the folder shut. As she turned off the office light and passed back through the quiet house, she realized how strange it felt to be there. It didn't feel like home anymore.

Just as she reached the front door, she heard footsteps behind her. She turned and saw her husband standing on the stairway. His beard was untrimmed and his legs looked thin beneath his bathrobe. He had lost weight.

"Amithi?" he said.

She put her hand on the doorknob.

"Please, wait." Naveen came down to the foyer and put a hand on her arm. His face was fragile, hopeful.

For a moment, Amithi felt sorry for him, but the pity was quickly replaced by fury. She pushed his hand away. "I just came to get my passport," she said. "I was hoping you would be at work."

"Jayana told me you are taking a trip to India next month," he said with a wounded expression.

"Is she returning your phone calls now?" Amithi asked.

Last she had heard, Jayana was still shutting Naveen out. Amithi had mixed emotions about it. On one hand, she appreciated her daughter's loyalty. On the other, she wanted them to have a good relationship. Even though Jayana was an adult, and a very independent one at that, Amithi didn't want her to grow to regret having drifted apart from her father.

"No," Naveen said. "I happened to run into her at a sandwich shop near campus."

"I want you to know that I never told Jayana to ignore you," Amithi said.

"No, of course not. I know you would not do that."

The pain in Naveen's eyes was something Amithi could empathize with, though she knew he had brought it upon himself. She, too, had lived with the fear of growing apart from Jayana, which made their renewed closeness all the more precious.

"Do you remember the last time we went to India as a family, when Jayana was a teenager?" Naveen asked. "She complained about having to go the whole plane ride there but then didn't want to leave by the time our trip was over."

Amithi remembered, angry that her memory of that trip—and nearly every memory of their family—was now tainted by Naveen's betrayal.

A silence ran between them, full of half a lifetime of emotions.

Finally, Naveen said, "I suppose I should tell you I am planning to take a trip to India at the same time you and Jayana are there. To visit my family."

Amithi clenched her fist around her passport, bending the cover. "This is *my* trip, Naveen," she said in an irritated tone. "I have rarely asked for anything for myself, in all these years."

"I know. I know." Naveen held up his hands, palms facing out. "And I promise I have no intention of interfering with your time with Jayana. I will be staying at my sister's house. I expect nothing of you, I swear. I simply want to be near where you are." He gestured around the dusty house. "Everything is empty without you, *jaanu*."

"*Jaanu*." A Hindi term of endearment meaning, literally, "my life."

Amithi exhaled. She doubted that Naveen expected nothing from her. When had that ever been true, of him or any husband?

"If you have no expectation of me, then why can you not go to India another time, after Jayana and I get home?" she asked.

Naveen's eyes revealed the truth before he said it. "I suppose I hope that, by being in the place where we first met, we might be able to remember how things used to be between us. I can still picture what you looked like the first time I saw you at your parents' house. I was nervous and sweating, but you were so beautiful in your blue sari, and so calm. You have always been the calm place in my life, Amithi. When I think of how I hurt you, how foolish I have been—" His voice wavered and he looked away.

Hearing Naveen's nostalgia for happier days set off a torrent of anger within Amithi's chest. How dare he long for something that he himself ruined? What selfishness to feel sorry for himself when he'd hurt her so deeply! His loneliness was evident, from his haphazard housekeeping to his unshaven face. But it was a result he could have avoided, had he thought about how his actions would affect his family.

"Those days are gone, Naveen," she said.

"I am so sorry, Amithi. You have every right to be angry with me. I understand if you do not want to see me while you are in India. But if you do, even if just once for a cup of tea, it will have made the whole trip worth it for me."

Amithi sighed. "How long will you be there?"

"Two weeks. It is all I could manage to be away from work. And you? When will you return?"

"I am not certain," Amithi said. "I'm going to spend some time in New York after I get back. There are some classes I've signed up for at FIT."

"FIT?" Naveen looked skeptical. "I have never heard of it. What sort of classes?"

"The Fashion Institute of Technology," she said, not expecting Naveen to understand. "They have some continuing education courses that are open to the public and look very interesting. There is one on design and pattern making that I think would help me with my tailoring work."

"That explains the charge I saw on the credit card bill."

Amithi felt defensive. "The classes are a bit pricey, but I can write them off as a business expense once my tailoring business starts to make a profit."

"I'm not worried about the cost," Naveen said. "But what is this about tailoring? I did not know you were working."

"You did not know I had any interests that didn't involve you," Amithi said with a rush of adrenaline.

Naveen looked as surprised to hear these words as Amithi was to say them. She had never before spoken so frankly with her husband.

"I always knew you liked to sew," he said. "And I know you used to design things before we were married. You mentioned it when we first met."

"I didn't know you remembered," Amithi said.

"I remember everything about the day we met." Naveen put his hands in his pockets. "I just wish I would have known that you were interested in taking classes. We could have figured out a way for you to do that."

"This is not about the *classes*, Naveen," said Amithi with growing frustration. "It is about the fact that you cheated and you lied."

Naveen looked at the tiled floor. "I know. I am so sorry, Amithi. I only wish things could go back to the way they were."

"That is not possible. The life we thought we had—it is nothing but a story, a fiction. And it is too late to rewrite it."

"Well, then, perhaps it is possible to start a new story instead," Naveen said in a tentative tone. "One in which I am a better husband to you."

"Perhaps," Amithi said.

"Have a cup of tea with me, then, when we are in India. Please. I promise I will ask nothing more of you than that. We could meet at that little café you like in the Old City."

"No," she said in a firm voice.

The hope fled from his face.

"I'll come to your sister's house, and you will cook breakfast for Jayana and me," she said. "Nothing more. Just breakfast."

Naveen looked startled at first, but then a smile spread across his lips. "Yes," he said eagerly. "I will make that filled bread you like— *aloo paratha*. And I'll get mangoes. The sweet, small ones from the market. Just wait. It will be the best breakfast you've ever tasted."

Amithi put her hand on the doorknob again. She opened the door this time, and stepped out into the sun.

Chapter 28

INVENTORY ITEM: *brooch*
APPROXIMATE DATE: *1960s*
CONDITION: *fair*
ITEM DESCRIPTION: *Faux gold starfish pin with rhinestone detailing. Some tarnish on edges.*
SOURCE: *garage sale*

Violet

THE GOATEED TATTOO ARTIST examined the brooch Violet handed him. The gold setting and blue stones glittered in the glow of the neon lights in the window of his shop.

"What do you think, Gary?" Violet asked. "Do you think you can do something like that?"

"Sure." He turned over the brooch in his enormous hands. "I've never done a starfish like this before, but I've done plenty of other marine life. Lots of dolphins, of course. Those were really popular for a while there. And I've done coral, shells . . . one lady even had me do that cute little fish from the movie. What's his name? Nemo?"

Violet laughed. "Good God. I do not want this tattoo in any way to resemble a cartoon fish."

Gary held his hands up. "Hey, I don't judge. I just give people what they want. Anyway, I know that's not your style." He walked around to Violet's side to get a better view of her arm. "The phoenix I did for you a few years ago is still looking good."

"That's why I came back," she said. "I trust you."

"I'm gonna have to hand-draw the design. Can you give me a few minutes?"

"Sure," Violet said.

As Gary sat down at his desk, Violet waited on an overstuffed fake leather couch, watching the evening foot traffic on Williamson Street. A couple with matching lip piercings strolled by the window, arm in arm. On the porch of a coffee shop across the street, boxes of vegetables stood in neat stacks. Violet watched as a woman loaded the contents of one of the boxes into a canvas bag. She guessed it was a pickup spot for one of the dozens of local community-supported farms that delivered vegetables to their shareholders every week.

Gary got up, holding a piece of paper and a stencil that went over it. "How does this look?" he asked, removing the stencil so Violet could see the drawing. "Is this what you had in mind?"

"It's beautiful," she said, touching one of the long, delicate legs of the starfish in the picture.

"Then have a seat."

Violet settled back into the reclining chair and rolled up her sleeve.

"Your bicep again?" Gary asked.

Violet nodded. "The other one this time."

"You know, I've gotta hand it to you. A lot of chicks want 'em somewhere you can't see 'em, like their hip or their back."

"Yeah, well I'm not most chicks."

Violet thought she detected a faint smile on his lips as he wiped her arm with rubbing alcohol, then pressed the stencil to it. When he removed it, there was a blue outline of what the tattoo would look like.

"So why the starfish?" he asked. "You don't have to tell me if you don't want, but I like hearing folks' stories if they're okay with talking about 'em."

"Me too. I listen to my customers' stories all the time," Violet said. "I picked a starfish because they can heal and regenerate, even if they are injured or lose a leg. I've had a lot of loss in my life lately."

She thought of Sam, and how much she longed to be in his easy presence again, to feel the strong warmth of his arms around her. She thought of Grandma Lou and of Betsy, who had become much like an adopted grandmother to Violet. She thought, too, about her old life in Bent Creek and how, in distancing herself from Jed, she'd necessarily had to distance herself from her parents, too, and all the echoes of the girl she used to be.

"Regeneration." Violet let out a half laugh. "That probably sounds really flaky, doesn't it?"

"Nah, it's cool. I've heard far flakier." Gary went to work putting together an intimidating contraption with a needle and tubes. Violet watched, trying not to get nervous. The whole point of getting the tattoo, after all, was to remind her that something good could come of pain.

He rubbed ointment over Violet's bicep and leaned toward her with a needle attached to a bag. "You ready?"

"Uh-huh."

"Remember to breathe." Gary switched on the machine.

Violet felt a prickling stab. Her arm radiated pain as the needle touched her skin with a buzzing sound. To keep herself from dwelling on all she'd lost, she focused instead on her new house, her new start. It might take a long time, but she was determined to grow whole again.

"Doing okay?" he asked.

She nodded, clenching the fist of her free hand.

The buzzing stopped and Gary lifted the needle. "Good work. We're done with the first line, and that's always the worst part."

Violet smiled. "It's always good to know the worst is behind you."

The next morning, Violet's arm still felt sore. She smoothed ointment on it and searched her closet for something to wear that would cover up the raw, red-looking tattoo for now but wouldn't rub against her skin. She startled when the doorbell rang. It was only eight thirty—an hour and a half before the shop would open.

She threw on a soft cotton T-shirt dress before running down the stairs to get the door. When she opened it, a man in a suit stood in front of her, clutching a briefcase. Violet's heart pounded. She remembered her run-in with the process server a few months earlier.

"May I help you?" she asked. She didn't invite him in.

The man set his briefcase down on the worn wooden slats of the porch. "Are you Violet Turner?"

"Yes. What is this regarding?" she asked, trying to keep the edge out of her voice.

"My law firm is handling Elizabeth Barrett's estate," he said. "And I've been instructed to contact all of the interested parties."

Violet exhaled. "Oh, well I'm not an interested party. I mean, she was a friend of mine, but I'm not a family member or heir or anything."

"According to Mrs. Barrett's will, you are to receive some of her possessions."

Violet sucked in her breath. "What?"

"Mrs. Barrett named you as a beneficiary in her will. You're the only human being, actually, that she named. Everything else is either going to the arts trust she set up or to various charities."

"You've got to be kidding. Not about the charities part, I mean. The part about me."

The man picked up his briefcase again and clicked it open. "Here's my card, and a copy of the will, so you can see for yourself. Betsy directed that I deliver the news to you in person, rather than calling or e-mailing."

Violet extended a shaking hand and took the papers from him.

"I should let you know that we have to set up the trust first, the Barrett Center for the Arts. And we need to pay off her medical bills with funds from the estate," he said. "Those are our priorities at the moment. As soon as we've done that, we'll contact you to make arrangements to give you the personal items she wanted you to have, probably within a month or so."

"Okay," Violet said, dumbfounded.

"We also need to have the items appraised for estate-tax purposes, so when that's done, we'll give you an itemized list of all the values for your own records." The man smiled. "I don't know much about fashion, but even so, I suspect several of the clothing items are of significant value."

Violet thought of her friend's lovely suits and dresses, her dozens of pairs of designer sunglasses and shoes. She was sad to think she'd never again see Betsy wearing any of them.

After the lawyer had left, Violet flipped open the document he'd given her and turned to the signature page with hands still trembling with shock. She saw that the will had been signed and dated over a year ago—before Violet's problems with the eviction and before she even knew about Betsy's illness. For some reason, this made Violet happy. Betsy had known about her troubles with her landlord, and Violet hoped her friend hadn't left her money just because of that. Like Betsy, Violet didn't like to be pitied. Knowing that Betsy had put her in the will out of pure affection, rather than charity, made the gift more meaningful.

Behind the last page of the will was a document that read "Memorandum Disposing of Personal Property" across the top. Betsy's lawyer had explained that this was the part of the estate plan that indicated where Betsy's specific possessions were supposed to go and told Violet where she should look for her own name. The memorandum was several pages long, with lists of Betsy's treasures and their intended recipients. Her silver collection was to go to the state historical society. Her artwork was itemized, with some pieces going to the trust that would run the Barrett Center for the Arts and some going to the contemporary art museum. Some of the items had instructions scribbled next to them, like "for the permanent collection" or "to be used in whatever manner most needed."

The last page listed Betsy's fur coats, handbag collection, and "the entire contents of the bedroom closet." Next to those items, Violet read the following phrase: "to Violet Turner, for her own personal enjoyment, or to use, donate, or sell as she sees fit."

Violet realized with a heavy heart that she would finally get to see all the contents of Betsy's closet—something she'd always been curious about—but regretted that her friend wouldn't be there to tell her the stories behind all of her beautiful clothes.

April came into the store that afternoon, toting a sleeping Kate in a car seat carrier. She set the carrier on the counter where she and Violet could both admire her.

"Welcome, Mama," Violet said. She surveyed April's ikat-print skirt and layers of beaded wooden necklaces she'd purchased from the shop. "You look way too good to have just had a baby. But why are you here? I told you I've got things under control. I thought you were going to take some time off."

"Oh, don't worry, I didn't come in to work," April said. "I just needed to get out of the house. Sitting around all day reminds me of being on bed rest. So what did I miss around here?"

Violet slid the copy of the will across the counter.

"What's this?" April picked it up. "Something about 'estate of Barrett'?"

Violet grinned. "I just found out Betsy left me everything in her closet, that sneaky darling."

"Seriously? That's incredible," April said, letting out a squeal.

Little Kate opened her eyes at the sound of her mother's voice, then yawned and closed them again.

"So," Violet said, "since I'm no longer on the brink of being evicted, and since I apparently will have some valuable items coming my way soon, it looks like I won't be quite so tight on funds as I have been in the past. It got me thinking about how I want to run things around here in the future."

"Oh, yeah? Have you reconsidered my idea about selling costumes?"

"Yeah, and I think we should do it, but I'm talking more about big-picture things."

"Like what?"

"Well, when you were gone, both before you had Kate and in the last few days, I realized how much value you bring to the store."

"Thanks," April said. "That means a lot to me."

"And I decided that, with your internship wrapping up, I'd like to offer you a position as a paid employee, if you think you'll have enough time to work a few hours a week once you get settled into your routine with classes and Kate and everything." Violet smiled. "Only if you want to. No pressure."

"Of course I want to," April said. "I honestly didn't think it was a possibility, though."

"You know, as much as I love the store, I love other things, too," Violet said. "And as long as I'm the only one running this place, I rarely have time for anything else. Seeing you with Kate, I've realized that someday, not now of course—I'm still busy settling into my new space—but hopefully in the not-too-far-off future, I'd love to have a family of my own." Violet leaned over and touched the baby's pink cheek.

"Really? Like you're going to adopt or do in vitro or something?" April put a hand over her mouth. "Sorry, was that too personal?"

Violet shrugged. "Maybe fostering. I don't know. I haven't gotten that far into the details yet. But I'm just saying it's something I want. And when it happens, I have no idea how I'd have enough time to both be a mother and run this place seven days a week. So, if you're still interested in working here . . ."

"I'm definitely interested," April said. "I'll probably have to work a pretty light schedule during the school year, though. I think my classes are gonna be pretty tough. I tested into some math classes that are usually reserved for juniors and seniors."

"That's fine. We can work around your schedule."

April grinned. "What made you change your mind?" she asked. "You have to admit you were pretty resistant to the idea of working with anyone at first. I'm pretty sure Betsy had to force us together."

"Yeah," said Violet. "But she knew what she was doing."

Chapter 29

INVENTORY ITEM: *costume*

APPROXIMATE DATE: *1995*

CONDITION: *excellent*

ITEM DESCRIPTION: *Circus tightrope-walker costume. Satin leotard with red and gold sequins.*

SOURCE: *Lane Lawton. Worn for an off-Broadway production in New York.*

April

APRIL WAS ARRANGING COCKTAIL dresses on hangers on a Tuesday in October, hoping to attract students shopping for homecoming, when the phone rang at the shop. She walked over to the sales counter and picked it up.

"It's me, Violet," said the breathless voice on the other end. "Are there any customers in the store?"

"No. We had a rush over the lunch hour, but things have calmed down," April said. "Amithi's upstairs working on some alterations."

"Okay, well can you close the store down for an hour or so? I need you to come meet me at 215 South Hamilton right away. I found something amazing, and I'm afraid if I don't act on it now, someone else will snatch it up."

April jotted down the address. "Sure, I'll come, but I don't think we need to close the shop. I can ask Amithi to watch the store while I'm gone."

"No, bring her along. I could use her help, too."

"What if we get busy again, though?" April asked. "With Halloween coming up, we might get some people in here looking for costumes. I have to say I told you so about the costumes thing. Ever since we put them out on the sales floor, they've been flying off the racks. Oh, remember that awesome circus costume of Lane's? Someone put it on hold yesterday and said they'd be back in to buy it this afternoon."

"Okay, well, just put a sign on the door that says you'll be back soon and close up the store. This won't take long, I promise."

April went upstairs to the sunroom, where Amithi sat bent over a sewing machine, working with a swath of shimmery black fabric.

"Violet just called," April shouted over the hum of the sewing machine. "She wants us to come meet her."

Amithi stopped the machine. "Right now? I have to finish taking in this dress before I leave for India tomorrow. I promised the customer I would get it done."

"Violet said to come right away."

"Why?" asked Amithi.

"I've learned that with Violet, sometimes it's best not to question."

April locked the shop doors. She and Amithi caught the bus and got off at South Hamilton Street near the capitol. April looked at the address she'd written down and tried to match it with one of the nearby buildings. All she could see was the courthouse, a bank, a parking garage, and some dilapidated rental houses with political yard signs for the upcoming election cycle cluttering their front lawns. Where could Violet possibly have found some sort of vintage treasure *here*? Maybe she found something on Craigslist—a priceless piece of couture stashed in the basement of one of these old houses.

She and Amithi walked up and down the block, looking at the address numbers: 210, 212 . . . but no 215. April stopped a man coming out of the courthouse with a briefcase.

"Excuse me, sir, do you know where I can find 215 South Hamilton?" she asked.

He pointed his thumb at the massive building over his shoulder. "That's the address of the courthouse."

Perplexed, April and Amithi climbed the stairs and went inside, where a security guard made them remove their coats and handbags and run them through a metal detector. April panicked, wondering if maybe Violet had been summoned to court for something to do with the lease on the old building. She thought Violet had worked with Karen to get that all cleared up before moving the shop into her mom's old house, but maybe there was some detail they'd overlooked.

"Excuse me," Amithi said to the security guard. "Have you seen a woman with short black hair come through here?"

The guard scratched his graying beard. "Was she wearing a wedding dress?"

Amithi shrugged as April said, "Um, I don't believe so."

"Almost all the women I've seen come through here in the last hour or so looked like lawyers. You know, they were wearing suits and carrying files and stuff. Only lady I've seen who didn't look like a lawyer had on a wedding dress."

"Hmmm," April said. "Well, thanks anyway. I guess we'll just wait here in the lobby until we see our friend."

"Oh, and the lady I saw, the one in the dress, she had tattoos. One of a bird, and something else. A starfish?"

Beyond the security guard, April caught sight of Violet coming out of the elevator, wearing the ivory, full-skirted 1950s gown April had purchased for her own wedding, and then returned, back in the spring.

Amithi gasped.

April rushed toward Violet. "Is this what I think it is?"

Violet hugged each of them as best she could without crushing the bouquet of red ranunculus dangling from her hand. "Sam and I are getting married and we need two witnesses. Come on!" Violet flashed a red-lipsticked smile, then beckoned her friends into the elevator.

"Of course we will be your witnesses," Amithi said. "How wonderful."

April wasn't quite so sure. Violet and Sam had been broken up for a couple of months now. Questions rose to her lips, but there were other people riding with them in the elevator—serious-looking, white-haired people wearing ties—so she just stood there in silence like everyone else.

They got off on the third floor and followed Violet into a courtroom, where Sam paced in front of the jury box like a defense attorney about to deliver his closing argument. His face lit up when he saw Violet and he buttoned his houndstooth blazer.

April was still too stunned to be able to articulate anything, so she just hovered near the door.

Amithi grabbed her gently by the arm. "I think we are supposed to go up to the front."

The bespectacled clerk looked up from her computer and asked, "Should I tell the judge we're ready?"

"Yes," Violet and Sam both said at the same time.

Chapter 30

INVENTORY ITEM: *wedding gown*

APPROXIMATE DATE: *1952*

CONDITION: *good, minor discoloration on lining*

ITEM DESCRIPTION: *Ivory, tea-length gown with scooped neckline and cap sleeves. Silk taffeta with crinoline under-structure.*

SOURCE: *Dress acquired from the couple's daughter. Later purchased and returned by April Morgan. Worn for the wedding of Violet Turner and Sam Lewis.*

Violet

VIOLET HAD BEEN PRUNING April's mother's peony plants on the side of the house on an October Sunday when she heard a car pull into the driveway. She had pulled off her gardening gloves and wiped her hands on the vintage Boy Scout button-down she liked to wear for yard work. Before buying the house, Violet wouldn't have guessed she'd enjoy weeding the flower beds and mowing the tiny lawn. But it turned out that being outside in the autumn air, caring for living things, had a calming effect on her.

She walked around to the front of the house, where Miles had awoken from his nap and now stood on the porch, barking at a white Subaru in the driveway.

Sam's car.

He got out and, in two steps, crossed the small expanse of grass separating him and Violet. For a moment, he looked as if he was going to throw his arms around her, and she, too, wanted nothing more than that. But caution and confusion paralyzed her. Sam must have sensed it, too, because he didn't move any closer.

He cleared his throat. "The shop looks great," he said. "As if it was meant to be here all along."

"Thanks," she said.

"Are you in the middle of something?"

"No. Just some gardening."

Violet wanted to scream, *Enough with the small talk!* He looked even more handsome now than the picture of him she'd been carrying around in her head since they broke up. He'd let his beard grow in a bit, and Violet had to stop herself from reaching up and putting her hands on his cheeks, tilting her head up to kiss him.

"I've done some soul searching," he said.

"Me too."

"If I look a bit worse for wear, it's because I've been camping out at Devil's Lake all weekend."

"It's okay," Violet said. "I'm all full of dirt anyway."

"It's a good look for you," he said. "And is that a new tattoo I see?"

Violet nodded.

Sam reached out and traced the outline of the starfish on Violet's bicep with his finger, sending a rush of longing through her.

"So did you find out anything about your soul?" she asked. "You know, in your search?"

Sam ran his fingers down her arm and caught her hand in his. "I spent the weekend hiking around the bluffs and canyons there.

Everywhere I went, I kept seeing all these families. You know, like big-eyed little girls toting walking sticks and curious boys collecting shells on the shore of the lake. I noticed the parents were always lagging behind them, chatting to each other, you know?"

Violet nodded. She could picture the parents, walking under the orange- and crimson-colored leaves, the children with their fuzzy sweatshirts and scraped knees. She was afraid to hear what Sam had to say next. Afraid to hope.

"For the first time, I could picture myself as one of those parents without feeling afraid," Sam said. "And I think it's because I pictured you, too, chasing after a kid in one of your impractical outfits."

Violet laughed, bathing in a sudden rush of pure joy. "Who are you calling impractical? I've got on a Boy Scout shirt. What's more practical than that?"

"Yeah, but look at your shoes." He pointed at Violet's high-heeled, lace-up ankle boots.

"Okay," she said. "But I promise you I walk better in these than in gym shoes."

"Seriously, though," he said. "I want to be with you, whatever that means. Anything I do with you is gonna be an adventure. Of course, I realize there are no guarantees that we'll be able to, you know, have a family. Or that, if we do, it would be anything like the ones I saw this weekend."

"Of course not," Violet said, still grinning. "It would be cuter."

Sam squeezed her hand and produced a blue velvet box from the pocket of his jeans. He opened it to reveal a vintage ring—a square diamond nestled in a silver art deco setting. He didn't even have to ask the question.

As soon as Violet saw the ring, her fears about being married again, about losing her freedom, fell away. She reached up to touch his face like she'd wanted to just a few moments earlier and said, "Let's do it."

*N*ow, on the steps outside the courthouse, they posed and waited for April to snap a picture. Sam pulled Violet close and lifted up her birdcage veil to kiss her. Men and women in suits walking in and out of the building stared at them, but she didn't care.

"I'm starving," Sam said as he pulled away. "I was too nervous all day to eat anything."

"Aw." Violet touched his cheek. "Cold feet, darling?"

"No, I was afraid *you'd* get them."

Violet pointed down at her peep-toe pumps, which were cream colored, with little blue bows on top of them. "It may be October, and maybe I'm not wearing the most practical shoes for this time of year, but my feet are nice and toasty. Let's go get something to eat, then. Pizza, anyone?"

"Don't you want me to get back to the store?" April asked.

"Oh, no. I'm your boss and I say you're coming with us to celebrate. The store can be closed for one afternoon. Call Charlie and tell him to come, too. And to bring that delicious little baby of yours."

"I can go keep an eye on the shop if you would like," offered Amithi. "I have an alteration I need to finish before I leave for my trip tomorrow."

"No, I want you to come, too," said Violet. "At least for a little while."

"Will someone tell me what's going on, besides the obvious fact that you just got married?" April asked. "I'm confused. I thought the two of you were broken up."

"Get in the car, and I'll tell you on our way to the restaurant," Violet said.

The four of them got into Sam's Subaru.

"Okay, so will you please tell me how all of this happened?" April asked. "When did you decide to do this?"

Sam looked at her in the rearview mirror. "About a week ago."

"A week?" April hit Violet lightly on the arm. "I've seen you almost every day at the store. You didn't say a thing. I didn't even know you were back together. And now you're married? You guys sure don't waste any time."

Sam stopped at a light and exchanged glances with Violet. "I'd already wasted enough time letting all my stupid fears hold me back," he said.

"Me too," said Violet. "So when Sam told me he'd changed his mind about something that was important to me, that was it. There was no reason to wait."

"But that was over a week ago," Sam said. "Turns out there's a six-day waiting period from the time when you apply for your marriage license to when you can actually get married, and today was the first day the judge could fit us in, so we went for it."

"How did you propose?" Amithi asked.

Sam turned to Violet. "Do you want to tell them?"

Violet laughed. "I guess you could say it was a mutual thing. I didn't really give Sam a chance to propose before I said yes."

"But you've only been dating since, what, July? That's only a few months," April said. "Not even, if you count the time you were broken up."

"It's not always necessary to know someone for a long time," said Amithi. "In India, plenty of people get married after knowing one another just a short while. I think it's wonderful that you've found one another. Time does not matter."

Out of the corner of her eye, Violet saw Amithi sniffling and dabbing at her cheeks with the edge of her blue scarf—the one with the peacocks on it that she'd almost sold to the store but then changed her mind about. Violet was glad to see that Amithi, who seemed to have been hardened by her husband's infidelity, could still be moved by love.

During the rest of the ride, Violet made phone calls, leaving messages for Karen and Tom, and other friends in town. She told everyone to join them at Greenbush Bar, the basement pizza joint where she and Sam had eaten many times before, including the evening of the recent Sunday when they'd gotten engaged.

Sam glanced over at Violet in the passenger seat. "You're going to shock the hell out of a lot of people when they get those messages."

"Good," Violet said. "If I've learned anything in the last few months, it's that there are plenty of bad surprises that creep up on you in life. It's nice to be able to announce a good surprise now and then."

"Why don't you ladies get out and I'll find a parking spot?" Sam asked. He pulled the car up in front of a small building on Regent Street with a sign over the door that said ITALIAN WORKMEN'S CLUB. American and Italian flags hung from the red brick façade.

Violet pushed through the door and walked down a narrow staircase to the basement of the building with April following close behind her. Violet stopped and turned around. "I hope you don't mind that I wore this dress."

"Not at all. I'm glad someone got to use it, since it didn't work out for me."

Violet smoothed the full skirt around her hips. "I'm surprised I fit into it. I think I lost some weight from all my worrying and running around for the revue. Did I tell you I've already had people contact me to ask when the next one will be?"

"Do you want there to be a next one?" April asked.

"Why not? It's a good way to make some extra money, and maybe this time we can give some of the proceeds to charity. I wanted to do that last time but didn't have enough money. I was thinking maybe we could donate to the fund Betsy set up for artists. You know, as a way of saying thank you for what she did for me."

They entered the low-ceilinged restaurant. Violet spotted Lane already at the bar, talking to Charlie, who held Kate on his lap. The baby, though still tiny, cooed at the sight of her mother.

Lane jumped up from her stool and hugged Violet. "I certainly was not expecting to be going to a *wedding* reception today. What a wonderful surprise."

"It's not exactly a wedding reception," Violet said. "Just drinks and pizza."

Kate started to wriggle and cry in Charlie's arms. April grabbed her and said, "I'm gonna see if she needs a diaper change."

As April walked away, Charlie asked, "Where's the groom?"

"Parking the car," Violet replied.

"What can I get you to drink?" Charlie asked Violet.

She ordered a glass of red wine, then looked down at her white dress and changed her mind. She asked for a glass of clear, sparkling Prosecco instead. When the dark-haired bartender came over with a stemmed glass, he winked at Violet. "Best wishes, *bella*."

Sam came in and walked over to the bar to embrace Violet. They kissed, and the whole restaurant clapped. It was only four thirty, but there were already a few tables of people eating dinner, mostly white-haired couples and young families. One little boy climbed on top of his chair, pumped his fists in the air, and yelled, "Kissy face!"

Violet and the rest of the wedding group settled into a large, round table. April returned from the restroom with Kate in her arms. Violet reached for the baby right away. She snuggled the warm bundle on her lap and caught Sam's eye. She couldn't imagine a better day.

"So, was it hard to decide against having a big wedding?" Lane asked.

Violet shook her head. She'd had a big wedding once before, back in Bent Creek, with all of her family and friends present. This time around, the small celebration suited her.

"I've never really liked fancy ceremonies," Sam said. "I just hoped

I'd be lucky enough one day to find someone to spend my life with and who is willing to put up with me."

"I am very happy for you," said Amithi. "But I must admit, if my daughter had gotten married without telling me, I would have been very angry."

"We called our parents just before the ceremony," Violet said. "We explained to them that we didn't invite anyone, so it's not as if we were leaving them out. We left everyone out—well, besides our two witnesses, who were required by law."

"How did they take it?" Lane asked.

"They were . . . surprised," Sam said. "Both of our parents are on their way down from Bent Creek as we speak, so they can celebrate with us tonight."

"My parents sounded ready to kill me," Violet added. "They calmed down a bit when I hinted that one of the reasons we were in such a hurry is that we want to have a family. The mere possibility of grandbabies shut them up pretty quickly."

"And, even though we haven't dated long, technically I've known Violet since high school, even though she didn't really know who I was." Sam loosened his black tie. "But, yeah, I'm sure it sounded pretty crazy to our parents. But I'm thirty-nine and Violet's thirty-eight. We're not teenagers."

Lane wagged a finger at Sam. "If you want your marriage to last, I wouldn't go around telling people your wife's age."

"Oh, I don't care," Violet said. "The further I get from my teens and twenties, the better."

"I do not think it matters how long you know someone," Amithi said in a quiet voice. "What is more important is trust. Without it, a marriage cannot survive." She reached into her purse and slid a small red pouch across the table.

Violet opened it and sucked in her breath.

"What is it?" April asked.

Violet reached into the box and held up a pair of gold earrings with shining red stones dangling from the ends.

Amithi smiled. "I have been carrying them around in my purse because I meant to take them to the jeweler to sell. But I could not bear the thought of them going to someone I did not know."

Violet closed the box. "I can't accept these. They're too valuable."

"If you do not accept them, I will be deeply insulted." Amithi crossed her arms in front of her chest. Then her face softened. "Please, take them."

Violet put on the earrings.

"They look beautiful on you. My mother would be proud to see you wear them. She and my father have been married for over sixty years. I hope that you, too, will have many years of happiness." Amithi got up from the table. "Now, I am sorry to have to leave the festivities, but I must go back to the store. I promised to get the dress I am working on to a customer by this evening before I leave town, since I will be gone for quite a while."

"Have a wonderful trip with your daughter," said Violet. "The sewing room will still be here for you when you get back."

"Did I tell you? When I return from India, I am going to New York to take some classes on fashion design. It is something I have always wanted to do but was too busy taking care of my family. I am hoping I can learn to do some of my own designs so that I can make more custom clothing instead of just doing alterations."

"That's wonderful," Violet said. She lowered her voice. "Have you decided what you're going to do about your husband?"

"We have plans to meet up when I'm in India. He's going to cook me breakfast. He has been sending me e-mails with pictures of different recipes he's been trying out." Amithi grinned. "And, from there, we'll see. I figure Naveen took three decades to tell me about what happened. The least he can do is give me as much time as I need to sort things out."

Violet got up and hugged Amithi. "I hope it goes well for you, whatever that might mean," she said.

"So, Violet," Lane said after Amithi had left, "I know you're wearing something old. You always are. And I saw that you've got blue bows on your shoes. Do you have something borrowed and something new?"

"Well, technically the dress is borrowed," Violet said. "Since it's going right back to the store after today, for someone else to buy and add to its story. Unless you want it, April."

April shook her head. "Not after the way things turned out last time."

Charlie's mouth twisted into a guilty smile. "I know I put you through hell, but things turned out fine eventually, don't you think?"

April glanced from Charlie to Kate, whom Violet was still holding. "Yes, I suppose they did."

Lane set down her glass and said, "Okay, so the dress is borrowed, the earrings are old, and there's blue on your shoes, but what about something new?"

"Do I have to have something new?" Violet asked. "I never wear anything new. Well, besides underwear, and sadly, today I'm wearing a pair I've had for a while." She glanced at Sam. "Sorry, honey."

Sam just grinned.

"I see something new," Charlie said.

Violet examined her outfit. "What's that?"

"Little Kate there, in your lap."

Violet looked down at the baby, who slept in her arms with her pink lips pursed.

"Does that count?" Lane asked.

"Oh, yes, she counts." Violet nuzzled the baby's velvety head and whispered, "And don't let anyone ever tell you that you don't, even if you make a thousand mistakes."

April raised her glass. "To second chances."

Glasses clinked around the table in the basement bar.

Violet reached out to tap Sam's glass and caught him admiring her new tattoo. The redness had finally healed, and the blue and green starfish stood out against her pale skin. She was happy with how it had turned out, but she still preferred the old tattoo, and looked down at it now. The phoenix rose, strong and graceful, just below the cap sleeves of her vintage gown.

Acknowledgments

THIS BOOK IS THE product of many hands. Heartfelt words of love and thanks go to my husband, Bill Parsons, for his patience throughout the process. I also would like to express deep gratitude to my parents, Frank and Kerry Gloss. They encouraged my writing from a young age and, more recently, provided countless hours of childcare, as did my wonderful in-laws, Bill and Peggy Parsons. I could not have written a word if my son had not been so well cared for in the hours I was away. Family is the fabric from which this story was stitched.

Special recognition goes to Christina Hogrebe and her colleagues at the Jane Rotrosen Agency for their expert guidance and advocacy for *Vintage*. I am exceedingly grateful, too, for Rachel Kahan, Trish Daly, and the team at William Morrow. Rachel's enthusiasm for this project was evident when, before we even spoke over the phone, she purchased a vintage Diane von Furstenberg dress from my online store. I knew then that Rachel would be the perfect editor for Violet, April, and Amithi's stories.

In addition, I wish to acknowledge my writing groups, the Novellas and the Inkwellians, and especially my critique partner, Rebecca Anderson-Brown. She read more drafts than anyone should be asked to read, quickly and often with little notice. Amy Robb contributed her heavy hand for the delete key, and Kavita Mohan and Padma Shankar gave invaluable insight into the Indian-American experience. Early readers Kori Yelle and Suzan Headley provided perspective from a distance. Kelly Harms shared her knowledge of the another experience, while Nick Wilkes, Autumn Burns, and Corinn Swinson helped me look the part.

Finally, I owe my appreciation to the staff of Barriques café on West Washington, for always letting me finish one last sentence after the lights flashed.